Rebound

Rebound

1962–1963

Ella Rea Murphy

Windstar
Books

30869 6259
R

Cover and interior design by Jane Hagaman
Cover photo © leonid_tit/istock
Editing by Dawn Kinzer
Proofreading by Cynthia Mitchell
Publicity provided by Sgarlat Publicity

Windstar Books
PO Box 581
Earlysville, VA 22936-9998

Printed and sold by Amazon. To order, please go to www.amazon.com.

ISBN 978-1974476473
10 9 8 7 6 5 4 3 2 1

To Bill, my longtime friend; Terri, my daughter; Greg, my son; Robin, my daughter-in-law; Stephanie, my granddaughter; Brian, her partner; Carol, my granddaughter; Alan, my grandson-in-law; and Sharon, my granddaughter.

Author's Note

For those of you who have been keeping up with Maria's adventures, you will notice that this book is set up much the same way as the previous ones. There will be large sections from different characters' points of view—sometimes a whole chapter, sometimes just a portion. The narrator(s) for each section will be designated after the chapter title and as headings within the chapter if there is more than one.

Contents

1. Starting Over

June 1962

(Maria)

The last two days had been terrible for Maria Fuller. She'd been living in a bubble waiting for the pain to go away. The bubble to protect her had popped after her husband's funeral yesterday. The waiting was over, she could come out and live—that is, if she knew how. George was finally at rest. His burial had taken place in Arlington Cemetery with full honors, a fact her mind acknowledged, but quickly relegated it to the unimportant. If only she'd been given the chance to say good-bye. *That* was important. Surprising, confused thoughts had appeared during the wait, allowing her very stable mind to unhinge a little. Her mind had slipped into the past, as if she were viewing their marriage in a giant kaleidoscope. With each turn of the cylinder, a different side appeared—some wonderful, some ugly.

Long before George had died, their marriage had become a meaningless, hollow, lifeless shell. She'd finally stopped using the children as an excuse for staying together. The simple truth—they weren't together. She'd lost him to his mistress.

However, after nearly thirteen years of marriage, she'd grown accustomed to their lifestyle. Maria hadn't been willing to give up financial security, standing in the community, country club friends, and basking in her husband's charisma.

He'd always been a man who poured energy into his career, never comfortable being home with her and the children. He loved his job, flying all over the globe, discovering new places for his magazine travel accounts. The magazines and the travel agencies loved the money his articles brought in by intriguing their wealthy subscribers to vacation in the undiscovered worldwide destinations, and the companies rewarded him handsomely.

George was generous, maintaining an expensive home outside of Washington, DC, complete with a cook and gardening services. He never questioned the household bills, sent his children to private schools and expensive summer camps, and occasionally took them flying with him on day trips. That's who he was on the surface and the profile he carefully maintained.

Underneath, there lived a troubled soul, struggling to love and be loved. That was the George Maria lived with, and it was painful to watch and be a part of .

Image was important to George, and it included a beautiful wife and two kids, preferably a boy and a girl. George had all three. He was lucky, but he didn't appreciate them. It especially hurt when she watched nine-year-old Amanda's desperate attempts to be noticed and loved by her father. She would follow him around like a puppy dog trying to get his attention, but rarely succeeding. Twelve-year-old Chris acted just the opposite, withdrawn and churlish around him, but silently begging for his father's love.

The loneliness she felt when he made his duty visits was worse than when he was gone. Just knowing he was in the house, but completely oblivious of her and his kids, was heartbreaking. He would spend most of the time in his study, constantly catching up on bills or working on his consulting business, paying little attention to any of them.

Pretending nothing was wrong and playing the game had become unbearable for her. It had made her feel old, frozen inside. She'd long ago stopped screaming or causing a scene with him because it didn't work. But fed up and worn down, stuffing her rage inside her, she'd finally decided to file for divorce. He and his mistress had won, and she'd felt a strange relief with her decision.

Looking back, it always amazed her that George, a Medal of Honor recipient, had been such a coward with her, pretending to the world that everything was perfectly normal between them. He, in essence, had cut off any chance for them to breathe life back into their marriage. Desperate for help, she'd called dear Dr. Rudolph time after time, begging for his intervention. George would show up for the counseling sessions resigned, silent, and resolute.

But perhaps something Dr. Rudolph had said had finally penetrated George's thinking, because obviously he'd changed before he died. Maria had his note to prove it, and that magical letter had turned her life around in an instant. Days before he left on his trip to the air show in Wisconsin, she'd sensed a softening in him for the first time in years, and she wondered what was behind it. Maria got her answer when she found his letter propped up on her bedroom pillow.

He said he loved her, then asked her forgiveness and begged for another chance, melting her heart. Lying on her bed and clutching his letter next to her cheek wet with tears, she'd reread it so many times, she'd memorized every word. She'd won him back, somehow! Emotions she hadn't felt in years came flooding back, and they swirled around in her mind and body. Maria couldn't wait to see him, and she rehearsed how she would act and what she would say when he came through the door from his trip. She was ready and eager to try again, but it didn't happen. The plane he was flying had flown into a covey of geese and crashed just before he nosed down to land.

Burying her face in her hands, a sick, guilty feeling also made its way through her body. *What was I thinking, letting Bill make love to me last night? I wasn't thinking, I was reacting, wanting to feel like a desired woman again, if only for an hour or so. It had been such a long time.* She comforted herself with the thought that Bill had loved her once. Perhaps he meant it last night when he told her he still loved her. So many burning questions were tearing at her, and she wished she could ask him now. Did they have a chance together? Or was it too late?

Beneath her desires was her constant questioning of herself. Why did the men in her life either forget or tire of her? What was wrong with her? Bill had forgotten her and his commitment to her when he joined the navy, and George had gotten tired of her after four or five years of marriage. Did other women feel that way? That they were never good enough? She and Dr. Rudolph had been working on her issue for years without resolving anything. Then she got George's letter.

But now, being alone for the first time after living with a man who took charge of everything, made her feel inadequate. Her mind slyly flirted with the "what if" game. *What if I can't cope alone? What if I can't pay the bills?*

While Maria sipped her coffee, her hands began to shake, spilling drops of liquid caffeine on her robe. *Oh, dear, am I that old?* Her mind began racing from one worrisome thought to another. *I'm a single parent now. How will I take care of the kids alone? Life, financially, as I have known it for the last thirteen years is over.* She took a deep breath, tried to focus and think rationally, but survival worries continued to whirl around in her head.

With blurry eyes, she laid her head in her hands. *What am I crying about? My life with George the last few years has been terrible. I've been doing everything around here—raising the kids, getting my college degree, and even landing a great job at a good magazine. My boss has promoted me several times, and my kids, folks, and Briggie love me.*

She straightened up and wiped her eyes. *I guess I'm crying for what it might have been.* She pulled George's heart-felt letter, written just before his ill-fated trip, from her robe's pocket. She read his words for the hundredth time, then stuffed the note back into her robe's pocket with a vengeance. *Why did he wait so long to tell me that he loved me and wanted to come back? Did his girlfriend toss him out?*

That question would never be answered. *It's over. Time to move on. Stop playing the victim.* Closing her eyes, she sat back and took some deep breaths. It felt good. She did it some more. As she slowly relaxed, her breath evened out, and suddenly a pinpoint of light in her mind grew until it filled her thoughts. As she watched, mesmerized, soft orchid-colored waves began rolling over each other. She'd never experienced anything like that before. They bathed her in a warm loving feeling. *What was it?* Comforted, suddenly she knew. It was George coming to her. It seemed ridiculous, but she knew his essence was there. She couldn't see him, but his loving presence let her know that he would always be there for her. His visitation passed as quickly as it had come. She rubbed her eyes, not ready to let go of him. *Oh, George darling, why, why, why?* Despite the agony of her loss, she treasured that moment together and would never forget it. It gave her courage to go on and face the day.

Maria reluctantly opened her eyes. Why was the house so unusually quiet? Where were the kids? They were probably sleeping, exhausted emotionally from their dad's funeral the day before.

Her phone rang, breaking the silence. "Stop it," she said, furious the noise had invaded her world, and she lunged to silence its irritating intrusion.

Maria wanted to slam the receiver back down, but her young, new secretary's crisp voice came through loud and clear from the other end. She spoke fast, offering unfeeling condolences. Maria made a mental note to talk to her about phone etiquette. The secretary sounded like she was ordering takeout for lunch. Even though she was only thirty-two, suddenly Maria felt old. She'd been just like her secretary at one time. Maria didn't blame her. She was one of the next generation of women who were more aggressive and working hard to take her job, but still not ready yet. Her secretary would need ten or fifteen years of experience before she could match Maria.

As she replied, her voice sounded flat to her ears. It was the first time she'd uttered a word that morning. "Thanks, call if you need me," she said abruptly and hung up. Maria had been rude, but at that moment, she felt so removed from her work she didn't care. She was still consumed with George's visit.

Straining, she could hear the familiar quiet shuffle of Briggie's feet coming down the hall, and Maria immediately felt better. *Good old Briggie. What would I have done without you all these years?*

Busying herself around the stove, Briggie poured herself a cup of coffee, heaved her large bulk into a chair, and stared at Maria. "Saints preserve us, you're white as a sheet. Bad night, no doubt."

"I feel detached, somehow."

"You're in shock. I've seen it several times in my forty-two years. It's perfectly understandable," Briggie stated, confidently.

"Is that what it is? One minute I'm reasonably okay, the next I'm feeling sorry for myself, or worse, not feeling anything," Maria whispered. "The funeral and all the interactions with people yesterday are blurry. Is that normal?"

"Me mither would have said, your mind took a bit of a 'walk-about.'"

"Briggie, this will shock you, but I felt George was here this morning."

"Saints preserve us, you did? Was he a ghost? Did he actually appear?"

"No, I didn't see him, I felt him. He filled me with peace and love. Something he never did those last few years. It was how he was when we were first married. Somehow, I know his death is part of a bigger plan for me, but I wish I knew what it is."

"Well, if you want to believe that, you can. I personally don't believe in ghosts."

"Briggie, he wasn't a ghost. His presence just filled my heart with his love," Maria repeated, slightly annoyed.

"I moost say that it was quite a funeral day for the likes of George." Briggie, speaking in her Irish brogue, had changed the subject. "I niver knew he was so important and had so many friends. I gather he was buried in a special place." She cocked her head and looked at Maria. "And all them military certainly know how to eat and drink. Did you iver see the like?"

Briggie's down-to-earth assessments of George's funeral guests made Maria grin for the first time. "Briggie, I forgot to tell you that George was buried at Arlington Cemetery in Washington, DC, as a decorated war hero. It's quite an honor. I wish you could have seen it, but I know you were busy slugging it out in Mom's kitchen, getting ready for all the locusts to descend afterward. Thanks, my friend, for feeding everyone. Please take it easy today, and come visit Mom and Winston with me and the kids."

"Thanks, but no thanks, me darlin'. I plan on putting me feet up and relaxing."

Again, that inconsiderate phone rang, breaking into their enjoyable conversation.

"Yes," Maria answered testily.

"Is this too early to be calling?" Her mother sounded hesitant. "Everyone over here is driving me crazy to see you. How are you anyway? Your dear stepfather has been bugging me to call you. Yesterday was a tough day to get through, I know."

"I don't know, Mom. I'm sort of in a funny place. Briggie's giving me advice and making me smile, but I can't forget what happened early this morning. I'm sure I felt George's presence. He was only here for a second, but he filled me with indescribable love. He promised to watch over us." As she spoke, Maria fought back tears. "Briggie doesn't believe me. She explains it as shock."

"Come see us now. It will do you good, and you'll save my sanity." Her mother's tone had almost become frantic. "Later on we can discuss George and your dream.

"I'll come get you if you don't come soon," her stepfather boomed into the phone.

"Okay, you two." Maria's spirits had sunk even more. "I'll get going, but it wasn't a dream, Mom."

Briggie stood there with her hands on her hips. "Let me get those two youngsters of yours up. You'll be wanting to see your friends and family, and it's good for the kids too."

"I guess so, but I dread it in a way."

"Nonsense, get dressed and I'll get those scalawags ready. Would you like that?"

"Oh, yes, I can't face their sad faces when they wake up.

"I'll give them a pep talk."

Whatever Briggie said to them seemed to have worked, because Chris and Amanda ate their breakfasts and didn't spar with each other like usual. Instead, they sat with solemn faces staring at each other until Maria sent them to the car.

At first, it was complete silence as Maria drove to their grandmother's home. Chris and Amanda acted unhappy and showed it openly. Looking at them in the rearview mirror, Maria saw two very confused looking youngsters. She didn't blame them. Their father's death had flipped all of their worlds upside down.

2. Where Do We Go from Here?

June 1962

(Maria)

"Mommy, I miss Daddy. I'll never see him again," Amanda said, breaking the silence with her sober little voice.

"Your dad is here, Amanda, encouraging us to be brave and start living again."

"Why do you say that?" Chris yelled at Maria. "He's gone. You or I can't talk to him, ever again. There is no God or heaven, or this would never have happened. It's all tommy rot. You're just saying that to make us and yourself feel better."

"No, Chris, I know he was here this morning sending us his love." How could Maria explain in a way her children could understand? "I could feel his presence, although I couldn't see him."

"You're crazy! I'm never going to see my dad again," Chris snapped, his voice breaking.

The rest of the way, her children's anger and misery flooded the car, pushing her into silence. But in spite of their mood, the warm breeze of spring was pouring through the open windows, and it fed her with renewed energy. Roadside bushes and trees were bursting out in a greenish tinge, a preview of their promised leafy beauty. Washington, DC, and the surrounding countryside were awash in spring.

As she turned into the long driveway, she took in the scene before them. "My gracious, your grandpa's driveway is full of cars! But I see a spot for us." She squeezed into a tiny space and turned off the car. "Relatives you've never met are anxiously waiting to get to know you. Won't that be fun?"

"Oh, Mom, stop trying so hard," Chris said, groaning. "I'm not five years old. They'll all be boring and not interested in me. I'm not going in!"

With no response from Amanda except to grab her hand when she opened the car door, they walked to the house. *I hope he comes, but I'm not going to force it.* It was better that way.

God, give me strength to face these well-meaning but inquisitive friends and relatives.

Happily, the first guests they saw were two very special people—Bill's parents, Alice and Bob Morgan. Maria immediately thought about the goodness and respect they had given her while she was dating Bill in college.

Alice enveloped her in her arms. "Words can't describe how we feel for you."

Maria closed her eyes and let Alice's gentle kindness permeate her whole being. Bob stood silently next to Alice. Moments later, Maria felt Amanda's fingers poking her, which brought her back to the present. "Meet my precious Amanda. My twelve-year-old son, Chris, is in our car, deciding what he wants to do." Could this feel any more awkward? She could at least save her daughter from having to stand there. Maria smiled at Amanda. "Go get some breakfast and sit with your grandma, honey. I'll be out soon."

"But Mom, what about Chris?" Just as Amanda spoke, her face lit up as she saw Chris scoot in, fly by his mother, and head for the patio.

Shrugging her shoulders in mock displeasure, Maria grinned. "That's kids for you." She quietly nudged Amanda toward the patio, then Maria's eyes met Alice's. "I've missed you and Bob so much. Thanks for making this long trip."

"We had to," Alice said. "We'll never forget all that George did for Bill in the hospital after his accident when you were in college. Bill told us the whole story about George's unusual thoughtfulness. Bill saw a side of George probably most people never knew. He said George seemed to consider him a wounded warrior, possibly like the men George served with during the war. He said that George had given him an inspiring pep talk that ultimately gave him hope that he would regain his health and memory. It meant the world to Bill."

Bob nodded. "What a guy. George also paid all those high-powered lawyers to help us win our court battle over Bill's innocent role in the multi-car accident. Bill said George seemed to understand how much pain he was in. That's why we came to comfort you and honor George," Bob said, tears rimming his eyes.

"Mother and I had seen pictures of Arlington Cemetery, but we never thought we'd be there. Bill told us George was a hero from

WWII, but to learn he was given the Medal of Honor made us really proud our son had met him. I wish we could have known him personally, but at least Bill did have a few precious hours with him.

"When we told Bill that George had died, he said he'd be there, too, if he had to move mountains, and he came." Bob stroked his jaw and cocked his head. "Did he have a chance to spend some time with you last night? I encouraged him to see you. You know that Mother and I always wished that you and he had married. But you married a fine man." Bob paused and looked at his wife, as if seeking her approval. "I know there was another very important reason Bill came. He still loves you, Maria. He's never gotten over you. He gets a certain look on his face whenever we mention you. If I tease him about it, he always gets angry and won't talk."

"To answer your question, yes, Bill stayed for a little while, but he had to get back to Washington, DC, for a scheduled flight to the west coast," Maria said, lying smoothly. To cover her uncomfortable feelings, she quickly asked, "Tell me about his daughter, Rosemary."

"She's a pretty little thing. Different from her mom," Bob growled.

"Land sakes, Dad!" Alice shot him a disapproving look. "Gerrie is a fine nurse, but she just has a little trouble understanding young ones. Rosemary spends a lot of time with us because Gerrie works very hard. Being divorced from Bill, Gerrie has developed a very active social life. It's hard being single." Her eyes, as always, held compassion. "I know Gerrie is lonely. But it doesn't leave too much time for Rosemary, I'm sorry to say," Alice said, wistfully looking at Maria. "Bill loves his daughter, and he's a good father when he sees her, but it isn't the same as living with her. He has a busy flying schedule for the airline."

As Maria listened, guilt over spending time with Bill the night before mixed with her ache over the loss of George.

"Because of all his flying experience in the Korean War, Bill is top dog as pilot on those huge planes that he flies all over the world." Bill's voice was laden with pride. "What he says, goes."

Alice poked her husband. "Dad, we're keeping Maria from seeing the rest of the company. Let's get a cup of coffee and mingle with everyone."

The minute Maria's gregarious brother-in-law, Don, saw her, he boomed loudly for her to sit down next to him. She made her way over to him and slid onto a chair.

10

"Did you and Bill end up together last night?" A smirk grew on his face. "Little sister, after you left, I saw him hightail it out of here with your maid, Briggie, in tow. You'd think the devil was chasing him."

Don had observed that? Best to give a simple answer and ignore his innuendo. "I forgot Briggie because I was so befuddled."

Don winked at her, took out a cigarette, and lit it. "I suppose he just dropped your cook off and left?"

"Yes," she said, lying, her face feeling warm.

"Little sister, you'd already gone last night when I invited your family to visit us for a summer vacation. When I called May yesterday to see if she felt better, I asked her. She sends her best and likes the idea of another family reunion this summer. Winston is for it, what do you think?"

"I don't know. I feel foggy. Forgive me, but this whole thing has thrown me for a loop. I have to consider my kids and my job. I'm one of several editors responsible for my monthly magazine." Maria took a sip of coffee. "I'll talk it over with the folks. What's the time frame?"

"Any time you all can get away. I'm not going anywhere for a while after this trip." He winked. "I've got farmers who want to see their veterinarian once in a while."

A shadow fell over her, and looking up, Maria saw her favorite doctor, Greyson, and his wife, Terri, standing there, holding hands.

"Move over, big guy," Greyson said. "We want to get in on this conversation, don't we, Terri?"

Terri gave her husband the kind of smile that a woman offered her man when still in love. "It's so good to see you again, Maria. Even though it's under such sad circumstances."

For a moment, Maria felt jealous to see two well-adjusted people who had stayed happily married. How did they do it? She could feel their affection for each other. It swirled around them as they talked. She'd known that feeling only for a few years with George.

"So, Doc, how's the best bone man in Chicago?" Don asked Greyson.

"Fixing them right and left. How's the vet business?"

"It pays the bills."

Ignoring the men, Maria focused on Terri. "It was so good of you and Greyson to come. You were the best boss I've ever worked for."

Don grinned. "She was your first and only boss, if memory serves."

"No, I was your kids' nanny during my high school years. But working for Terri was my first *paid* job." Maria sounded a bit curt, but she couldn't help remembering how cheap they'd been, never paying her a penny. Her sister always implied that Maria was lucky to have place to live with her during the summers. Her unresolved anger toward May and the way her sister had taken her for granted surprised Maria.

Turning to Terri, she said, "You were so fair. You worked harder than any of us, bent over backward to give me days off, and listened to my problems with all the snooty guests."

Looking a little embarrassed by Maria's heart-felt compliments, Terri patted her hand and smiled. "Did I hear someone talking about a trip to the Midwest? If so, I want to invite you to visit us. We live in a suburb of Chicago, near La Grange where you grew up, Maria. We'd like you to come and meet our two girls."

"If we go, we'll certainly come and visit you. I still have your old business card after all these years, Terri, but I need an update so I can call you."

After digging around in her ample bag, Terri handed a business card to her. "You were the best, Maria," she said quietly. "I really missed you when you went back East with George."

"I wish I'd had an inkling of what I was getting into, but that's in the past, and I have two great kids—Christopher, twelve, and Amanda, nine."

"I didn't get a chance to meet George, but I did see your children when I peeked into the kitchen. Your boy is handsome, I imagine like his father, and your daughter is a cutie. You can be so proud." Terri smiled, but her eyes held a hint of concern. "It sounds like you had some troubles."

A loud voice from the doorway interrupted their conversation. Maria would know that voice anywhere. Susie, her old roommate from college was standing there. "Isn't this nice? A regular coffee-klatch club, I see. Can I join you? " Not waiting for an answer, she strode across the slate floor, squeezed in next to Maria, smiled, and gave her a quick hug.

"Well, 'roomie,'" Maria said, "thanks for coming all the way from Omaha, Nebraska, to be with us. You know, you haven't changed a bit from our college days." Maria was so happy to see her old friend, she was beaming. "Where's that husband of yours?"

"Richard's talking with Winston and your mother. They'll be out here in a minute. I can't believe thirteen years have passed since we came to your and George's wedding. Too bad George chickened out," Susie teased.

"You would bring that up again after all these years," Maria said, slightly irritated. "For everyone's information, George didn't chicken out. He blacked out and ended up in the hospital, but came home a couple of days later." *Susie has a way of trying to make me feel uncomfortable, but she won't.* Smiling at everyone she said, "Besides, we had a lot of fun without a wedding, didn't we?"

"Yeah, we did, but I'm glad I'd met him at college. What a handsome brute. Too bad his witch of a mother came to the wedding. Her name was Lady Bancroft, everybody. She acted like she was the Queen of England and was out for Maria's hide." Susie's crowed. "Did she go back to England?"

"She did and called several times, but good ol' Winston took care of her," Maria said, glancing around the room. Where was Richard? If only he'd appear and take Susie's mind off the past. Why did she have to take so much pleasure in sharing Maria's history with the whole world?

A moment later, Richard appeared in the doorway. "Nellie asked me to say that the pancakes and bacon are coming out in a moment."

Susie waved him over. "Come sit with us, Richard."

Sauntering over, he said, "Sorry about George," and sat down next to Susie in a chair. Speaking to everyone within earshot, he said, "I met George when he came to our school, and I really liked him. He was quite a guy. I knew he'd fought in WWII but didn't know until yesterday that he was a war hero. I wish I'd spent more time with him and had known him better."

If only they had really known him like I did, maybe they wouldn't be calling him a hero. "You have a family, now, don't you?" Greyson asked Richard.

Richard's chest puffed up. "Yeah, two great boys, six and eight, who will work with me in my coffee bean business in a few years."

"If they make it to adulthood," Susie muttered under her breath. "Little boys are a handful, and it's hard to love them sometimes."

Moments later, Nellie's husband, Dean, Winston's longtime handyman and friend, came in carrying a gigantic tray of pancakes and bacon for everyone.

Nellie, Ruth and Winston's cook and maid, smiled triumphantly beside him. "Dig in, folks. We're making more, and they'll be out in jig time." She turned to Maria. "The kids are in the kitchen eating their heads off."

"Maria," Susie said, "let's keep in touch, now that our kids are bigger. I haven't been very communicative, but I've missed you."

"Why don't we meet at Don and May's this summer? You could drive east from Nebraska, and we'll drive west from Washington." Maria asked, "Oh, and Susie, would you send me Carol and Sharon's phone numbers? I've lost both of them."

Susie nodded. "We'll talk more when you know your plans."

Before Don left, he was very insistent that Winston, Ruth, and Maria commit to a visit, but Winston held him off by saying very emphatically that they'd only promise to talk it over.

As the morning slipped away, a slight shift of energy signaled everyone's wish to be on their way. Wishful promises to keep in touch were called back and forth among the guests as everyone walked out.

"Ah," Maria said, stretching her legs out. "This is nice. I'm tired of making conversation. What a wild time this has been." Gratefully accepting a hot cup of coffee from Nellie, she sipped it carefully, savoring the flavor. She eyed her folks. "Thanks for being there for me, again. Am I ever going to be able to just live? It seems I'm always leaning on you both for support."

"That's what a family is for. We help each other. There will come a time when you may need to help us, God forbid." Ruth's brow furrowed and she glanced quickly at Winston.

"By Jove, your mother's right. Too many families live too far apart these days, looking for the illusive brass ring in some big city. Years ago, families lived nearer to each other. Nowadays, workers from agencies have to do the job families used to do for each other."

Winston seemed to be just warming up. "George was a great American hero, and I'll never forget his sacrifice and service to his country, but now we have to "circle our wagons." You need us, Maria, and we need you and those wonderful kids of yours. They've made our lives mean something. Right, Ruth?" He massaged the back of his neck. "I wish he'd been better to you and the kids. We knew how hard it was for you," he added softly.

"Don't feel bad, Winston. George left me a wonderful letter, asking to be forgiven. He wanted to start over with me again when he returned from the air show."

"By Jove, he did? Well, it means a lot to me knowing that." Winton's face lit up with pleasure.

Her mother brushed away a few tears with her fingers. "Oh, Maria, I'm so glad he finally saw the light."

"And this may surprise you, but I feel he's with us, Mom. Like I told you on the phone, he filled me with love this morning. He's never going to leave us until we're okay. He promised."

"I hope you aren't cracking under the strain, Maria. Perhaps you imagined it," Winston said, patting her hand lovingly.

"Oh, Winston, I wish I could convince you, but let's talk about the trip, instead. That's something we all agree on. It would be fun to get away, but there's one problem. Bill and I want to see each other more."

Her mother's eyebrows raised. "You and Bill?"

3. The Dropped Bombshell

June 1962

(Maria)

Were they going to understand? Or were they going to tell her she was moving too fast and making a big mistake? "Look, I know I just buried my husband, but seeing Bill brought back feelings for him that had been put on hold for so long because of the Korean War. He stayed with me all night, and the next morning, he promised he'd call and come for a few days so we could get to know each other again.

"How I wish I knew then what I know now. I can't forget how impetuous and angry I was at him for not writing to me, even though you tried to tell me that he was probably hanging on by his fingernails during his flight naval training, trying not to wash out. I didn't want to understand. I wanted instant everything. When you told me to be patient, I wasn't. When you said his letters to me and my letters to him may have been lost because of the situation, I didn't believe you. Those two kids would have been his, and we would still be happily married if I'd waited and given him a chance." *If only I had listened.*

Her mother and Winston stared at her, their faces a mass of disbelief from her confession.

"I know, folks, I've shocked you, but I've decided to be more open and not go around pretending ever again."

Appearing upset, her mother fanned herself with a paper napkin. "I guess I'm glad that you and Bill have connected again," she said, sounding concerned. "I've always felt you two had something special. He may be an answer to a prayer." She leaned over and touched her daughter's hand. "If we go, you could call him or his folks and leave word as to where we're going to be."

"I will, Mom, but his schedule is such he's rarely in his Chicago apartment, except to sleep. He doesn't check in with his folks very often and is basically hard to reach. I don't want to miss him *again*," she said, with a little catch in her throat.

"Don't look back and wish *what if*. There was a reason why you and George married. Think about those two wonderful children you have." Ruth held her daughter's hand tenderly for a moment.

"Well, ladies, this makes up my mind," Winston said, breaking his silence. "We all need to get away and have a vacation. Besides, I'd like to see, first hand, how my investment in Ed's clinic is doing. Wouldn't you like to see your old boyfriend again?"

"You mean my old married boyfriend? I don't know." Secretly, Maria wondered if Ed had ever forgiven her for leaving Illinois so abruptly with George all those many years ago when she was so young and foolish.

"You're quiet, Maria," her mother said. "Did we say anything to upset you?" She studied her daughter's face. "How does the trip sound to you?"

"As I said, I'd rather stay right here, because of Bill, but I must think of connecting our family. I want my children to know their cousins. I'll call Alice and Bob, give them phone numbers, etc., and call Bill's apartment and hope for the best."

"I'd like to see my other grandchildren before they're all grown up," her mother added softly.

Winston slapped his knee. "By Jove, let's go then."

"With George gone, I don't know how the kids will feel leaving their home for a trip. They're pretty upset. Besides, Chris has been looking forward to soccer camp."

"Let's talk to them." Winston flipped on the intercom. "Nellie, are the kids in the kitchen with you? Send them out, will you?"

They soon appeared. "Ah, there you two scallywags are." Winston patted the couch. "Sit down with Grandpa." Once they settled, he maneuvered in and sat between them. "We have a question for you both. How would you like to visit your relatives this summer?"

A broad smile morphed her son's sour expression. "Uncle Don's a hoot. He promised he'd take me fishing on his lake and out on his vet calls."

His enthusiastic response surprised Maria.

By the fear in Amanda's eyes, it was obvious she didn't feel the same excitement. "Will my cousins be nice?" Her voice was full of concern. "Maybe they won't like me."

"Oh, honey, just be yourself, and they'll like you. Besides, Uncle Don has lots of dogs and cats on their farm. You can play with them all the time," Maria said, encouragingly.

Amanda's face lit up. "Really, Mom, do they really have them? I would love that. Do you suppose I could have one of their dogs? I've always wanted one."

"We'll have to see," Maria said, not wanting to dash her daughter's hopes, but secretly wishing she could avoid dealing with the trouble of having a puppy.

"That means, Squirt, that Mom doesn't want you to have one," Chris said with an evil tone.

"That wasn't nice or necessary, Christopher," Maria said, giving him a shriveling glare.

After that, the trip became their magic elixir to help their recovery. Together, Maria promised herself, she and her children would make a new and better life in the future.

With that pledge, and distinctly remembering George's promise to be there for her forever, Maria's anger and resentment softened. A sense of peace slipped quietly into her life for the first time in a long while, and something else happened. A sense of freedom, forgotten since college, emerged.

Maria's boss called with his condolences, told her to take as much time as she needed before she came back, and assured her that her position was hers for as long as she wanted it. After a week, she was ready to go back. She missed the stimulation of work and the camaraderie of her staff who were all dedicated in producing an exciting, interesting magazine for women across the country. All of them felt the time pressure to produce next month's magazine, spending endless hours to ensure the spot of one of the top selling magazines. Maria was continually pleased and encouraged to redouble her efforts with their determination.

Although her home fires were burning brightly in Briggie's dedicated and lovable hands, Maria's guilt of leaving her children in the care of another woman bothered her continually. Adding to her guilt was the fact that she didn't have to work. George had left her financially secure. Maria worked because it gave her personal fulfillment. She liked being rewarded for her own accomplishments.

Maria, like many other women, had moved into the workforce in larger and larger numbers. Many of their accomplishments had begun popping up and earning enough recognition in areas of politics, medicine, and business to make news. As articles came across Maria's desk, touting some female's abilities or contributions to the world, they began to be part of the magazine's focus for the next issue, along with the much-anticipated next chapter of an exciting love story, recipes, and tips on the most stylish clothes and hairdos to please the homebodies.

Maria felt a driving need to validate women in all walks of life and let them know they had power, were being heard, and were becoming a force for good in the country.

During the day, Maria presented a strong, in-charge woman in the office and mother to her family at home, but nights were a different story. Growing up, sleeping soundly had never been an issue for her, but as her marriage had begun unraveling, her sleep pattern became as erratic as her life. Resorting to playing the denial game, pretending George was out of town traveling, but knowing down deep that he was with his mistress, her wild dreams had made sleeping more and more difficult.

But every time she was ready to call her lawyer and start divorce proceedings, George would appear, full of stories about his travels, delighting the kids, and leaving her wondering if she was going crazy. If he stayed overnight, his utter charm destroyed her resolve, and she gave way to his ardent love making, For the next day or two, he would almost be content to catch up on family life, and she would begin to hope again. But once he started packing his bag, she knew he was going. He never offered any clues as to where he was going or when he was coming back. Questioning him was useless. She had tried that before.

Persistent, confusing dreams of George during those last five years before he died had caused her endless nights of wakefulness. Ugly visions of George trying to reach her, but being held away by demonic creatures in one scenario after another, had been frightening her over and over. But miraculously, after his funeral, and his visitation, she'd felt completely at peace with him for the first time in years. Maria had once again embraced his love for her, and the nightmares had stopped.

They were replaced by gentle dreams about Bill, occurring after they spent the night together. They always centered on her being unable to find him, even though she could hear him somewhere out in a haze. They never alarmed her, they were just very unsatisfying.

Turning to meditation, she hoped for answers about Bill, but when she read her meditation guide book, it said that successful mediation had to be about the person meditating, not someone else. Occasionally, she would wake around two in the morning after a dream about Bill. Maria would then wrap up in a big comforter, sit on her couch, and try to allow God to speak to her in the silence. Closing her eyes, she'd wait, but her monkey mind never rested. One problem after another begging to be solved, popped into her thoughts and interfered. Thinking about forgiving Bill for not coming back, after he'd promised, seemed unattainable. How did people do it? Meditation didn't work for her.

After Bill rekindled her feelings for him, no matter whether she was busy at work or home mothering her family, something would trigger a remembrance of him. Maria imagined him in his captain's uniform flying to some distant place in the world, and she wondered if he ever thought of her. She had been so sure he would call, but he hadn't. The world was his oyster, and he was out there living it up. She evidently wasn't high on his priority list. No call because he simply didn't love her.

Maria turned to her long-time friend and shrink, Dr. Peter Rudolph, for help. In the past whenever she'd called, distraught over George's attitude and absences, he'd continually tried to assure her that she was a normal, well-functioning woman. Peter had always insisted it was George's problem, not hers, but she had spent years with him arguing about her inadequacies with men, never quite convinced he was right.

Once, after a particularly troubled night full of reservations as to how to proceed, she'd prayed fervently for understanding. Sleeping fitfully until dawn when the sun came peeping into her room, the promise of a good day brought her a gift.

Take this time and make the most of it. Don't waste another second thinking about the past. Think about your future. Become an adult.

The message that surfaced in her thoughts sounded just like her dear old dad's admonition to become independent, no matter whether she married or not. He always said that men could die or leave. Bill left and George did both. At that moment, she'd finally had enough of the old. *I'm worth the freedom I've earned. It's time to live again.*

She'd been ready to hear her own advice. It was an exhilarating feeling. No more procrastination. She'd make a long overdue call to her dear foster sister, Elena.

Winston had casually placed Elena's number on Maria's desk a few days ago. She smiled at his gentle nudge to keep the family together. Her beloved stepfather had become more of a father than her own. Since marrying Betty, her dad had become a stranger to her, immersed in his life with his new two small children. It was almost like she didn't exist. Winston had been so generous with her whole family. The latest example of his big heart was taking off from his huge State Department position to help Elena apartment hunt and then underwriting her until, as he put it, *she takes off and makes a fortune.*

When she heard Elena's soft, slightly accented voice, say "Hello," Maria realized how much she had missed her.

"Hi, I just wanted to call, see how you are and how you like your new digs, ask you to come see us, and invite you to come with us on a trip to the Midwest this summer. Whew, there, I've said it all. I've missed you and want you and my kids to know my side of the family. We need to pull the family together."

"I, too, have missed you and the children and have been mourning my dear George, but please understand that my life has changed. I like living near all my friends here in Washington. They're full of energy and inspire me to work hard. Trying to recover from George's death has been very hard for me, and I'm just getting back to painting again. I owe everything to him."

"So, you won't be using the room that George built on the house for your work?"

"No, and I'm sorry, but it is too isolated. I need people who live in the art world around me. It helps me forget George and live a new life. I have a new friend, Kathy Gibbs, who is finding ways to show my work. She has two local galleries that are going to take some of my paintings and maybe some of my sculptures. She has offered to be my manager, and I feel very happy about that."

Elena's sweet, but firm, rebuff surprised and hurt Maria. Feeling rejected and angry, Maria was also a wee bit jealous of Elena's complete freedom to live independently, to have a passion that she was good at, and to have plenty of like-minded friends around her. *All I've ever done is be married and raise kids. No, that's not true, I've finished college and have a very good job, plus I have a wonderful family.*

"That probably means no as to taking a trip with us to the Midwest."

"Yes, Maria, I find there are not enough hours in the day to do what I want to do with my work."

How fast these kids grow up, Maria thought but, trying to sound like an adult, said, "Elena, I understand your wish to surround yourself

21

with friends who are also artists, but I hope you don't forget us. We all miss you. You're very talented and will go far. Your sculptures and paintings are gorgeous. If Kathy can help you, I'm delighted."

Her younger foster sister had politely brushed her off and essentially said she wanted her own life and to leave her alone. Trying to maintain an understanding attitude, Maria said, "You have the whole world out there waiting for you to share your God-given talents. We are cheering you on. George is too. Make us all proud."

Maria needed to shake off Elena's rejection. Chalk it up to being young and dedicated. *Elena has a plan for doing what she wants to do, and I need one too. The trip will be a good place to start.*

Calling her mother, Maria gave her a report that Elena's life was busy and happy. Maria also explained that Elena didn't have time to visit them in the near future or take a trip with them.

"I'm glad for her, Maria. She's finding her way. Heavens knows we've all been there. She'll be back when she needs us."

"How's Winston doing planning our trip?" Maria asked, still irritated with Elena's quick dismissal.

"I think he was feeling worn out with his work, but the trip has given him a new focus. He's decided our trip should be at least three or four weeks and is making reservations along the way in interesting little towns. He says he wants to soak up the Midwestern culture."

"That's wonderful. It's nice to have someone besides me planning. My work is so all consuming. Will you help me by shopping for the kids? They've outgrown everything. Since going back to work, I find my deadlines have a way of creeping up on me."

"You know me, I love to shop. I'll buttonhole those grandchildren of mine and get them ready."

"You always give me a lift, Mom. Thanks, I'm getting excited about the trip."

The next couple of weeks flashed by so fast, Maria felt under more pressure than usual to leave her work in capable hands and organize for the trip. Her dreams, now nondescript, had allowed her to sleep through the night, reaping huge benefits for her during the day.

The day before she was to leave on vacation, her boss called her into his office and gave her a reserved, tiny, parting pep talk. "Enjoy yourself. You deserve a change."

For him to say anything at all was monumental, and his words made her want to scream and throw her arms around him, but good judgment kicked in, and she just smiled and thanked him. Inside, she was dancing.

Everybody was excited about the trip when she got home from work, and so was she to some degree. So why did she begin to feel so apprehensive as the evening wore on? Perhaps facing the fact that she didn't feel ready for this trip. She felt a certain edginess as she was going to bed but ignored it.

In the middle of the night, she woke—sweaty, heart beating wildly, scared to death. Jumping up, she ran to her bedroom door, locked it, and turned on all the lights. It made her feel safer. Wrapping up in her soft, warm robe, she began to pace, going over her terrifying nightmare of a horrible intruder who chased her all through the woods, almost catching her before she woke up. Was it a warning?

Awake the rest of the night, she called her mother as soon as she dared, to say that she wasn't going on the trip. When her mother tried to question her, Maria could only express her fear that her dream was a warning that trouble lay ahead for them. Her mother said they'd be over as soon as they could, and they'd talk. It was hardly light out when they arrived. Maria stood in the kitchen, hugging her mother, and wailing that she couldn't go with them on the trip. When her mother asked her why, Maria sobbed and told them through her tears about her nightmare.

Her mother searched Maria's face. "The dream was about you, honey, not some bogeyman. Don't you realize that? What are you afraid of that must pertain to this trip?"

Maria stared at both her mother and Winston. "I guess I'm ashamed of the way I treated Ed and left him so abruptly to go with George. I never wrote and apologized or did anything to explain. It's something I've been ignoring all these years." She put her head in her hands. "Am I afraid of facing him again?"

"Possibly." Her mother brushed hair back from Maria's face, like she had done when Maria was a child. "But he won't hurt you. He's a nice guy."

"Well, we're going, my girl, and with your children if they want to go," Winston said, emphatically.

How dare he suggest they'd go without her? "You're not leaving me behind." *I'm going. I'm changing my life.*

"That's the spirit. Go with us. Make things right with Ed and have a good time!" A delighted grin grew on Winston's face.

Her parents stayed and got the kids up while Maria checked with Briggie as to her plans with Nellie and Dean while she was away, gave her May's phone number, and asked her to contact her if Bill called. Then she glanced at Winston and smiled. "I'm ready." But the knot in her stomach tightened.

Would she run into Ed while they visited Don and May? And if so, how would she ever make amends?

4. Discoveries

July 1962
(Maria)

"Nothing like the smell of a new car, the open road," Winston proclaimed to all the eager occupants in his car, and, under his breath, he muttered, "None of the headaches of an old one."

"Thanks, Chris, for helping me with all our luggage. You ladies certainly brought a lot of clothes. Now, hang onto your hat, I'm going to give you the ride of your lives!"

"You can't frighten me, Stepdaddy." Maria stretched back against the seat. "It's pure luxury to have you drive."

"Well, you see, I need to be sure everything is working perfectly before I entrust this vehicle to you women." he said, with a delightful chuckle.

Maria patted his shoulder. "I'll let that chauvinistic remark pass because of my good mood."

"Grandpa, you promised we can stop early so we can swim in the motel pools," Amanda said. "Are we going to?"

"Of course, I factored that important feature into our trip all the way. I want to swim too." True to his word, Winston spared no expense. Every motel or hotel they stayed at all had beautiful pools.

Each time they encountered anyone during the trip who even looked faintly friendly, Winston would remark, "Salt of the earth, these Midwesterners."

"Do any of these towns look familiar to you, Maria, or didn't you notice with George in the car?" Ruth teased, as their car ate up the miles.

"They hardly registered with me back then. I think I was at my wits end trying to understand George. He was a hard man to read, and I was pretty naïve."

Her mother's innocent question forced Maria to face her feelings about him, once again, but she was pleasantly surprised to find her anger had melted away. Their life together was over, buried in a gentle place. All of the TV fix-it shows used the new catch phrase *emotional abuse*. Just like they said, it lasted only as long as someone let it.

Maria knew one thing. She'd never play the victim again. Feeling free from job deadlines and the day-to-day family responsibilities, she reached over and hugged her daughter.

"When will we be there?" Amanda asked for the hundredth time. "I've read my comic books over and over. I'm sick of them. I want to get out and run around."

Maria couldn't complain. Amanda and Chris had both been good travelers the past two days. All they seemed to need was plenty of hamburgers and swimming pools.

"Look there, everyone, at the big sign. 'Welcome to Illinois!'" Winston's voice boomed. "We'll be there before you know it."

"Grandpa may be a tad optimistic, children," Ruth said quietly, patting her kind-hearted husband's knee.

"I've been waiting to show you something that might interest you." Maria pulled out a Christmas picture of Don's whole family standing next to their renovated farmhouse. "Do you want to know their names?"

"No, Mom," Chris said, sounding bored. "I'll remember them when they introduce themselves to me." He let out a large sigh. "I'm more curious about the tractor."

Amanda was only interested in the two dogs in the picture. Slightly put down by her kids, Maria tucked her photo away. *So much for that.*

Her mother glanced back at Maria. "I'm going to call May when we stop for lunch and give them a heads-up as to when we think we'll be arriving."

She was smiling when she came back to the car after lunch. "May was so pleasant. She invited us for supper."

Winston laughed. "Great people, these Midwesterners, so generous. I love their name for dinner. Okay, family, we're going for supper with the Dawsons!"

"Perhaps May has more time and isn't so tired, now that most of her family is grown." Her mother sounded hopeful. "She seemed very happy."

How wonderful if that were true. *The success of our visit with the Dawsons will depend on May's attitude. I know my sister. Let's hope for the best.*

26

As dusk closed in around them, Winston's foot got heavier and heavier on the gas pedal. "I want to find the farm before the landscape merges into shadowy images."

Ruth and Maria held on for dear life as Winston's speed on the turns on the back roads increased, throwing everyone around.

"Faster, Grandpa," Chris yelled, coming to life. "Drive like a maniac."

Amanda stared out the window at the darkness. "Grandpa, are we lost?"

"Eureka, if memory serves me right from Don's detailed map, that's their fence. We're almost there!" Winston grabbed the handle to his left. "Roll down your windows and smell the sweet scent of the Midwest."

The minute they did, an incredibly foul odor wafted into the car.

"Phew!" Amanda covered her nose. "What's that smell?"

"Pigs, my girl. Uncle Don grows them to sell." Maria swallowed a chuckle. This would be a new experience for Maria's innocent suburban child raised around manicured lawns and swimming pools.

As they turned into the wide unpaved drive, the light from a tall pole suddenly flooded the whole area. Dogs began barking and wagging their tails, geese were squawking and fluttering around, and kitties were dodging both the dogs and the geese.

"Mom, did you ever see so many animals in one place before?" Amanda sounded absolutely delighted, and she jumped out of the car the moment it stopped.

Slightly stiff from sitting, Winston and her mother were more reticent leaving the car. They moved slowly, but finally stood and stretched beside the vehicle while Maria surveyed the farmhouse. A moment later, the kitchen door flew open, and two adults came hurrying out into the flooded light.

"Welcome, welcome," Don said loudly, grabbing Winston's hand and pumping it up and down. "Good job, you old coot, finding your way here."

Maria glanced at Winston after Don's sharp remark, but heard him laugh and say, "Well, I've never been called an old coot before, but I guess I'll let it pass. Our eastern favorite is, 'old goat.'"

Chris stood there laughing hard, attaching himself to the men while Amanda raced all over the tall grass trying to catch one of the kitties too quick for her. In her element in the furry kingdom of the farm, she finally caught an old tabby. Struggling to hold her, Amanda gripped her tightly and walked toward the kitchen door.

May blocked the entrance. "Not so fast, my child. Cats aren't allowed in my house. They belong outside. You can play with her tomorrow, and June will help you catch the babies. Now, hurry in before the mosquitoes carry us all off."

Amanda looked a little shaken by her aunt's directness, but she reluctantly put the cat down and slapped a mosquito. "Who's June?"

"She's your cousin, young lady. Come in and meet her."

June smiled at Amanda through the screen. "Come sit next to me at supper. I didn't go out because I hate mosquitoes."

Giving June an adoring smile, Amanda sat down quietly next to her. "Are you a teenager? I don't know any, except for you." Amanda looked starry-eyed at June, then leaned in closer. "Does it always stink so bad? I don't know if I can eat. I've never been on a pig farm before."

June laughed. "It's awful, but after a while, you won't notice it so much."

"Come in and sit down, everyone, before my dinner gets ruined," May yelled, passing a plate of fried chicken to Amanda.

"Does the food always smell so good on the farm?" Amanda grabbed a chicken leg, all crispy and brown.

June laughed. "Mom is a good cook. You'll love her farm food. Tomorrow, I'll show you some pups."

"Really?" she squealed. "I'm going to have so much fun being here. I was afraid you would be mean, but you're nice," Amanda said, lowering her voice. "I couldn't have a pet at my house because of my dad, but he died. Here, I can play with them as long as I like." Beaming at her cousin, she added softly, "Maybe I can take one of them home if you say it's okay, and I can talk my mother into it."

"Winston, how about learning a great game called cribbage after dinner?" Don asked at the other end of the big dining room table. "You, too, Chris, you'll be a natural," he said, with a gleam in his eye.

"You old smarty, you want some built-in unsuspecting opponents," Maria called from the kitchen, "Some things never change. I remember the wild games you and Ed use to play when he worked for you."

Other things never change either. Maria plopped another spoon of beans into the serving dish. *On this farm, the division of labor is very clear. May and all females work on the inside, and Don and all males work outside.*

28

After a huge farm meal, topped off with homemade blueberry pie, the women were left with the clean-up while Winston and Chris learned how to play cribbage. May's incessant chatter began wearing thin on Maria. May had never learned to let someone else talk. She'd briefly nod and acknowledge any comment that either Ruth and Maria interjected, but immediately return to her constant patter of trivia about her life. Besides being boring, it seemed to Maria that May had used every pot and pan in her kitchen to make their meal, and she couldn't keep from complaining as they finally finished.

"You always were looking for ways not to work when you stayed with us as a teenager," May snapped.

"No, May, I just saw smarter ways to do the stupid jobs you made me do, with less effort and better results."

May gave her younger sister an irritated look. "That's water over the dam. I want to talk about something else. I'm so excited." Her tone seemed rather secretive in nature, something Maria had rarely witnessed before. "I'm taking a course in drawing, and my teacher said I'm ready for oils next semester. Can you believe that?" She asked, actually blushing and fanning herself with a dish towel. "It's something I've dreamed about doing, forever. My teacher feels I have talent," she said, lowering her voice. "He told me so the other day," May's cheeks reddened even more. She began to pull out samples of her work from a large folder tucked back in her kitchen closet.

As May showed them her sketches, Maria couldn't help but admire the work. *My sister is talented. Perhaps she's always had this talent, but had to ignore this part of her when she was tied down with five children and lots of responsibilities.* "May, these sketches are beautiful!" Maria was being honest, and their mother joined in with her own praise. May's eyes lit up. "You really mean it?"

A ringing phone broke the silence. "Oh bother," May said, pausing to answer it. "Don, it's Ed, and he wants to talk to you."

What did Ed want? Her stomach twisted into a knot, and her mouth suddenly felt like it was full of cotton. Years ago, after her marriage, he'd sent one quickly scrawled note to her about his own wedding. He'd become a guilty memory.

Her usual effervescent brother-in-law became very subdued, and his tone serious as he talked with Ed. A few minutes later, he hung up the phone and took a deep breath. "Ed's wife has left him again, and he doesn't know what to do, so I invited him out to see all of you tomorrow. I hope that's okay with everyone," he said, looking straight at Maria.

Besides her stomach being upset, her heart had begun to beat faster, knowing she would have to face him again—something she hadn't planned on at all.

I know all about abandonment. We'll have that in common. But what pushed his wife into leaving him? Perhaps it was out of desperation. Maybe she couldn't stand another minute of Ed? I know about those feelings, too.

"Do they see a marriage counselor?" Maria didn't wait for an answer. "We spent our whole married life with one. George suffered from child abuse and the agonies of WWII, and he took it out on me," she said grimly, looking at her shocked audience.

"We didn't know," May said, sounding surprised at Maria's revelation. "We thought you had married the man of your dreams."

"So did I, but I didn't know George at all."

"I don't think Ed or his wife would go to one, but maybe they did," Don said. "But there isn't one around where they live."

"But I bet there are plenty in Chicago," Maria snapped back. Something inside her wanted to shock her smug Midwestern family and their values. They had theirs and to heck with everyone else. "What's the matter with you people? Are all of you so perfect that you don't even know about shrinks? Or do you choose not to know? Aren't there any desperate veterans out here like George with PTSD, or were all farmers exempt from the war? Are you living in the current century? Don't you realize there is a whole nation of people out there, hungry, homeless, and struggling?"

Maria looked at her self-satisfied chubby sister who was the typical farm wife. A woman who worked hard in her house and garden, raised hard-working kids, but never had to worry about anything. She had long-suffering Don, who to Maria's knowledge, had never looked at another woman, made a ton of money, and gave May everything she wanted.

What would they have thought if she'd mentioned George's five-year relationship with his mistress? Maria had kept it a secret only to protect her children and their memories of their father.

After a few moments, a subdued Don shifted his stance. "Ed offered to show Winston how his investment in the clinic has turned out," he said thoughtfully.

"By Jove, I'd certainly like to do that. He's kept me abreast of everything all these years, and I've made a lot of money from that clinic." Winston said, sounding like he wanted to change and soften the conversation.

"This is Ed's second marriage, and it sounds like it's in trouble." Don in a sad voice. "Poor guy, he just wasn't able to marry the girl he wanted to in the first place," he said, glancing at Maria.

"Let's see more of your wonderful work, May. I'm thrilled that you're finally able to pursue your dream." Her mother offered a gentle smile. "Maria, come enjoy May's work with me."

Maria responded to her mother's plea and focused on another sketch her sister had pulled from the closet. "Mom, doesn't May's artwork remind you a little of Elena's? You have the same natural talent."

"Was she the one who escaped with George from Puerto Rico before you married him?"

"Yes, Mom and Winston adopted her when she was a gangly teenager and raised her. She's all grown up and starting to have art exhibits of her work. Maybe you will too, someday."

An excited and delighted look spread over May's face. "Do you really think I'm good enough? I haven't had the courage to show anyone else my work. Your comments mean the world to me. Perhaps I can meet Elena someday and show her my paintings."

Maria saw a different person emerging from the brittle shell that had been May's protection for years. If what they'd said to her would be a catalyst for May to show her work, their trip was already a success. Under May's bluster lay a sensitive artist who was easier to love, making Maria feel closer to her sister than she ever had.

A genuine smile lit up May's face. "Perhaps we can see more of each other than we have in the past."

"I was thinking the same thing, sis."

"Our kids are basically gone now with only occasional visits. June sleeps here, but that's all. She's always doing something at school. I'm alone more than I have ever been, and that has given me the chance to paint. I actually look forward to getting up every day now."

Their mother gave a firm nod. "Let's do it then."

Maria grabbed May's folders of drawings, sketches, and her two oil paintings of the farm house. "Why don't we get out of this kitchen and show the menfolk how good you are. Have you ever shared any of this with Don?"

"No, I didn't think he'd be interested." May's voice carried a note of sadness.

"How do you know until you make him notice?" Maria moved closer to the kitchen door, hoping her mother and sister would follow. "Men need a visual picture, and they need to be given a big push when it comes to understanding women and what we can do. They can't imagine women out there competing with men in all walks of life."

My, I sound brave. Why was I such a chicken all those years with George?

5. Telling It Like It Is

July 1962

(Maria)

Marching into the living area, Maria waved the two paintings of the farm house and surrounding landscape under the men's noses, disrupting their cribbage game.

Maria ignored their grunts of displeasure. "Look at this amazing work, the detail, and color in these pictures. Aren't they beautiful? Don, your wife painted these pictures! I'm going to buy one of them from her and hang it in my study. I'm sick of all the pictures of war planes George put in there. May, if you paint some pictures of your farm animals, I'll buy them too. I'm going to make some big changes in my home.

"May has a lot of talent and needs some support, dear brother-in-law," Maria said firmly as she began covering their game board with sketches, one after another. The men at first only glanced at the artwork, but then began looking closer, making favorable grunts and positive comments.

Don gave a low whistle of approval. "These are pretty darn good."

Winston, the consummate diplomat, supported the discussion by offering to buy two of her delicate, detailed sketches of the water birds on Don's pond.

"I don't know what to charge for them, so I'll give them to you," May said, sounding stunned. "I'll also ask my teacher how and where to have a showing when he thinks I'm ready. Thank you all so much!" May looked like she might burst with happiness.

"My dear lady, never give your work away. Put a price on it. Then people will value it," Winston implored, taking one of May's paintings of water birds and inspecting it closely. Maria smiled at Winston. *I love you for being you. I wish I could find a Winston for me.* "He's right, you know, May. Look what other artists charge in the galleries and price yours accordingly."

"Okay, I will. But please take the pictures as gifts this time."

Feeling triumphant, Maria gave her sister and mother a squeeze. "I'm tired." She stifled a yawn. "Amanda's gone to bed, and so am I." She stopped for a moment to watch Don, Winston, and Chris, now completely absorbed in their game again. "Hey, time for bed, Chris," she said, but he ignored her. She shrugged her shoulders, too tired to play mother.

As she was climbing the stairs, Chris called, "Mom, I'm learning how to play cribbage."

"Okay, son, see you in the morning." *Chris is growing up and learning more than cribbage. It's wonderful he has his uncle and Winston. Both are good men.*

Peeking into June's room, she saw her daughter, already asleep in her clothes, sprawled across one bed and June in the other, reading. *No tucking in needed tonight, she's doing some growing up too.* Maria waved at June, closed the door, and jumped into the shiny new shower in the remodeled bathroom.

Refreshed and relaxed, she didn't remember anything more until morning. Stretching, she hugged herself and realized that she hadn't had one bad dream since she'd started on the trip. That occasional feeling of loneliness she'd also felt before they had left was gone.

Maria was aware her daughter had crept into her room. She was in that delightful place between sleeping and waking.

"Are you awake, Mommy? I want you to come with me to see Uncle Don," Amanda whispered urgently in her mother's ear.

"Sure, honey," Maria croaked, and stretched again, luxuriously, also realizing she didn't have to go to work. She sat up and hugged her daughter. "I'm wearing my new jeans that I bought for the trip. You wear one of your new shorts and tops Grandma bought you. We'll surprise Uncle Don and Aunt May in our new togs."

They heard Don before they saw him, rattling around in May's kitchen. "What have we here, a genie in the kitchen?" Maria teased her one and only favorite brother-in-law. Sitting down at the kitchen table, she asked, "Do my eyes deceive me or are you cooking? I thought only womenfolk worked in the kitchen in your house!"

"People change, even me, little sister. I've been up, done the outside chores by myself since my boys are gone, and made breakfast for all of you. Hope you like pancakes and bacon. That's all I can cook." He smiled at them both. "It's nice to have you here. The old house gets pretty quiet with just May and me rattling around in it. June's gone most of the time now too." He flipped several pancakes. "Tell me how your life is out there in the East. How have you been since the funeral?"

"We miss Daddy," Amanda piped up, "but we go to camp, have swimming lessons, and Mommy works. Briggie takes care of us until Mommy gets home at night."

"Sounds like you have a pretty important job, little sister. You're one of the new women out there earning a living and not at home. How is it?"

"It's fulfilling, has lots of pressure, but beats staying home and being bored."

"I'll never understand it, but it's happening everywhere." Don said disparagingly. "Women were made to stay at home and raise the kids."

"But what happens when the kids have gone, or your husband leaves you, or is killed?" Maria snapped back. "What do you do then?"

"Uncle Don, can I have one of your puppies to take home with me?" Amanda blurted out, interrupting their discussion.

"It's fine with me, but your mother has to say yes," Don answered, grinning at Maria. "Now eat your breakfast before it gets cold, and don't make your Uncle Don feel bad because you don't like my cooking."

"Don't think asking Uncle Don in front of me will make me say yes, Missy! We'll talk about it later."

Don slid onto a chair at the table. "I want to clear the air and let you know that I feel bad for snubbing you when you and George tried to see us before you left for the East years ago. I guess we were all pretty disappointed that you left Ed high and dry."

Amanda looked at her mother, then turned to her uncle. "Who's Ed, and why was he high and dry?"

Don grinned at her. "I guess I'd better be careful what I say around here. I forget that I have an audience."

"You're right about that," Maria said, feeling irked. *I wish Don would mind his own business and let me mind mine.*

"Amanda, when you finish your breakfast, there's a big tree swing out back that I used to swing your cousins on—and took an occasional swing myself. Go try it out, and tell me if you like it."

Amanda's eyes lit up, and she shoved the rest of her pancake into her mouth and ran out to find the swing.

"Little sister, I want to make amends to you while you're here.

Mother and I have planned some nice things for all of us to do, like seeing my favorite ball team, the White Sox, play in Chicago. We'd also like to take the kids to the Brookfield Zoo, and I know Winston would like to inspect Ed's clinic, especially since he invested in the business. I'll even go to Marshall Field's if I have to and let you gals shop."

"I appreciate the fact that you felt bad about me choosing George over Ed. But remember, George did ask me to marry him at Christmas that year. Ed wasn't ready to commit to me that whole winter before he graduated. When his vet business picked up, he changed and was very pushy with me, to say the least. All he thought about was himself and his needs. I really didn't know him very well.

"But during that time in '49, I felt like a juggler keeping a dozen balls in the air. My life had become a mass of confusion. I'd given up on George, and I thought he'd either decided against marrying me or had died. After that, I accepted Bill's engagement ring before he left for his new reporter's job in Washington, DC. Early that summer, Bill enlisted in the naval air force program and was off training to fly for the navy before the Korean War started. All our letters to each other got lost because of it. I thought he'd lost interest in me, and it actually devastated me. Otherwise, I wouldn't have encouraged Ed at all.

"And then my big surprise arrived. George appeared at my summer job, and you know the rest. Anyway, that's my story and water over the dam, my friend. Life's too short to linger in the past. Let's have a good time. My trip out here has been a godsend. Being here with you and May—" Maria's heart jumped at the sound of a truck pulling into the yard.

Moments later, she saw Ed standing outside the screen door, smiling and talking to Amanda, who had come running to see who was there.

Maria heard her daughter say, "I'm Amanda, Mommy's little girl."

When Ed opened the door, Amanda scurried past him, plunked herself down next to her mother, and smiled at him.

Ed smiled back. "I'm Ed, an old friend of your mother's."

"Sit down, old buddy." Don gestured toward an empty chair. "You're in luck. I've made my wonderful pancakes."

"Amanda, you didn't swing very long. Didn't you like it?" Don offered her another slice of bacon.

"Yes, I did, but I like to listen to all the grown-up talk," Amanda said, before taking a tiny bite of bacon. She stared at Ed, her eyes filled with curiosity. "Are you still high and dry?"

Ed laughed, but looked confused. "I think so, young lady."

"Good, because Uncle Don said that when Mommy left, you were high and dry."

Maria had to put her hand over her mouth to keep from laughing at Ed's continued confused look. "Sweetie, go find June and play with the puppies. Maybe we can take one home with us." Maybe that possibility would redirect her inquisitive daughter for a few minutes.

"Really, Mom?" Amanda threw her arms around Maria. "I'll ask June which one she thinks I should take." She grinned at their new guest. "It was fun talking to you, Ed, but I want to pick out my puppy." She flung the screen door open and ran outside.

Ed sat down next to Maria and took the mug of steaming coffee that Don offered him. "Is she always so friendly?"

"She likes you, otherwise she would have been silent," Maria said, smiling at him. As she sat there watching Ed, she felt an old intoxicating pull toward him that she hadn't felt for years. She couldn't explain the draw, it just was there. His male energy swirled around her so strongly as he sipped his coffee and joked with Don, she almost felt sick. She glanced at his profile, something she'd always loved. He still had a slight overbite and dimples in his cheeks. The scent from his freshly washed head of short, brown curly hair, combined with the fragrance of his shaving lotion, sent lusty signals to her nervous system and made her body tingle. Instead of laughing with him as he joked with Don, she felt overcome with his nearness.

"So, what brings you out so early?" Don glanced from Ed to Maria with a grin on his face. "Maria still looks like a kid, doesn't she? She hasn't put on a pound. If anything, she's skinnier. How long has it been since you two have seen each other?" Don paused for a moment and cocked his head, as though listening—but for what? "Gosh darn that woman of mine. I hear her calling for me to do something. She's never satisfied."

"Doc, I wanted to borrow your stethoscope. Mine's broken," Ed called out to Don as he disappeared. He downed the rest of his coffee, then his big brown eyes gazed into hers. "Would you dare take a walk with me?" he asked softly.

His question made her almost tongue-tied, but Maria cleared her throat and prepared to speak. "Okay. My little girl is in heaven with all the attention June is giving her to pick out a puppy. She won't miss me for a while, and Chris, my almost teenager, is probably still asleep."

Getting up and holding the screen door open for her, Ed called to Don, "We're going to find that stethoscope."

6. Catching Up

July 1962

(María)

Maria couldn't deny the excitement she felt as they strolled along the rather overgrown path to Don's lake. The cool morning air felt so good, she threw her head back and took a deep breath. "I smell the rich farm land of Illinois. It's good to be here. It makes me feel like a kid again." She held her arms out and twirled around, laughing for no reason. Her exuberance made her want to run. Giving him a challenging look, she broke into a trot toward the lake, feeling her hair flying in the breeze.

It didn't take long for Ed to catch up to her. "You're still full of fun, aren't you? You don't act like the grieving widow," he said, with a smirk on his face.

"I see the years haven't dulled your sharp remarks." *He has an uncanny way of uncovering me. I hate it.* "This may come as a surprise to you, but I know George has finally found peace, something he never had on earth. I also know he wants the best for all of us. Does that sound naïve to you?" How would Ed respond to what she'd blurted out?

"No, that's about the best explanation I've heard about living with the death of someone loved. Does that 'best' you mentioned include me?"

It was such a blunt question, Maria was left speechless for a moment. "Of course it includes you."

Tension was building between them, and she didn't like it. She peered out at the mist hanging over the lake. "Isn't the lake surreal and beautiful? It seems a shame to invade it while all the wading birds are fishing and enjoying their breakfast out there."

"Then, let's stop for a moment and talk. I want to get something straight."

"So, what's on your mind?" This situation—being here with Ed—still felt awkward. "You go first, and then I have a couple of questions for you, too."

Quickly, without any hesitation, he grasped her hand. "Your hand is cold, Maria. Why?"

"Because I have a lot of feelings rolling around inside me. Don't you?"

"Yes," he said, pulling her closer to him as they walked.

The silence is deafening. This isn't going to be easy. She needed to break the ice. "Let's sit down," she said, but then wished she hadn't because the dew-soaked grass made her pants damp. "I wish I'd brought a blanket with us."

Ed eased himself down close to her, knees bent, but he was smart enough not to sit. He threw a pebble into the water.

She watched the ripples from the pebble spread out across the still lake. "The lake is so beautiful, it seems a shame to talk, but we need to, so who's going first?"

"You are—you have the most to explain."

She turned and held his gaze. "Have you forgiven me for leaving you?" Her eyes filled with unexplained tears. "I've wondered for years."

He leaned over and put his arms around her. "Don't cry, honey." He tilted her chin up, and his big, brown eyes searched her face. "Seeing you looking so miserable knocks all the fight out of me," he whispered. Then he brushed her lips with a gentle kiss. "I've never forgotten you," he said, softly. "For a long time, I felt like a horse had kicked me in my gut every time I thought about you. Then, I hated what you did to me, but I could never hate you, Maria, never.

"When Don told me you were getting married, I knew it was all over for us. I think I decided to get even. I married a beautiful, wealthy breeder's daughter who had been coming on strong for all the wrong reasons. She'd never worked a day in her life and was spoiled rotten, but so sexy I couldn't keep my hands off her. She had one big problem, however. She let a lot of other guys put their hands on her, so after five years and a series of affairs, I called it quits.

"After a year or so, I started dating again—a gal whom I'd first met when I landed in St. Charles years before. This time, I thought she'd be a better partner for me because she was intelligent, able to carry on a decent conversation, and worked at the local newspaper. I figured she'd understand my late hours as a veterinarian because she sometimes worked late, too.

"Funny thing, I never wondered why she wasn't married or going with someone when we started dating. She would never tell me her age, but I thought she must be close to mine. Maria, you never know anyone until you live with them. To put it mildly, she isn't very affectionate. Right from the start, she requested that we sleep in separate bedrooms with the excuse that we both would sleep better.

"She uses every opportunity to keep from having an intimate relationship with me. I think it's because of what her father did to her. But she won't tell me what he did. She's also paranoid with my late hours as a vet. I can't tell you how many times she's shown up unannounced at a farm and driven the farmer's wife crazy. To get rid of her, the wives have resorted to bringing her down to the barn to show her that I'm really there. Other nights when I get home, we have huge fights over her wild imagination that I am cheating on her. She even accused me of having an affair with Maisie, Hugh's fifty-year-old wife. We had a big one last night, and she's gone to stay with her mother in Chicago.

"Maria, I couldn't cheat if I wanted to and live in a farming community. It would be all over town in two days. When I said *I do*, I said good-bye to any extracurricular activities with anyone."

"Do those extracurricular activities include kissing me? Or doesn't that count? And, you've never referred to either one of your wives by their names."

"Kissing you has a special place in my heart," he said, touching her face, tenderly. "As for my wives, Babs was my first, and Jackie is my second."

"Also, my friend, you haven't answered my question. Have you forgiven me?"

"I told you I could never hate you. Isn't that enough for you?"

"If that's all you can say, we'll have to leave it at that." *This conversation is like getting into quicksand—just like I felt with George when I struck a nerve.*

"It's your turn on the hot seat." Those big, soft eyes staring into Maria's unnerved her. "How was your marriage?"

"We had our ups and downs, but we worked them out, for the most part." *Why are we on the subject of my marriage again? Until he says he has or hasn't forgiven me, I'm clamming up.*

"How did you do it? I'm stymied. I don't know what to do." Ed's confession melted her resolve.

"It's hard for all of us. We just got lucky with our doctor. They're hard to find. We went to see Dr. Peter Rudolph, a great marriage counselor and psychiatrist."

"I never dreamed you were having problems. I guess I thought . . . Maria, I've messed up my life. I've had unhappy wives and no kids."

"Maybe it wasn't in your plan."

He gave her a puzzled look. "I don't know what plan you're talking about."

"I believe we're all born with a preordained plan in our mind that we're supposed to follow."

"Are you?"

"I tried. I know George and I were supposed to have our two kids. Maybe that's why we got married. Only we weren't thinking about children then.

"Maria, you touch on things I've never thought about. Did your counselor talk about plans and souls?

"No, he was trying to help us see how we unwittingly hurt each other."

"Think your Dr. Rudolf could help me?"

"He's in Washington, DC. You'd have to come and stay with us," she blurted out. The minute she said it, she wished she hadn't. "I'm sorry, Ed. I didn't mean to imply that you should come alone. You're still married."

"Our marriage is over, Maria," he said with finality. Ed stood up, skipped a couple more stones over the water, then kneeled back down. "Is there a chance for us? I've always loved you, you know."

"Ed, you forget, you're still married! I'm not a home wrecker." *I can't tell Ed the agony I suffered with George and his mistress. When I think of it now, I'm embarrassed I didn't leave sooner.*

Thinking about her foolishness with George irritated her and made her edgy. She wanted to move. "I'm putting my bare feet in the water and cooling off in more ways than one. Come on."

"How about a ride in Doc's rowboat instead?" He followed her to the water's edge. "We won't get wet."

"Okay, sport," she said, helping him turn the boat over and drag it down to the water.

"You know, I've never taken time to go fishing with Doc," he said as they put the boat into the water. "What's the matter with me?"

That question was loaded. She ignored it. "You had to jump-start your practice, and that takes determination and guts. I'm impressed with your success."

"Thanks for your vote of confidence. It means a lot. " He suddenly got up to give her a quick kiss, and the boat rocked, startling Maria. Over they went into the lake.

As they flipped over, she remembered tipping over the sailboat with George. The memory made her giggle as she surfaced. Ed came bobbing up, sputtering, and upon hearing her laugh, he chuckled too.

"You're such a good sport, Maria. I'm sorry."

"No need, the dunk broke the mood and made us laugh."

They swam the little boat back to shore, pulled it out, drained out the water, and leaned it against a log.

Maria smiled. "What say we go back and dry out too."

Ed had a devilish look on his face. "Can I finish what I tried to do in the lake?"

She didn't answer—she just kept grinning at him.

He wrapped his arms around her and slowly touched her lips with his. When she didn't resist, he said softly, "Let's see if I can squeeze some water out of us."

He kissed her again, sending currents of electricity rippling through her. She didn't want him to stop and impetuously kissed him back when he drew away.

He immediately kissed her again, and he began breathing heavily.

"Ed, we have to stop," Maria said, pulling away.

"I felt the old magic between us," he whispered. "Did you?"

"You don't have to ask. You know I did, but that's the easy part for us. It's always been that way. We were so obsessed with sex in college, we never really got to know each other very well. I used to lose all self-control around you, but I can't anymore. I have two wonderful kids back at the house I have to consider. I'd like to know you as a person and for you to know me, and my children, as well."

Ed's whole demeanor changed, his face became serious.

He probably hasn't even thought about my children. I wonder if he even likes kids. Amanda was certainly taken by him.

"You're right, Maria. I'd like to take some time off while you're here to get to know you better and make friends with Amanda and Chris. I'll check with Doc as to his plans for your visit. I also need to find out what my vet partner is willing to do so I can see you as much as I can."

They walked back, slowly, quietly, not holding hands. Maria was mulling over what had just happened, and she was pleased she'd mentioned the importance of her children.

Just before they went over the rise in the landscape, Ed said, "I want you to know I did plan on seeing you, hoping to find out if we might have a future. I won't forget what we talked about. When I'm around you, I do impetuous things, like now." He took her in his arms again, and Maria didn't resist. "There's got to be a chance for us," he whispered. "Thanks for coming back." He brushed his lips lightly over hers. "When we get back to the farm, I'm going to hop in my truck and leave. I just want to think about us and not have to make a lot of small talk with everyone. Tell Doc I'll call him when I know my plans."

"I will," she said quietly, giving him a strong and steady gaze. "Ed, I won't say that I didn't enjoy your kisses, but I can't let my loneliness get in the way of making sound decisions. I hope you understand," she said, with resignation.

"I know," he said," but tonight when I'm lying in that bed alone, I'll remember your lips and soft body in my arms." He took her hand, then releasing it, he walked quickly back to the farm and disappeared in his truck.

Don and May had planned a whole week of activities for them to enjoy. True to his word, Don took them to a White Sox game, complete with hot dogs, popcorn, and Coke for the kids and beer for the adults. After a day's rest at the farm, they spent the next day at the famous Brookfield Zoo. There was wildness and beauty in the large enclosures for the animals, replicating, to some extent, their original homes. Some of the animals ignored the visitors, and some hid in the vegetation. The big cats tended to pace back and forth with a restless energy, never hiding, mesmerizing the crowds.

On a man-made island, the chimps lived together in tribes and seemed to enjoy showing off their athletic skills in front of the crowds, swinging from branch to branch of well-worn trees. But by late afternoon, Amanda had expressed that she was hungry and hot. She'd experienced enough of the zoo. "Mom," Chris said, rolling his eyes, "my sister is moaning and groaning. I'm hungry, too. What about a big, juicy hamburger somewhere?"

"I know just the place—the White Castle, if it's still in existence." Maria hoped everyone would agree. It had been a long day. "When I was young, we kids went there every chance we could if we had twenty-five cents. How about it?" When no one offered any objections or alternatives, Maria sighed with relief and directed Don to their objective, much to Chris and Amanda's delight.

As they pulled into the crowded parking lot, Winston groaned. "I guess one wouldn't have cocktails here before dining, judging from the spartan décor. Have you ever seen so many youngsters in one place before?" He released a loud sigh. "Let's get in line."

They finished their hamburgers and headed for home. With the children dozing and the adults tuckered out, the ride back to Don and May's was unusually silent.

The following morning, the men seemed unusually enthusiastic as they waved farewell to their women as May's station wagon pulled out of the driveway.

"Good-bye! Good-bye!" Amanda yelled out the car window.

May had a determined look on her face as she sat ramrod straight, propped up with several pillows to help her see over the dashboard. "This car was made for a big man, not a little woman like me."

May glanced over her shoulder. "Amanda, I bet you've never ridden on our famous 'L.' Your grandmother, your mother, and I used to take it to the Chicago Loop and Marshall Field's huge department store. We're going there today, and you're in for a big adventure."

They parked alongside an entrance to the train in Oak Park, climbed the long flight of stairs to the train platform, and waited with all the other passengers. Moments later, a train rumbling down the tracks stopped and opened its doors. May herded everyone quickly into a car. "We're going to eat first in the Walnut Room before we shop, and it's my treat," she announced over the noise. "Don gave me the money, so don't argue."

Twenty minutes later, they walked off the train into the huge Marshall Field's department store and were whisked in the spacious elevators up to the eighth floor to the elegant, beautifully walnut-paneled room. Immediately, Maria's memories of better times with her mother and sister long ago came welling up inside her. It was mainly because her mother was always happy when they were there. But besides that, the thrill of always being allowed to order what she wanted to eat was so exciting. At home, whatever her mother made for dinner had to be eaten with no complaints.

Afterward, her mother had always taken them to see light-hearted movies of the forties in the magnificent Chicago Theater. They were always greeted with the sounds of glorious musical scores from the huge organ filling the room as a prelude to the highly anticipated movie.

Amanda and June were planning something for just the two

of them. Watching them giggling during lunch, Maria wondered what they had in mind. She trusted June, who seemed level-headed enough, but decided to reinforce her order to be on time. "Girls, don't be late. Meet us at 4:00 sharp at the 'L' entrance. Any questions?" she asked, catching their eyes as she spoke. "Remember what I said and have fun."

The women scattered in all directions in the store, promising to meet promptly at 4:00 p.m. Occasionally, Maria caught a glimpse of Amanda and June riding the escalators up and down between floors. Later, she saw them disappear into the toy department.

When they all met right on time, Amanda had a dot of chocolate on her cheek.

Maria wiped Amanda's face with her handkerchief, then showed her the dark smudge. "Where did that come from, honey?"

The girls giggled. "June bought me a chocolate sundae." Amanda grinned at her cousin. "Wasn't she nice?"

Maria smiled at both of them and nodded. She remembered how much fun it was to have a friend and share a treat together.

The blaze in the fire pit was a welcome sight for the women when they returned, tired and hungry. They bustled around, adding a large garden salad, buns, marshmallows, and drinks to the roasted hotdogs, rounding out their supper.

The night sky had quietly descended while they were eating, lit by millions of stars. Her mother pointed to the twinkling display. "Out here in the country, the stars look like diamonds sparkling down on us!"

"I've never seen them so bright!" Winston said, tipping back in his chair to observe them.

"They are quite a show." Don put another log on the fire, making flames lick out in all directions. "Get your sticks ready. It's marshmallow time."

"Gosh, this so much fun on the farm, Uncle Don," Amanda said, as she stuffed a browned marshmallow in her mouth.

Slowly, the fire burned down and had a primal effect, mesmerizing everyone.

"I'd like to stay here all summer," Chris said, breaking the mood. He glanced at his mother, then Don.

Maria ignored her son's casual comment, assuming he was caught up in the moment, but Don didn't, judging by his smile.

May stood and stretched. "Time for clean-up. It's been a long day, and I'm ready for bed.

"Aunt May, I love your farm and all the kitties and puppies," Amanda said.

The sound of the phone pierced the night air, causing everyone to look at Don. "Probably a farmer with a sick cow," he said and ran inside to answer it. Maria heard him say, "Sure thing, Ed. I was going to phone you up, but I've been busy working Winston and Chris around the farm to pay for their suppers. We'll meet you any day you say. Next Monday sounds fine. You'll make reservations for us at the St. Charles Hotel? Great, ol' buddy. I'll even wear a clean pair of jeans." A quiet pause indicated Ed was speaking again on the other end. "You want Maria? Okay, I'll put her on."

Maria went inside and accepted the receiver from Don. With all ears expectantly listening, she said, "Hi, I guess we're on for next Monday."

"I know you can't talk. I just wanted to say I've been mulling over everything that happened between us, and I can't wait to see you again."

Maria could feel all ears straining to hear and just replied, "See you Monday."

"What did he say, Mommy?"

"He said he was looking forward to seeing everybody." Maria looked at her mother and received a guarded smile.

7. Weighing All Options
Late July–Early August 1962
(Maria)

The following Monday, bright and early, Winston drove his roomy but cumbersome station wagon slowly out of the farm driveway with five reasonably happy adults and two tired and silent children in tow. Of course, Don sat with Winston in front, with the rest of the women and children relegated to the back. No one ever challenged that.

Winston rolled down his window. "How do you know which road is which, Don? There are no signs here. They all look alike to me,"

"I finally know my way around, but I've been lost my share of times."

"How's Ed doing?" Winston tapped his fingers on the steering wheel. "He seems like a smart vet."

"He's a better vet than I am, but don't tell him I said so. He's also quite a surgeon, always going to conferences and using every new technique he learns."

As the men were conversing in the front, May whispered to Maria, "Since you've given me so much encouragement about my art, I'm thinking about getting a little day job in an art supply store so I can meet other artists. I'm so bored at home.

"Why are you whispering? Speak up. You have a right to look for a job. I think you'll find yourself looking forward to each day, seeing other people besides Don."

"I don't know how he feels about it."

"It's your life, May. You need to live it. In case you haven't heard, we won the right to vote, and supposedly we are first class citizens, even though a lot of men don't realize that yet," Maria remarked, hotly.

It was midmorning when they drove through the center of St. Charles to the beautifully quaint St. Charles Hotel and parked under its portico. Moments later, Ed came striding through the lobby doors.

He poked his head through Winston's open car window. "I've made all the arrangements. Just stay in your car and follow my truck to the clinic, Winston." He paused for a moment. "To make more room in the car, why don't you ride with me, Maria?"

"My, my." May sniffed as Maria laughed, got out, and climbed into the truck's cab.

She grinned at Ed. "You realize you have a car full of people watching us."

A slight smile slipped onto his face as he put his arm around her. "I know."

"Are you sure you should be doing this? It got us into all kinds of trouble once. I bet you don't remember the first time you did this to me."

"I remember everything about that Thanksgiving weekend with you," he said, his voice catching as his arm tightened around her. They rode that way to the clinic in silence.

Gathering his visitors inside the clinic, Ed introduced his partner, Glen, and his office assistant, Hugh. As he led them through the clinic, Ed explained how their surgeries were handled. Maria was struck by how spotlessly clean the rooms were, but she wasn't surprised, because Ed had always been so squeaky clean himself.

"Can I see the animals?" Amanda piped up.

"That's our next stop." Ed took them to several small recovery rooms—one for cats and the other for dogs. In each large room, the animals appeared comfortable in their clean cages.

"Someday, I'm going to work in a clinic," Amanda announced, but no one heard her little voice except her mother.

Typical male, Ed was busy explaining the life of a veterinarian to Chris, who looked bored and was shifting from one foot to the other.

"The boss is having a good time showing off our clinic," Glen said to Maria as they stood next to each other. He seems very up today. Does it have anything to do with you?"

"I don't think so, we're just getting reacquainted."

Glen grinned at her. "Before I left this morning, Sharon asked me to invite all of you over to the house. I know she's excited to see you again, Maria. That's all she's been talking about. Shall I call her and tell her you're coming?"

"Sure, Glen, we'd love to."

"By the way, I never thanked you for introducing Sharon to me when we were all at Iowa State together. She's a great gal, my best friend, and smart, too."

"I'm glad I did it. You two sound like you make a good team and have a great marriage. Don't let anything happen to it."

"Ed told me you're a recent widow. I'm sorry that happened, but I'm glad you came to see us." Glen tilted his head. His eyes were full of questions. "Whatever happened to you and Bill? At school, I thought he was number one with you."

"The Korean War happened. It's a long story, better left unsaid." Smiling she asked, "Will we see you this afternoon?"

"No, someone has to run the show with the senior partner goofing off," he said loud enough for Ed and Hugh to hear.

Hugh sidled up to her. "It's great to see you again. You look just as pretty as you did when I first met you, and the boss thinks so, too."

"Flattery will do it every time, you rascal." She grinned, pleased with his compliments. "It's good to see you walking so well. Tell me, when was your operation? I remember you still in your wheel chair at Don's years ago."

"Well, let's see . . . Terri's husband, Doc Bentley, gave me my legs back for free before he went to that damned Korean War, twelve or thirteen years ago, right after I met him at Don's."

"Who took his legs?" Amanda looked aghast. "I'm glad the doctor was able to give them back to him. Where did the doctor find them?"

"I'll explain later, honey," Maria whispered.

As they filed out, Ed caught up with Maria. "Would you ride with me?" he asked softly. Winston, follow me for a little ride through the countryside to Sharon and Glen's place!" A few miles outside of town, Ed casually pointed out his home to Maria.

"You have a big house."

"Yeah, and it's a mess. My wives didn't fix it up, and now, living alone, I don't care."

Maria ignored his chilling remark as she climbed out of the truck to join her waiting daughter, who was jumping up and down in excitement. "Ed, who do those ponies behind that fence belong to? I wish I could have one," Amanda said softly. She kept turning around to look at them as she walked to the front door, and she almost tripped over a small tricycle.

A small naked boy bolted out of the house in front of them, but Ed scooped him up. "Where are your clothes, Timmy?" The child began squirming and yelling to be put down.

"So there you are, mister. I've been looking all over the house and yard for you," a pretty young woman said, breathing hard and looking embarrassed. "Hello, everyone, welcome. I'm Sharon, a long-time friend of Maria's. We went to Iowa State together. And thanks, Ed. I'll take my little rascal. I don't understand two year olds," she said, shaking her head. "I never planned on a kid like this. Forgive us, folks." Inviting them in, she put Timmy on her hip. "It's so good to see you again, Maria. It's been too long."

Smiling at Sharon, Maria let Ed make introductions all around among the adults.

"I'd like you all to meet Violet, my five-year-old daughter and my big helper," Sharon added. "You've already met Timmy." Looking at Ed, she asked, "Would you hold Violet's hand? She just adores you."

"Of course, I will." He grinned down at his little charge.

Violet immediately clamped her tiny hand into his and returned his big smile.

"Everyone, excuse the messy house. Just shut your eyes and follow me out into the back yard. It's our favorite place to be. As you'll see, I prefer gardening to housekeeping."

As they stepped outside, they were greeted with a yard bursting with color. Bluebird boxes were alive with little baby birds making chirping sounds as their parents flew endlessly back and forth to feed them, and trellises of flowering plants perfumed the yard and enticed butterflies and honeybees to compete for their nectar. A large vegetable garden filled in the back section of the yard, full of ripening red tomatoes and thick, dark green leafy greens growing in rows. A grape arbor was loaded with succulent bunches of purple grapes just begging to be eaten. Behind all of it were several bee hive boxes hidden in between bushes.

"Mommy, look," Amanda whispered, as a delicate butterfly landed on her shoulder, its wings rhythmically undulating as it rested there. She froze until after a moment or two, it fluttered away.

"Butterflies are good luck, Amanda," Ed said.

Amanda gave Ed a big smile. "The lady's yard is a magical place." With Timmy clinging to her hip, Sharon answered all their questions, naming her flowers, plants, butterflies, and birds. She was a veritable encyclopedia when it came to knowing what interesting things were growing in her backyard. When everyone seemed satisfied, Sharon held up a clump of purple grapes. "Try these. They're delicious." Ed used his pocket knife and handed them to eager outstretched hands.

"Mommy, these are yummy!" Amanda wiped juice from her chin. "Can we have a garden like this at home?"

"Honey, I don't have the time or inspiration to do the work this requires."

"I'll help," her daughter replied, naïvely.

"When the temperature zooms upward and you have your swimming lessons, you'll not want to work in the garden." To change the subject, Maria asked, "Sharon, show us what's in that huge building behind your yard."

"It's the work I do for several seed companies." Sounding excited at the prospect of sharing her passion, Sharon led the way.

As they trooped into the weather controlled building, kept it at a constant seventy-two degrees, a few sighs were heard.

Winston wiped his brow. "By Jove, this is nice in here."

Looking over multiple rows of green shoots with labels, stretching for hundreds of yards, they listened and followed Sharon as she guided them around the huge building, giving expert explanations of the experiments she was implementing. When she finished, Winston asked if she had any help with all the heavy work to keep the plants growing.

"Yes, I have a team of high school youngsters interested in the environment and how to grow the seeds who do all the grunt work for me. Their school awards them credits.

Wow! My old dorm mate has always had such passion and interest in botany. Someday, she'll be recognized for her work.

As they walked back into the house, Maria said, "Sharon, I'm sorry we haven't kept in better touch, but now I'm recovering and will be a better friend."

"I'm glad. Glen told me about your husband, and I'm sorry. It must be terrible to lose your partner so unexpectedly. As for me, I'm up to my neck with the kids and my work and haven't been the best friend either. But you're here now, and that's what counts. I'll let you in on a little secret. Ed has been on pins and needles since he found out you were coming. Ed's really been a great senior partner for Glen, as well as our friend."

"Speak of the devil, here he comes now," Maria said. *I'm amazed by how well he is liked.* "He looks like he's ready to offer us something. I wonder what it is?" Ed's grin reminded her of a big kid bursting with a surprise.

"Gals, I'm buying lunch today at the local root beer stand." His eyes twinkled. "Want to come with us, Sharon?"

"Thanks, but no thanks. Timmy will ruin it for everyone. He's too wild." Sharon kissed her son playfully. "Take Violet, she'd love it. Just drop her off at the clinic afterward. She'll play with the animals, and Glen will bring her home with him."

"Come again!" Sharon called out the front door, holding onto a squirming Timmy. "I promise to be better organized next time. Maria, I'll get Carol's number for you." She ducked inside for a moment, then returned and handed a slip of paper to Maria.

"Thanks! We'll keep in touch, Sharon."

Violet and Amanda were waiting by Ed's truck with determined looks on their faces.

Violet grabbed his hand. "I'm sitting on Uncle Ed's lap."

"I'm going to sit on my mommy's lap," Amanda said, apparently not wanting to be outdone.

Ed winked at Maria. "I guess we'll have company to the root beer stand, whether we want it or not."

As they bounced along, Amanda asked, "How can you drive with Violet on your lap?"

"It's not easy, but she doesn't weigh much. Do you want a turn, too?"

"Yes," Amanda answered, emphatically, "but there's no room for me." She glared at Violet.

A bit of jealousy was evident between the girls vying for Ed's favor.

At the root beer stand, Ed was the perfect host, making everyone comfortable at their large picnic table, taking and returning with their orders, while seating Maria at a more intimate table for two under a big tree away from the family.

After watching him rush back and forth for several minutes carrying everyone's orders of hamburgers and root beer floats, she asked, "What took you so long?" He burst into laughter for the first time that day. "You're what I need in my life—a sense of humor."

Maria felt emboldened by his compliment. "Stop. You're making all the men jealous, you're delighting my mother and sister, and you're causing Violet and Amanda to fight for your attention. And, to top it off, I saw you and Winston both trying to pay for lunch. What are you trying to prove?"

"I guess I want you to think about me as someone special," he said, holding her eyes with his for a second. "As for my success with little girls, that's easy. It's one woman in particular that I'm trying hard to impress, but I don't know if I'm getting anywhere."

Take it easy, Maria. Change the conversation. "You like spending money on me, don't you?"

Ed nodded. "Yeah, it takes a lot of vet calls to buy your lunch, but

I'll manage somehow." He took a swig of his root beer. "You look like you have something more on your mind. A penny for your thoughts," he said, grinning as he sat down to eat his lunch.

"What do you think about seeing Terri and Grey tomorrow? I'd like to touch base with my old boss before we hit the road for Washington. I was wondering if you could take time from your work and drive over with us to see them. After Grey helped Hugh regain the use of his legs, I thought you might like to thank him personally. When I call them, can I include you?"

"Don't call them," he said, his face a dark cloud.

"Why not? We're leaving the following day for home."

"Because I want to see you alone—not with a bunch of people. Besides, driving there one day and taking off the next is ridiculous. Your kids would much rather stay on the farm for the last day and not with all those strangers."

"Hmm, maybe you're right." Maria set her hamburger down, and wiped ketchup off her lip. "I tend to try to pack too much in sometimes. I would love to swim in Don's lake just once before I leave, Amanda loves to play with the animals, and Chris would rather go on calls with Don." She took a sip of her cold drink. "Okay, I'll ask the folks. I'm sure they would like to have the day to pack up properly. I think I was being a tad foolish."

"And I want you to spend your last day with me."

She laughed. "You sound like I'm going to be executed!"

Ed chuckled, too. "Maybe you are in a way—going back to Washington and leaving me," he said, quickly getting up and giving her a hug.

She pushed him away. "Ed, I think we got a little carried away at the lake. I need to slow down."

"For god sakes, it was only a kiss."

"It was a lot more than that, and you know it. You're married and have a wife who probably still hopes there's a chance for the two of you. Until you're divorced, there will be no more kisses or anything else."

Ed's face darkened again, plus he looked embarrassed. "Okay, okay, I get it. Spend tomorrow any way you want. I won't be there."

8. Laying Their Cards on the Table

Late July–Early August 1962
(Maria)

Maria bolted up from their table and joined the rest of their party. *I have to draw the line somewhere. Ed's mad, but too bad. I keep thinking about his poor wife.*

Smiling at everyone she said, "I think we should spend our last day on the farm and not with the Bentley's. It's too much. What do you think?"

"I agree," her mother quickly said. "I just didn't want to disappoint you or Terri. Why don't you call and explain your change of heart? I'm sure she'll understand. We'll be out here again to see May and Don, and you can see her then. Winston, do you agree?"

"Of course," he said looking at Don. "And it will give me a chance to beat you—just once—at cribbage, and swim in your lake."

May started to clean up their table. "And I'll have time to pick some vegetables from our garden and send them home with you—especially our wonderful tomatoes."

"So, it's settled then. I'll call her now." Maria walked slowly to the hot, little phone booth. dreading to have to cancel the visit. She really wanted to renew her friendship with her old boss and valued friend.

Delighted with Terri's understanding, Maria hung up and stepped out of the booth.

Ed stood there, looking miserable. "Did you mean what you said?"

"Yes, of course I did, but can't we stop this fighting? Let's enjoy the rest of the day. I don't want to meddle in your personal life. I know you're angry at me, but you shouldn't be. You should be glad I don't want to influence your decision about ending your marriage.

"I took your advice. We're not going to Terri's. You see, I do listen to you."

"Okay," he said, sounding reluctant, but he smiled.

Maria took Ed's hand and walked over to sit with everyone and be part of the happy group.

Don was entertaining them with stories about difficult animals he had to treat and, far worse, their owners.

"Good, you are joining us, my boy," Winston said, studying Ed. "Can you spare the time tonight for a swim and supper, as you call it, at Maisie's? And tonight, dinner's on me. You were too quick for me today."

"I'll probably burn the midnight oil tonight doing paperwork, and I may even have to make some calls if there's an emergency. I'll let you know about tomorrow." Ed glanced at Maria. "It all depends."

"Let's get going," Don said. "I need to make some vet calls, myself, back at the hotel."

Amanda raced to Ed's truck and made it just ahead of Violet. She scrambled into the cab and tried to close the door, but Violet was too fast and hopped in too.

"Winston, would you do me a favor and take those two little feuding girls with you and drop Violet off at the office? Her daddy will take her home." Ed rubbed the back of his neck. "I'd like to talk to Maria alone."

"Of course, my man. I'll go get those two little Indians."

"Thanks, Winston."

"You lead the way back. These country roads are still a puzzle to me, and I don't want to get lost with this crew. We all need a swim in the pool. Your Midwestern summers are hotter than Washington, I do believe." He paused. "Maria deserves some genuine attention," he said quietly. "She's had quite a time of it."

Winston waved the group over. "Everyone, come with me. Ed and Maria are going to lead the way. Amanda and Violet, we're going to swim and then to Maisie's for supper." He smiled at his wife. "We men have decided."

"I like your stepfather," Ed said. "He's quite a guy."

"I see you two have been talking about who is riding with whom, and I'm with you," said Maria.

"Yes, I need to apologize, so I can see you again." He gave a small smile and gestured toward his truck. "Please get in."

"I think the term that describes both of our situations is REBOUND—in capital letters—you with Jackie and me with my memories."

Ed was silent for a minute or two. "That's plain enough. I hadn't thought of our situations as similar, but they are. You don't mince words, and I guess I like that, but whatever happened to that sweet, giggling girl I knew in college?" he asked as he drove out onto the highway with Winston close behind.

"She grew up." Maria paused. *How could she ever trust a man again.* "I'm not sure I'll want to remarry. There are three lives riding on my decisions now, and I can't make another mistake."

"Hey, no one's talking about marriage, least of all, me. You remember me, noncommittal Ed. But I would like to start seeing you again, if you're interested. I can fly out to Washington for long weekends this summer and fall, and we can explore the possibilities between us." Despite needing to keep his focus on the road, he held her gaze for a moment. "No strings, okay?"

"There's a third party here who isn't being considered—Jackie."

"Okay, that wasn't very nice, but I did warn Jackie we were through if she left."

"Let me tell you a little story about George and me so you know you're not alone in this miserable situation. I had decided to file for divorce the day before George's plane crashed. Flying geese clogged his plane's engines, causing them to stop, and his plane fell like a stone. There was no need to file once I got the news.

"We'd gone for marriage counseling for years, but it didn't work," she said, bitterly. "I finally wised up. George was never going to leave his mistress. After realizing that, I gave up on the marriage, but I went to the shrink for personal therapy to get my head on straight."

"Wow, what made you tell me all of this?"

"To ask you to consider counseling. With no third party, it might work for you."

"I was all for it because I knew after a year or so that we were in deep trouble. I actually begged Jackie to consider therapy. I even suggested she ask her witch of a mother to help us because she's lived in Chicago for a long time and might know a good doctor, but Jackie refused." Ed sounded so angry and upset. His eyes darkened and Maria could see the muscles in his jaw clench. "I think I know why. She's afraid she'd have to tell me and the counselor about her father's relationship with her. I think he raped her."

"Oh, my gosh, poor Jackie!

"Yeah, and I bet that mother of hers turned a blind eye to the whole thing."

"How awful! To have a mother like that. You must give her another chance!

"Thanks for being so honest with me, Ed. We do have a great deal in common when it comes to miserable marriages, but I'm not proud of that. I'm now in the process of self-discovery, and I need time to figure out my life so I don't make any more mistakes."

"You're certainly clear about what you will and won't do. At least I know where I stand. I don't like it, but I couldn't leave things the way they were, having you think I was a complete ass." Ed's demeanor changed slightly, and something about him made Maria ache when she heard him say quietly, "There's a big part of me that I don't understand when I get so mad."

"We all have parts of ourselves we don't like that pop up at inopportune times."

"I'm sorry I have to work, but Glen can't take up all the slack. I've ignored the office too much. I guess I thought we'd see each other and everything would be rosy. But it's not so easy. We're both different, and I don't know how to interest you. I'll meet you in the morning at the hotel, and we'll go from there." He leaned over and brushed her cheek with his lips. "I'll get you to giggle yet."

She could hear everyone playing in the pool when she walked into the hotel lobby, still thinking about Ed's confession. Violet and Amanda were splashing around together, several young boys with Chris were doing cannonballs off the diving board, and the rest of her family were sitting under two large sun umbrellas sipping tall drinks.

"I see we still have Violet with us."

"She convinced her father that she'd be perfectly okay, and, so far, she's having the time of her life with Amanda." Winston handed her a glass of beer. "Here's your favorite summer drink. Down it before I do." Winston took a gulp of his cocktail. "When is Ed joining us?"

"I'm not sure."

"Well, little sister, how was the ride back from the root beer stand?" Don said with an evil chuckle.

"My sister has the right to a little privacy. Stop being so nosy!" May snapped.

Maria stifled a smile. *I can't believe my ears. My sister is actually sticking up for me!*

For the next hour, as the sun sank lower, the adults enjoyed a relaxing hiatus, ignoring the wild antics of the youngsters burning the last of their energy supply in the pool.

Suddenly, the pool noise stopped and Amanda, Violet, and Chris were standing there, the water droplets from their suits dripping on the deck. Amanda was the most vocal, complaining about being hungry.

"We can fix that," Maria said. "Here are your clothes. Go get dressed in the locker room, and Amanda, please help Violet."

After a Midwestern supper at Maisie's quaint café, as Winston called it, he congratulated Maisie on her service and hospitality, completely unaware that Don was paying the waitress. Walking out, Don challenged him to a cribbage game later that evening. He said the stakes were high. The loser had to buy dinner for everyone the next time they met.

"Why don't we gals take a walk around the town while the men take Violet home and play cribbage," Maria's mother suggested as they left the café. "The weather is lovely, there's no traffic, and no mosquitoes."

Hopping up and down alongside Maria, her grandmother, and May, Amanda moaned. "I really want a puppy, but I don't think I can take one home because all the hotels say *no pets allowed.*"

"Judging by the way your mother and Ed were talking, maybe he's going to visit. He could bring the pup," May said, with a slight smirk on her face.

"Really, Aunt May? Is he coming, Mommy?"

"Not in the foreseeable future," Maria said firmly, glaring at May. "He's got to take care of his wife."

"All right, gals, I think we're all tired," their mother said. "Let's go back to the hotel and turn in. We'll have a long day tomorrow with packing up for home." Their mother wagged her finger at Maria and May. "You two sisters be nice to each other."

Exhausted by the day's activities, Amanda passed out the minute her head hit the pillow. That delighted Maria, who was anxious to talk with her folks. She tapped softly on their adjoining door, walked in, and sat down on her mother's bed. "I want to talk to you both when Winston gets out of the shower. I know you're wondering what's going on between Ed and me."

Winston came into the room in his pajamas, drying his full head of white hair.

Her mother sat up a bit straighter. "Winston, Maria wants to talk to us."

Winston stopped rubbing his head with the towel and glanced at them both. "Hmm, I sense a problem."

58

"I need your opinion about Ed. He's pushing me pretty hard, and it worries me. He's charming, but I saw an angry side to him today. I know he's frustrated, but I can't be the reason he breaks up with Jackie. I won't do to Jackie what George and his mistress did to me. Besides, I really don't know him."

"Of course, Maria. You're much better than that," Winston said, sitting down on his bed with his towel draped over his shoulders. "I like Ed, and maybe I did hope he'd give you a lift after what you've been through, but you must hold your ground. Don't be hasty. He can't solve your problems, and you can't solve his. Plus, you have no financial worries, thanks to George.

"Honey," her mother added, "it's hard at first being alone, but many new avenues will open up to you if you just give yourself time to heal."

"As for the pup," Winston said, "if you want Amanda to have one, we'll smuggle it into the hotels."

Her mother shook her head. "May tells me the puppies aren't old enough to leave their mother for another few weeks, so that settles that problem."

"Mom, it doesn't," Maria said, slightly irked with her mother's casual dismissal of Amanda's needs. "She's just a little girl. Losing her dad, however distant he was, has been hard on her. I can't be heartless. She needs something to love."

9. Wrapping Things Up

August 1962

(Maria)

The next morning, Maria was awake when Ed called. His crisp tone stating he had an emergency and should be back by ten to say good-bye indicated something was wrong. He was either still mad at her or tired from working so late last night.

"Okay, Ed." She was ready to end the conversation and hang up when he said, "I called my wife late last night, and I'd like to talk to you about it."

"Ed, I can't stand the thought of hurting Jackie. Remember that." Maria hung up before he could say another word. *It was all too painful, she needed some space from him.*

"Mommy, was that Uncle Ed?" Amanda asked, leaping into her mother's bed. "Do you like him? I do. He's nice to me and he's funny.

"Who decided to call Ed, Uncle Ed?"

"Me! That's what Violet calls him." Amanda made herself comfortable. "Why is he called a vet? What is that?"

"My, you're just bursting with questions this morning. Ed's called a vet, short for veterinarian, because he's an animal doctor. I met him when he worked for your Uncle Don."

"So, Uncle Don is a vet, too? I thought he was a farmer."

"He's both, but he's really a vet first. His work pays all the bills."

With that big question answered, Amanda lay down next to her mom and cuddled up close. "Mom, I love you so much." She kissed Maria's cheek.

Tears filled Maria's eyes. *Thank you, God, for giving me my little girl.* Maria wrapped her arms around Amanda and gave her a hug. "I love you, my little sweetie."

Lying there, she anguished about Chris. *I love him as much or more than Amanda, but I can't gush over him. He wants to be an independent young man, but it's hard to let go.*

It was easy with Amanda. She loved being hugged. "Cutie, let's take a shower together, and I'll wash your hair when I wash mine. Then we'll go down to the lobby and look in the gift shop. Maybe we can find a nice 'thank you' gift for your aunt and uncle."

"What are we thanking them for?"

"Your aunt and uncle have made us feel welcome, fed us wonderful meals, taken us on sightseeing trips, and stopped their work schedule to make our trip special."

They found a hurricane lamp for May's picnic table, and some lavender soap for May, but nothing for Ed. What he needed she couldn't give him.

On the way out, Amanda picked up a soft, furry stuffed puppy with long, floppy ears. She held it close. "Please, Mommy, can I have it? It looks like the real puppy I'm going to get."

Maria knew Ed wouldn't be coming to see them, so she gave into Amanda's request.

Everyone was up early for their final breakfast at Maisie's. They met in the lobby and walked purposefully down Main Street, knowing their trip was over. Only Chris, who walked alone bringing up the rear, seemed oblivious and wrapped up in himself.

Maisie greeted them exuberantly and welcomed them in. The aroma of freshly made coffee floated in the air, adding to their enjoyment. The place was almost empty except for a few regulars who sat at the counter. "Sit anywhere, folks, and I'll bring you some coffee. Menus are on the table."

"Ed must be running late," Maria said. *Maybe he's not coming. If so, so much for that.*

"He'll be here." Her mother opened up a menu. "If I know human nature, he's not going to let you leave without saying good-bye."

They'd just finished eating when Ed joined them, looking and acting distant.

As if on cue, Don and Winston invited him to join them for one last day together.

Ed glanced at Maria. "I'm on the fence. I have a full day's work to do today."

"I've been waiting for you," Maisie said, bringing him a steaming cup of coffee. "How's my secret boyfriend?"

61

"Just waiting for you." Ed grinned for the first time since he'd walked in.

Maisie rested her hand on Ed's shoulder. "I hope you folks will be coming back to see Ed again. He's our pride and joy. Everyone loves Doc."

"My dear lady, we love your Midwest hospitality. We shall be back, soon!" Winston handed her money for their breakfasts and included a generous tip.

"Uncle Ed, can I ride with you back to Aunt May's farm today? Did you fix some sick animal this morning? Mommy told me what you do every day, just like Uncle Don," Amanda said, sounding very pleased with herself.

"Well, Petunia, I'm not sure I can."

Amanda giggled. "Uncle Ed, I'm not a flower," she said shyly.

"You are to me," he said, holding his coffee cup and sitting down between Amanda and Chris.

Maria suddenly felt let down with him not sitting next to her. Ed was overdoing it with her kids. *Why the big uncle act with them? It's too soon. Maria, isn't this what you wanted? Are you jealous? You silly goose, you should be happy he likes them so much.*

"Please come, Uncle Ed," Amanda begged. "Ask him to come, Mommy."

Chris looked up at her. "Yeah, Mom, I'd like to talk to Ed about doing some work for him."

With Ed watching, both of her children were pushing her into a corner. It was obvious that Ed knew what was happening and was enjoying it. If she didn't say yes, they'd be upset.

"It's fine with me," she said, almost defensively and worrying about the unknown consequences.

"I want to ride with Ed, Mom. I have lots of questions for him," Chris said, more enthusiastically than her son had been for several days.

Amanda practically jumped out of her seat. "Me, too! I want to ride with him. Can I, can I?"

Maria locked eyes with Ed. "Are you sure you can spare the time?"

"I can, if you can. It's important to all of us."

They drove in two vehicles, and before Maria knew it, Winston was pulling into the farmyard.

Chris startled her by racing up to her door. He opened it and leaned in. "Mom, I need to talk to you."

By his tone, it sounded like he thought it an urgent matter, but what could be so important? "Can't it wait until later? We just got home."

"No, I want to talk now!" Chris yelled defiantly. "A few days ago, Uncle Don invited me to stay with him for the rest of the summer and learn all about farming and vet medicine. This morning, riding over here with Ed, I asked him what he thought, and he agreed it would be a great experience for me. He even offered to let me work with him, too. What do you say?"

"So, that's why you've been acting so strange? That's what's been on your mind?" Her brother-in-law was a rat not talking to her first. Don knew she'd have trouble saying no to Chris. "What about soccer camp? I thought you were looking forward to it."

"I was until I came out here and got to know Uncle Don better and met Ed. I might be interested in being a vet. Who knows?"

"If Uncle Don wants you, I guess you can stay. He'll have to ship you home in a cattle car when it's time to go back to school," Maria said with a grin.

Amanda, who had been eavesdropping, gasped. "Mommy, you wouldn't make him ride home with all those cows, would you?"

Chris laughed. "Amanda, it wouldn't be too bad, and it would be free."

She scowled at her brother. "You both are teasing me."

"We were just kidding around," Maria said, putting her arm around her.

Amanda smiled at her mother. "You never used to tease when Daddy was here. You're happier."

Maria was aware of Ed standing nearby during their family discussion.

"Chris, that uncle of yours will fill your head with a lot of nonsense and off-color jokes. Try to take it all with a grain of salt. Have fun, work hard, and don't get hurt. And please call me once in a while."

"Thanks, Mom. I promise I'll keep in touch." Chris raced back to Don and Ed where he pumped his uncle's hand first, then Ed's. They had a deal with her son, and he was growing up.

After all the bags were unloaded from the car, Ed stepped closer to Maria. "I've been waiting to talk to you. If you're at all interested, that is." He tossed his head and threw his shoulders back and waited.

"Things are moving too fast for me, Ed. I'm confused as to what to do. It would be so much easier if you were divorced, but you're not. I like you and want to know you better."

"I'm upset. I hope it wasn't too obvious this morning. I had to know if you wanted me to spend more time with you." The pain in his voice sounded like he might burst.

"We can't talk here. Help me take the luggage in, and then we'll slip away." Maria was venturing into dangerous territory. She felt trapped and needed to let her mother know what was happening. "Mom, say a prayer for me to act like an adult and say and do the right thing," she whispered before she dropped her luggage in the bedroom and ran back outside to meet Ed.

"Let's walk by Don's lake and into the forest behind it." Maria headed in that direction. "I've rarely been down there. I'd like to see it, and no one will bother us."

"Good, whatever you say. I'm at my wit's end, Maria."

Ed's fast pace made her almost run to keep up with him. "Whoa, there! Let's calm down a little," she said, breathing hard.

"Sorry, I forget myself." He turned in a complete circle, appearing to survey the area. "This is a pretty place. It reminds me of the property behind my house in St. Charles. A farmer owns a lot of it, but I always said I'd buy it if I had someone who was interested in the place, besides me," he said, looking as though he expected a reaction from her.

Maria sat on an old fallen log and patted the rough bark next to her. "Sit down with me and tell me what you are thinking."

"Well . . ." He sighed. "When I got home, your story about counseling inspired me and made me decide to call Jackie, ready to compromise. I was all pumped up. I offered to meet her anyplace instead of talking over the phone. She said she wouldn't consider it until I agreed with the set of rules she and her mother had made to save our marriage. First of all, she said, I have to work a normal week like most husbands and be home by six, every night. I wanted to say that's impossible, but I waited to hear her out. The next statement out of her mouth was the deal breaker. She demanded her bedroom have a lock on the door."

"What did you say?"

"It doesn't take much imagination to understand what the lock meant. I can't live with a paranoid nut who doesn't trust me when I'm out making a living or who needs a lock on her door. She acts as if I might rape her."

"Maybe you were right when you suggested that's what her father did to her. *How I hurt for Jackie and Ed. She needs a good doctor, and Ed needs a good friend. What I say or do right now might change my life in ways I'm not prepared to live with. I've got to be careful.* "So, what do you plan to do?"

"I'm filing for divorce, ASAP. She won't go for counseling."

"I'm stunned by Jackie's conditions. They almost force you to file. Yet I hope you aren't being hasty. I wish you well. It's going to be rough for you for a while."

"Can I call you?"

"Yes, but not until you have talked with Jackie some more and have exhausted every avenue with her." *I don't want to be the reason he gives up. It would make me feel so guilty.*

"I'm done talking." Ed pinched the area between his eyes, as though he had a headache. "I'm filing."

"So, you're not going to try one more time? Maybe Jackie has thought it over and is willing to make a compromise."

"As I remember, you said George wouldn't leave his mistress, even with counseling. What makes you think she'll change?" He grabbed Maria as if to shake her, but stopped, wrapped his arms around her, and tried to kiss her.

"This is exactly why I didn't want to get involved," she said, squirming.

He held her so tightly, she couldn't move. Ed kissed her, lightly at first, then staring into her eyes, saw what he was looking for and gave her a hot smoldering kiss that made her body shake. Before she knew it, she was on the ground, and Ed was kissing her neck and face and slowly rolling on top of her.

"Stop it, Ed, stop!" She shoved his chest. "This won't solve any of yours or my problems." Maria slapped him hard. Then she pushed him off her, sat up, and shook the leaves out of her hair. "Will you act like an adult?"

"Don't tell me you didn't like it."

"I admit that I lost it for a moment or two, but not for long."

"Long enough to let me know we still have the old magic."

"That old magic, as you call it, won't sustain a real relationship. Unless we feel connected in many other ways, we won't stay together. We don't even know each other. We were young and crazy in college—only dating for three weekends and ending up in bed a lot!"

"I never forgot those weekends. It was dynamite for me. As I remember, you never complained about my love making."

"I agree we have chemistry, but I ask you, what do we do with each other the other twenty-three and a half hours in the day?"

"You let me come spend time with you and find out."

"Let's start by calling each other in the evenings after my family is in bed."

"That's not enough for me. Don't you want to see me, too?"

"Ed, if it's right, we'll have the rest of our lives together. Let's take it step by step. I don't know exactly for how long, but I do know I won't be pushed. If you don't like that, you're free to find someone you think will be better for you."

"And that goes for you, too?" he asked, looking very uncomfortable.

"Of course, what's sauce for the goose is sauce for the gander."

"Okay, that does it," he said, frustrated. "I need to go back to work. I've got to think about everything we've talked about. I don't know if I like the way this has turned out. You're so different than you were in college."

"Haven't you heard that the 19th Amendment guarantees me first-class status, just like you?" Maria asked and laughed.

"Come on, let's go before I kiss you again. I'm going to hop in my truck and keep on going when we get back. I'll probably call you once you get back to Washington, but I'm not promising."

Maria watched his truck roar out of the yard, sighed, and called to Amanda who was playing with her pup, "Come in, honey, and help me pack. Tomorrow, we're leaving bright and early. Our vacation is over."

The following morning amid laughter, hugs, and promises of future reunions, the two families gathered by Winston's big station wagon for a few final remarks.

Amanda hugged her cousin. "June, please make sure Uncle Ed gets the right puppy when he comes to see Mommy."

"I'll do it, sis, if Ed can't," Chris said, thoughtfully, looking taller and skinnier than ever.

"I know you'll be fine, but I'll miss you, son," Maria said, wanting to hug him.

"Thanks for letting me stay, Mom. I really like it here," he said, quietly.

"I'll make him work to earn his keep, sis," Don said, giving her a little hug.

Winston waved his hand in the air. "Enough talk, let's go."

Maria drove the first leg of the trip home to give herself time to think and begin to sort out her feelings about Ed. Winston navigated, while Maria's mother sat in the back seat with her arm around her crying granddaughter.

"We'll come back soon, honey," her mother said. "And Chris will bring your puppy."

"I'm counting on it. I miss my puppy," Amanda wailed, tearfully burying her face in her grandmother's shoulder. After a few moments, she said, "I'll miss June and Uncle Ed, too. I hope he comes."

"I don't know, sweetie." Her grandmother said. "He has to change some grown-up things first."

As the car ate up the miles and home loomed closer and closer, Amanda began talking excitedly about seeing her friends again, eating her favorite chocolate cookies that Briggie makes, and playing cribbage with Grandpa.

Maria, on the other hand, kept reassuring herself that her life was good and she liked her work. But she dreaded the nights. During the trip, she'd been so immersed in all the family activities, plus all the fun and laughter, she hadn't been lonely. And, of course, Ed had been a constant and sometimes worrisome diversion, but now she thought about Bill again for the first time in almost two weeks and his promise to call, and she wondered if he was thinking about her.

10. Shifting Gears

August 1962

(Maria)

Briggie threw her arms around Amanda first and then Maria. "It's so good to have me family home. I missed you and was bored. I have a grand meal for all of you, folks included. Nellie and Dean went to see some old friends today, or I would have invited them too."

"Oh, Briggie, I've missed you and your company." *What would Amanda and I do without this sweet woman?* "If you weren't here, I couldn't stay in this house alone."

"Me darlin' girl, I agree." Briggie glanced around the room. "Where's your brother, Amanda? Did you lose him?"

"He's staying with Uncle Don for the rest of the summer," Amanda announced, looking like she was very important passing on family news.

"Help me with dinner, Amanda. Fill the water glasses and give each person one." Maria's tone had a sad quality to it. "I wish we could eat outside, but our patio is too small." *If only we had enlarged it when George was still interested in us.*

Moments later, Winston and her mother arrived with a plate of watermelon slices and a bowl of fresh pineapple chunks for dessert.

"Briggie, my girl, it smells wonderful in here. You certainly can cook a great meal. You know how I love roast chicken!" Winston wet his lips as he watched her expertly cut up the bird and place slices on a platter.

"Sit down folks. Amanda and I will serve you," Maria said.

It had been a long drive back, and they were all starving. "I want to thank the heavens for bringing us safely home and being here together eating Briggie's homemade comfort food," Winston said. "It's good medicine."

"I agree." Maria's mother dabbed her mouth with a napkin. "The best part of going away is coming home."

A big grin spread across Briggie's face. "You moost eat with us until the likes of Dean and Nellie return. Then I'll know you are well cared for."

Amanda picked up her glass of milk. "Mommy, I hear a car."

Moments later, the front door opened, and Elena burst into the room, breathless. "Thanks for your call, letting me know when you were arriving, Maria. Otherwise, I might have missed your homecoming."

Elena gave Briggie a quick hug. "I'm afraid I've neglected you, Briggie, but I've been working frantically getting ready for my exciting exhibit. Kathy has been pushing me to complete a couple of sculptures and one picture I've had a terrible time finishing, but they're done!"

"Relax, me girl, and have some food." Briggie pulled out an empty chair from the table. "Here, sit down and eat this plate of chicken and mashed potatoes."

"Yum, I can't remember when I've had food like this."

Winston spooned peas onto his plate. "So, are you ready for your exhibit?"

"Almost." Elena scooped up a big bite of mashed potatoes, and after downing it, grinned. "This is delicious, I'm starved." Looking at everyone watching her, she said, "Enough about me. How was your trip?"

"I'm getting a puppy when Uncle Ed brings her out on the plane with him and Chris. Chris is staying with Uncle Don and Aunt May," Amanda said, her face beaming.

Maria sighed, but she still had to smile at her daughter. There was no way Maria could avoid taking on a puppy—Amanda was too excited about the prospect. "We had a good time with my sister and brother-in-law and seeing some of the sights."

"You left out Uncle Ed, Mommy. He's a vet and very nice. I can't wait to see him again. He calls me his little petunia," Amanda said proudly.

Elena was smiling as she ate and listened, but her facial expression suddenly changed. "I almost forgot, Maria. While I was here one day picking up some of my clothes, the phone rang. I picked it up, and a man named Bill asked for you.

"I said you were away on a trip, and he asked who he was talking to and I told him. He said he had time between flights and wondered if I remembered him from George's funeral. I said, I thought so. He asked if I would have dinner with him. I felt sorry for him because he sounded lonely, so I agreed. We had a nice time, and he asked if he could repeat the evening again, sometime, between his flights. I really don't want to because I am so busy with my work, and Kathy doesn't like the idea, but I didn't feel right saying no."

Maria suddenly froze. *How could Bill do that to me?*

Her anguish must have shown because Elena asked, "Is it all right with you? Is he someone special to you?"

Maria saw both Winston and her mother look at her. "We go back a long way, but he's not special anymore," she lied. *I feel so used. How could he have forgotten his promises that night? Didn't he mean any of them? I'll know one way or another if he calls me.* She'd know one way or another if he called again. *again.*

"Elena, did Bill ask for another number where he could reach you?" asked Maria's mother sounding irritated.

Elena's face flushed. "Did I do something wrong?" she stammered. "I did give him my studio phone number."

Maria had to stand up. She suddenly felt like running around the room, screaming. She hugged her foster sister. "Bill is free to do what he wants," she said stiffly. "If you want to see him, please do."

"I hope he doesn't call. I'm too busy, I don't really like him, and Kathy will be upset. Now, I must go, but I promise I'll be back to see all of you, dear family." She jumped up, and said good-bye, avoiding Maria's eyes.

"You've outdone yourself, Briggie," Winston announced, as the front door closed. "We'll see you again tomorrow night if your invitation still holds. It will help our vacation blues," he said, glancing worriedly at Maria.

"Hugs before I go," her mother said. "Maria, call me if you need me."

"Thanks, Mom, I may need some TLC."

With the house quiet, Elena gone, and Amanda visiting Briggie in her room, Maria held back her tears as she unpacked and stuffed her dirty clothes in the washer. When the ancient washer started making its normal racket, Maria shut the door, turned and pounded her fists against the wall, sobbing, promising herself never to believe that bastard again.

"Mom, Mom, where are you?" Amanda called for her.

"I'm in the utility room," she yelled back, quickly drying her eyes and rubbing her sore fists.

"Mommy, your face is all blotchy, and your eyes are red. You miss

Uncle Don and Aunt May, don't you? Don't cry, come and see my treasures from the trip. They'll cheer you up."

"Okay, I will. I love you, sweet pea."

"Mommy, what's a sweet pea?"

"It's a lovely flower, one of my favorites."

Amanda grabbed her mother's hand, and they walked slowly to her room. "Look at this cool stuff." Amanda dumped her bag of treasures out on the table. She handed Maria a stone flecked with tiny, shiny particles.

"I see you have all sorts of nice things—a big pod full of fluff, a little dried up flower, and lots of pretty stones."

"Uncle Ed gave me the pod and flower. Uncle Don and I found the stones."

"Put them away safely, then let's have a game of cribbage before I tuck you in."

"Mommy, I didn't know you can play cribbage. Where did you learn?"

"I lived with Uncle Don and Aunt May every summer when I was young. Uncle Don wouldn't let me escape and taught me cribbage. I was an easy mark, but after a while I got better and better and beat him—sometimes."

Amanda's eyes lit up as she found her cribbage board in her suitcase, partially hidden by all her dirty clothes. "Here it is! Uncle Don gave it to me. I thought I'd forgotten it."

Maria couldn't concentrate. Confusing thoughts of Ed and Bill kept whirling around in her head. She didn't want to play cribbage. All she wanted to do was go to bed and sleep.

"Mommy, Mommy, I won!" Amanda squealed with delight. "Let's play again tomorrow night. Maybe you'll be lucky and win."

"Yes, but now it's bedtime for both of us."

"Mommy, do you like Uncle Ed?" Amanda asked, out of the blue.

"I don't know him very well, never did, even in college. He may never want to come."

"If he doesn't come, will Chris bring my puppy?"

"Yes, for the hundredth time," Maria said, slightly irritated.

As Maria turned out the light in Amanda's room, Amanda said, "I love you, and I'm glad to be home."

"I love you, too, my little cribbage player. Sleep well, honey."

"Mom, if I wake up in the middle of the night, can I sleep with you? I liked being in your room when we were away."

"Of course you can. Just come and snuggle up to me."

Maria had forgotten how lonely her big house was once she was home. With Chris in Illinois and Elena living in Washington, DC, Maria thanked God Briggie was still with her and Amanda. Sitting there in the study thinking and drumming her nails, she toyed with the idea of moving to a smaller house, but stopped when she realized it would mean living quite a distance from her folks. There were no townhouses out here. She did however, make one decision.

She studied George's memorabilia placed all over the room and the pictures of war planes hanging on the walls. Maria would redo the room, hang her sister's painting over her desk, and get rid of George.

She felt better after making that decision and made another one. She was going to stop her vacation blues by breaking her self-imposed rule—she called Ed. Her hand was shaking slightly when she dialed his number. She was being pretty aggressive, but she didn't care. Maria was feeling so lonely, she could scream. When he answered in that sexy, deep voice of his, she shivered.

"Hi," she said, hesitantly.

"My, this is a surprise. I didn't expect a call. You miss me? I miss you. But the cold hard reality of work has helped. I vaccinated a hundred pigs today and have another vaccination session tomorrow. Ugh, my shoulders are sore from pushing fat pigs around. I prefer working with horses, but I can't disappoint my farmers."

Maria sensed a slightly distant attitude as he talked so lightly about his work. It had been a mistake calling him. She didn't give a damn about his farmers or his shoulders.

"Ed, I just put Amanda to bed, I'm facing a mountain of work tomorrow at the office, my bills are long overdue, and I have vacation blues. And, you know what? This house is too big."

"So, why did you call?"

"Because of what I just said. I guess I hoped for a little TLC. You sound mad at me. I'm just trying to be friendly and tell you how I feel. I thought you might be interested."

"That's a lot of bull. I don't want to hear about your problems, and I'm not up for a lot of late night therapy sessions. I'm not gay, and I want some sex in my life. I know you do too, if you're honest with yourself."

"I'm sorry I called," she said and hung up.

11. Plain Talk

August 1962
(Maria)

Lying in the dark in her bed after a soothing shower, she forced herself to think about Ed's honest remarks. He had a rough way of not mincing any words. Was he right about her wanting sex? Maybe she did, but she still thought she was right about not jumping in bed with him and two-timing his wife. *Ugh, men! He has a short fuse, and I don't like him or any other man right now.*

She opened her windows wide and listened to the night concert performed by the late summer insects. They played their tunes monotonously, lulling her mind, and she began drifting off to sleep. The sharp ring of her phone shocked her awake. She grabbed it to silence the noise.

"Maria, I'm sorry for sounding like such a shit. I don't know what gets into me. I couldn't sleep until I called and apologized," Ed said, quietly.

"Thanks for that, Ed. I wish things were better between us. I was lonely and wanted to talk to you, but I guess I got you at a bad time. Where did that nice guy go that I knew?"

"I wasn't married to a bitch then. I guess I was taking out my frustration on you. I'm definitely going ahead with the divorce, but it may take a while. I want to see you anyway. Do you want that too?" He paused, then chuckled. "Besides, maybe you're up for more?"

"I'll ignore that last remark." Maria took a deep breath. "May I ask you something personal?"

"Maybe. I'll answer if it has something to do with sex. What is it?"

"Did you ever love Jackie? I mean, really love her?"

"I'm not sure what your definition of love is. In fact, I don't know what my definition is, either. I'm a guy who shows his wife he loves her by working hard to make her life nice. I want her to feel secure. I guess I want to protect her. Is that so bad?"

"No, that's admirable. But did you ever tell her you loved her?"

"No, I'm not good with words, but I tried to show it by the way I made love to her. I wanted to help her enjoy it, so she felt very loved, but I didn't get many chances."

"Did you succeed?"

"I almost broke through a few times, but something scary held her back."

"But women love to be told—"

"You need a lesson in what men want and need." Ed gave a small grunt on the other end of the line. "They want a loving wife who enjoys sex and encourages their husbands in bed. When a guy has that, he'll go out every day and slay a dragon for her."

"Maybe that's enough for a while, but sooner or later, there's got to be more, a mutual appreciation for each other. One in which they enjoy each other's company outside of the bedroom, doing things together, laughing at the same things, feeling comfortable with each other.

"I tried in every way to keep George interested in me, besides sex, but he left me for another woman. I couldn't compete. Perhaps I wasn't sexy enough because I had kids who needed attention, a home to run, and a job to fulfill part of me. But whenever George came through that door, the kids and I gave him everything we could. It still wasn't enough. I don't want that again."

"Maria," Ed said, softly, "I remember how great it was with you, on those close, snowy weekends. If you hadn't thrown me over for George, we'd still be married."

"I'm not so sure, Ed. We didn't really know each other. We were naïve and hadn't experienced any tough times together."

"I had high hopes when I saw you again, Maria, but as we talked about ourselves, I realized you were much different than what I remembered. I guess we both grew up."

"I *used* to be nineteen, single, and a sort of wild college kid who had a crush on you. I'm now thirty-two, with two children who depend upon me, and a failed marriage that has made me very untrusting and unsure of myself."

"We sound alike, only I'm one bad marriage up on you. Let's stop second guessing each other on the phone. I'd like to see you, by yourself, without all the family around and see if we have anything going for us. Want to take a chance?"

"I do, but only if you agree to see Peter, a shrink who saved my life when I was drowning in George's affair. One never knows their partner until they live with them, and then I'm not so sure one ever really does."

"Amen to that." Ed was quiet for a moment. "If I say no to seeing the shrink, does that end our relationship?"

"No, but it won't be the kind of relationship that will make me want to sleep with you."

"Wow, you play hardball. Okay, set up a meeting with this guy. I'll try it once, but that's all, how about weekend after next?"

"You're forgetting our agreement. Remember, our relationship will always be purely platonic until you have Jackie's word she's done and will give you a divorce. I'm not going to break up a marriage!"

"Wow, you are tough. I don't know who hurts the most. We are the proverbial walking wounded! But there's something about you I can't get enough of," he said. "Can I call you, maybe every night?"

"Only call when you aren't mad. I don't mind your problems, but not your anger. And, in exchange you must give me support. Otherwise, I'll hang up. I do need to complain about my life once in a while. I keep hoping that beneath your masculine exterior that needs to talk about sex, there is a person I could be interested in. Is there someone like that inside you?"

The phone was silent. *Where was he? Did he hang up?* Maria was poised to hang up when she heard, "I've never had a woman dig into my head like you do. I've also never thought I was any more interested in sex than any other normal male."

"Well, I do. I'm hoping that Dr. Rudolph will help you uncover more of who you really are."

"No one, especially any woman, has ever been as interested in me as you are. I feel bad I got so mad at you when you hung up. Maybe your shrink can help me. When you left Illinois, I missed you so much. Maria, I really need you."

With Ed's self-analysis and sounding like he was open for help, Maria felt a trickle of hope and excitement, inside. *Am I being foolish and reading more into this conversation than is really there?*

And why have I neglected to tell Ed about George's change of heart in his letter? I guess I never really believed it.

The next thing she knew, her alarm jarred her awake. It was morning, and she'd slept all night. Ed's call gave her new enthusiasm for getting up, meeting her responsibilities, and going to work. That same little thrill about Ed's possible visit surfaced and stayed with her all day. As she left a sleeping household to attend an important meeting with her boss that had been scheduled after her return, she said a little prayer to God and his angels for having Briggie there to make their household run smoothly.

They'd hit it off, eight years earlier, when Briggie had come to interview for a cook's position. She'd been Maria's staunch friend ever since, running the house efficiently, cooking, cleaning, but most importantly, providing a loving influence on Chris and Amanda.

The next two weeks seemed to fly by. Putting in long hours at work playing catch-up, deciphering George's system of paying the bills so she could pay her creditors, and spending as much time with Amanda as she could, took all of Maria's energy.

But at night, when the busy day was over, Ed's visit kept slipping into her mind, with fantasies about their future. *Was she expecting too much?*

Feeling extremely tired after work one evening, she changed into her pajamas and old robe she hadn't had on since the funeral. George's letter of confession and plea to return was still in the pocket, plus a key, hard and small at the bottom of the envelope. In her state of confusion after he was killed, she'd overlooked a lot of things, including filing his heart-felt plea away in a safe place. She held the tiny key in her hand, looking for its lock in George's desk.

Suddenly she saw it, and sure enough, the key fit. Inside, was a thin bank book. Maria opened it, and the sum of one hundred thousand dollars jumped off the page. She quickly closed the book, reopened it, and looked again. The numbers were still there. A fortune had been stashed in the bank—another secret he'd kept from her. Those funds meant complete freedom from financial worry, but raised many questions.

Why hadn't George told her about the money? Why was he so secretive? Didn't he trust her after all their years of marriage? She shook her head in dismay. He'd obviously made secret plans for that money, but changed his mind when he'd written her. Maybe he'd decided she was worth the money, and the cash was part of his peace offering.

The next day, she made a long overdue call to his lawyer to make sure his will and papers were, as George claimed in his letter, all in order. His lawyer gave her more financial good news. The two hundred and fifty thousand dollar accident insurance policy that George carried on his plane would be awarded to her after the insurance company reexamined the wreckage. If it were true that George's plane had crashed due to a covey of geese that had flown into his engine, not pilot error, she would be receiving a huge check in a month or two.

With no more financial worries, Maria wondered about quitting her job, but what would she do? *After Ed's visit, I'll think about it, but now I'm just going to think about Ed.*

The morning he was to arrive, even Briggie had caught the excitement bug. "He's pretty special, eh, me darlin'? Briggie asked in her lilting Irish brogue. "Me girl, it's good to see a sparkle in your eyes again. I remember seeing that light when I first came to work for you, but after a while, when George was gone more than he was home, that sparkle disappeared. Saints preserve us, I used to hate George for being so thoughtless to you, but since he died, I don't feel that way anymore. As for this new fellow, you must insist on better treatment."

"Dear Briggie, although he's filed for divorce, Ed's still married, so I have to think very carefully about what I'm getting into with him. One bad marriage is enough to last me a lifetime." Maria grinned. "I'll make a deal with you. If you go grocery shopping, I'll clean the guest room and bathroom."

"You have a bargain, missy." Briggie hurried as fast as her sore feet would allow her to go out to her old jalopy and rattle off to the grocery store.

Maria grabbed her cleaning supplies with determination to keep her part of the deal. She was just finishing polishing the mirror in the bathroom when she heard Briggie's old jalopy stop at the kitchen door after a couple of belches from the engine.

"I bought some fresh vegetables and other assorted goodies," Briggie announced when Maria peeked into the kitchen. "I'm going to cook from my heart and pray as I do it. My dear old mither always said to do that when you want somethin'."

"What do you want, Briggie?"

"Never you mind. Just drive safely pickin' up that friend of yours."

Amanda stumbled half asleep into the kitchen and sat down at the kitchen table, her face hidden by her long, tousled hair.

"Is it the day Uncle Ed comes?"

"It is, honey, so get dressed in your best shorts and top. Make sure they're clean. Have Briggie help you brush out your snarls. We'll be going in a half hour."

Back in five minutes, fully dressed, Amanda yelled, "I'm so excited to get my puppy!" Briggie worked on her hair. "Ouch, take it easy," Amanda yelped as she popped a fat strawberry in her mouth.

"Come on, sweetie, time to go," Maria called from the hallway.

Briggie put a small container of strawberries and a piece of toast in Amanda's hands as she bounded out of the kitchen, her blue eyes alive with anticipation. For an instant, Maria saw George in her daughter's eyes. She also felt he was there cheering their little girl on and sending her boundless amounts of love. It had been a long time since Amanda had been so excited.

All the way to the airport, Amanda babbled on about her new puppy. If Ed didn't bring the dog, her daughter would be devastated.

But perhaps it would be she who would be devastated if things didn't work out for them. She also felt like she was going to be judged by a man again, and she didn't like it.

12. Endless Possibilities

Late August 1962
(Maria/Ed)

Maria

"We made it in time, honey. I was worried with all that traffic," Maria said, breathlessly, as they approached the airline gate.

"There he is, Mommy! I see Uncle Ed." Jumping up and down, Amanda began yelling, "Over here, Uncle Ed, over here!"

Goodness, he's handsome!

A crisp-looking jacket was slung over his shoulder, and he carried a small bag. Ed's eyes held hers for a moment before he bent down to hug Amanda. "How's my girl?"

"Fine. Where's my puppy?" she asked, her eyes filling with tears.

"No tears. She's just minutes away, Petunia. I wouldn't have left her for the world. I gave her a little injection to make her sleepy for the flight, and she may be a little dopey. Hold her next to you so she feels safe, and she'll be fine in a little while."

"Oh, thank you, Uncle Ed. I'm so glad you're an animal doctor. You can fix her if she gets sick." Amanda took his hand and swung it back and forth. "I told my friends that a real animal doctor was coming, and they want to see what you look like. Can I bring them over to look at you sometime?"

Maria chuckled. "You're really popular with nine-year-olds. Did you know that?" Her eyes dared him to disagree.

"Bring them over any time, Petunia," he replied, grinning at Maria.

"My friends are all jealous because I'm the only one getting a puppy. They say their parents don't want messy dogs in their homes. Wiggles won't be messy, will she, Mommy?"

"That depends on you."

"You've named her, I see," Ed said, ignoring Maria's sobering tone. "I like it. We'll get her a license tag with her name and your telephone number on it, in case she runs away."

"Runs away?" Amanda's face filled with worry. "Oh, my goodness, having a real puppy isn't like having a stuffed one, is it?"

"She'll be fine, Amanda." *I need to soften Ed's rough comment.* "I'll ask Dean to fence in the back yard."

Out of ear shot, Maria said, "Amanda worries enough for a nine-year-old. Please watch what you say to her. She adores you, but she has incredibly tender feelings."

"Will do." Ed grinned at Maria. "I hope her mother will follow her lead."

Maria quirked her eyebrow. "I didn't realize you liked women who worry."

"So this is how it's going to be, is it, sparring with you, all the time. I like it. It keeps me on my toes. That's something my other two women weren't able to do." Taking Amanda's hand, Ed asked, "Are you ready to claim your puppy from the animal department?"

Amanda watched as Ed carefully extracted a tiny, sleeping puppy from the container and said, "You can hold her when we get to the car."

He helped Amanda settle Wiggles in the back seat in her lap with a towel over her legs to protect them from Wiggles' sharp little nails. "Are you comfortable, Amanda? Wiggles is."

"Yes." Amanda gave Ed an adoring smile.

He climbed into the passenger's seat. "What else do you have time for when Amanda's around?"

"Are you worried I don't have time for a personal life?"

"It crossed my mind," he answered quietly. "I thought about it after we talked at night." He hesitated for a minute, looked back at Amanda, then leaned over and brushed her hair with his lips and whispered, "Your hair smells so good."

"You old charmer," she whispered. "Help me get through Washington traffic by letting me concentrate. You wouldn't want us to end up in the hospital, just when we're finally getting to know each other a little."

Ed laughed, settled back, and began fiddling with the radio. "I'd like to find the news."

"Don't turn it on. Just enjoy this beautiful city with me as we drive. Check out the buildings. We can't stop now, but if you want, we'll make a big day of it in the city sometime. I've all kinds of things we can do this week to have fun." She glanced at him for a second and a slow, pulsating feeling of excitement began making her hands cold and her face flushed. *I hope he doesn't notice,* she thought as she watched the traffic on both sides of her car in the three lanes zooming faster than she.

"Maria, how do you do it all and work too?"

"I don't. I have a woman who poses as a cook for our family and a nanny for Amanda, but in reality is a saint. She's Irish with a thick brogue, her name is Briggie, and she's become part of our beloved family ever since George hired her. She was the bargaining chip to entice me to come back after I'd left."

"You left him? Life with George must have been bad, I take it."

"It had a few highs and a lot of lows."

"I guess I could have afforded a cook for Jackie, but I don't think it would have made a particle of difference with her."

"You'll never know unless you try."

"You certainly know how to make one second guess themselves," he said, sharply, but quiet enough that Amanda may have not heard.

He was staring at her as she drove, and it made her nervous. "A penny for your thoughts."

"I'm beginning to wonder if this trip was a mistake trying to get involved with you. You live in a different league than me. I'm just a poor farm boy with lots of rough edges that need to be smoothed off."

"First of all, I don't buy that poor farm boy stuff, she whispered. But we can discuss that later. Our friend in the back seat has very good hearing."

"Wiggie is waking up!" Amanda yelled from the backseat. "She's looking around. She's so cute. I just love her, Uncle Ed. Thanks so much for bringing her to me."

"You are so welcome, Petunia." He turned around, smiled at Amanda, then caught her mother's eye. "Someone in this car appreciates me. She's quite a kid, Maria. I wish she were mine."

"No you don't, but thanks for being so nice to her. That adds to your point count." Lowering her voice, she said, "I made an appointment for a session with Dr. Rudolph tomorrow."

"Ugh, I was wishing you'd forget, but if that's the only way I have a chance with you, so be it," Ed responded in a resigned voice.

"I must warn you. He doesn't hold back, but he gets results," Maria said even more softly. "Aren't you interested in finding out about your bursts of anger?"

Ed leaned over. "He didn't get very good results with you and Prince Charming, did he? I'm not sold on this guy."

"He saved me from going into a depression. I wouldn't be the person you see before you if he hadn't been there for me. Besides, George did change enough to write me a letter the day before he died, saying he was sorry and asking me to take him back."

"Really? Why didn't you mention it before? Would you have?"

"I don't know. Maybe I didn't believe him, but now it's a moot point." Maria put her finger to Ed's lips and glanced over her shoulder. "Our little passenger and her puppy are sound asleep in the back seat," Maria said softly.

The city's traffic disappeared, and more and more green landscape appeared as Maria drove. *We're almost home. It's pretty out here, isn't it?* She turned into her driveway.

"Wow, this is a beautiful place. George did all right, didn't he?"

"He made a lot of money." She drove into the garage and stopped.

"Goody, Mommy, we're home," Amanda yelled. "We fell asleep back here."

"I'm glad you did, Now, you'll have plenty of energy for Wiggles."

"He and I are alike in that way. A man's home is his castle."

I hope that's the only thing that they have in common. A tiny premonition fluttered through her, and she shivered.

Ed stepped out of the car. "I'll help you with the pup, Amanda."

"Don't let her get away, Uncle Ed. I'd die if she did."

"She's too little to run. By the time she is, your mom said you'll have a fence around the backyard." As he was talking, he put Wiggles down, and she squatted a little and watered the grass. "Okay, she's all set for a while. Pick her up, and let's go in and meet your Irish cook and show off your dog." Ed put his arm around Amanda.

Briggie was standing by the window, observing when they came in.

"Hello, you're Briggie, I bet. I'm Ed McDermott."

Briggie beamed. "Nice to meet you, Ed. Where's your brogue?"

"Back in Ireland, I guess. I was born and raised in Illinois. My grandparents came over during the potato famine in 1848."

"Well, Ed McDermott, I'll be making you a grand dinner, and I hope you enjoy yourself here. But I will warn you, right off, that Maria is very special to me," she said, giving him a sharp look. "She's the best you'll ever find. Make no mistake aboot that."

"That's why I'm here. We go back a long ways." He flashed a grin. "Excuse me, I forgot my bag." He headed back into the garage.

Ed

In the garage, Ed's eye caught a low, long, covered car in the other bay. Pulling off the cover, he ran his hands lightly over its dark red surface, recovered it and grabbed his bag. *I've always wanted one of these babies. But owning a sports car always seemed too frivolous for an old dirt farmer like me.*

Ed went back to the house. Maria was in the kitchen in shorts. She and Briggie were absorbed in watching Wiggles struggling to walk to Amanda, who was lying on the floor encouraging her.

"Well, that's a picture—three adoring females. I need to grow fur, I guess," Ed said, with a chuckle. "I hate to break this up, but where do I sleep, Maria?"

"I'll show you. Follow me down the hall." Maria led the way. "This is it, Chris's bedroom, but with clean sheets. I'm sorry you have to share the bathroom with Amanda, but at least she's not a teenager. I'm just down the hall in case you need anything."

"If I told you what I needed, it would end the visit."

She gave him a wry look. "Perhaps your session with Peter will really end our visit."

13. Breaking the Ice
Early September 1962
(Ed/Maria)

Ed

Ed stood in front of the mirror and felt his rough face. He took out his electric shaver and did a quick touch-up job, felt his face again, and smiled. On his way to the kitchen, he stopped, sniffed the air, and walked to the kitchen.

"You look refreshed." Maria's fingers caressed his jaw line.

He held her hand to his face, searching her eyes with his.

"Let's have lunch," she said, pulling her hand free as her cheeks turned pink.

"You have the scent in your hair that I smelled in the hall. What is it?"

"Lavender. It reminds me of the out-of-doors, all fresh and clean."

"When was your last big meal?" Briggie asked, breaking their intimate moment. "I love to feed a hungry, handsome Irishman, such as you."

Ed chuckled. "Briggie, it's been a while since a woman has asked me to lunch and flattered me all in the same breath. I'm yours."

"Go on with your blarney, me fine Irishman. Keep it up, and you'll niver get rid of me." Briggie winked at him. "Now for the important things in life." She rubbed her hands together. "A hearty roast beef sandwich for you, Ed, and me special chicken salad for you, Maria. Amanda and I will have our old favorite, grilled cheese.

"Now, get Wiggie out from under me feet afore I squish her. I'll be ready in a couple of minutes. Why don't you all go out on the patio, and take this dog with you."

Ed took Maria's hand, and he put his other arm around Amanda. "Get your dog and show me around your backyard."

Amanda held Wiggie as the three of them strolled together.

"Did George do all the work around here?" *How do I compete with the obvious wealthy lifestyle Maria's accustomed too? A gorgeous home, manicured grounds, not to mention a cook and nanny for Amanda.*

"At first. He liked getting his hands dirty. But as time went on, he got so busy and was gone for long stretches on his travel assignments, and that made it impossible for him to keep up with the yard work. Now Chris mows when he's available, and I have a lawn service most of the time."

"I take it George traveled a lot."

"He did, flying his plane all over this country and parts of the world to places he thought would interest magazine readers. He took great pictures and wrote interesting descriptions of the places, and the magazines couldn't get enough of his work. He was a natural at knowing what would intrigue readers."

"Did you ever go with him?"

"Before Chris was born, I traveled with him for a few months. But after a while, he never asked me."

"It was awful, Uncle Ed. I never saw my daddy."

Ed reached down and gave Amanda's head a comforting pat. "While I'm here, let me earn my keep and mow your lawn."

Maria perked up. "Great! Can you run the mower?"

"Can I run the mower?" Ed gave a belly laugh. "Remember, I was a farm boy long before I was a vet."

"I hear Briggie calling us." Maria turned back toward the house. "We'd better eat before she has a stroke. She hates it when she has everything ready and no one comes."

Their sandwiches were sitting on the small table on their cramped patio.

"If you want anything else, just holler and send Amanda in for it," Briggie called through the window. "Me feet are hurting like banshees."

"That's too bad, Briggie. Are your feet sore all the time?" Ed called back.

"Yes, me friend, they are!"

"I'll tell you a little secret, Ed," Maria whispered.

Amanda leaned over closer to her mother and whispered, "I love secrets. My friends and I tell them to each other all the time."

"Keep this a secret, young lady. Briggie's been complaining about her feet since we hired her. I've tried everything. I've sent her to foot specialists, used home remedies, and nothing works. The best thing we've found is Epsom salts in a pan of warm water."

With Amanda repeatedly getting up to bring her wandering puppy back to the patio, Maria finally suggested that Wiggles be put in her bed in the utility room while they ate.

"I'll put her to bed in my bedroom so she can sleep with me," Amanda said.

Maria shook her head. "No, not until she's trained! It's the utility room for her."

"Mommy, puppies are a lot of work, aren't they?"

"That's true, but they're fun too. It's nice to have a furry pet at your age. Now, what are you going to do with her while you go to your friend's house today?"

"I'll put her in the utility room until I get back."

"What about her food that we bought her? Have you fed her? Also, does she have water in her bowl?"

"Gosh, Mommy, there's a lot to do, isn't there?"

"You'll get the hang of it. You are a smart Petunia," Ed said, smiling at her.

"Oh, Uncle Ed, you're teasing me again. Daddy never did. I like it," Amanda said, looking adoringly at him.

Maria

I wish Amanda wasn't so needy. What if Ed and I never make it together? How will Amanda feel? I'd like to protect her from more pain, but how? "Finish your lunch and get ready to see your friends. We'll drop you off on our way to see Grandma and Grandpa."

After lunch, the three of them headed for the garage. An idea popped into Maria's head and she pulled a set of keys from her purse. "Want to drive George's car while you're here? It's a lot of fun." She tossed him the keys and watched as a huge smile made his eyes sparkle.

"I checked this baby out when I was getting my duffle. It's quite a car. I bet it would burn up the highway." He pulled off the cover, folded and laid it carefully on a shelf, and climbed in.

Ed turned the key and the engine roared to life. "Hop in, gals, and enjoy the ride." Moments later, they were cruising down the well-maintained country road. The sun flashed through the trees on either side of them in short bursts. Large homes, partially obscured by lush vegetation were tucked in behind their long driveways, and manicured lawns swept out to the roadside.

Maria touched Ed's arm. "Pull in here." Amanda stood up, leaned over from the back, kissed her mother's cheek, and bounded out of the car.

"Have fun, honey. We'll be back by five to pick you up."

A few minutes later, Maria said the same thing again. "Pull in here."

"Wow, your family is wealthy. Look at that house and this circular driveway. I never dreamed Winston owned a place like this. He's such a regular guy."

"Old money doesn't have to put on airs."

"So life has been good for you."

"Since Winston married my mom."

Little did Ed know how tough her life had been before her mother met Winston. Her teenage years had been the absolute pits. She was only thirteen and had just graduated from eighth grade when her father told her he was leaving. Stunned and heartsick, she was left in their big home with her mother. Neither her father or married older sister had given her a choice. She was her mother's only support. They had opted out.

Maria witnessed her mother's slow dissent into an alcoholic breakdown after the messy divorce. Maria became the go-between for her father and mother for all communication. Every week she made the duty run to her father's office for household money. She rarely missed a week all during high school.

When she left for college, her mother had recovered partially from the divorce and was accepting social invitations again.

Her mother called that fall and told Maria she planned to marry again. Was her mother ready for such a huge commitment? What if her boyfriend was looking for a lonely, vunerable widow? Winston wasn't. He had a big job in the State Department and was a widower and was lonely. They had now been happily married for thirteen years.

"Hey, girl, where'd you go on me?" Ed touched her arm. "Can you tell me who's this big fellow coming? He looks like a linebacker."

"That's Dean. He's Winston's chauffeur and bodyguard."

"Bodyguard?"

"Yes, I'll tell you about him when we're alone."

Dean opened Maria's door. "Hello, Maria. Madam and Winston are waiting for you and your friend on the patio. Hello, sir, my name is Dean."

"Hi, I'm Ed McDermott." Ed stuck out his hand as he got out of the car, but Dean just stood there. There was an awkward moment until Dean shook Ed's hand.

"What's with this guy?" Ed whispered. "He has the grip of a bouncer, but doesn't shake hands. I'd hate to get on his wrong side."

"He's not supposed to shake hands with the guests," she whispered back.

Winston was standing and waiting on the patio. "How was the flight? On time, I hope." Winston enthusiastically shook Ed's hand.

"It was, and I'm glad to be here."

"How is the clinic doing? Am I making a lot of money on my investment?"

"Of course, I'm running it."

Her mother stood and gave Maria a quick hug before taking Ed's hand. "You're a wonderful doctor. The people are lucky to have you."

Winston gestured toward extra chairs sitting around the patio table. "How about joining us for a drink?" asked

"Perfect. I'll have a beer, Stepdaddy. How about you, Doc?" Maria hadn't felt this excited in a long time.

"Beer sounds good to me." Awestruck, Ed waved his hand around the patio. "I see you have a beautiful pool. Do you all swim?"

Her mother smiled, looking pleased. "Absolutely, every chance we get. We just got out a little while ago so we would be ready for your visit."

Ed held out Maria's chair for her. "Winston, have you lived here long?"

"For more years than I wish to acknowledge."

"It's a beautiful place."

"Thanks. Now, drink up, my boy."

Ed sat next to Maria. "I could get used to this." She smiled at him and sipped her beer, feeling content.

"Maria, Ed, we'd like to take you out for dinner at the club and a play in Washington tomorrow evening. How does that sound?"

Ed appeared surprised, but he smiled and looked expectantly at Maria, who said they'd love to.

"But Mom, I do have a problem. Poor Briggie's feet hurt. Could she and Amanda stay here with Nellie and Dean? Then Nellie could help out with Amanda, and Briggie would have some adult conversation."

"I don't see any reason why not," her mother said. "Why don't you ask her, and at the same time introduce her to Ed.

Maria winced at her mother's suggestion. *I hope Nellie will be cordial. She doesn't form friendships fast, especially with my male friends.*

Winston buzzed Nellie on his new intercom. "I had to get a new one," he said apologetically. "The old one was so bad, I had to resort to yelling into the kitchen."

"He loves his new toy," Ruth said with a wink. "The old one worked just fine."

Nellie appeared in the doorway, stopped, and then looked at Ed for a moment too long. "You buzzed me, Winston?"

"Nellie, I have a favor to ask," Maria said. "We're going to dinner and a play tomorrow night with my friend, Ed, who is visiting from Illinois. Would you and Dean have Amanda and Briggie over while we're gone? It would be nice for Briggie to see you, and Amanda loves to come."

"Certainly, Maria," Nellie replied stiffly, casting a very cool look in Ed's direction.

Before she could leave, Ed quickly stood up. "Thanks for helping us out. I'm glad to meet you. I knew Maria in college." He gave Nellie an engaging smile, and Nellie grudgingly gave him a slight nod of acknowledgment.

He's very aware that he is stepping on dead toes. What a smooth operator, reading the whole situation! Maria looked at him with a newfound appreciation.

Winston handed Ed another drink. "It's a great day for a beer and a swim. How about it? It's hot enough to fry an egg."

"I didn't think about swimming. I don't have a suit."

"That's my fault, folks" Maria said. "I forgot to tell Ed to bring one, but that's okay. You can use one of the rentals that Winston keeps for just such occasions. How much are you charging these days?"

Winston laughed so hard at her joke, he had to get up and walk around before he could stop. "You little devil, teasing Ed. He probably believes you."

Her mother pointed toward a small building next to the pool. "My friend, go in that cabana over there and take your pick. Nellie washes them every week no matter what, even if there hasn't been a guest here for a month."

"And you, Maria, borrow one of mine. Winston has given me so many you can keep it. He loves that I'll swim with him."

When Ed stepped out of the cabana, Dean and Winston were stringing up a net across the middle of the pool.

Maria watched Ed walk across the patio. *His frame has filled out since I last saw him in a swim suit. He's all muscle.*

"We're going to play water polo, Ed. I talked Dean into joining us. To make it fair, I put him on the ladies' team. You and I will stand them." Winston looked quite pleased with his plan.

When Ed asked about the rules, Winston said there was only one rule—no drowning.

Dean single-handily beat Ed and Winston. The women were never quite fast enough to help him, although Maria made several valiant saves for their team and came up sputtering. Winston admitted defeat after a wild hour or so and climbed out of the pool.

They all moved to chairs placed around the pool to lounge, dry off, and recover from their activity. Ed rubbed his head with a towel. "That was more fun than I've had in a long time. I may put a pool in my place."

"Capital, my friend. A man can't work all the time, and besides, think of all the cute bathing beauties who will be attracted to your pool." Winston draped a towel around his neck. "Now, what about a cocktail before we get ready for dinner at Maria's? I'd say we've all earned one. I'll fix us a man's drink of scotch and soda and the ladies a light summer cocktail."

Maria screamed with mock displeasure. "Stepdaddy, your subtle male chauvinism is showing again. What if I ordered scotch on the rocks?"

"Never you mind, young lady. I'll make you your favorite—a strawberry daiquiri." Minutes later Winston returned with a tray filled with drinks.

Maria sipped her drink and winked at Winston. "This is pretty good."

Ed took a drink of his scotch. "Now this is living. You run quite a resort, Winston. I'll be spoiled when I go back to work." Ed leaned back in his chair. "May I ask you about your work?"

Maria perked up with Ed's question and listened. It was an unwritten rule not to question Winston about his State Department work.

"I've been there almost all of my working career. A lot of what I do is classified. That's why I rarely mention my work. It's better that way."

"Do you share what you do with other people there?"

"We cooperate in certain matters but are very careful. It's safer. I believe you are one of the few people outside of work except for George with whom I've ever even discussed my work."

With the effects of the exercise and scotch contributing to a soft and mellowing mood for Ed, he seemed reticent to move when Maria said they had better go and pick up Amanda.

"I'm glad someone is thinking about our schedule, because I'm on vacation."

Her mother finished her drink, then stood and began filling the tray with empty glasses. "What time do you want us for dinner, Maria?"

"Come by five thirty. Amanda will be starving by then, and so will I."

Winston walked them to the car. "I'm bringing some of my special sipping whiskey for dessert.

The minute they entered Maria's home, Ed began commenting on the wonderful odors wafting around the house. His compliments made Briggie blush. Looking into the refrigerator, Maria saw chilled cracked Maryland crab with asparagus for starters. In the warming oven, broiled stuffed mushrooms with shrimp were waiting along with French rolls. "Everything looks yummy, Briggie. Amanda and I will serve and make everyone clean up to save your feet."

Later, during dinner, Ed expressed how much he was enjoying the meal. "Do you eat like this every night?"

Standing in the kitchen doorway, Briggie overheard him. "It's a rare day when I have an Irishman at my table."

"Well, Briggie, this ole' Irish farm boy certainly thanks you."

"Oh, go wan with your blarney," she replied, beaming from ear to ear.

"Anytime you want to work for us, Briggie, we'll make it worth your while," Winston said, chuckling, adding to Briggie's delight.

"Grandma, Grandpa, do you want to see my new puppy?" Amanda scooted to the edge of her chair. "Mommy said I had to keep her in the utility room until after dinner."

Maria's mother gave Amanda a warm smile. "I think we're all finished. Bring the puppy out on the patio, and we'll meet you there."

"I'll need a couple of glasses, Maria, for my sipping whiskey," Winston said.

Maria set the small glasses down on the outdoor table. "What do the women get to drink, Stepdaddy?"

Ed grinned at her as he watched Winston pour two small glasses of amber fluid. "You get a taste of mine."

She waved his outstretched hand away. "I'm full. I just wanted to tease Winston. I drank more today than I usually do in a week. How about you, Mom?"

Her mother shook her head. "I'm so full, all I want is some water."

"Grandma, Grandpa, isn't she the cutest dog you've ever seen?" Amanda held the puppy in front of them. "I'm going to show you what she does when I put her down. She walks funny and falls over sometimes. Just watch." Wiggles waddled over to the edge of the two-inch high patio, promptly fell off into the grass, and then rolled on her belly, making everyone laugh.

"See what I mean?" Amanda squealed.

"My, the night air is lovely. Feel the breeze, and listen to those summer insects," Ruth suggested. "They're outdoing themselves with their noisy music tonight."

Winston and Ed sipped their drinks quietly, and Amanda busily followed Wiggles around the yard while Maria and her mother relaxed, looking up at the stars.

Ed broke the silence by asking, "Winston, have you given any thought to retiring?"

"My, my," Winston replied, with an interested look. "It's crossed my mind once or twice. Why do you ask?"

"My folks just retired. I helped them move into a retirement community, something new. It has all kinds of activities, plus medical care on the premises. I'm not suggesting in any way that you should or would consider that type of life. I just wondered if you've thought about not working so hard."

"I have several ideas rolling around in my head that I haven't even discussed with Ruth. I'm going to be sixty-three soon and need to give it some thought."

"What do you think of the Midwest?" Ed asked, suddenly coughing from the fiery liquid.

"Did that whiskey go down the wrong pipe?" Winston sounded anxious to change the direction of the conversation.

"Amanda, I think your puppy is trying to get into the house." Her mother had saved Winston from any more questions about the Midwest by changing the subject. "Maybe she wants a drink of water. Or maybe she wants to get into her bed."

"Honey, I agree with Grandma. Take your puppy inside, put her to bed, and you do the same thing." Maria smiled at Amanda. "You've had a long day, and the new book you got from the library sounded pretty good to me. I think it's a mystery."

"I will. I'm bored. I'd rather read." Amanda scooped up her puppy and disappeared.

Maria let out a sigh of relief. "Well, that's a change. Wiggles is going to be a good addition."

Winston poured another drink. "She deserves a pet. She's a winner."

"I'd better check on my girl and that puppy of hers. Don't talk about me while I'm gone." Maria picked up a couple of empty glasses and headed into the house.

Ed

"What are your plans for tomorrow?" Winston casually asked Ed.

Ed shrugged his shoulders. "Maria has something in mind for us."

"Trust Maria, she knows what's fun. Perhaps she'll take you into the city."

Ed felt as if Winston were fishing for answers.

"Having you here is a big step for her," Winston went on. "She had a hard life with George. I know you're interested in her or you wouldn't be here, but I want to caution you both to go slowly and get to know each other.

"I knew George as well as anyone knows another person. He was barely twenty and ready to fly in the war when I met him. He distinguished himself and became a real war hero, earned the Purple Heart and Medal of Honor. After the war, he fought in 'the war on drugs' as an undercover agent for three years until he was captured and almost died at the hands of a crazed young drug king. George loved danger, excitement, and flying. Men admired him in the State Department. He had a wide circle of very influential friends, but when it came to being a married man with all the responsibilities, he had a lot to learn. He couldn't help it, it was who he was. He wasn't a family man. He tolerated Chris, but ignored Amanda. That's why Maria goes the extra mile with her."

"Maria has mentioned a few things about George, and I know she's been burned. So have I. I'm just a country boy, not sophisticated like George, but I don't think he knew what he wanted. I hope I can figure it out." Ed held out his glass. "I could use a refill, Winston."

"Of course, my friend. This kind of talk makes you need another one, doesn't it?

"Ruth can attest to everything I've just said. It's been a long, rocky road for Maria, but fortunately, not for us," Winston said, fondly looking at Ruth and holding her hand.

Ed took another sip of his drink, then cleared his throat. "I've known Maria since she was fourteen. She caught my eye for the first time when I heard her infectious laugh. She was playing 'hide and seek' with her nieces that summer day. Although she was just a teenager, she had a way about her that made me happy when I was around her. When I found out she was going to Iowa State, my alma mater, I thought I'd look her up. But I got busy, had another girlfriend, and didn't see Maria again until I gave her a ride home to Don and May's for Thanksgiving.

"I started dating her quite by accident after Christmas. My current girlfriend and I had parted company and I was lonely. Maria popped into my mind and I looked her up. After a few dates, although I thought she was the one for me, I was young and foolish and put my business plans ahead of her.

"When I realized that I was actually going to be able to make a good living, I asked her to marry me, but it was too late. She'd already met George and was engaged, but hadn't heard from him. He had fallen off the face of the earth. She hadn't heard from him for months. He'd never been able to tell her he was with Army Intelligence. Maria thought he was dead, and she'd accepted another man's proposal. But her fiancé, Bill, who was serving in the Korean War, had lost contact with her, too. His letters snafued somewhere and were never delivered to her, so she thought he might be dead.

"When she told me that, I rushed over hoping to convince her to give me a chance, when George came walking into the resort, where she was working that summer, alive and well. I knew then that I was out in the cold." Ed stood up, stretched, ran his fingers through his curly hair and was quiet for a moment.

"On the rebound, I married a gal I hardly knew and things didn't work out. After five years, we called it quits. I repeated the mistake of marrying someone else I didn't know very well, and now I'm in the process of getting a divorce.

"I actually hadn't planned on ever seeing Maria again, but then you all came out for a family reunion, and I couldn't stay away. I told myself I just wanted to renew a friendship, but I was lying. I still love her. Now, I'm here, trying to sort out my life and see if we have enough in common to make it—but I don't think so." He stared off into space for a moment or two and sat down.

14. Solace, Soul Searching, and Struggle

Early September 1962
(Maria)

Maria had been standing inside the house listening to Ed tell her folks about himself. He'd portrayed the picture quite accurately and she believed his assessment of their chances. "I'm back," she called through the screen, giving Ed a chance to collect himself. "Both Amanda and the puppy are out like lights."

"It's late and we need to go home." Her mother stood and started to collect her things. "It was a nice evening, and I loved the chance to talk with you, Ed. I wish you well and appreciate all that you have shared with us tonight. See you tomorrow. Come on, Winston, take me home."

After her folks left, Maria locked up and stopped at Ed's open bedroom door on her way to her own bedroom. "I'm glad you're here. This house is too big now that my artsy sister, Elena, is gone. Her empty bedroom is an awful reminder that she doesn't come home anymore. She has a new life. I'd hoped you would meet her, but it looks like it won't happen this visit."

Maria stepped just inside his room. "You look comfy." She pretended to look interested in the magazine in his hands. "I don't want to disturb you, but I'm curious. What are you reading?"

"Oh, I think you have other things on your mind other than my reading habits. That's why you didn't keep going down to your lonely bed."

Maria blushed. "Okay, I'm interested in spending more time." It felt uncomfortable admitting her true intention. "Where do we begin?"

"Come sit down on my bed for starters. I can read my monthly vet magazine anytime." He tossed it on the floor and patted the bed. "Come on, I'm harmless."

Maria hesitated, but then sat down, looked at him, and smiled.

"Well, this is awkward," he said. "We have a lot of history, but that's no help right now."

"Do you want to talk about today? Did you like it?"

"I did, but I think you're too close to your folks. Winston was fishing for answers when you were tucking Amanda in. Did you tell them about me seeing your shrink?"

"No, but I guess I'm guilty about relying on them because George was gone so much. If I marry again, it will be to a guy who likes to be home. In defense of my folks, they've stuck by me all the years George and I were married." Maria didn't know what she would have done without her parents. "As you can see, I come as part of a package with children and grandparents. Perhaps we're too much for you."

Ed smiled a sexy grin. "I remember how you and I lived together on those cold and snowy nights." His brow furrowed. "As far as the rest of the family, I'll have to wait and see. I would be kidding you if I said it's going to be easy."

"What do you mean?"

"Taking on another man's children is a hard thing, but I do like them."

"Well, I appreciate your honesty. I hope Peter, my therapist, can help you, personally. I'll see you tomorrow for breakfast." Maria started to get up, but Ed put out his hand to stop her.

"I promised myself you would have to make the first move, but I can't stand not at least kissing you. I've been dreaming about a lot more, but a kiss or two will make me feel better."

"Now I feel awkward. Should I close my eyes and pucker-up?"

"Don't, honey, you don't have to perform. That's the last thing I want."

"Well, that's a relief. We have a long way to go, Ed. Take it easy on me."

"I'll try, but I don't seem to know how. I want too much too fast. Maybe the doctor can tell me why."

Maria got up, smiled at him from the doorway, and blew him a kiss.

"The following morning, the intoxicating aroma of fresh brewed coffee filled the house.

96

"I smelled coffee as soon as I opened my bedroom door, and I followed my nose to the kitchen." Pulling his chair as close as possible to Maria, Ed sniffed her hair. "You smell good, too, almost as good as the coffee. Lavender is nice."

She grinned at him, leaned closer, and sniffed his neck. "I'm a sucker for your shaving lotion."

Briggie stood nearby with a pan in her hands. "How aboot some good ole Irish oatmeal for the likes of you? It puts hair on your chest." She handed him a steaming bowl. "Try it with maple syrup. There's none finer. I'll get you some coffee to wake you up while you eat."

Ed obediently spooned a bite into his mouth and smiled. "Pass the syrup, please." He studied Briggie with a slight furrow of concern on his face. "How are your feet this morning?"

"Saints preserve you, thanks for asking." Briggie gave him a wide smile. "They're better."

"Would you mind if an animal doctor takes a look at them sometime?"

"My dear friend, we're all animals, only we're the human kind," Briggie said, laughing at her little joke. "Maria, I like this Irishman. He has a big heart." Under her breath, she mumbled, "That's more than George ever had."

Ed grinned. "You've got a bit of the old blarney in you, my girl."

"I hate to break up this love fest, but we have an important appointment this morning," Maria announced in a concerned tone. "Briggie would you mind helping with Amanda and her puppy? Just tell Amanda what to do, don't you do it. She has to learn to care for her dog."

Briggie grinned and gave a small salute. "I agree. I'll crack the old whip."

"Also, you don't have to cook tonight. The folks are taking all of us out for dinner at the club and then are treating Ed and me to a play in Washington. You and Amanda have been invited to visit with Nellie and Dean after dinner. Winston bought them a big television set."

"What a glorious time we'll be havin' this evening." Briggie clapped her hands. "I can't wait to see it."

Later in the garage, Ed leaned against Maria's car and wrapped his arms around her waist. "You're so aware of everyone's feelings, and you try to make things run smoothly. I love you for it. I need you in my life."

"Why? To make your life run like a clock? What about what I need? Thanks, but no thanks. I did that for George, and he used my efficiency as a way to belittle me. He called me a great housekeeper. I wasn't exciting enough, I guess. Only his mistress supplied that." Pain from the past began to surface, and Maria's heart pounded as she became heated. "I'm a woman with feelings, who happens to have two children to raise, not someone you hire from an agency!"

"I hit a nerve. Sorry, but I didn't mean it in a bad way."

"I know I'm pretty intense at times. I find stuff boiling up out of me that isn't rational."

"So do I," Ed said with a tone of regret.

"George was a master of making me feel like I didn't exist. After a while, as he became more and more caught up in his new life, in desperation, I asked him to go with me to see Peter. He went reluctantly, but it was too late. Nothing worked, because George was gone emotionally. Maybe he'd always been absent. Amanda was five and Chris was almost nine at the time."

She buried her face in Ed's shoulder for a moment, then she raised her eyes to meet his gaze. "Forgive me. I didn't mean to burden you. Let's go see Peter."

"You haven't gotten over him, have you?" Ed's eyes were full of concern as he held her close. "This isn't going to be easy for either of us."

"I have, most of the time, but sometimes, I feel so mad—"

Ed shook the keys. "Come on, we'll beat this thing, together. But now I must tell you about the love affair that most men have, including me, with machines of all kinds—especially little red sports cars. I promise they'll be my only mistresses."

"Don't promise me anything," she said in a bristly tone. "I've had enough promises to last me a lifetime."

"I've hit another nerve. You are real flesh and blood, aren't you?" he said as he removed the car cover, almost tenderly.

"Ed, I remember your new car at Iowa State. You were so proud of that vehicle. You wouldn't let anyone smoke in it, including yourself."

"I was a little over the top then, but I'm better now," he said and laughed.

He drove effortlessly through the traffic to their appointment. If he was nervous about it, he never let on. He'd been raised to be farm-tough, strong, and never show any nerves.

They were early for the appointment. Maria watched Peter drive up, park his sports car askew—taking up two parking places—and run up the walk behind them.

"It's nice for the doctor to be there before his patients, but I'm not. Sorry folks, I overslept. My girlfriend and I had a late night, and I'm slightly hung over. Give me five minutes and then come in. On Saturday, I don't have a secretary, because I don't usually work on the weekends. But because I'm in love with your girlfriend and have been for years, I'll be nice to both of you."

Ed gave Maria a puzzled look. "Is this guy for real?"

"Wait until he bores into you. You'll wonder if he isn't the devil."

"This is a first for me. It's only because of you that I'm going to try to deal with this nut."

"I know," she said, softly. "I appreciate that. It's been five minutes, shall we?"

Peter was feverishly writing something as they came in. He looked up and gave them a little grin. Then he directed his focus on Ed. "Let's get right to it. You're here to see if you and Maria should tie the knot. Am I right?"

Maria muffled a chuckle. Peter was a rascal. He'd already gotten Ed's attention.

"No, I think we're just trying to find out if we're compatible." Ed sounded irritated.

"Don't play any games with me. I charge too much money for that. Don't dance around the real reason you're here. You're both scared to commit because of past mistakes, right?"

Neither one of them answered him, so he continued. "I usually have individual sessions with each partner to discover their child-hood traumas, spaced out over time using regression hypnotherapy. It helps my patients uncover secrets their minds have conveniently forgotten. How does that grab you, Doc?" Peter's eyes bore into Ed's.

"I don't know. How do you do it?" he asked with a suspicious edge to his voice.

Peter was stirring up Ed on purpose—working to break his outer shell of protection. Maria remembered him doing the same thing to George. "I'll take you back to some of the defining moments in your childhood. Usually traumatic and buried in your mind to pro-tect you, but they're all part of you and very important. Afterward, I'll give you a tape of your session and suggest that you play it over with

Maria before your next visit." He sat behind his desk, tapping the tips of his fingers together waiting.

"What if I say no?"

"Then I'll use Maria as a guinea pig and hypnotize her while you watch to show you what I mean. She's done it so many times, it will be no problem for her." Peter folded his hands on his desk. "Which is it, you or her?"

Ed looked stricken. "You play hardball, don't you? I'm here as a favor to Maria, and I guess I'll try it, but I feel I'm over my head with all this mumbo jumbo. I don't think it will work, but I'll give it my best shot."

"Keep that attitude, and you'll make progress. Your subconscious listens." Peter leaned back in his chair. "Do you want Maria to stay until you go under?"

"Yeah, to keep you honest, Doc."

Peter grinned. "Lie down on my fancy sofa, take your shoes off, loosen your belt, and get comfortable." He stopped giving instructions while Ed positioned himself on the couch. "Now, focus on the small silver vase on the shelf and close your eyes. I'll start counting backward from twenty down to zero. With each descending number, I want you to open your eyes, look at the vase, then close them slowly until I get to zero. But you won't know that because you'll be out. Before we start, I'm telling you now that when you're hypnotized, you will not—I repeat *will not*—be able to raise your ring finger on your right hand when I ask you to do it. Do you understand?"

Ed gave him an irritated look. "Of course, I understand."

He went under quickly.

Peter used his finger test. "He's out, Maria. Please leave us. I'll call you when we're finished."

15. Uncovering Ed

September 1962
(Ed/Maria)

Ed

Peter waved good-bye as Maria closed his door, then he turned to Ed. "I'm going to count backward by year to the year where something very important happened to you. Whatever happened, you've buried it.

When Peter reached Ed's sixth year, Ed broke in with the high little voice of a child. "I'm in my old, dirty bedroom, and my mother is screaming at me that I'm no good. She says I'm just like my no-good father and will never amount to anything, just like him.

"I don't know what I've done, and I'm crying," Ed said, sobbing. "My mother screams smart boys don't cry—just dumb ones like you. She's holding a paper from school and waving it in front of me, saying you're stupid. She wants me to write those arithmetic problems over and do them correctly. Otherwise, she'll beat me within an inch of my life. She throws the paper at me and marches out, screaming, you'll get no supper, you stupid kid."

Ed lay on the couch and continued to sob, the tears running down his face onto his shirt.

Peter went to his door, opened it, asked Maria back in, and sat down, preparing to wait.

Maria

Maria knew Peter was happy with Ed's regression because he sat there smiling, tapping his fingers together, and nodding his head.

It seemed like an eternity before Ed stopped crying. Peter remained quiet and didn't move. He finally got up and stood over

Ed. "I'll count to ten, slowly," Peter said in a strong voice. You'll wake up on ten and feel good and ready to enjoy the rest of the day."

Ed opened his eyes, looked around, sat up, and felt his shirt. Then he put his shoes on. "Why is my shirt wet? How'd I do? I remember trying to lift my finger and not being able to do it." He offered Maria a groggy smile, but otherwise didn't move.

"To use a phrase Maria has heard before, we hit pay dirt on the first pass with you. I asked Maria to leave the room after you went under so the session would be new to her too. I want the tape to hit you right between the eyes, Ed," he said, pacing around the room. "Your shirt is wet from tears. Isn't that wonderful? I had a professor tell me once that people who can't cry or get angry are the hardest ones to help. You're a very good subject. I can help you a lot, and I like that because then I can send you a big bill."

Ed laughed for the first time. Peter had hooked him. Hopefully, Ed would receive therapy that would help him live well for the rest of his life.

"So, can you come Monday, Wednesday, and Friday next week? Maria told me you'll be flying back to Chicago next Saturday. I'll stir you up, pick your brain, make you mad, sad, but never happy throughout our work together. The more I can open you up, the better." Peter held up his hand. "Don't get up just yet. Wait a little longer. Hypnosis is a big deal."

Peter kept up a running conversation with Maria about her life, her kids, a conference he was going to in Chicago, but all the while, he kept an eye on Ed.

"You can get up now."

"Thanks, Doc, I feel different," Ed said, shaking Peter's hand and looking relieved. Peter grinned. "I can tell you wrestle animals for a living. You have a grip that could hurt people like me."

While walking out to their car, Maria asked, "What do you think, handsome? Peter's a neat guy, isn't he?"

Ed stopped in his tracks. "It's been a long time since you called me handsome. Does it mean you like me more?"

"Don't push your luck, big boy." She gave him a gentle shove and laughed.

"Now that it's over, I can tell you I was a little nervous. But Peter's a regular guy. By the way, he has the handshake of a wrestler. Judging from his build, I bet he was one. Now tell me, do you think I really cried?"

"George did, and he was tough. He had to be, with the OSS during the Second World War. We'll find out tomorrow morning. We can listen to the tape Peter gave us before Amanda gets up."

"I feel relieved, and I don't know why," Ed said, getting into the sports car. "Added to that is being with you. Maybe you're the reason, or it's a combination of you and Peter's work with me. I feel euphoric—like there is a God."

"I hate to mention it at this monumental moment, but we need to go to the grocery store for Briggie. She only needs a few things," Maria said, apologetically.

"Honey, never apologize for doing good things for your family. I'm not George. I like seeing you in action. It gives me a chance to see how you operate. It helps me know you better."

"You are a charmer, I'll say that for you," she said, shaking her head in disbelief.

"You make it easy for me."

"We'll see how easy you think it is when you see the huge grocery store we have to shop in. I grew up with mom and pop stores where the owner helped everyone. No one helps anyone in there. Now there are signs telling customers which aisle to find things in, but they have everything. It's one more indication that America is moving into a bigger, more impersonal, faster age, and it's hard for me to like it or keep up."

Back in her garage, she loaded Ed's arms with grocery bags.

He peered over the bags and laughed. "I'd hate to think how many bags I'd carry in if you really needed to shop."

Maria returned his chuckles. "Thanks for helping me. I'm not used to such treatment." *I wish I would stop comparing Ed to George, but it's hard. I can't remember George ever going to any store with me.* She gave Ed a little peck on the check.

Her kiss and compliment brought a surprised smile to his face. "I'll help you every day for a kiss or two. He leaned over with his arms full and kissed the top of her head. "I'll do better later, if you let me."

Briggie was standing in the center of her kitchen. "Well, you big Irishman, it's good you're makin' yourself useful. Do you have any older brothers you could send me way?" She turned away quickly after her question. "I've made some burgers for lunch. Does this Irishman eat them?"

"I do when they're made by a beautiful Irish lady."

"Go wan with your blarney, Ed."

After lunch, Ed excused himself and carried his dishes to the sink. "This ol' farm boy is going to mow the back forty. I need to do something to earn my keep. Besides, I'm not used to having so much free time."

"I heard you ask Ed about having any brothers, Briggie," Maria said, poking Briggie.

"I was just giving him some of the blarney he's been giving me." But she paused and said sadly, "I'm too fat and not very pretty. No man would ever be interested in me."

"Briggie, you're only ten years older than me. There's someone out there just waiting for you. I want to help you. Tell me what I need to do."

"I'm not sure. Maybe it's too late for me."

Just then, Amanda appeared at the door holding Wiggles. "Mommy, Wiggles stinks."

"Get your bathing suit on, my girl. We're going to change that right now by bathing her in our tub in the garage. I'll show you how, but after that, you'll be in charge of keeping her clean."

Briggie heard all the laughing in the garage and went to see what was so funny.

Both Amanda and Maria were in their bathing suits—Amanda in the tub with Wiggles and Maria outside helping to hold her as Amanda attempted to wash the puppy. They were laughing hysterically because Wiggles kept shaking the water off and spraying both of them.

"Mommy, it's a good thing you and I have bathing suits on!" Amanda screamed.

"Your laughter is blessed by the angels. I haven't seen the two of you so happy for a long time," Briggie said, her eyes filled with joyful tears.

Maria looked at her dear friend. "I know, and it feels wonderful," she said quietly.

Surprising them all, Winston and Maria's mother walked up behind Briggie.

"Hi! Ruth and I were out shopping, and we thought we'd stop by. I see Ed out there doing his bit, and you two are soaked. Bring Wiggles and yourselves outside to dry. We'll be on the patio cheering Ed on." Winston pointed to the lawn. "Ed looks like a pro out there. Is he a farm boy?" he asked loudly, over the noise of mower.

Maria lifted the puppy from the tub and wrapped her in a towel. "Yes, he grew up not far from Don and May's farm."

"How did things go with Peter, this morning?" her mother asked, searching Maria's face.

"Good! Peter was pleased, and Ed liked him. He's going to see him three more times."

Ed spotted them, waved, stopped the mower, and strolled over.

"We've been critiquing your work out there, and we think you should go over all of it again, cutting it an inch shorter," Maria said, her eyes dancing with devilment.

Her mother gently patted Ed on the shoulder. "She's a tease, Ed, but ignore her. She only does it when she's happy."

"She's a lot of fun." Ed winked at her mother. "It's one of the reasons I came to visit."

Winston gave a nod toward the lawn. "Are you almost finished out there?"

"Yes, I'm essentially done."

"Well, how about a round of golf this afternoon?"

"I don't know how."

"Well, my man, I'll give you your first lesson. A strong, young man like you will be a great golfer. You'll learn easily. My dear wife is learning, and she's not a youngster." He gave a sly smile, then glanced at his wife as though asking for her forgiveness.

"What do you think, Maria? Do you want to come and take a lesson from Winston?" Ed tilted his head as though assessing her athletic ability. "Or did you become a pro playing with George?"

"I never learned, because George never encouraged me to try. He liked being away from me both at work and at play, and I didn't want to be where George didn't want me." She caught Winston's eye, and raised her eyebrow. "I'll go swimming with Amanda and her friends."

Winston's face reddened, and he looked aghast. "Maria, forgive me. You and George lived down the road from me, and I was too busy with my work to take time to really understand how much you were suffering in your marriage. I didn't realize you never played with George!" Winston said, sadly. "I have a great idea. Maria, come and let me make up for my mistake. I'll hire a pro to give you both a lesson, and I'll work with Ruth. How does that strike you?"

"That's fine, Stepdaddy, I'd love to learn. George told me once that I wasn't coordinated enough to be able to play golf. My self-esteem had been shaken, and I believed him.

"We'll clean up and meet you folks at the club by three. But I'll pay for our lessons," Ed added, firmly.

"Fine, Ed, we'll see you all then." Her mother tugged at Winston's sleeve and started to move him toward their car.

As Maria showered, she did the comparing game again between Ed and her late husband. She didn't like stacking their qualities next to each other, and it wasn't very productive, but she couldn't help it. George had grown up rich, he'd gone to the best private boarding schools and college, and he had plenty of time for sports. He never worked, had lots of money, and never went hungry.

Ed, on the other hand, went to a public school, worked all of his young years after school on his parents' farm, and he had no time for sports. Money was tight, and when he went to college, he worked two and three jobs to pay for it. Ed was never able to just be a college student.

"Mommy," Amanda yelled into the bathroom. "We need to pick up my friends. Hurry! Ed told me to get you going."

"I'm sorry, I just lost track of time in the shower," Maria said as she ran to the kitchen.

"We'll make it, Petunia! Take it easy," Ed said.

Although Ed tried to act relaxed, he wasn't. Maria could feel it. She wanted to reassure him but hesitated to acknowledge it. She knew why—he was way out of his element.

16. Learning to Play Together

September 1962

(Maria)

After depositing the kids at the club pool with last minute instructions for them to behave, Maria and Ed found the club pro waiting for them at the practice tees. Standing in front of them, the pro demonstrated the golf swing over and over, having them swing their clubs at the same time. It seemed easy, and she was anxious to hit that elusive little ball. Ed was in front of her, and soon she watched in amazement as each of his balls soared far up into the sky and dropped out there, sometimes two hundred and fifty yards away. He was a natural.

She, on the other hand, was having a terrible time trying to connect with that illusive little orb. "You're peeking," the pro kept telling her. He infuriated her, and she stubbornly ignored him and kept missing. Why couldn't she do it? She started to sweat as she kept whacking away.

Maria finally gave up. "What do you mean?"

"You're looking up to see where the ball went before you've finished hitting it."

"Oh," she said, her face feeling hot. *I'm going to keep my head down if it's the last thing I do!* When her club finally connected with the ball, she screamed. "I did it!" Maria danced around with delight.

A half an hour later, both of them enthusiastically thanked the pro. Ed paid him with a generous tip and shook his hand.

"I feel like a kid, Maria. This has been more fun than I've had in a long time." Ed's brown eyes sparkled. "Let's play every day next week. That is, if you want to."

"You would say that. It's so easy for you! I don't know if I'll ever get the hang of it." Secretly, she was thrilled he wanted to enjoy her company and include her in his fun.

"Don't be so upset. You'll figure it out," he said, exuberant over his golf prowess. He picked her up off her feet and held her close. "How can I be so lucky to have found you after all these years?"

A small group of golf onlookers clapped their approval.

Ed waved at everyone. "You should try this with your wives or girlfriends!" He walked off the tee. "Where to?"

"Well, Lothario, we'll practice on the putting green with Winston and my mother."

"So, what do you think, Ed?" Winston leaned on his golf club. "You looked like a regular from what I could tell from here. And Maria, you'll be a good golfer when you learn to stop peeking."

"I know, I know, Stepdaddy." Maria let out an exaggerated sigh. "That's what the pro said, over and over."

"I suppose we'd better get going so we won't be rushed tonight," Ruth reminded them. "Drop by for cocktails before dinner." As they walked off the green, her mother matched Ed's stride for a moment. "I'm glad you're with us," she said quietly. "You have a nice way with Maria."

Winston nodded and grinned. "Be sure to visit us again so we can play golf." He walked next to Maria. "Tell Amanda to bring her cribbage board tonight, so she can teach Dean and Nellie to play while we're gone."

After they gathered Amanda and her giggling friends for the drive home, the back was filled with whispers and occasional laughter. They deposited her last friend at her house, and Amanda asked if she could sit in front for the rest of the way home.

"Of course," Maria said, getting into the back seat.

Maria watched her young daughter's face with some concern. She was falling in love with Ed. How would her Amanda stand it if they decided to call it quits? "I'm so glad you brought me my puppy and came to the pool with us. My friends love you. You're so funny and nice, Uncle Ed," Amanda said, grinning at him, adoringly.

Maria's heart hurt for Amanda, and it made her mad at George all over again. Her daughter had never known a father's love. George fed and clothed her, willingly paid her tuition to private school, but never paid the slightest bit of attention to her. Amanda was looking for a father and Ed was it.

When they got home, Briggie met them, all dressed and ready to go. "Nellie called and said they've found a special program on the 'telly' that they think we will all enjoy," she said enthusiastically. "We'll have a grand time, Amanda. Nellie promised popcorn, too."

"Briggie, if you like watching television, I'll buy you one this week for your very own." It would be a nice way for Maria to show her appreciation for the care that Briggie always gave her and Amanda. "You can have it in your bedroom where you can put your feet up and enjoy a program or two. I also think one would be nice in George's old study." Maria gave Ed a coaxing smile. "We could use your help, Ed, to move those heavy boxes around, not to mention your brains to get them working."

"Saints preserve us, who would have thought that one day we could sit in our own home and be entertained? It's like going to the movies. What will they think of next?"

"Let's all get ready, so we won't be late," Maria said.

Ed popped his head into Maria's open bedroom door. "Thanks for today. Just when I think I have you figured out, you surprise me. You'll try anything within reason, won't you? From therapy with me to golf lessons in one day. Wow!" He leaned against the doorframe. "I've always wondered about golf, but never felt I had the time to try. I feel like I have to work all the time," he said, sadly.

"I feel that way too, lots of times."

"When Winston invited me back, I couldn't help but wonder if I'd also get another invitation from you."

"It all depends on what happens with your divorce proceedings. I can't think about a future with you until your divorce is final." Maria sat down on the end of her bed. "I'm also concerned about Amanda. Ed, she idolizes you. Are you aware of that? If things don't work out for us, she'll be devastated."

"I didn't realize," he stammered. "I've never had to consider kids before."

"There are a lot of things we have to consider."

When Ed finished dressing, he found Maria with Amanda and her puppy out on the patio.

"Uncle Ed, how do you like the ribbon in my hair?"

"You look beautiful, Petunia." "You really think so?" Amanda twirled around the room. "Mommy, Uncle Ed said I was beautiful."

Maria gave Ed a sharp look. *Take it easy with the compliments.* "You two ready to go?"

"Petunia, you must sit by me tonight at dinner, so I can enjoy your company."

Amanda giggled. "You're my boyfriend. My friends said they were jealous because you look like a movie star. Can they come and look at you?"

"We'll have to see," Ed said, as he helped Briggie into the small front seat of the car.

As soon as they arrived, Amanda rushed into the house. "Grandpa, I brought the cribbage board, but not my puppy. She's home in her bed. Do we have time for a game?"

"Of course, we'll play after I get everyone a drink. I have lemonade for you and Briggie."

With Winston engaged in a cribbage game with Amanda, Ed was able to sit on the couch with Maria and sip his scotch and soda. "This is nice." he whispered.

Winston's stereo's music filled the room with gorgeous sound, and Maria shut her eyes. She sipped her beer and let the music wash over her. It felt so good to relax.

After draining the last drop from his glass, Winston looked at his watch. "We'll have to continue our game tomorrow, Amanda. I'm hungry. It's time to go."

"Dean will drive us all over to the club in the big car," Maria's mother said, wisely. When they pulled into the country club's parking lot, everyone got out except Dean.

"Where's Dean? Why didn't he come in with us?" Ed asked.

Maria shrugged her shoulders. "It has to do with his work. He shadows Winston whenever he's out in public. I don't know where Dean goes, but make no mistake about it, he's not far from Winston."

Ed gave her an incredulous look and shook his head. "What am I missing?"

Maria smiled. "I'll fill you in later." She glanced around. "Where's Shirley, our friendly hostess?"

"She's back living in Georgia near her adored married nephew, Franklin, and his wife, Diana, who is expecting their first baby," Ruth replied. "Ed, poor Diana was married to crazy Luis who had George kidnapped. Luis is in prison and Diana deserves her happiness with Franklin."

After a delightful dinner, Dean materialized at the exact moment they needed him. He dropped Amanda and Briggie off with Nellie and drove the others into Washington, DC, to the theatre.

"In case you're wondering, we're going to see *Brigadoon,* the story of a magical city that appears once every hundred year in Scotland. It's not Ireland, but it's as close as I could get," her mother apologized.

Ed smiled. "I've never seen a professional play. No time, no money, and too far away from Chicago, living out in the corn fields of Illinois and Iowa."

After discharging his passengers, Dean pulled out smoothly and drove away.

"Where's Dean going?" Ed whispered in Maria's ear.

"He really interests you, doesn't he? He'll be around. Just relax and enjoy the show. Don't worry about the cloak and dagger stuff."

17. Ignore the Pain of Rejection, Life Is What You Make It

September 1962
(Maria)

As masses of people streamed into the theater, Ed touched Maria's arm. "Look over there. Isn't that Bill Morgan with a good-looking woman in tow? It's been a long time since I've seen him. Maybe we can catch up with them tonight."

Maria felt like someone had punched her in the gut, causing her to stumble slightly.

Ed instantly grabbed her. "What wrong?"

"Oh, nothing, my heel caught on the sidewalk," she lied. Her face felt warm, and her hands were suddenly cold. *So, this is how Bill honors his promises. He really is a bastard, dating Elena, my foster sister!*

She grabbed Ed's arm tightly. "The good-looking woman is Elena. She nursed George back to health after his captors had beaten him almost to death. George brought her out of Puerto Rico, escaping his captors, and asked my mother and Winston to take her into their home. They did and raised her. She's a beautiful person and a gifted artist."

"Well, old Bill's doing all right for himself. She's pretty," Ed replied. "You were engaged to him. Was your engagement just a war-time thing?"

"He acted like it was. He was so caught up in the Korean War flying for the navy and trying to stay alive, his few letters never caught up with me until I had agreed to marry George. He ended up marrying a navy nurse, but is divorced." Maria called, "Mom, Winston, look over there. Bill and Elena are walking into the theatre." Maria tried to keep any bitterness out of her tone.

From the amazed looks on their faces, they must have been wondering how Bill and Elena had gotten together. She'd explain later, but she'd leave out one huge detail.

During the first act, Maria sat in her seat, not enjoying the lighthearted play. All she could think of was Bill and how he'd hurt her. She kept going over the promises Bill had made to her that wild and wonderful night after George's funeral. She twisted her handbill, inadvertently, until it was in shreds.

During intermission, Ed searched out Bill. She watched them shake hands, and, before she knew it, Ed was leading them back to her, her mother, and Winston.

Bill had a guilty, stunned expression on his face as he approached her. Elena seemed unconcerned. She had no idea what Bill had said and done the night they'd spent together.

Maria stood there waiting, her heart racing, trying desperately to look and sound like seeing him with her foster sister was perfectly normal. She choked back a mixture of anger and sadness for what might have been, and pasting on a ridiculous smile, she said, simply, "Hello."

Completely unaware, Winston, always the consummate host said, "Good to see you again, my boy. Why don't you and Elena come out tomorrow while Ed's here and have dinner with us? On second thought, bring your bathing suits for a swim in the pool. We can have a game of water polo."

Bill glanced at Maria. She held herself firmly in check, not showing any noticeable reaction. "We'll have to make it an early visit," he said, sounding a bit hesitant. "I'm on duty tomorrow evening and flying to California."

"Anything you say. We'll be waiting for you, son," Winston replied in a fatherly tone.

Again, Bill glanced at Maria. "Okay, we'll see you all tomorrow," he said smoothly, as though there should be no reason at all to decline.

"The lights have dimmed for the final act, everyone," her mother announced to her little party.

And so have our lights, Bill. Forever!

As Dean drove them home, her mother brought up seeing Bill and Elena together. "Elena seemed so subdued. She's usually happy."

"Maybe we'll find out tomorrow." Winston reached for his wife's hand. "She feels a little awkward about how she met Bill."

Elena's no fool. She remembers how miserable I felt, waiting to hear from Bill during the Korean war. She knows there's still something there.

Amanda was bubbling with happiness as she hopped into the car, excited to talk. "Mommy, we watched a wonderful show on television. There were dancers and jugglers leaping around. Briggie and I loved their television."

"Good, honey," Maria said, trying to sound enthusiastic. "But don't forget to take Wiggles out before you go to bed."

"What's wrong, Mommy? You sound sort of mad."

Briggie gave Maria a questioning look. "Yes, me girl, what's wrong?"

"I'm not mad, Amanda. Just tired." But she couldn't fool Amanda. She'd grown up in George's house and was tuned in to Maria's feelings.

Helping Amanda get ready for bed and listening to her daughter's youthful excitement had a calming effect on Maria. Perhaps she was being unfair to Bill. He was just dating Elena, and she was getting to know Ed. But there was a difference. Ed hadn't promised her anything.

Ed poked his handsome face into Amanda's bedroom. "Come on, Petunia, get into bed, and I'll tell you a funny story."

She could hear the two of them laughing, and it was so precious it almost made her cry. Amanda's father had never tucked Amanda into bed once during his lifetime, much less made her laugh with a good story. Small wonder she idolized Ed.

She stood in Amanda's doorway. "Hey, you two. Time for you to go to sleep, Amanda. You'll see Uncle Ed tomorrow." A huge wave of concern washed over her as she realized how everything she did, including seeing Ed, affected everyone else, especially Amanda.

Ed came out smiling. "I've tucked one in, now it's your turn." He walked her to her bedroom door.

I know he wants to come in, but he can't. Now that Bill saw me tonight, perhaps he'll call to explain.

Ed didn't move—he just looked at her. Feeling terribly awkward again, and searching for a kind word for him, she said, "You've captured Amanda's heart. She loved your story. You could be a writer, if you'd give yourself half a chance. God's given you a gift for storytelling." Why did she say that? Where did that thought even come from?

"Maria, I'm a vet, not a writer. Telling a story to your interested little girl gives me an excuse to enjoy a part of me that I like, but telling stories doesn't pay the bills."

"If you don't want to write them down, let me. Tell me the story you told Amanda tonight. You can see how much she enjoyed it. Imagine hundreds of little kids, just like Amanda, loving every one of your stories. I'm very excited about this. If I let you into my bedroom tonight, it will be only to record your story. It's too early for anything else."

"I'll settle for anything. You never know where it might lead," He dropped onto the sofa in her room. "I wondered how I'd get in here, but I never figured it would be this way."

Maria grinned at him. "This is the sofa. It's a long way from the bed. Now, I want to share a few of your stories from college that I wrote down and stored in my desk. Those weekends when we went on calls together produced many good tales."

"Gosh, Maria, you wrote them all down? No one has ever encouraged me with my stories—or in all the little things you've done for me this week."

At that moment, she saw a side of Ed that was so endearing, she began to hope.

His face lit up. "I can remember my dad coming into my room at night after my mother was asleep and telling me tales about the fairies and elves in Ireland. My dad's mother had tucked him into bed with a story like that every night. His stories encouraged me to think about my own, and I used to spend time as a little kid thinking up more. It was a way for me to escape my angry mother. She wanted me to be tough, not cry, show no feelings, and never write any sissy stuff like girls did."

"She sounds like she was the man in the family."

"I never thought of that! She certainly wanted a man around the house, and I was it."

"How did your dad get along with your mom?"

"He didn't, he drank. Now that we've discussed my childhood ad nauseam, can I at least put my arm around you while I charm you with my stories? I promise not to do anything else unless you wink at me."

"I never wink." Maria waved her pen and notebook under his nose. "I've always thought that Irishmen had a bit of fairy dust in their blood, and that made it easy for them to be writers, poets, and musicians. And *you* are full of fairy dust." She smiled. "I like that about you."

"Now that you've given me a fat head, before I tell you the story, I want to say that Peter helped me a lot this morning. I wasn't prepared

115

to like him at all, much less feel he was a good shrink. But I trust him, and I need his help so I can find out why I shoot myself in my foot all the time."

"Thanks for your honesty. If you'd backed out of your appointment, I would have written you off. I can't waste my time on another relationship that's doomed before it starts. I know myself much better because of Peter, but still don't know what I did wrong with George. Peter has said, over and over, not to blame myself for George's problems, but it's hard.

"But you know what? I think both of us wanted to fix our lovers. You married a nymphomaniac and then a sexually abused woman, and I married an emotionally scarred veteran."

"Wow, I never thought of that. We are alike. Maybe we have a chance, Maria, because both of us are independent."

"I'll tell you something else. I think if we'd married when we were young, we wouldn't have made it. I was too immature with a lot of baggage, like you."

Ed sat studying her face and intently absorbing what she had confided to him. "Maybe you're right about us. I'm a doctor and wanted to marry and heal my spouses."

"I'm the daughter of a doctor and kept thinking I could heal George."

"What an evening! Maybe I didn't waste the last ten years. I was learning a lot about women that will help me not make the same mistakes with you."

"Enough psychoanalyzing, let's get started on your magical stories. All of a sudden, I feel full of energy." An hour later, Maria's hand began cramping from writing as Ed poured out one funny, clever story after another to her.

"These stories will make a wonderful children's book, maybe two. In my business, I have friends in the publishing world who would gladly look at your book. Elena is a fantastic artist and would help us with illustrations if I asked her."

"I think you're dreaming, Maria. The tales are just little stories, nothing more."

"I disagree. I've been in the publishing field long enough to know good material when I see it. Think of this, we could be quite a team with your imagination and my expertise. We could make it happen!"

"I'll tell you one thing, I like your enthusiasm." Ed's gaze softened. "Could we seal our partnership with a kiss?"

Excited with her new idea and feeling so impressed with a side of him she'd never known before, she let down her guard and moved ever so slightly toward him.

He immediately put his arms around her. His body warmth and gentle domination were impossible to ignore. He kissed her lightly at first, barely touching her lips with his. She felt his breath on her face as he tightened his hold of her body, pulling her into him. She groaned from a need so primal, it surprised her. It triggered him to kiss her harder, slipping his tongue into her mouth. Their reserve was breaking down, she could feel it.

"Enough, dear storyteller, this isn't fair to you, physically. It's too much." She tried to pull away. "Go! I'll see you tomorrow morning."

"Oh, baby, you can't make me go now," he said, breathing heavily. "Please let me make love to you."

Maria fought the rising emotions that threatened to choke her. "I can't, Ed. I can't do what George's mistress did to me for five years."

18. Finding Common Ground

September 1962
(Maria)

Maria awoke with the sun trying to creep in through her blinds. *What was I thinking last night? I'm the mother of two children, and I let a married man kiss me until we almost lost it. No more of that.* She groaned and turned over.

How was she going to handle seeing Elena with Bill later that day? Why didn't he try to call her last night? Was she so old? She buried her face in her pillow and groaned again.

She quickly showered and dressed, found her tape recorder, hurried to Ed's door, then hesitated. How was he going to handle the pain that had to be expressed on that tape? Peter had said he'd hit pay dirt. That meant only one thing. As she stood there, she asked for help from Archangel Michael to make Ed strong and to be able to accept his childhood with all the good and bad it had to offer.

Opening his door, quietly, she took a deep breath. Watching him sleep was almost too personal. She felt like a voyeur, somehow. He hadn't lost any of his good looks over the years with his brown curly hair, slight over-bite, and dimple in his chin. *Enough!* She jiggled the bed, and Ed's eyes flew open.

He yawned. "Hi, what's going on?"

"Are you ready to hear your tape?"

"Oh, that. I wish I knew what I'd said."

"You will soon."

"Let me shower and shave first," he said, with a certain edge to his voice. When he returned, he looked wonderful, but he didn't sound comfortable. "I'm not ready for this."

"As Peter said, the gloves have to come off." Maria turned on the tape and sat on the edge of the bed next to him.

All through the tape, Ed sat mesmerized, listening to his little boy's voice telling how he felt between sobs from the brutal attack by his mother. Tears silently ran down Ed's cheeks. Maria had never seen him cry before.

"I knew she was a witch," he whispered, "but I never thought she was a bitch, too. Down deep inside me, I always had an indescribable feeling of dread around her."

Maria turned off the tape and sat quietly next to him. A strong urge to hold him surged inside her, but she fought off the feeling. He needed to be left alone to mull over his tape, but how could she walk out without doing something to comfort him? "I had to do this, too, and it really hurt, but I learned a lot about myself. Peter said I had to find out where the pain was so I could get rid of it, little by little. I was finally able to forgive my mother. I know a lot more about me than I did when I knew you. I still have some down times, but they're gone, for the most part."

"It helps knowing you went through this too, Maria. It makes me feel closer to you."

"Are you ready to face Amanda and Briggie?" Maria gently touched his face with her hand with concern in her voice. "Later on, Bill and Elena will be here, too."

"I like being here in my bedroom alone with you, even if it is only to pry into my soul. How about a comfort kiss after all I went through this morning?" he asked with a grin.

"Have you really recovered so quickly?"

"No, but I have to seize the moment."

"I have to get going, my friend. You are an unbelievable kisser. It loosens all of my controls. I find I can't trust myself. It can't happen again until you're free."

When Elena and Bill walked into the house, unannounced, later that morning, Maria and Ed were having a comfortable second cup of coffee with Briggie, and they were all watching Amanda play with Wiggles, waddling around the kitchen floor.

"Bill, it's good to see you again," Ed said. "You're looking much better than the last time I saw you. When did you get your memory back?" Ed got up and shook Bill's hand. "Remember the wild games of pool we played that afternoon? I was half drunk on beer and can't even remember the final score, can you?"

"I'm sure you won, Ed, you were quite a player," Bill said, with a laugh. "And my memory returned quite fast after I had a personal experience that triggered it. His eyes lingered on Maria for a second.

Maria swallowed and took a deep breath. "Bill, I'd like you to meet my dear friend, Briggie. Do you remember her in the kitchen cooking to feed the hordes of people at George's funeral?" An inner rage made her want to challenge him. "You do remember the funeral, don't you? Oh, and I must caution you. Amanda has a new little puppy that's under your feet as we speak."

"It's a good thing I'm not a few years younger and my feet didn't hurt," Briggie said in her thick brogue. "I might try to win you away with me cooking."

Bill's infectious laugh at Briggie's teasing triggered so many memories they shared when they were madly in love, it cut into Maria like a knife. For a moment, she couldn't breathe.

"Elena, watch my new puppy!" Amanda yelled from where she sat on the floor. "Her name is Wiggles. Isn't she cute?"

Wiggles, unknowingly, had become comic relief for everyone as she waddled around the kitchen, licking up crumbs.

Maria got her foster sister's attention. "Elena, I'm not sure I introduced you properly last night to Dr. Ed McDermott. He's a veterinarian visiting from Illinois."

"Oh!" Elena smiled at Ed. "Did you fly from Chicago? It's nice you came to see Maria. She's my dear sister, you know."

Maria caught an inscrutable look on Bill's face that defied explanation. Suddenly, he took Elena's hand and asked to see her studio.

Her heart sank. *Maria, focus on reality.* Obviously it was too early for them to have fallen in love. It didn't happen that way. Besides, Elena was so different from Bill. She was wrapped up in her passion for the arts. They wouldn't make it—Bill would tire of her after a while. He was just enjoying the chase.

Her mean-spirited thoughts made her compensate. "My, the weather is so nice, why don't we sit out on the patio and enjoy a cup of coffee with Briggie's cinnamon rolls?" she said with as much charm as possible.

With Wiggles under one arm, Amanda grabbed several rolls, then stuffed one in her mouth and the other in her pocket. She took her puppy outside and dutifully followed it all over the yard.

"Giving both Maria and Bill a subtle, questioning glance, "Ed asked, "Are you up for a tour around Maria's little world? Would you like to see the farm, Bill?"

"Sure." Bill followed Ed outside.

Soon they were gesturing and talking to each other. Again and again, Bill's laugh reverberated in Maria's ears. *That rascal, Ed. He's telling Bill naughty jokes. They're actually having a good time. I wish I knew what Bill was thinking and what the look he gave me meant.*

On the patio, Amanda's constant chatter to Elena made her laugh continuously. She seemed entranced, listening to every facet of her little niece's world. Maria needed to laugh more. Where had her sense of humor gone? Things didn't tickle her funny bone like they used to.

"Elena, tell us where and when your next show will be and we'll come. Don't be a stranger, either," She still couldn't wrap her mind around the fact that Bill was there with Elena. Not in a thousand years did she think that would have ever happened.

Elena answered Maria by shyly reaching over and taking her hand. "I've missed you, but I feel so awkward because of Bill. I don't know what to make of him. He's very insistent about seeing me. I don't think he realizes how important my work is to me and Kathy. He gets very impatient when I don't want him to come over, even when I explain how busy I am." Elena's face reflected such anguish. "I wish he would be more understanding. Somehow, I don't feel right with him. And dear Maria, I will definitely come to see you as soon as I can." She paused and seemed to think for a moment. "I like your friend, Ed. When I know the exact dates of the show, I'll call you. I'm sure my manager, Kathy, knows them," Elena added, in her soft, Spanish accent.

Maria could hear Briggie banging around in the kitchen, whipping up lunch for everyone. *Thank you, God, for giving me Briggie.*

"Come in and fill your plates," Briggie yelled out the kitchen window a minute later.

Maria scooped up the puppy who had been trying hard to get lost. Her mistress had forgotten Wiggles, spellbound watching Elena sketch a picture of her puppy.

Amanda squealed. "It looks just like her, Elena! How do you do it? Please do another one," she begged, jumping up and down.

Elena turned to a clean page in her sketch pad. "I will if you let me draw you holding the puppy in your arms."

At lunch, Amanda passed Elena's sketches around to everyone.

When they reached Ed, he looked at them carefully. "I've never known a real artist before. Do you paint as well as you draw? You've captured Amanda in just a few strokes."

"Thank you, but I don't do what I do by myself," Elena said and blushed.

Ed's eyebrows raised. "Nobody helped you draw those pictures."

"I'm never alone when I work. I get inspiration from a higher source."

Judging by the looks on everyone's faces, Elena's comment had caused some thought. It certainly raised some questions for Maria. Did Ed get his storytelling ability from that same place? Did everyone who creates get help? Was that what people meant when they said they had a God-given talent?

"Elena's inspiration may come from the heavens, but I can tell you firsthand that she needs a strong back here on earth to lift some of those creations of hers." Bill's tone had a tinge of irritation in it. "That clay is heavy!" His blue eyes flashed at Maria.

Did Bill like his place in Elena's life? Maria couldn't tell. But one thing was clear—he didn't mean a word of what he'd said to her the night they were together. He'd forgotten about it completely. *Good luck, Bill. I hope you're always on top because if you ever fall, I'll never pick you up again,* Maria thought, bitterly.

Somehow, Maria made it through lunch. But the day wasn't over yet. "My mother and Winston have invited us over for a swim and refreshments this afternoon. Whenever you're ready, we can drive over there—that is, if you'd like to go."

19. Putting Two and Two Together

September 1962

(Maria)

Like magic, the idea of swimming on such a hot day was the impetus for everyone to hurry, get into two cars, and drive to Winston's place. Only Briggie remained behind, probably thrilled to be able to put up her feet and relax.

Already dressed in his swimming trunks, Winston surprised them at the front door. "Let the games begin!"

Pandemonium reigned as the teams formed. "Bill and Ed cannot be on the same side," Maria announced loudly.

Amanda insisted on playing on Ed's team. Ed enlisted Dean for his side, which promptly caused Bill to ask Winston to play with his team. Maria's mother joined Winston to play with Bill, while Ed asked Maria. Elena said she wouldn't play at all. Her preference was to sketch the whole wild scene.

Bill was everywhere, diving, jumping, twisting, and turning, trying to win, but in the end, with Dean's power, he and Ed prevailed, pleasing Maria immensely.

The deck was covered with water from all the sloshing the game had generated. Elena had taken refuge under an umbrella near the house. When everyone dragged themselves out of the pool, the men had a heated discussion as to who had won, but Winston intervened, offering drinks to soothe bruised egos.

Everyone was thirsty, and they consumed a variety of beverages, keeping Nellie scurrying back and forth bringing everyone's favorite. As the afternoon dragged on, Bill's growing impatience to leave became obvious. He kept checking his watch and pacing around while Elena ignored him. Finally, he leaned over to her and whispered something.

She nodded yes, but continued to add lines to the various pictures she had sketched of everyone in the pool, turning them this way and that and cocking her head to add another line or two here and there.

Bill has met his match with Elena, Maria thought, gleefully. *He runs a poor second to Elena's artwork. Knowing Bill, he's wishing for a sexual interlude with Elena before he flies, but it's obvious she's oblivious.* It soothed Maria, somehow.

Looking pleased, Elena handed her mother the various sketches of the water polo games for her reaction.

"You've captured the excitement on the faces of us all!" Her mother passed the drawings around the group. Everyone except Bill laughed at the way she'd drawn their contorted faces diving for the ball.

Elena smiled, looking pleased. "They're really silly, but fun."

"Nonsense," Winston said. "I'm going to ask Nellie and Dean to get them framed, and we'll put them on the patio house wall for all to see. They're amazing."

Maria held up several sketches. "I claim the pictures of Amanda and Wiggles for my bare study walls."

Winston looked up from the paper he was holding. "What happened to George's fighter pilot pictures?"

"They've gone to be with George, wherever he is." Maria returned Winston's questioning look without smiling.

Elena rose gracefully and gathered her art materials. Bill moved immediately, put his hand on her back, and tried to guide her quickly out to his car. But she ignored his impatience, stopping innumerable times, talking and hugging Amanda and Maria, kissing her mother and Winston, and finally saying a few words to Dean before hugging her dear friend, Nellie.

Bill looked fit to be tied, and Maria loved watching him squirm. Elena's determination and grit, the same strengths she showed escaping Puerto Rico, were there. She wouldn't be rushed when it came to showing the respect and love she felt for the family who saved her.

"I miss her," Nellie said, forlornly. "How I wish she could come more often. She's like the child I never had. If only they could have stayed for the crab cakes I made for us tonight."

"I love your crab cakes, Nellie," Amanda said, "and your chocolate chip cookies."

Ed gave Amanda's hair a gentle tug. "How about a cribbage game, my little Petunia?"

"Really?" Amanda's eyes sparkled like fireworks on the Fourth of July. "I'd love to play with you."

With Winston coaching Amanda and Nellie in the kitchen whipping up a small supper, Maria took the opportunity to talk to her mother, who was arranging the patio chairs around the outdoor table. "I wish Elena and Bill had been a little forthcoming about their relationship."

Her mother gave Maria a puzzled look. "Why is it important to you?"

Maria squirmed a little. "It's not," she lied.

"Maybe she's been waiting to find out if you still have feelings for Bill. Now that she's seen you with Ed, she may let Bill into her life. But if you noticed, Elena won't be pushed."

Moments later, Amanda squealed. "I won! I beat you, Uncle Ed!"

It took only one look to know that Ed had blown the game to make Amanda happy. He really was a dear man.

After Nellie had proudly served her delicious crab cakes and enjoyed the praise everyone heaped upon her, Maria saw Amanda drooping and yawning.

"Mom, I'm tired. I'm too big to crawl into your lap, so let's go home."

Ed smiled at Amanda. "Right, Petunia, we'll let your grandma and grandpa have a moment to themselves."

"Uncle Ed, can I always be on your team when we play water polo?" Amanda put her hand in his as they walked to the car. "Will you tell me a story and tuck me in, too?"

Maria heard the door to Amanda's bedroom close.

A moment later, Ed peeked in Maria's room. "One short story, and she was out like a light."

"Thank you for tucking her in."

"Do you want to work on my book, among other things?"

"What other things?" Maria quirked her eyebrow and laughed. "I should say no, but I can't wait to hear your next story, Uncle Ed. Come in and shut the door. I don't want Briggie to hear us. She'll think we're up to no good."

"I hope she's right." Ed stepped across the threshold and shut the door behind him. "Ah . . . I'm in again." He gave her a devilish smile and reached for her.

She artfully ducked his arms and dove for the sofa.

A big grin spread across his face. "Do you want to play a little?"

"No, I'm waiting for you to intrigue me with your stories, not your physical abilities."

"Before we start, I have a question that I have to ask." His eyes were flashing with concern. "What's up with you and Bill?"

"Were you eavesdropping on me and Mom?"

He gave her a sheepish look. "Sort of."

"Bill isn't a subject for us to discuss. Let's work on your stories."

"I don't like it. How does he figure in our lives?" He put his arms around her. "Would you like it if I said I didn't want to talk about Jackie?"

"Listen, octopus arms," she said, as she extricated herself and pushed him away, "after your kindness with Amanda on this trip, you have soared on my love meter. You are so darn sweet to her, it almost makes me cry."

"Gosh, Maria, it's easy to like her, she's a lot like you. But . . ." His manner became serious again. "What's going on with you? You ducked my questions about Bill. Why?"

"There's nothing going on! If you noticed, Bill is head-over-heels in love with Elena. I suggest that you work on your life, your divorce and counseling with Peter, and our relationship."

"So, that's it then." Ed threw up his arms in frustration. "I don't like it, but I guess I'll have to live with it for now." They sat on the sofa looking uncomfortably at each other.

She reached over and gently touched his face. "Come on, Ed, think about everything we've done, and all you've learned about yourself this week."

"One thing, for sure—the tape has given me some relief knowing that I wasn't crazy for the scary feelings I felt around my mother. She hated me and my dad."

"I'll tell you something I haven't told anyone before. When Peter uncovered my terrible guilt about my parent's divorce, I've never felt so relieved. For ages, I was sure I'd caused it. He set me free from that ridiculous idea and many more, since then."

Ed's big, brown eyes softened, and he slowly moved closer.

She pushed him away. "I think we should call it a day. I'm tired. Aren't you?"

"I think there are two extra people in this room—Jackie and Bill," Ed snapped.

"I'm human, Ed. Bill and I have history. So do you. Don't make it any harder for me. Your divorce will take time, and what happened between Bill and me will fade, too."

"I think you're really waiting for Bill, but pretending to me that you're championing the perfect marriage with no sex until all the Is are dotted and the Ts crossed."

Maria couldn't believe that Ed had guessed her feelings about Bill and was trying to protect his domain. "What you think won't change my mind. I do believe if all women would say no to married men, a lot of heartache could be avoided." Maria rubbed her temples. "Listen, my friend, we're both tired and not in a good frame of mind, so no work tonight. Go to bed. I'll see you for our early morning appointment," she said softly, then she stood up and waited until he reluctantly walked out.

Ed was dressed and enjoying a cup of coffee with Briggie when Maria came into the kitchen the following morning, shaking her keys at him and smiling. "We'll see you in a couple of hours, Briggie."

He didn't return her smile, but instead gave her a resigned look. It didn't bother her. Her therapy with Peter had made her tougher.

Ed's unerring sense of direction made their second trip to Peter's office easy. Peter was waiting for them, but Maria knew his smile was a facade to cover his plan to break Ed's defenses. He was a master at uncovering tender areas that were hidden and needed to be exposed so that healing could begin.

"Do you want me to stay, Peter?" Maria was willing to do whatever would make him feel comfortable.

"For the moment, and listen carefully."

Peter directed his attention on Ed. "So, what did you think when you heard how the suffering little boy inside you felt?"

"I never knew he was still in there, and I was surprised by the amount of rage and downright meanness my mom felt for me and my dad."

"Do you think either of you deserved it?"

"No. She put us on the defensive." Ed's face was a mass of pain. "I always felt I was doing something wrong, but I couldn't put my finger on it. Hearing the tape validated my assumptions."

"If she felt like a threatening woman to you, do all women threaten you?"

Ed pondered Peter's question for a moment. "I don't know. I didn't understand my two wives, but my sexual needs made me ignore any questions I might have had about my feelings toward them," he answered, tapping his fingers nervously.

"Do you understand what makes Maria tick?"

"Not really." Ed's tone indicated his confusion. "When she seemed interested in me a long time ago, and then turned around and married George, I was furious." Ed's voice was filled with anger.

"Would it be fair to say that women you have an emotional bond with make you angry, and your anger surprises you? In fact, you sort of expect it, but you don't like it?"

"No, I don't expect it!" Ed was sounding even more angry with each question Peter threw at him.

"Wasn't that what you experienced with your mother?"

"That's different. She's my mother, not my wife."

"But she's a woman, isn't she?"

Ed crossed his arms over his chest and glared at Peter. "Doc, you've got me all mixed up."

Peter ignored Ed's angry confusion. "What did you want to do when your mom was so mean to you and your dad?"

"I wanted to hit her, beat her, scare her, and tape her mouth shut so she couldn't say those unfair things to me anymore!" Ed said, almost screaming at Peter.

"So, why didn't you do something?"

"Because I was little and she was big." Ed's voice sounded bitter. "But I swore when I grew up, I'd punish her."

"So, did you?"

"No, she was my mom," he answered softly. "I couldn't do that to the person who gave birth to me and raised me," Ed said, sounding disgusted that Peter would ask such a question.

Peter leaned across his desk, his eyes boring into Ed's. "How about your ex-wives and Maria?"

"Well, I never wanted my wives to get the upper hand. Maybe I was afraid that they'd punish me. But don't lump Maria in with them." Suddenly, Ed put his hands over his mouth, surprised at his last comment.

"Like your mom did," Peter said.

Ed sat there for a minute as though he was trying to accept what Peter had just said. "I had, and probably still have, a lot of anger toward my mother." He took a deep breath. "You're trying to tell me that I tried to get even with my mother by getting even with my wives."

128

"Bingo, you just put two and two together. You could do it to Maria, too, by the way.

"She's a woman." Peter leaned back in his chair. "Congratulations, you're getting it. All children take pictures of their parents' actions toward them and toward each other. The kids know in their gut whether they're loved or not, which parent is partial to them, and whether their parents love or dislike each other. Rarely are these things spoken, but everyone knows.

"Ed, because you knew inside from an early age that your mother, for whatever reasons, didn't like men or boys, what was your reaction?"

"To never let my mother get the best of me, and to always protect me and my father," Ed said, with grim determination in his voice.

"Now, substitute your wives and Maria in place of your mother and what do you have?"

Ed looked perplexed. "I guess to protect myself, I wasn't going to give them an inch. But Maria's different," he said slowly.

"Is she? After the honeymoon phase wears off, will she become part of the problem?"

When Ed didn't answer, Peter put his fingers together. "You win the prize for self-awareness this morning. It is the sweetest prize in the world, because it enables you to manage your life more successfully, and it may save your next marriage." He glanced at Maria. "I gather you and Maria are dating. I've taped this conversation and will add your next hypnosis to it so you can review everything when you go home.

"Maria, why don't you go out and sit under a tree while we do this? I'll call you when we finish the next regression."

20. Peeling Away the Layers
September 1962
(Ed/Maria)

Ed

"Now, lie down and think back to when you won an award, large or small, as a teenager, and your parents' reactions to your success. Shut your eyes. You'll go under faster and faster with each session because your mind is very smart and learns quickly."

Peter counted back to Ed's teenage years, and when Peter hit the magic number of eighteen, Ed stopped him and spoke in a young male voice.

"I'm standing in my living room in my cap and gown. I had to walk home from graduation. I'm holding my diploma from high school. I have several medals around my neck and two checks in my pocket from local businesses for being the outstanding student of the senior class. The money will help me start the five-year vet med program in the fall at Iowa State.

"I'm showing my dad my medals and checks. He overslept from too much drinking and didn't make it to my graduation. He's all apologetic, and I'm telling him it's okay. He tells me how proud he is of me. Our conversation stops when my mother comes in complaining about my dad being worthless because he missed my graduation.

"She turns to me and says, 'A lot of good those medals and checks are going to do you. You'll end up just like you father, a good for nothing.' I feel like I'll explode and hit her if I don't get out of there fast. I go upstairs and swear that I'll be the best damned vet there is, make lots of money, and show that bitch of a mother how good I am."

Peter went to the door and called Maria back inside.

María

María watched the color of Ed's face turn from red back to his normal complexion as Peter brought him out of the hypnosis.

"Congratulations, Ed. So far today, you're my star pupil. Of course, you're also my first patient. But I could do cartwheels, I'm so happy with the work you've done today," Peter said with exuberance. "Listening to this tape will give you a lot more insight."

Peter turned to María and grinned. "María, you've got to learn to be quiet at these sessions."

He shook Ed's hand and opened the door to send them out. "We ran over a bit today, but I wanted to give you the one-two punch, Ed. We have limited time available with you living in the Midwest and only visiting here once in a while."

María eased into the conversation with Peter about his mother and his wives. "Did Peter's questions about comparing your attitude toward your mother and how that may have influenced the way you treated your wives seem logical?"

"I'm still trying to accept what he said, especially about you. I can't believe that my feelings about my mother have anything to do with the way I treated my wives or the way I'll treat you."

"It takes time to let the things he says become reality. At least it did for me."

"When do we hear about you? I feel like this therapy is one-sided."

"I've been seeing him for years, and when I get to know you better, I'll tell you more about me. Besides, Peter wants to give you a jump-start."

"Okay, enough for one day! Let's have some fun. How about some golf and anything else that comes to mind?" Ed's eyes were full of mischief.

"Maybe in your perfect world, but not mine. I can see going to work for a couple of hours to keep my job for me, but nothing else." María gave him a stubborn look. "You promised to play cribbage with Amanda, and I would be eternally grateful if you would take her to her swimming lesson. That would free Briggie up to go to the grocery store and cook you a delicious dinner.

"After you finish all your family obligations, call Winston and play some golf with him this afternoon. I'll be home later," she said briskly. Thinking twice about how she sounded, she leaned over in her seat and gave him a kiss on the cheek.

"Can you spare it?" said Ed in a resigned tone. "I was hoping by this time you would have warmed up a little." He changed subjects. "I need to call the clinic and see how Glen is doing. He's the best, but farmers are funny. They hate change and will want to see me. I want them to get used to him, so I can come out here, get beat up by my shrink, turned down by my girl, and play father to her daughter." Ed winked, then leaned over and returned the kiss on the cheek.

"Handsome, you're working your way into our world and charming us all doing it. You're hard to resist." It was getting more and more difficult to keep some emotional and physical distance. Good thing she had to work today and that they lived so far apart. Maria needed space from Ed—at least until his divorce.

Work wore her out, and she was glad the household was quiet and happy when she got home. Briggie had dinner ready for them. Ed had played golf with Winston and was telling Amanda a story when Maria joined them in the kitchen.

Early next morning, they listened to Ed's tape together before Amanda got up.

Ed's silence indicated that he was upset, but he wouldn't discuss it with her. She felt he was definitely uncomfortable because of the two very tender subjects on the tape—his drive to succeed and his father's weaknesses.

The following day, they drove to his appointment with Peter in silence.

As soon as they walked into his office, Peter acknowledged that he picked up on Ed's resistance to be there. But that seemed to energize him, and he waded into Ed. "What did you think of your graduation and the way your parents ignored it?"

"I was angry and disappointed that neither of them came. I felt like they didn't value me enough to make the effort. I wished my dad didn't drink so much. He might have come if he'd been sober, but my mother was probably so awful to him, he just gave up and drank. I'm also mad at him, deep down, for not doing his share of the work on the farm and forcing me to do his job."

"What about your mother's reference to you turning out like 'your no-good father' after winning those awards?"

Ed sat there choking back his tears while Peter remained silent. He walked around his desk and sat down on the sofa with Ed. Peter motioned for Maria to leave as he hugged Ed like a child. Ed broke down into uncontrollable sobs, and as she closed the door, Maria could hear Peter encouraging him to cry it out.

While Maria waited for Ed, she walked around the grounds and finally sat down on a bench under a beautiful tree. It was a relief to be outside. She didn't want to become more embroiled in Ed's life than she was already. He was still a married man.

A different Ed came out to find her. His face had a composed look to it. The nervousness she'd felt in him when they were driving to the appointment had been replaced by a calmness and a willingness to talk.

"Peter certainly doesn't waste any time. He made me let go of some nasty stuff I've been carrying around for a long time."

"I'm so glad, Ed. Your mood is lighter." Maria was jubilant. "I've had time to think about us while you were with Peter, and I think it's time for me to excuse myself from your sessions. Go see Peter alone on Friday. It will be better that way. If there's anything you want to share with me afterward that would be fine. Otherwise, we won't talk about it. We need some distance."

"Yeah, there's a lot of manure that I don't want you to smell while I'm working with Peter." Ed's face screwed up in a grimace. "I want us to reap the benefits, but getting there will take some hard work that you can't help me with. Only Peter can. I want to protect you from my ugly stuff. You've had enough. I'd like to spend our time together having fun and hopefully bringing us closer."

On Friday, she played hooky from work and waited until Ed had left for his final session in George's sports car. Maria dropped Amanda off for her swimming lesson, bought groceries for Ed's farewell dinner, and stopped by to see her mother for a long overdue talk.

Maria found her in the kitchen helping Nellie rearrange the pantry. "I need to talk, Mom."

"Of course, let's have a cup of coffee out on the patio."

"I don't have long because I have a lot of groceries in the trunk, but I wanted to invite you and Winston over for Ed's last dinner. And I also want to talk to you about Bill, Ed, and me."

"I've been wondering about that."

"This is difficult, but I have to tell you. When I saw Bill at George's funeral, he came over afterward and said he wanted to resume our relationship. He promised me he'd see me every time he flew to Washington, DC. I was thrilled because I'm still in love with him,

Mom. But as you know, he's now dating Elena. It crushed me when I met them at the theatre. I hardly remember the play. All I could think about was, how could he do that to me?"

"What about Ed?"

Ed and I are in the early stages of a relationship, but he's a married man, and I'm not sure what will come of it. He's charming, but there's a lot beneath the surface that isn't so nice. I hope Peter can help him."

Her mother gave Maria a sympathetic look. "I'm sorry about Bill. I always thought he was a wonderful fellow."

"Mom, should I encourage Ed, or should I wait and hope Bill will call?"

"Advice is easy to dispense, but here goes. I'd wait, whether Bill calls or not. But quite frankly, Bill looks like a man who's enjoying the chase with Elena. As for loving her, I don't think so. To be crude, it's all lust at this point. They don't seem compatible."

"Elena confided in me that she really wants to have the freedom to pursue her dreams."

"And what about George? Have you forgiven him yet? Until you do that, you won't be able to focus on Ed. Take care of Amanda and Chris, keep the house going with Briggie's help, and devote energy to your wonderful job. It provides you with something of your own and a sense of accomplishment, which you need right now. Don't rely on a man to make you happy. Only you can do that."

"I have forgiven George in a lot of ways. During his visit the morning after the funeral, I felt his love just pouring out to me, Mom. At that moment, he was the man I fell in love with on the Keys. I think about that feeling a lot, and it's helped me erase a lot of the pain." Maria was thankful for the emotional healing she'd experienced.

"I do need time. I don't want to make any mistakes. A lot is riding on my choices." Maria stood up and hugged her mother. "Sorry I have to go. See you tonight for dinner. I love you, Mom. Thanks for your advice. I'm so glad I have you."

Ed returned from his session looking even calmer than before. Peter had obviously removed another block that Ed had been lugging around.

Maria prepared his lunch, then sat down with him. "Things must have gone well with Peter." It would do him some good to have some fun. "Let's go to the club for one last fling—swimming for Amanda and her friends and golf for us. I'm going to learn how to hit that little ball or throw my shoulder out trying."

"Just take it easy and keep your head down," he teased, his eyes full of mischief.

She tried to whack him, but he held her hands. "Easy there." He studied her with those expressive eyes. "I need to talk to you tonight. There's a reason I'm here, but I don't know what it is."

"I'll be waiting," was all she could say.

That night, after Amanda had fallen asleep, Ed tapped lightly on Maria's door.

"Are you coming in or just saying good night?"

He cocked his head. "Are you inviting me in?"

Maria sat down on her sofa and patted the cushion next to her. "So, talk to me."

"Peter asked me why I'd come to DC. All I could say was that I knew I was supposed to be here."

"It is odd after all these years that we're seeing each other," Maria said, searching his face.

"I've never had a week like this before. I wasn't prepared for your generous hospitality, Amanda's adoration, Briggie's friendliness, and your folks' acceptance of me. I was raised so differently. I've never known people who lived like you and your family."

"I'm glad, Ed. It's been a new start for us, and it helps that Amanda loves you. But I wonder about Chris. My children are my responsibility, and they're a big part of my life."

"Both my wives were childless when I married them, so this is new territory for me." Ed took a deep breath. "And now for the big question. What do you honestly think of me? After spending a week with me, do you still feel optimistic about us?" He sounded hopeful.

"I'm very drawn to you sexually, but you know that," Maria said.

Ed gave her one of his charming smiles. "Like any guy, I came out here with fantasies of sleeping with you. I was disappointed when you turned me down." A slight blush was obvious beneath his tanned face. "But as the week went on, it wasn't as important as before, because of your genuine interest in helping me. You introduced me to Peter and took me into your family. I liked all the nice things you and your folks planned to make my trip feel like a vacation. When you showed excitement over my stories, enough to write them down and offer to see if they were good enough to publish, I was blown away. Frankly, I'm a little embarrassed that my attitude was so shallow."

"I just wanted you to enjoy your precious week of vacation. You deserve it." Ed was such a genuinely nice person. The fact that he told her how much his week with her and her family meant to him melted her heart.

He took and tenderly caressed her hand. "Do you feel we have a chance to make it?"

"That's a fair question to ask." How honest could she be right now? He'd been so vulnerable with what he just shared. The last thing she wanted to do was hurt him. "I know you're my friend." She cocked her head. "If love is a combination of all those things you said I did for you, perhaps there's hope for us. I have to see what you're willing to put into our relationship, too. Think about that," she said, poking him lightly with her finger. "You pass the test for being an intelligent and humane doctor, you like my kids, and you make a lot of money because of all of your abilities. But I honestly don't really know you yet. I feel an urgency about you. George had it too. It was like he wasn't comfortable in his own skin. Maybe, all smart, very masculine guys have it. I don't know . . . I never had any brothers."

"That urgency, as you call it, pays the bills and allows me to come see you," he said, with an edge to his voice.

"I didn't mean it as a criticism. I can't explain it. I just hope it's a good thing."

"I'll ask Peter about it. I'm willing to work with him for as long as it takes. All I can promise is to try to make our relationship better and better after my divorce."

"Don't make any vows until you really understand what you're committing to. I've had enough hasty promises to last me a lifetime."

"Okay, I've been warned." Ed nodded in acceptance. "Let me tell you what I learned today from Peter, which makes sense. It's called 'Dr. Rudolph's Reality Check.' He said to use it when I don't understand why I had an argument with you. It's a series of questions to ask myself to check if I was misinterpreting a situation in a misguided way because of some of my perceptions. He also gave me the tape of today's session and his private phone number. I can call him, night or day."

Peter must really like you to give you his private number. He has a huge practice and cherishes his privacy."

It doesn't matter to me if he likes me. I just want him to help me. You're the one who matters to me." A teasing twinkle appeared in his eyes. "How about a kiss to send me on my way?" he asked with an expectant smile.

"Why not, you've earned it." She held out her arms.

Saturday morning, Maria insisted Ed drive the little red sports car to the airport one last time. He didn't argue. Amanda chattered all the way there, making it easier for Ed and Maria not to talk. They had said it all the night before.

Hugging them, he promised to call, then he ran down the ramp and quickly disappeared.

21. Exploring Each Other

Early November 1962

(Maria)

Ed kept his promise and did call every night. Sometimes, his calls came late at night after Maria had given up on him. He always had a legitimate reason involving a sick animal for his tardiness. Ed's divorce proceedings, and the problems he was having, began to overshadow everything else in their conversations, and that bothered Maria.

On Peter's advice, he'd hastened the proceedings with more expediency by insisting on shortened intervals between meetings with his wife and her lawyer to force her to negotiate.

At first, she'd refused to even get a lawyer to represent her. She called Ed continually, denying they were having any problems. When Ed accused her of being in denial, she would cry and hang up. After breaking several meeting dates, her lawyer cajoled Jackie and her mother to come to the table with the promise of a big alimony settlement. When Ed said that Jackie had begged for reconciliation, Maria started to cry.

When Ed asked her why she was crying, Maria could only explain that Jackie didn't know what to do, and she felt sympathy for the woman.

After that, Ed's discussions about his divorce proceedings stopped until late one night, early in November, when he called and woke her up.

She fumbled with the phone. "Hi," she finally croaked, "I hope that critter that kept you from calling earlier is okay. Do you know what time it is?"

"Sorry, I've been dying to call you for days, but wanted to wait until I could give you my good news. I'm free," he said, his voice full of emotion.

Maria waited as he struggled to maintain his composure. When he was able to talk, he said, "To get out, I had to agree to a very generous alimony settlement. But I don't mind. To be fair, Jackie tried. She just has a lot of demons to deal with, and I realize now, I do too."

"Can you afford it?"

"Yes, business is booming and my freedom is priceless. It's been an emotional roller coaster for me, but with you and Peter behind me, I made it. Thanks, sweetheart. When can I see you? I'm dreaming about a little celebration when I come." he breathed into the phone.

"When can you?" She wished she was as excited as he was.

"Next weekend. Unless Russia fires Cuban missiles at us before then. I think President Kennedy has won, and the Russians are backing down. I've worked every weekend the past few months for two reasons. To give my partner time with his family and to earn a celebration trip."

"Do you think it's going to happen?"

"What, the missile threat or me coming?"

"Don't joke. I'm worried sick because of living near DC."

"I'm sure the Russians were bluffing. It was essentially over in late October. President Kennedy didn't knuckle under. I'm sure he threatened retaliation."

"Sometimes I wonder if we'll ever be safe again."

"I'll use every weapon in my arsenal to make you feel better when I see you Saturday."

By the time of Ed's long awaited visit, the November weather was getting nippy. Amanda and Maria had arrived early at the airport in order to not to miss him stride up the ramp—this time carrying an overcoat and wearing a backpack. He walked with a confidant manner that was different from before.

"It's good to be here," he said simply, without any fanfare. Holding Amanda's hand, Ed slipped his arm around Maria's waist, and together they moved as a single unit to the car.

Amanda grinned up at him. "Uncle Ed, what are you wearing?"

"It's something all hikers use to carry their possessions. It's called a backpack. It frees up my hands to give you a present from Sharon, Amanda. She said she hopes you like it."

"Gee, that's so nice, Uncle Ed," Amanda squealed. "Can Sharon be my aunt, Mommy?"

Before Maria could reply, Ed had maneuvered Amanda into

the back seat with her present. "Your mom is going to sit up front with me."

"Very clever, my friend," Maria said, giving him a smile of approval.

"I hope I can still outwit nine-year-olds."

A scream from the back seat made Maria jump.

"I love Nancy Drew mysteries. I haven't read this one. I usually have to wait and get them from the library."

Ed threw a smile over his shoulder. "Read it while I drive. It will make the ride go faster."

"Ah, silence, how nice it is," Maria uttered quietly.

"So, Rosebud, what are our plans for today and tonight?"

"Let me surprise you," she replied, her eyes catching his.

"Are we going to play golf?"

"Yes, I've lined up a game with Winston and Mom. We tee off at one. It's perfect weather, plus we're still here," she whispered.

"Is Amanda worried? It looks like President Kennedy has backed the Russians down."

"She doesn't understand it, and it frightens her. I asked Chris and Briggie not to watch the news if Amanda was around. Chris prefers to play his Beatles records in his bedroom anyway, so loud I think he'll go deaf. I can't understand why he likes them so much."

"Turning to a more interesting topic—golf," Ed said, sounding excited. "I've been looking forward to driving a golf ball or two, among other things. I must confess I practiced on a public driving range a few times this fall."

"I wish I had. I'll do my best to not embarrass myself. Amanda has play practice after school, and Briggie offered to drive and pick her up, so hopefully, I can concentrate."

Briggie had rich, hot chicken soup with dumplings ready for everyone. After lunch, Ed and Maria met Winston and her mother at the country club for nine holes and Ed played well. His practice had paid off. Maria finally gave up and drove Ed around in the golf cart.

Still uppermost in her mind was the huge elephant she'd seen in the corner that morning. He hadn't visited her in a long time, but she knew he was coming. Until she solved her dilemma as to whether to wait for Bill to come to his senses and call her or to forget him and gamble her and her family's future on Ed and his trustworthiness, the elephant would haunt her.

A very important side issue was Chris's total dislike of Ed. Ever since he'd returned from his summer stay with Don, Chris had discouraged her from seeing Ed. When she'd tried to pin him down as to his objections, he simply said he didn't trust Ed. She'd overheard Amanda scolding Chris a week ago, telling him Ed was really nice and he should like him and Chris growling in return.

Although not describing Ed's visit as a divorce celebration of sorts, Winston and her mother wanted to show their support for Ed by inviting them to dinner at the club that night. Winston enjoyed Ed's company, and he loved to talk about the Midwest and Ed's profitable business. Her mother was always the congenial hostess, but noncommittal in her approval.

The club was beautifully decorated with myriad pungent yellow and white chrysanthemums and fat orange pumpkins grouped artistically around the club's entrance and dining room. Striped green and yellow gourds lying in small woven cornucopias decorated the center of each dining table.

At the last minute, Chris had decided to come. Maria had heard him mutter something about checking out the jerk to Amanda. After several drinks, with encouragement from Amanda, Ed began embellishing his stories, making them funnier and funnier by painting some of his customers with a ridiculous brush.

He was so entertaining, and Winston laughed so hard he had to wipe his eyes on his napkin several times. "My boy, you should be on television. Your material is priceless."

During dinner, Maria felt Ed's hand on her knee making its way up her leg hidden under the table cloth. He grinned at her as she artfully pushed his hand away. His actions made her feel slightly nauseated. *I have a tiger by the tail, and I don't know how to deal with him.*

Ed was higher, emotionally, than she had ever seen him. It must have been a combination of feeling free, his appreciative audience, a couple of scotch and sodas, and excitement for a new beginning. While they drove home, he teased Amanda, talked with Maria, and ignored Chris.

He even volunteered to tuck Amanda in with a special story he'd been saving for her, but Maria wasn't fooled by his zealous attitude. She went to her bedroom and sat on the sofa, knowing full well what he wanted from her and wishing he were Bill. She scolded herself. Ed was a great guy, and he'd been there when she needed him. Suddenly, the house was quiet, and Ed was in her bedroom, unannounced.

He sat down next to Maria. "It's just you and me now," he said, watching her every move.

"Why do I feel like your prey?"

"Don't think that. Have I ever done anything that you didn't want?"

"No, but you've pushed," she said softly.

"Then just take it easy. I'm here for the duration. We have plenty of time." He slowly wrapped his arms around her body and nuzzled her neck. "You're wearing lavender."

She pushed him back a little. "Ed, let's do what you just told me. I haven't been around you for months. I may be a big disappointment. It's been years since a man has made love to me." The night with Bill didn't count. She wasn't coherent. *Oh, Maria, who are you kidding?*

"I've been in dry dock for quite a while, myself," he whispered. "Don't worry about a thing. They tell me it's like riding a bicycle. You never forget."

"If I get up enough courage to let you in my bed, I want you to sleep in Elena's bedroom afterward. I don't want Chris to know. He's not very keen on you."

"Anything you say," Ed said. "I'm going to shower." He leaped up exuberantly.

She heard him singing off key with the water running as she sat there panicking.

I'm not sure I can do this. It's been years since college. What if he doesn't like the way I am now, and I never see him again after this weekend?

She sat on her sofa, frozen.

"Come in and let me give you a massage," he called from the shower. "It'll relax you."

When she didn't answer, she heard the water turn off, and then suddenly, he was standing there, his beautiful naked, muscular body just waiting for her.

"You're still dressed. Where's my little nymphomaniac from college?"

"She's thirty-three, has had two children, and is left with saggy breasts."

"Stats say that women peak sexually in their thirties." He smiled seductively at her and sat down next to her.

He smelled of soap and testosterone and her need for his attention bubbled to the surface.

"Come on," he said and slipped his bare arm around her, pulled her close, and teased, "now there, that's not so bad. I'll not push you

142

any further than you want. I have too much to lose. I guess I thought you'd be as anxious to celebrate my freedom as I am. Is there any way I can turn you on?"

"Chris and his friends are always saying things turn them on. You sound just like them."

"It's the sixties," he said, as he opened his arms, coaxing her.

"When did we decide that you were going to spend your visit in my bed?"

"You didn't come between Jackie and me, promising me wild, passionate nights once I signed the divorce papers. Although I wished you had. But come on, what do you have to lose?" his eyes sparkling. He gently took her chin in his hand, turned her head, found her lips with his and kissed her softly. Then his lips traveled over her face kissing her eyes, cheeks and finally finishing on her neck.

All of her reserve began crumbling. Part of her held back, but part of her wanted him.

"Okay, handsome, I'll try. Make some magic for me." Maria slipped into his arms, feeling his hard, firm muscled body next to her.

"Can I help you undress?" He whispered as he reached around her, lifted her sweater off, unhooked her bra and asked, "Now, that wasn't so bad, was it?

She didn't answer. She just got up, finished undressing, and snuggled into bed.

He was right next to her before she knew it. His power enfolding her almost made her jump out of bed. He began kissing her gently at first, but slowly more and more insistently. He stopped, and his long, sensitive fingers began moving lightly all over her body, seeking out the sensitive and delicate places, causing her to lose track of her emotions.

"Want more?" he asked, almost on top of her.

Not waiting for an answer, he ducked his head down, and began kissing her body, especially her breasts, making her nipples hard. His breathing changed as his mouth moved all over her body, kissing places that hadn't been touched in years. "It's been so long," he whispered. "Please, Maria, I've got gel for you."

She hadn't expected to thaw out so quickly, but his utter charm and gentle approach had made her want him. She groaned and waited as he expertly used the gel on her and a condom. Seconds later, she felt his fire, and there was only one way to put it out.

Maria didn't remember exactly what happened after that. She knew only that she was being held in a long, intensive, rhythmic sex dance with him that was building into a tidal wave. It was so electrifying that it made her lose all control. Maria lost all awareness of time as their dance became more and more urgent. She felt him continually reposition himself, holding her tighter and tighter, allowing her body to respond to him more in a wild paroxysm of sexual ecstasy.

Nothing mattered to her. Her rational mind had no control. She wanted more and more, until suddenly she felt a blessed release. She clung to him unable to comprehend all of what had happened between them.

Ed held her tightly for a few moments, then he let her go, and laid quietly next to her. He began breathing normally. "You made it, didn't you?" he asked, with satisfaction. "We've still got it, haven't we?" He kissed her softly. "I told you, it's just like riding a bicycle," he said, then laughed.

"I can't explain it. I just went away somewhere and never wanted to return. You took me with you. I'm embarrassed, and I don't know why."

"Your body ignored all your rules and broke free. Don't be embarrassed by enjoying a God-given gift," he said, pulling her over onto his chest and stroking her hair.

"You have a way with you that's better than ever. Have you been practicing?" She giggled. "Practice makes perfect," he said, kissing her nose. "I finally got you to giggle. Want some more?"

She squeaked. "I don't believe you."

He laughed. "Just teasing. I'm good, but I'm not superman." He gave her a sly smile. "You've been practicing too, my little Rosebud."

She tried to slap him, but he grabbed her hands, pinning them to her body.

"We'll have no kinky sex in this house, lover boy."

"How do you know if it's kinky unless you've 'played.'"

"Remember, I'm in magazine publishing. Plenty of erotica comes across my desk."

"So, my little innocent has grown up."

"I grew up when George left to live with his mistress. I had to. He relegated me to being the mother of his children and housekeeper, but that was all."

"Did you have an affair afterward?"

"No, but I was offered many conference trips by a couple of hunky editors in my office, quite a few times." She wrinkled up her face in disgust. "Tonight was a big hurdle for me to get over. It's added a whole new dimension to your visit. It helped me see how much I've missed waiting for George to come back. I should have called you up to see if you were free. She giggled again.

"It's settled a lot of questions in my mind too, my adorable little enchantress."

She turned on her side, and Ed curled up behind her. "If the play station is closed, can I at least have a toy to hang onto? I've dreamed about your big, soft breasts for months."

"Sure, until I want to sleep on my stomach, handsome," she murmured.

In the morning, the moment she moved and opened her eyes, he was there, watching her. He smiled wickedly. "Are you sore? I wouldn't want to have that on my conscious."

She laughed and ran for the bathroom. "No, you did everything right. Want to shower?"

"Do I? Are you up for everything?"

"I can see you are," she giggled.

"You're still a fresh kid, you know that," he said as he pinched her bottom. "Move over so I can brush my teeth, too. You've got to learn to share."

"I shared a lot of me last night with you, didn't I?"

"Not quite enough," he said as he turned on the shower and grinned at her.

After their shower, as they were dressing, Maria asked, "Do you feel like I do about our relationship? We're great together, sexually, but I don't want to rush anything."

"Yeah, I'm glad we aren't lying to each other. All I can do is come out here until we decide we love each other enough to get married or call it quits, my little Rosebud."

"What about settling for a nice love affair?" Her question had a ring of sincerity. What if Bill contacted her?

"It may be the sixties, but I don't buy that free love stuff."

"Usually, it's the woman who says that," Maria said, her eyes searching his.

"Yeah, I surprise myself."

"That's my point. We're getting to know each other more, but we have a long way to go. For instance, I didn't know that you didn't approve of having multiple sex partners, and I'm glad you feel that way. And another thing, neither one of us has declared our undying love for each other."

"Yeah, I know, Maria, but I think we're much more honest with each other not saying something we don't feel. This is just the beginning. I can honestly say that no matter what happens between us, being with you again is the best thing that has happened to me since we were in college."

They were having coffee with Briggie when Amanda came in, shortly followed by Chris. Ed waited until both of them had eaten, and then he said, "What about showing me some of your favorite places in Washington? I've never seen any of them."

"I'd like to go to the Arlington Cemetery and see my dad's grave again," Chris immediately said, seriously.

"Certainly." Ed nodded in complete agreement. "We'll go."

Amanda groaned. "Do we have to? I hate the feeling I get there."

"Tell you what, Amanda. We'll stop for lunch anywhere you want and have a big water polo game in your grandparents' pool afterward. You can be my partner." Looking at Maria he said, "You'd better call and tell them I just invited all of us to their house this afternoon. I hope they're going to be home."

"Thanks, Doc, I hope they don't have other plans," she said, grinning.

That night when they were in bed, Maria melted under his warm gaze. "It was fun today. Thanks for being so good to my kids."

"Is my credit rating going up? Will it climb if I take you for lunch tomorrow?"

"I'm working for part of the day. I have some deadlines to meet."

"Point me in the right direction, and I'll pick you up from work."

Late the next morning, he called Maria and asked for a quick tour of her office before they went for lunch. "I want to make my presence known to those guys who are interested in you, he said, then laughed. After lunch, he insisted on buying her some sexy lingerie.

As they strolled out of the store with some outfits that made her blush in the dressing room, she asked, "Don't you like my sturdy, cotton panties?"

"No, they don't fit your profile."

"How do you know my profile, as you put it, when I don't? But thanks for your interest in my work and how I look. George never cared about either after a few years. He never visited my office, and I could have walked around naked and he wouldn't have noticed."

"That fool," he muttered. "On a better note, I asked Chris to meet me after school today. I thought I would clear the air with him. Wish

146

me luck. He didn't act like he wanted to do it, but I was persistent. I may be late, so go ahead and eat. I'll call you." He kissed her long and hard in front of her office building.

Maria watched Ed drive away. A realization hit her hard, making her gasp. She was falling in love with him.

22. Male Bonding

November 1962

(Ed)

That afternoon after school, Chris stood waiting for Ed. He sprang into the car. "Let's get out of here. I don't want the guys to see me with you," he said disdainfully.

Ed gunned George's sports car, and they left the high school campus as fast as they could without breaking the speed limit.

"We're going somewhere that's far away." Chris leaned back in the seat. "I don't want to run into any of my friends. I'll give you directions." After driving for a while, Chris sat up and pointed to a small restaurant at the side of the road. "Pull in here."

"Good, I thought we were going to end up in DC."

After ordering two cokes, Ed eyed Chris. No time better than the present. Time to take a chance. "I asked you to meet with me so we can get to know each other. I've tried, but you seem to dislike me."

"I'm not interested. You coming out here is turning our lives upside down." Chris stuck his straw in his coke and took a sip. "I wish I were anywhere but here with you," he muttered.

"I'm sorry you feel that way, Chris. We could be friends. What do you have to lose? Your dad is gone. I know I can't replace him, but I can be like an interested uncle to you. Tell me what you like about school, sports or music, or perhaps, girls."

"You think I want to confide in you? I don't. I don't like you, and I don't trust you. What do you want from us, especially my mother? You think you can make my life all better? First of all, no matter, even if you were Jesus Christ, you couldn't replace my dad, even as my uncle." His tone was defiant. "Are you a fortune hunter? They prey on wealthy women like my mom.

"My dad was out there trying to stop the all the drugs coming into this country when you were in college, all safe and secure. He was actually captured and held for ransom by a drug lord. He was a decorated hero in WWII, tough and strong, and wanted me to be the same. He always lectured me to play to win and be proud of myself." Chris's eyes bored into Ed. "I admired my father and intend to make him proud. He took good care of us, kept our home going, sent me and my sister to good private schools, and gave my mother all the money she needed."

Chris's voice quavered, and he suddenly choked up. "I wish he'd lived so I could have known him," he whispered. Looking embarrassed by his show of feelings, he roughly wiped tears from his eyes. "Are you satisfied now?" he growled, his face all blotchy.

"I'm sure your dad thought he was doing everything he could for you. Men don't say what they feel many times. They show it by being good providers and your dad was that." In his heart, Ed felt so close to Chris. They shared the wish to know their fathers better.

Chris sat there recovering from his outburst. "You never lived with him, so don't tell me how he really was," he said belligerently, then quickly wiped his eyes on his sleeve. "As far as school goes, I like it okay, but I don't know where I'll be going to school next year because of you," he snapped. "My life is on hold. I'm going out for the wrestling team in spite of you." He sat there with his jaw clenched, glaring at Ed.

"Next year, if your mom and I do get married, you can go to a brand new high school in St. Charles, and I'll come to your meets."

Chris looked Ed squarely in the eyes. "Talk is cheap. Don't offer something like that and never show up. Some farmer will have an animal that's sick and I'll never see you. You come around wanting to be all 'palsy-walsy.' You make me sick. I don't know you from Adam," Chris said out of the side of his mouth before he began sucking hard on his straw.

When Ed didn't respond, Chris said, quietly, "I did appreciate you taking me to see my father's grave. I couldn't ask my mom. I want to make my father proud, but I don't know how yet." All the fight had gone out of him. "Have you known my mom for a long time?"

"We've known each other since she was fourteen and I was nineteen. We go back a long way. Do you want more information?"

"No, that's enough. But tell me, what is going to happen to me and our family?"

"Are you hungry?" Ed asked, ignoring Chris's unanswerable question. "I'll order some hamburgers and call Briggie so she doesn't worry." Ed was only gone a minute before returning to their booth. "What if I said I'm thinking about possible marriage?"

"Until you showed up, I thought of my mother as just a mom. I didn't think she'd ever get married again after my dad. I didn't think that old people like you and her would want to get married. I knew she was a college girl, married my dad, and didn't graduate from college until my sister was two or three. I didn't know she dated you in college."

"I intend to do the right thing by your mom, Amanda, and I hope you, if you'll let me."

"Yeah, as I said before, talk is cheap. I'll see how you are when things aren't so rosy."

They ate their hamburgers in silence.

"I'm glad we had this talk," Ed said while driving home. "I hope we can be friends in the future."

"I'm not like the women in our family. You have to prove yourself." By Chris's tone, he meant business. "You can't charm me. You'll have to make good on your promises."

23. A Leap of Faith

Winter 1962 –Spring 1963
(Ed/Maria)

Ed

Ed became a regular visitor to the Fuller household and added his very male personality to the mix of males to females. He nourished Amanda's need for a father figure with his genuine interest in her. He also attempted to close the gap between himself and Chris by attending as many of Chris's athletic events on Saturdays as possible.

He bit the bullet and bared his soul to Dr. Peter Rudolph on almost every visit. His aim, he told Peter, was to keep his part of the bargain with Maria to help them have a deep and enduring relationship. Taking to heart Peter's wise counsel that "what will be will be" and relax, Ed did feel more confident accepting the level of sophistication he found in Maria and her family. Maria even teased that he was easier to be around and more comfortable in his own skin.

Because of Sharon's long distance interest, with each visit he brought Amanda a new Nancy Drew book to read and add to her collection. Knowing Maria loved his animal stories, he found himself writing them in his head while driving to make a vet call to a farmer or breeder. Later, he would quickly scribble them down for safe keeping so he could present them to her for her journals. Pleasing her pleased him more than he'd ever thought possible. They were good for each other.

His stories were always mixture of humor, fantasy, and gentle wisdom about woodland creatures. Maria said she was fascinated by the way his mind worked, and she loved his artistic, imaginative side. When she hugged and kissed him in appreciation for his work, she filled him with hope and made his visits impossible to forget when he had to return to his vet world.

María

When Ed left, Maria always missed him, but knowing he would be back helped her remain at peace. It was a new feeling for her. During those first years that she was married to George, she was thrilled by his attentions to her, and she always tried to keep his interest, but she never felt content. After he left her emotionally, with Peter's help, she was able to develop a more independent spirit within herself, but she still wasn't satisfied with her life. Little by little, living for her children, her family, and her work, she did acquire a real feeling of thankfulness, but not contentment.

But after Ed secretly began sharing her bed, and they became close working allies on his stories, a measure of contentment emerged.

Ed began hinting that they consider a more lasting arrangement. It was too soon for her, and she pretended she didn't get his message. One day he came right out and asked if she was willing to tie the knot.

She'd been dreading that question. It would mean a huge change for her and the family, and she wasn't sure she loved him enough to marry him. Although flattered by his attentions, she knew she didn't love him the way she'd loved Bill or George. Playing for time, she told him she had to consider uprooting the children and moving away from her mother and stepfather.

Sexually, she had no reservations about him. He was an incredible lover and continually made her feel like a very special, desired woman. To his credit, he was a well-respected veterinarian by the farm and breeder community. Winston liked him as a man. But she had a bigger question that plagued her. Did he really know what he was getting into, accepting a ready-made family?

After flying out to see her all winter and early spring, one day he returned from seeing Peter and asked her to take a ride with him so he could share some important news.

Here it comes, he's going to ask me again.

"Okay," she said, with reservation.

"Peter has turned me loose. Unless I'm naughty or need a tune-up, he doesn't want to see me again. When I said that I'd be indebted to him for all he's done for me, he laughed and joked about how I would be in debt after seeing his final bill."

152

Ed took her hand and massaged the palm with his thumb. "He's been a great guy. It was hard work seeing him all the time, but there's been a big payoff. I feel better about myself than I ever have, and I feel we'll do fine, together." He looked into her eyes, and his gaze didn't waver. "What do you think?"

"Is that question another proposal?"

"Guess I didn't phrase that very well. I'm a little rough around the edges. But I'm sure we'll have a good marriage, Maria."

"Your work with Peter has made you much more confidant, but have you really considered taking on all of us? Remember, I come as a package."

Ed's face fell with her comment. "Peter suggested that we have a family meeting with your folks present so everything can be discussed openly."

That darn Peter and his suggestions. "I can agree to having a meeting tonight to talk, but I can't agree to a commitment yet. I'm still not sure." Her intuition urged caution, and that irritating elephant was still in her room driving her crazy waiting for a decision.

When Ed left to watch Chris in a wrestling match at the junior high school, Maria gathered up her courage to call Elena on the pretext of asking about her shows, but her real intention was to find out about Bill.

She closed and locked her bedroom door and dialed Elena's number. As it rang, Maria thought about all the postcards Elena had sent her from all over the country. What did Bill think of Elena traveling so much?

"Hi, Elena, I just wanted to touch base with you. It's been too long since we talked."

"Dear Maria, I apologize. I've been so busy, and now I'm late for a party in my honor."

"I totally understand. I just wanted to know how your shows are going."

"They're very successful according to Kathy, but as always, Bill is upset with me not always being here when he flies to Washington. We have big fights all the time over my career, and Kathy hates him. Sometimes, I wish he would go away."

"But you two are still together?"

"Yes," Elena said, sounding tired. "But I'm not sure it's worth it. He wants more than I want to give. I'm sorry, dear sister, but I must fly. Kathy is standing at the door, tapping her foot. I love you and will try to see you all soon."

Hearing that Bill hadn't lost interest, however unsuited she thought they were for each other, Maria wished Elena well and hung up. But she couldn't deny feeling sad. *That's it then. Bill is definitely gone. Ed is the only game in town.*

She sat in her bedroom thinking about what might have been with Bill, but finally pulled herself together, called her mother, and invited them to come over for a meeting that night.

Chris came home from the wrestling match with a scowl on his face. "I already know there's going to be a meeting. Ed told me. But I don't want to come and hear Ed brag that he's marrying you," he said, his voice filled with anger.

Amanda was thrilled when Maria invited her. "Mommy, are you and Ed getting married?"

"Not yet, my little matchmaker."

When her mother and Winston arrived, Briggie nestled down next to them, and Maria heard her whisper, "I'm afraid my life is going to change."

Her mother patted Briggie's hand. "You'll always have a place in our home."

Ed stood in front of the family seated in the living room. "Glad we're all together for our meeting. We're missing one young fellow who is very important, but we'll carry on without him." Ed threw up his hands in mock disgust. "I've asked Maria to marry me more than once, and I'm here to plead my case. If we become a family, I need your input as to when and where. Early spring is better for me before all the baby animals are born in Illinois." He stood in front of Maria. "Are you ready to tie the knot with me?" he asked quietly.

The room was silent as they waited for her answer.

"When you put it that way, how can I refuse, in front of God and everyone," she replied sarcastically and laughed. *That was dirty pool.* "For practical purposes, the last Saturday in April is best because it's before eighth grade graduation and Winston's retirement party. It may interfere with some of the new farm babies, but I can't help that."

No one spoke.

Ed looked around the room. "Having heard no complaints from the rest of you, we'll tie the knot on the last Saturday of April."

His wording irritated her. Why did he keep saying "tie the knot"? It sounded like they were going to be bound together in some terrible manner. Was she doing the right thing? Maria studied each of her family members. Everyone was so quiet—too quiet. Her son stood glowering in the background, and Briggie had a strange look on her face. It all wasn't very encouraging.

"Mom, can I have a new dress to wear?"

Leave it to Amanda to brighten up things. "Of course, my dear. I want all of us to look our best."

The meeting was breaking up when Winston cleared his throat. "This exciting news means we've got to get our houses ready to sell," he said with a sparkle in his eyes, surprising everyone. Except Maria's mother—she didn't seem surprised at all.

Ed looked at Winston, Maria's mother, and then Maria. "Have I missed something here?"

"No, my boy. With my retirement, we decided we'd go with the family and find a nice place to live near you, but I swore Ruth to secrecy until you two were committed."

"Well, that makes me feel better." Ed's shoulders visibly relaxed and he grinned. "I haven't known how to approach you, but when I came to visit you last fall, I gave my builder the okay to design and build a townhouse adjacent to our home just in case you might consider it. I knew it would increase the value of the place, even if my marriage plans failed."

Winston seemed overwhelmed, and he put his hand to his chin, a sign that meant he was really concerned. He took his wife's arm and walked her into the hall.

It wasn't long before they returned. "We'd be happy to accept your offer with a couple of conditions," Winston said. "If we decide to stay in your compound, we'll buy the place, and if we don't stay, there will be no bad feelings among us. Agreed? It will be a new experience for all of us, and it might be too much togetherness."

"And we all lived happily ever after," Amanda said, laughing and throwing her arms around her grandmother.

A few nights later, the phone rang and Maria heard a voice from the past—Carol. Thrilled and guilty that she hadn't called Carol, she heard her old dorm mate ask, "What's up, Maria?"

"Plenty, but you go first."

"I'm swamped with our new baby boy. Alan and I don't know what's hit us. I can't work, I'm so tired. That baby is sometimes up all night long. When does it get better?"

Maria understood being a first-time mom. She'd listen as long as her friend needed. "Does Alan help with the baby?"

"Yes, when he can, but he's so busy being a star reporter for the *Iowa Progress* that he falls asleep feeding the baby. I'm so glad we traveled all over the world before we decided to have a family. Having a baby is hard work!" She let out a loud sigh. "So, enough about me, what's up with you?"

"Well, first the bad news. George died in a plane crash last spring. I didn't feel like contacting anyone about it. I'm sorry to admit I haven't kept up with a lot of my friends because of my life, but things are much better, and I'm marrying Ed McDermott this spring. You may remember him when he came to see me that summer at the resort. We're moving to St. Charles to live with him later this summer. I have two children, Chris and Amanda. Chris will be thirteen in May and Amanda just turned ten in February."

"Congratulations, sister Chi Omega and fellow waitress. I'm so glad I called. I'm sorry George died. I never met him but was glad you two got together. At least you have two nice kids to remember him by. What ever happened to Bill? Weren't you engaged to him? Did he make it through the war? When did Ed come back into the picture? after George died? I do remember him when he visited you at the resort. He was a great looking guy."

"So many questions, Carol! I'll try to fill you in if you're ready for it." They talked until Carol's baby began screaming at the top of his lungs.

"I've got to go and take care of Alan Jr. Call me when you move. We'll be within driving distance of each other. We can talk some more. I also want to show off Alan Jr. and meet your husband and kids.

"We can talk to our heart's content when I move. Go take care of your baby. Bye for now, Carol."

Smiling to herself as she hung up, Maria promised herself to have a reunion with Carol and Sharon when she moved. It would be so easy with Ed. Unlike George, he liked having people around, and she wanted some friends.

24. A Fresh Beginning

Late Spring–Early Summer 1963
(Maria)

Maria wanted a church wedding, but it was out of the question. All of the churches had been booked a year in advance. She had to settle for a justice of the peace.

A week before the wedding, Ed called one night, all upset. "I forgot to get us wedding rings," he said. "I know I promised to do it, but I've been running 'out straight' with work. Would you get them? Get me a heavy band that I won't lose. I have to take it off every time I give an animal examination."

"Sure." She might as well get used to Ed's rough side. She was marrying a vet, but she'd fill their lives with beauty, music, and the finer things of life.

They were married the last Saturday in April in a small ceremony with family members and beloved servants attending, with the exception of Elena, who was traveling in Europe.

Maria wore an off-white silk suit with a crown of baby's breath in her hair, and she carried a small bouquet of white roses. Amanda was absolutely thrilled with her small wrist corsage of pink roses to match her dress. The rest of the women wore light, seasonal dresses, and the men complemented them in their usual dark suits with a sprig of baby's breath in their lapels.

The ceremony was over in a blink of an eye. Such a life-changing event like her marriage should have taken longer than that.

Afterward, before she had time to realize she was married, Ed was cradling her in his arms and whispering, "You won't be sorry."

"I'd better not be," she whispered back. She was committed, feeling all right about their marriage, but not delirious with happiness.

He laughed and gave her a light kiss.

Dean whisked the wedding party to the country club in the big black car. Her life was moving very fast, and suddenly she was standing in the center of the elegantly appointed country club main party room, smiling for pictures with Ed and the rest of the family. Her mother had warned her to get the best, and she'd hired a professional photographer.

The room was filled with her mother and stepfather's friends and acquaintances. She didn't have anyone she wanted to ask, and Ed was a complete stranger to people in town. It gave her pause to realize how barren her life had been with George, not to have made a single friend to invite. That was going to change!

Although neither Ed nor she knew most of the people, it was nice to have such pleasant well-wishers around them. Ed charmed them all by telling funny stories about his life as a vet. Maria was proud of the way he handled himself and the nice impression he left with everyone that afternoon.

He also amazed her with his dancing skills when he took her in his arms and whirled her around the room to the melodies of the fifties and sixties. "I see you've taken lessons since college," she said, as she offered him a genuine smile.

"I had to so as to not embarrass myself at those breeders' parties, and now I'm really happy I did." As he held her in his arms, he glanced around the room with a smile on his face. "Your mother went to a lot of trouble to make our wedding so memorable. This place, the guests, and the band are all high class. I thanked her and Winston for giving us a night on the town in Washington. But I'm going to take you on a real honeymoon when you move to St. Charles."

Maria smiled at his promise, not believing it. The only real wedding gift that Maria wanted had been given to her. Winston and her mother were moving to St. Charles with her, Briggie, and the children. Leaving her job with the magazine had been hard. She felt as if her independence were being threatened and that she was slipping into the delegated role of wife and mother. At work, she was a professional and had the respect of the office. She liked her feeling of competence in her job, her interaction with her co-workers, and most of all, the excitement of making the deadlines every month. She would miss all that.

During the afternoon, Maria discovered Amanda sitting with Chris and Briggie, eating big dishes of ice cream with hunks of wedding cake on the side. "I see you are all in your glory, eating all the ice cream and cake you want and no one to say no. We'll be leaving in a little while. Ed and I are going to have an overnight together at a big hotel in town, and Amanda, you're going to stay with your best friend, Heather. We'll drop you off today and pick you up tomorrow on our way home."

After that, Amanda began asking her when were they going and gave Maria no peace. The moment the party was over, Amanda spoke of nothing else until she'd been dropped off at her friend's home. Waiting in the car to see her safely in, Maria knew all was well when she heard Heather scream and saw her drag Amanda into her house.

"Well, Rosebud, it's been a long time in coming, but it's finally here. We're married, and it's going to be the best thing we've ever done. You and Peter woke me up to life." Ed shifted George's old sports car into gear and roared down the road to DC.

"Remember me climbing out of my dorm window, falling into your arms, and driving through that terrible snowstorm to get to the inn?" I wasn't scared then, but I am now. Slow down, handsome. We need to return in one piece. We have children to consider."

"Boy, do I remember. I thought about us for months afterward. But I was such a sap, weighed down with ridiculous worries about my future. I guess I didn't trust myself."

"How could you with all the terrible things your mother had put in your head?"

"Peter worked with me on those things all winter, and I think I've licked them."

"Oh, look, I can just see the lights of the city. It's a pretty place," she said, feeling better than she had felt about the day now that it was finally over. That morning, the elephant had almost disappeared, but not quite.

When they arrived, Ed told the young valet attendant rather forcefully, "I don't want to see one tiny scratch, bump, or dent on this car. If it's in perfect condition, I'll give you a big tip. If not, I'll see the manager."

For one bone-chilling moment, she thought George was talking. It was a side of Ed that she hoped would be their only similarity. Ed's confidence level had surged since seeing Peter, and with that change, he was far more sure of himself with her and not so angry.

"I need a bellhop to carry our luggage," Ed said in his new take-charge manner while registering at the front desk. "I want to carry my new wife over the threshold of the honeymoon suite."

The manager glanced at the register. "Dr. McDermott, I'm so delighted you've chosen us for you honeymoon. It has been paid for by Mr. and Mrs. Winston Brooks. I will send a complimentary basket of fruit and a bottle of champagne to your suite."

The bored bellhop opened their door, then stood back while Ed did what he promised, sweeping Maria off her feet and into the suite. The bellhop stood waiting for his tip and barely smiled as he pocketed the money and closed the door behind him.

"Come join me on the balcony," Maria said, looking out over the Potomac. "Isn't the city beautiful at night? I'm actually excited for the first time in a while."

Ed came up behind her, wrapped his arms around her, and breathed into her hair. "Are you hungry?"

"To tell the truth, I am. I didn't really eat a thing all afternoon."

"Room Service will be here in a few minutes, and I'll feed you, fill you up with champagne, and make love to you, in that order."

"I'm not going anywhere, so take it easy, handsome. I don't want to be the subject of the waiter's conversation when he talks with his buddies."

A tap on the door brought Ed to attention.

Let the games begin.

Moments later, Ed held a big basket of fruit and cheese in his arms. "This should tide you over."

A large pop sounded, and she knew he would soon be serving her champagne. He was different these days. He'd acquired a new assurance. She could feel his testosterone level rising, but he was trying to be smooth and not drag her into the bedroom. He wanted her to want him, and that intrigued her.

She dug into the fruit basket and picked out a bunch of juicy red grapes. When he came out on the balcony with a glass of bubbly in each hand, she said, "Open your mouth," and popped a grape into his and then hers. He grinned and handed her a glass.

"Sit on my lap, and let's get in the mood." He'd taken off his tie, unbuttoned his shirt part way, and wore no shoes.

"I'll be right back." She flew into the bedroom, tore off her wedding suit, and slipped into a robe.

She carefully sat down in his lap and took a sip of her champagne. "How do you like the lingerie you bought me?"

"Where is it? Underneath that robe?" Ed gently slid his hand inside, then gave her a sly smile. "You little devil, you're naked."

160

"As long as you don't tear it off, no one will know except us. Take off your clothes, too, and put on the complimentary robe. We might as well get smashed together," Maria downed the rest of her champagne. "I need some more. Where's the bottle?" She was feeling good! What did she have to lose?

Ed tilted his head back to look at her and laughed. "What's gotten into you? Where's that sedate mom I see around Chris and Amanda?"

"She's home, and your wild child is here to wear you out tonight," she said slyly, then poured herself another glass of bubbly.

She sipped her drink and finished off the grapes while Ed went inside to change. She liked being away from her other life, and she loved the feeling of freedom she had sitting out on the balcony looking at the exotic lights of the city.

"Grrrr," he roared as he came out in his robe and flashed her. Laughing, he sat down on the other lounge chair and patted his lap for her.

"Have another drink," she said, slightly slurring her words and slipping into his lap.

"You little imp! I've never seen you drunk except on that first date of ours in college. Why are you so wild?" His breathing was coming a little faster than usual, and he was pouring himself another glass.

"It's the first time in a very long time that I don't have to worry about the kids hearing us. I just want to break free and be me. It's lots of fun."

"I guess I haven't thought about you like this for a long time. Although, I do remember you and I having some pretty wild times at the Tucked Inn, now that I think about it. I have a lot to look forward to with you, especially if I take you away on a vacation by ourselves."

"I've never said this since college, but you're one big stud." She reached inside his robe and began fondling his balls and penis.

He roared again, picked her up in his arms as he stood up with her wiggling all the way, then carried her to the bed and dropped her. "Don't move, unless you want to get pregnant. I'll be back, baby proofed."

"You would make an adorable father," she called.

"I think that magazine company you work for sells girlie magazines, and you write the dialogue," he said when he returned.

"I've grown up and know enough to keep you on your toes, if I can escape once in a while from my role of mother."

"Come with me and help me christen that big tub in the bathroom."

"As I remember, you were big on doing it in the tub at the Berkmar. Bring the bubbly."

"You drank it all. Don't worry, we don't need any."

His mood had changed from a wild, playful one to a sexy man hungry for what he needed and wanted from her. With the water filling the enormous tub, he placed towels on the back, helped her wrap her hair up in a towel and get in, carefully because of her drunken state, and poured in a bottle of something that made the water foam with suds.

"Where did you get that, and what is it?"

"It says bubble bath on the bottle. Judging by the water, it really is. I guess I shouldn't have put the whole bottle in."

"I love it, Ed. I'm going to get some when I live in St. Charles, and we can get in our tub and make love with bubbles everywhere."

"Is that a promise? I'm going home and have the builder put a gigantic tub in our bathroom, next to the shower." He lay back and the bubbles swirled all over him. "Are you still feeling tipsy?"

"Yes, but I like it. Make love to me. The warm water really makes me feel sexy."

He rolled over on top of her, adjusted the towel behind her head, kissed her, and whispered, "I'll give you a ride of a lifetime, Mrs. McDermott," and he began to make good on his promise. The champagne, the warm water, and the charged atmosphere made her cling to him as the speed and rhythm of his lovemaking caused her so much pleasure that she had one orgasm after another. It had never happened to her with him before.

"You are amazing, Maria," he murmured. He seemed relaxed and sexually satisfied. "I'm so lucky that you're so responsive to me. Being like that is what I need to keep me alive. I love you, my darling wife."

"That's a first," she said.

"What is?"

"Telling me you love me."

He looked shocked by her words. "Oh, my God, I thought you knew."

"I figured as much, but a woman likes to hear it once in a while. Don't look like I just hit you with a two-by-four. We'd better shower off the bubbles or we'll itch."

As he rubbed her dry, he kept saying, "I really love you, Maria," until she put her finger to his lips.

"I know." She sensed real peace in him and hated to break the mood, but they needed to eat. "If you want a repeat performance from me later tonight, you'd better feed me. Hunger makes me frigid."

"The way I feel right this moment, I'd take you to the moon, if I could. Let's go, baby. Anything you want, I'll get it for you."

"I'd like a chance to wear my sexy new dress. Let's go downstairs to eat," said Maria.

Maria put on her electric blue evening dress, complete with a slit up the side, and the back of the dress so low, it almost reached her panties.

"Wow, you're asking for trouble in that dress, and I'm ready to give it to you," he said, his eyes sparkling. He slipped his hand down her bare back, making her squeal. Holding her tightly, he whispered, "We'd better go for dinner. I'm going to need a lot of energy tonight."

Of the four restaurants in the hotel, they chose the smallest one, overlooking the Potomac River, and asked to dine out on the terrace. It was unseasonably warm and comfortable. Maria talked Ed into trying fresh lobster from Maine.

"I don't have a clue as to how to eat this big red crustacean sitting in front of me."

"Handsome, why don't we ask the waiter to show us how?" *I don't want to embarrass him because he's never eaten a lobster. I'll pretend I'm a beginner, too.*

"I don't believe you don't know how to eat lobster, living with your family. Just tell me what to do. I may call you bossy afterward, but I'll eat this ugly guy."

She looked around at everyone eating so primly. They weren't eating messy lobsters—they knew better. It had been a mistake to order.

"I love lobster, but they are messy," she said smiling at Ed who was dissecting his lobster with the concentration and control of a surgeon and doing a good job of it.

He looked up from his task. "This is quite an experience. It's fun and we'll do it next time on the coast of Maine at a lobster pot overlooking the ocean. I want to show you the world, Mrs. McDermott."

Instead of making her happy, his remark had chilled her to the bone. George had said almost the identical thing when they were helplessly in love with each other.

They later returned to their room full, relaxed, and feeling fine. "Let's strip and sit on our balcony," Maria teased. "I'll wear my robe, and you can wear your shorts."

"The city is beautiful at night. I never realized it would be all lit up." Ed yawned, then stretched his legs out in front of him and sat quietly for the longest time. "I'm going to follow Peter's advice—travel with you and not work so hard. Did you do much traveling with George?"

"No, I didn't, although he talked a good game when we were first married. But soon he was busy getting his business started, buying a plane, getting consulting jobs with travel magazines, and doing all the other things it takes to get started. He was also renovating the house he'd bought for us. Added to that, he was going for therapy with Peter and a group of veterans. To make things more complicated, I got pregnant right off the bat, so it was a busy time, and we had no time for trips.

"After Chris was born, I was a mess, emotionally. George was bored with family life and lost interest in us. I guess it wasn't what either of us had bargained for. But I had to take care of Chris, so I gave up and moved back with my folks for several years. When George convinced me to try it again with him, I moved back in, and we struggled for years to make a go of it. When Amanda was five, he left me emotionally for another woman. He never asked for a divorce. George wanted to have his cake and eat it, too. I finally decided to file for divorce the spring he was killed in his plane accident. And you know the rest.

"Funny thing, the weekend before he died, he put a letter on my bed asking to come back, saying that it was all over with the woman."

Ed looked over at her and took her hand. "You don't have to say any more. I've been in love with you for so long, nothing you could say would make a particle of difference."

"But it does to me," she said, tears rimming her eyes. "I know lots about you, but you really don't know much about me. I've never felt comfortable enough to tell you until now.

"I never dreamed I'd marry a man who would do what my dad did to my mom, but I did. George was a dynamic kind of guy and so was my dad. My dad was a wonderful doctor and took good care of us. But just like George, he had a mistress—his secretary. He was on the fence, just like George. He couldn't leave, and he couldn't stay. Then he got her pregnant and had to go. George never let that happen.

"His cheating hurt me so much. I still hadn't recovered last summer when I—"

"Shush." Ed reached for her. "Come sit on my lap." He gently guided her head to rest on his chest. "I promise I will never cheat

164

on you. I've wanted you for so long. My dad never looked at another woman and neither will I." Ed stroked her hair, and they looked out at the twinkling lights for a while. "I always wondered why Bill never contacted you that summer after you two were engaged. I know he was training to be a pilot for the Korean conflict, but that's all I know."

"It was the war's fault that I never heard from him until it was too late. Winston told me repeatedly that during WWII, mail was lost, sent on the wrong ship, thrown away, or blown-up in accidents, and men never heard from their wives and sweethearts. He gave me many scenarios as to why I hadn't heard from Bill, and I believed him, up to a point. When I finally heard from Bill, he asked me why I hadn't waited for him. I wrote him and apologized. Privately, I wished I hadn't been so foolish not to wait a little longer, but George was very persistent and fooled me."

"I think he fooled himself more than he fooled you, Maria. I don't think he ever thought he'd cheat on you. I've been fooling myself in so many ways, but Peter set me straight this past year. I'm a small-town boy who never wanted to fly, had a veterinarian student deferment, and wanted to save animals, not the country. I just wanted a wife I could love, who loved me, and who would help me make a living. That's why I married you, Maria."

Ed kissed the top of her head. "But I have one more question. I've heard you insinuate several times that you were afraid of George. Was he an abuser?"

"In defense of George, he suffered terribly in WWII. He was just twenty-one when the OSS chose him to work with the resistance movement behind enemy lines. Because he was so proficient in French, German, and Dutch, he was just the man they wanted. As a child, he'd spent lots of time overseas with his English mother learning different languages. He'd signed up to be a fighter pilot and was flying with the air corps when he was sent to oversee and coordinate the resistance movement."

Maria sat up so she could see Ed's reaction to what she was sharing. "He never got over the war and was sort of crazy at times, spending years in therapy with Peter and a group of veterans all trying to get better. To be fair, he had a way about him that was charismatic and exciting to be around, but sometimes very scary. We all knew not to cross him when he was in one of his down moods."

Ed's face was sober. "I think George was afraid to face painful things, just like me. I've stuffed hurt down inside me for years. Peter helped me."

Maria gently stroked Ed's face with her fingers. "I'm so glad he did. When I went to Peter on my own, after I'd given up trying to make my marriage work with George, Peter worked with me for a long time, making me face my fear of George over and over again, until it began to dissolve and then finally disappeared.

"The other thing that Peter helped me get rid of was feeling it was my fault for the way George treated me. George had everybody fooled, including himself, with his charm, wit, and sexy demeanor. Men respected him, women loved him, and even Winston thought the world of him. It makes me sad to think about George's life while he was on this earth. But I know he's in a better place. I forgive him. He knows it and is at peace."

Maria lay cuddled up on Ed's lap. "Come on, handsome. "Let's go to bed before your legs are paralyzed. I'm tired. Too much bubbly, and too many emotions and sex for one day," she said and laughed. She ran into the bedroom, threw off her robe, and crawled into bed naked.

Ed lay down beside Maria and held her close. "Thanks for taking a chance with me. I'll never let you down, and I'll kill myself first before I ever frighten you, so help me God."

"I believe you, handsome. Now we begin the best part of our lives together."

25. Moving Pains

Late Spring–Early Summer 1963
(Maria)

They checked out early the following morning, closer emotionally than they had ever thought possible. Ed inspected the car, gave the valet a big tip, and they picked up Amanda, who was tired and cranky from staying up half the night with her girlfriend.

"Welcome to my world, handsome," Maria said as they listened to Amanda whine.

When she and Amanda took Ed to the airport, she promised she'd have everything packed when he came back.

"I'll call you every night, sweetheart, and tell you how many babies were born that day. I'm sorry I can't be with you every step of the way, but I have to keep things going at the other end for all of us." He patted Amanda's head. "Petunia, my surprise for you and your family will be ready by the time you come."

"Is it a pony?" Amanda asked in her innocent way.

"No, Petunia, your mother and brother wouldn't want one of those."

"What is it?"

He chuckled. "You'll see it when you get there."

Maria reached over and grabbed his hand. "One other thing, my darling husband." She gazed into his loving eyes. "I want to invite Briggie to come live with us if she wants to. She's helped me raise my kids, and she's stood by me through thick and thin."

Ed thought for a moment. "I like her and her Irish brogue. If you want her and she's willing, that's all that matters to me. She'll help you from getting too tired, which will make my life more enjoyable," he said, smiling broadly. He gave her a quick kiss, jumped out of the car, and disappeared inside the airport.

Ed had made her feel alive again. If anyone would have told her how her life would change after George died, she wouldn't have believed them. Ed had become an important figure to all of them. As Amanda chattered all the way home, Maria tried to respond, but her mind raced from one thing to another about the move. She was so engrossed in what she had to do, she was on auto pilot and in the garage before she realized it.

"Briggie, where are you? I've got a question for you," she called, running into the kitchen.

"What is it, me darlin'? I've been sitting here having a cup, thinking about all the things we've got to do to get you out of here and into your new home. Have a cup with me, and help me plan."

"Briggie, what would you say about going with us to Illinois?"

"Saints preserve me, are you sure?" Her eyes held disbelief, but her tone sounded hopeful. "Now, tell me the truth, did that Irishman of yours agree?"

"Of course! He loves you." Maria was stretching the truth a little, but she wanted Briggie to agree.

Briggie took a sip of her coffee. The next thing Maria knew, Briggie was crying. Amanda came running in with the puppy in her arms to see what was the matter.

"Forgive me, 'tis a silly old girl that I am, blubbering away. I'm going to Illinois with you, Amanda."

"I never thought you weren't going, Briggie. Daddy wouldn't have left you here," Amanda said, confidently.

"Well, let's get started with our big move." Briggie began singing one little Irish ditty after another at the top of her lungs.

Her mother dropped by one afternoon after Maria was home from work. "Guess what Nellie and Dean just told us? They're going to start a decoration, renovation, and restoration business for people of Washington, DC. Winston offered to tell everyone he knows about their business, and I'm going to spread the word at the club and hospital."

"Winston wants your okay for him to do the negotiations for our two prime properties with a real estate agent he's known for years. You know Winston, he's a master dealing with people with all his experience working in the State Department. He'll be fair, but firm, Maria, and I know he'll get a good price for our properties."

In May, when Chris was out of school, he asked to fly by himself to Chicago with Wiggles. Ed had asked him to work for him and Dr. Glen in the clinic. He had an invitation to stay with Dr. Glen and Sharon with the understanding he would help Sharon with her seed beds. Wiggles was also welcome if Chris would take care of her. Surprised by her son's request, Maria called Ed to find out why he hadn't asked her first. Ed said she should trust the men in her life more.

Amanda wasn't happy when Maria told her Wiggles was going with Chris, but brightened up when Maria told her how much fun Wiggles would have in Sharon's pretty fenced-in back yard.

"We won't have to worry about Wiggles when the movers come, when we're driving, or when we get there. Wiggles will be happily running around Sharon's yard chasing little critters."

Amanda laughed. "Mommy, you are right."

After much discussion, Winston's new station wagon and George's little sports car were the two cars they would drive to the Midwest. All the other vehicles were to be sold.

Maria made a duty call to George's father, Christopher, to explain the coming changes in her life. Although she'd never warmed up to him, and he'd never offered any help or shown any interest in her or his grandchildren, she felt he needed to know. Hearing a sadness in his voice, it made her impulsively give him her new address and extend an invitation to visit them. After all, he was the children's real grandfather. When he said that he would definitely come, she didn't believe him, but encouraged him because it was the right thing to do.

Maria's hardest call was to Elena. Besides Nellie and Dean, she was the only person Maria would really miss. After confirming the dates of Elena's next art show, Maria promised to attend. Knowing she would see her foster sister at the showing made saying good-bye less painful.

Elena was her usual delightful and gracious self, saying she was anxious for them to see her new work. She also mentioned her future show in Chicago and said she would keep in touch so they could have a reunion there when her dear manager, Kathy, firmed up the dates. Maria had mixed feelings as Elena talked. She was happy for Elena's incredible artistic ability and independence, but her new personality was emerging, leaving the sweet, young girl behind.

"If I'm still seeing Bill, he'll meet me in Chicago, but I really don't know about us. My work is so demanding it upsets him, and we have the same arguments over and over again about pursuing my dreams. I don't think they include him, because he wants too much from me personally." Elena was quiet for a moment. "We finally have a personal relationship, but it still isn't easy. My first love is my art, and I need a great deal of time to devote to it. He doesn't like that fact, and it upsets my ability to work."

"My advice to you is to be true to yourself. Be the great artist you were meant to be. If Bill fits into your picture, good. If not, then it's not supposed to happen."

Bill loves the tension and excitement that Elena provides. He's having to prove himself to her all the time because she's not available like he's used too. I wonder if he knows what an amazing artist she is. Elena has a need to produce beautiful pieces of art for the world. Bill needs a challenge. He may end up marrying her, but he'll always be trying to be number one in her life, yet never quite making it.

When Ed called, Maria gave him the dates for Elena's exhibit. "I hope you can come. Bill may be there, and I hope you two can share a few stories and become friends. Plus, you'll see some great artwork."

Two weeks later, Winston, Ruth, Ed, and Maria attended Elena's beautiful art show in Washington. As the evening wore on, Bill finally appeared. Maria watched as Elena immediately put him to work, making wooden crates to transport her delicate sculptures and pictures. He left and returned carrying several large paintings all wrapped securely, presumably for guests who had purchased them. While putting them down carefully, he was immediately accosted by a young woman who seemed very irritated by the way they were wrapped.

Maria had noticed that the same woman had been hovering around Elena all evening, acting very much in charge. A disgusted look grew on Bill's face as she began shaking her fist at him. He turned around, and it looked as if he were going to leave, when he looked up and saw Maria. Bill paused for a moment, then strode across the room toward them. "Congratulations, Maria. Elena told me you got married, but didn't say when."

"Early spring," Ed had answered before Maria could get a word in. "I spent the year working on Maria, and she finally agreed. I just wore her down," Ed said, laughing as he put his arm tightly around Maria's waist, then smiled smugly at Bill.

Bill turned to Winston. "Elena told me you retired this spring. Congratulations, sir. What are your plans?"

"We talked Ed into letting us live in St. Charles near our daughter and grandkids," Winston boomed out loudly with a chuckle. "Spectacular show our little Elena has put on. I always knew she was good when she was living with us, but we never dreamed she would go onto doing this kind of work." Winston eyed Bill. "What do you think of your girl now, Bill?"

"She's amazing. She's so talented, but every time we get together, she puts me to work carrying boxes of canvases, paints, and clay from one place to another. Did you ever pick up sculpture clay? It's heavy. When I'm finished, I feel like I've been working out in the gym all weekend." He forced a little laugh, but his face and body language told a different story.

Poor mixed-up guy. But it isn't my concern. He made his choice, and so have I.

"We're moving to the Midwest soon," Maria said, volunteering their future plans. "Ed has to go back tomorrow, catch up with his practice, and then come back to help us move."

"I hope you'll see my folks again when you get settled. Iowa isn't too far from Illinois. They always ask about you." A fleeting look of angst passed over Bill's face. "My daughter, Rosemary, also lives out there, and I'd like you all to meet her. She's nine, about the same age as Amanda. Perhaps I can bring her for a visit sometime after you're settled."

There it was—that sweet quality Maria remembered so well. It was obvious that he loved his daughter.

"Please do and bring your folks with Rosemary." Maria's face lit up with real interest. "I would love to see them again. And perhaps, my Amanda and Rosemary will become friends. We could meet up again and discuss the details when Elena brings her wonderful show to Chicago."

"Come and I'll take you and Rosemary to see some beautiful horses," Ed said generously. "And of course, I'll have some jokes to share."

Bill chuckled. "Thanks, I'd like to have Rosemary know such a nice family." Bill trained his blue eyes on Maria for a long instant. Then he turned away. "I'd better find out what the boss wants me to do." Bill exited smoothly after shaking hands with the men and smiling at the women.

Maria followed him with her eyes as he found Elena, and the expression on his face was serious. Maria had felt something when he had looked at her but had ignored it. His eyes were talking to her, but what was he saying? Anyway, it was too late.

Even with Elena's successful art exhibit, Maria had misgivings about leaving her. She was still a very sweet, vulnerable young woman.

Maria didn't want Bill to hurt her; he had a way of getting what he wanted.

Why did he bring up visiting us with his daughter at such an inopportune moment? Perhaps he'll explain himself if and when he comes to visit.

Life went by in a whirl for Maria the next few weeks. The closer the time came to pick up her hardworking husband at the airport, the more she found she hadn't completed all she had planned for the move.

Poor guy, he'd spent the past year on a plane, enduring Peter's constant pressure to make changes in his life, trying to befriend her children, and hoping she'd agree to marry him. She couldn't have asked for anything more from him. He'd passed her tests.

When he came up the ramp, looking fit and handsome, several young businesswomen were walking along next to him, engaging him in conversation.

"Over here, Daddy!" Amanda called. He smiled and waved as Amanda broke loose and ran to meet him.

He picked her up. "How's Daddy's girl doing?" He gave her a big kiss and hug. She screamed with delight from his attention, grabbed his hand, and never let go until he said, "I can't drive and hold your hand, Petunia, but I bet your mom wouldn't mind if you sat in the front seat next to me while I take us home."

From the moment he arrived until the morning of their departure, they were busy. It was like a nightmare because of all the continual decisions she had to make. Thank heavens for Ed's confident attitude, cooperative spirit, and strong back. All thoughts of sex were the furthest from her mind, and Ed was very understanding about it.

Crumpling up her final list of last-minute things to do, Maria turned to Ed.

"Here's to the rest of our lives together." She tossed the wad into the trash bag and kissed him.

"It's going to be terrific, honey. Let's get this show on the road and go get your folks."

When Ed pulled the front door shut for the final time, snapped the lockbox in place, and jumped back into the sports car, Maria relaxed.

I've finally got it right. Everyone I love is with me except for Chris, who is waiting for us there, and the two other most important people in my life will soon be joining us.

Pulling into Winston's driveway for the last time was a nostalgic moment for her, bringing tears to her eyes. At nineteen, when she came to visit, hesitant, naïve, to this very house, she was swept up into the loving arms of her mother and her new husband, Winston, and they never let go. She needed to remember that the only thing that mattered was that they were a family and that they all loved one another. What more could she want? Winston was in his car, ready and waiting for them. "Come with us, Briggie, into our much more luxurious vehicle," he thundered.

Briggie extricated herself from the low bucket seat and hobbled over to his car, jerked the back door open, and heaved herself in.

"I'm so glad this part is over!" Maria's mother waved to them. "Ed, lead the way to our promised land."

Winston had to have the last word and called from his window, "Capital! By Jove we're on our way."

26. Change and Challenges

Summer 1963

(Maria)

Maria felt heartsick standing at the entryway of her new home. It was such a disappointment. It reminded her of a sadly neglected barn where unhappy people had lived, but wanted out. Not even a scrap of a lifeless rug or mat was there to trap the inevitable dust and dirt that came with the perennial flow of a family and friends.

It didn't seem very old. Ed had told her he'd built the house as a wedding present for his first wife, and after they divorced and he remarried, his second wife was the recipient. But it was obvious that his wives' interests didn't include any homemaking skills.

Maria shuddered, thinking about the amount of work it would take to make it livable. But she'd conquer the monstrosity, little by little.

What exactly did she expect? She hadn't married Ed because of his decorating skills. He loved her, wasn't that enough?

She remembered she'd glimpsed the outside of the place last summer. Ed had casually pointed it out when they were driving by. It seemed out of place and uglier than before. It reminded her of a huge, white boulder jutting out from the gentle rise of the land, pushed there by glaciers.

A one-story house painted in soft beige tones and nestled into the landscape would have been nice. Perhaps a few more bushes around the foundation would improve the home's appearance. She'd think about that later. For now, she'd live with the house. She had to. She was stuck with it.

Ed's deep voice jerked her back to the moment. "What's the matter, honey? Are you sick? Why are you standing there like you're paralyzed? Tell me where to put these bags so I can finish emptying the car." A frown creased his brow. "We'll fix whatever's bothering you, I promise. Just don't act like you're disappointed around the kids. Tonight, when we're alone, we'll talk."

Maria looked into his big brown eyes and listened to his innocent questions and concerns. "You said the magic words . . . we'll fix it." She reached up and lightly touched Ed's face to reassure him that his words were appreciated, then grinned. "Now, slave, put all the luggage and boxes over against the wall under the stairs. When the movers come, I want a clear path for them."

"What was Daddy saying to you, Mommy? Are you mad at him?" Amanda's little face was filled with worry.

Maria was amazed at the sensitivity of her little girl. Amanda could detect any small aberration in the feelings between her and Ed, and Maria knew why. Amanda had grown up around her real father, unable to understand his distant behavior toward her. Ed was the absolute opposite, talking, laughing, and teasing her, letting her know she was special to him. When she put Amanda to bed that night, she'd explain that Ed didn't mind Maria teasing him.

"Why aren't you listening to me?" Amanda whined. "I want to see my bedroom."

Maria sat down on the hot, dusty stairs and pulled her little girl into her lap. Amanda's face was covered with tiny bubbles of sweat. Hugging her, Maria said, "Sweetness, I don't know which room is yours. I've never been in here before. Let's go upstairs and pick one out. I'm sure there are a several bedrooms just waiting to be your first choice."

"Mommy, when I grow up, I want to know everything just like you do so I can fix everything and make things nice." She cuddled in her mother's lap.

Ed came in with the last load and announced he was going to help Winston unload their car. He stopped, leaned down, and looked at Amanda. "How's Daddy's girl doing? Just come to me if your mommy can't solve whatever's bothering you. I'm good at this stuff." He kissed her nose and grinned at Maria.

Gratitude for his thoughtfulness made Maria smile. Amanda leaped off of her mother's lap, and energized by Ed's attention, hugged him with all her might. "I love you, Daddy. Now, let's go and find my room, Mommy."

"What a little taskmaster you are," Maria teased, as she stood up, ready to mount those dirty, scarred stairs. But a familiar voice stopped her.

"For an Irishwoman, this is awfully hot weather. Me old country was never like this."

"Briggie, why don't you let me find you a chair. Then you can sit down until I figure out where your bedroom is located. Amanda, come with me and help me find a chair for Briggie. I'll also get us all a glass of water, and then we'll go exploring and find your bedroom, Briggie. Amanda, you can be my little detective."

"Mommy, will this old kitchen chair hold Briggie? Her legs look big and red."

"I hope so. Have a glass of water first, Amanda. You look hot and thirsty."

One lonely coffee mug and several old jelly jars stood together on the counter. "These have seen better days," Maria said as she rinsed them out, filled them, and gave Amanda a drink. "I'll bring the chair, and you bring Briggie the glass of water after you finish yours."

Without any furniture available, making Briggie comfortable was a tall order. Maria left her and Amanda sitting on the bottom stair of the staircase drinking their water together. The chair had collapsed with Briggie's weight, and she'd gone head over teacup, but thankfully was all right. Back in the kitchen for refills, the taste of the cool water had been a delicious surprise. So was the large kitchen, equipped with expensive appliances. Ed hadn't spared any money there, and that night she'd tell him how much she appreciated his generosity and good taste.

The house also came with beautiful windows, easily opened, and made of varnished wood. No paint stuck to the casements in these expensive windows. A hot afternoon breeze drifted into the room and stirred the air. She suddenly had an uneasy thought. How would they sleep at night without a fan? Midwestern heat waves were awful.

The shadows of the late afternoon were slowly taking form in the kitchen as the sun thankfully lost its hold on the sky, dropping behind a few big trees in the front of the house.

Maria glanced down at the filthy linoleum floor. She could barely make out the pattern and original color. A lot of heavy boots had ground dirt into that floor. She shivered. She'd have to scrub the floor before she could put their beautiful table and chairs under the lovely bay window. Maria put her hands on her hips. Where was the rest of the furniture?

Ed's wives must have cleaned him out, both literally and financially. How did they miss the coffee mug and glasses? No need for a second-hand furniture man to take away unwanted junk. There was plenty of room for everything she owned and more.

"Come on, Mommy, let's play detective and find the bedrooms," Amanda said, pulling her mother out of the kitchen and down the hall. Maria's quiet moment was over.

With her finger to her lips, Amanda tiptoed carefully to the room just behind the kitchen, peered in like detectives she'd seen on television, and turned to her mother. "It isn't that room" she whispered. "There are all kinds of shelves in there." She quietly closed the door.

Amused, Maria followed her little friend to the next room, where she repeated the whole scenario. "This is it, Mommy! This is Briggie's room!" Amanda squealed, then clapped her hand over her mouth as if she'd just alerted the bad guys. She regained her composure. "There's a little bed in there, not Briggie's big one," she whispered. "I hope Briggie doesn't fall out of that one." She giggled at her own joke.

Maria peeked in, pretending to act like a sleuth for Amanda's sake.

"Oh, Mommy, you don't know how to be a good detective. You're just a mommy," Amanda said in a superior tone. "I'm the detective."

"Okay, you little sleuth, let's get Briggie so she can lie down." Maria was grateful there was a little bed for Briggie to lie down on until the movers delivered her own. How did it happen that Ed's wives had missed the bed? She chuckled a little as she pictured the stark little room as a convent nun's cell in the twelfth century. The only things lacking were a Bible and a candle by the bed.

"I'm not a sleuth." Amanda gave her a questioning look. "I'm a detective, Mommy, aren't I?"

"Honey, it's just another way of saying detective." Maria wished she hadn't said anything and Amanda would stop chattering. It was getting on her nerves.

Briggie was just where they'd left her, sitting on the bottom step with her feet sprawled out and her ample girth protruding out in front of her. Well, at least her face wasn't so red now.

Briggie's health had concerned Maria for some time, but not enough to do anything about it. She felt guilty about her neglect of her faithful friend the past couple of years, using George's sudden death and her new role as a working single parent as an excuse. Now that she was married, she hoped Ed could recommend a good doctor for Briggie. An instant feeling of security filled her when thinking about him.

"It's good to see you smiling, Missy," Briggie said, looking up at her. "Lead me to me room so I can stretch out for a bit. I don't know what I'll do about dinner for us." Briggie sounded worried, and her mouth pursed tightly.

"Nothing, Briggie. I've decided that we're all going out to Maisie's Café." Maria would wait to see if Ed suggested it first, but even if he didn't, they'd go anyway.

"You'll love Maisie, and the food is good. Not as good as yours, but okay for restaurant fare." Maria took Briggie's hand to help her stand and get her balance. "We'll fix up your room as soon as we can," she said apologetically.

Briggie's lips relaxed into a big, relieved smile with Maria's announcement about dinner. When they reached Briggie's room, she hesitated at the door. "Don't you worry about me room. In Ireland, me sisters and I shared two beds in one room and felt lucky to have them," she said quietly. "Thanks for not expecting me kitchen to be up and running right away. It's a little puzzling to me."

Looking into those gentle pale green-blue eyes of her longtime supporter through those last tough, lonely years with George, Maria smiled. "It's okay, Briggie. Now please lie down and rest for me," she said quietly. "Little by little, we'll make this place into a home." If only she felt as confident as she sounded.

27. Taking the Good with the Bad

Summer 1963
(Maria)

Maria could feel Briggie's eyes on her as she made her way back up the dusty hall, suddenly tired from all she was facing. Finally, she heard Briggie's door close. Her dear friend and ally had laid down to rest.

Amanda was amusing herself, running up and down the stairs while she waited for her mother. "All right, my little jumping jack, let's go. I wish I had some of your energy."

As they climbed the staircase, Maria ignored the dirty, scarred stairs and focused on the staircase itself. It was a work of art with delicately turned wooden poles holding the polished banister in place. An artist, masquerading as a carpenter, had made that staircase. But had he worn hobnail boots while he worked? Someone had.

On the second floor, the sounds of their footsteps echoed as they clattered down the bare hall floor. Running ahead, Amanda quickly picked out the biggest bedroom for herself, forgetting all about playing detective.

"I love the windows, Mommy." Suddenly she shrieked, making Maria jump. "I can see a pool, Mommy. Daddy didn't tell us that he had a pool, did he? That was his surprise, wasn't it? Isn't it wonderful to have our very own pool and not have to go to Grandma and Grandpa's house to swim?"

Maria loved Amanda's quick assessment of her room choice and delight with the pool.

Ed was a rascal, keeping the pool a secret from all of them and letting them discover it on their own. He continually surprised her with his sweet, unpretentious manner. He was almost too good to be true, and it worried her for a second.

Amanda's choice of rooms was a wise one. Her big windows gave her cross ventilation in the summer and warmed the room with the sun in the winter.

"Good choice, my girl. You'll like your room."

Having claimed her prize, Amanda was gone, peeking into every other room, identifying them for Maria in a loud voice as she ran from one to another.

"Here's the bathroom, Mommy, and another bedroom with shelves in it, but no furniture." Turning to the other side of the hall she called, "This should be Chris's room, and this one for company. She loped down to the other end of the hall and shrieked. "Look at this room, Mommy! It has a big bed in it, and it's huge."

Amanda's voice became muffled as Maria walked down to see where her energetic daughter had disappeared. She found her inside one of the large walk-in closets, talking a mile a minute to herself.

"Here you are, in Daddy's closet. What are you babbling about?"

"Mommy, Daddy has a lot of clothes. Did you know that? What are these?" Amanda held up a pair of western riding boots.

"They're boots. You know that."

"Mommy, I want a pair, too. Oh, Mommy, please, please get me a pair," Amanda whined, then smiled at her mother.

That little rascal was beginning to really get on Maria's nerves. Cowboy boots were the last thing Maria was going to buy. "We'll go looking, sometime, but I think we'd better get a pony before we get boots."

"I'll ask Daddy if I can have a pony and some boots," Amanda said with the confident tone of a little girl who had no idea what she was asking for.

"Daddy's awfully busy right now, " Maria said, almost snapping at her. "Don't ask him now."

"I want to ask him. He won't get mad at me like my other dad. He'll hug me and talk to me about my boots and a pony." Amanda spoke in an irritating, superior tone.

Maybe because the closet was hot with no air moving, or because she was hungry, but for whatever reason, Maria wanted the afternoon to be over. She also wanted Amanda to shut up and be granted fifteen minutes of quiet.

Trying to control herself, Maria said, "Okay, my little detective, I'm going to faint if we don't get out of this hot closet."

Amanda's face registered worry at hearing her mother's words. She quickly ran out of the closet. "Don't faint, Mommy. Don't do that."

When Maria smiled, Amanda relaxed. "Gee, Mom, you and Daddy have the whole front of the house for your bedroom. I can see way down to the road from your windows. Yours is the best bedroom ever."

A glance around the room almost made her sick to her stomach. What a disaster. It was barren and reminded her of some of those scenes in movies shot in run-down motel rooms. That was the only way to describe it. No shades, curtains, or drapes on the windows—no rugs on the floor. What kind of woman would want to undress or sleep in there? She felt like a big, heavy stone had just rolled onto her chest. It would take her years to make the place livable. Tears began to well up in her eyes. She didn't want Amanda to see her cry.

But Amanda took one look at her and started to dance nervously. "Don't cry, Mommy, I'll be good. Tell me what I did."

Maria gathered Amanda into her arms and hugged her tightly until Amanda quieted down. "You didn't do anything wrong. Mommy's just tired. I know how exciting and also how scary new places are, honey." Maria smoothed Amanda's hair, using a mother's touch, in an effort to reassure her daughter. "We're all going be fine. Your life will be better than you can imagine now that your daddy is with us. The sad years are over."

Amanda perked up. "I want to see Grandma and Grandpa. I'm going to tell them about my bedroom and the pool." She took her mother's hand and pulled her toward the stairs. "When will my furniture come, Mommy? Where are Chris and Wiggles? I want to see my dog." She practically bounced down the stairs.

"I don't know about the furniture, Chris is at the clinic helping Dr. Glen with the animals, and Wiggles is playing happily at Dr. Glen's house with Sharon. You remember Sharon. She sent you all those Nancy Drew books. You can ask Chris all about Wiggles when you see him tonight at dinner."

Amanda let go of her mother's hand and disappeared through the French doors.

"Stay there for a while," Maria called to her daughter. "I'll be in the study making a list." She ducked into Ed's study to assess the room she intended to share with Ed, something she'd never felt she had a right to do married to George. "Ugh," she muttered. "I'm buying new office furniture for this room. All of this has got to go, especially that beat-up sofa." She had just started her "to buy list" when she heard Amanda's faint scream of delight. She found her in the kitchen talking to Ed.

"Mommy said to ask you," Amanda said, her voice filled with excitement.

Ed was listening while gulping down a jelly glass of water. Her darling husband had a grin on his face as he whispered something in Amanda's ear. He looked up at Maria. "Now, go and see your grandma," he said and gave Amanda's backside a little tap.

"Don't forget, Daddy," she said, then ran out to the patio.

Ed opened his arms to Maria, his brown eyes dancing. "Have I got a surprise for you," he said, taking her in his arms and swinging her around.

"I've had enough surprises for one day," she said. Maria was plain worn out, but her mood softened with his touch. "What is it?" He was kindness, itself, but why did it worry her? Since they'd married, every day that they spent together had heightened her feelings about how intelligent and dedicated he was to them. She was more in love with him now than she'd thought possible.

Plus, he didn't realize how handsome he was with that dimple in his chin, his slight overbite, his big expressive eyes, and his brown, curly hair falling over his forehead. What a guy!

"This is an executive decision coming from the two heads of the households," Ed gave Maria a big smile. "Winston and I decided that we're all going to spend a night at the St. Charles Hotel with dinner and breakfast at Maisie's included. Now, I won't take no for an answer" He pulled her tightly to him, nibbled her ear, then kissed her. The intensity of his kiss told her what that smile meant. He wanted to celebrate with an intimate night with her.

"You like to kiss Mommy, don't you?" Amanda said, interrupting their quiet moment. "You really like her. My other daddy never kissed Mommy."

"Where did you come from? I thought I sent you to see your grandparents. And as for your mommy, she'll do as long as she minds me." Laughing, Ed held Maria's arms down to her sides so she couldn't hit him.

"Mommy, you mustn't try to hit Daddy. He's so nice, just mind him. I do, except sometimes," Amanda said, with a guilty grin on her face. "Daddy, what did you tell Mommy?"

"We're going for an overnight to our favorite hotel and out for dinner at Maisie's."

"Oh, Daddy, you are so fun. I love you," Amanda said, adoringly. "I almost forgot, Grandpa wants to know when you want to go for dinner."

"Tell him we'll go in fifteen minutes, and we both need to drive. Now scoot, my little messenger."

Ed turned back to Maria. "I have a knack with little girls—it's the big ones that stump me. Better alert Briggie."

Chris was waiting for them when they pulled up in front of Maisie's Café. With him was Hugh, Maisie's husband and Ed's right-hand man in the clinic.

"It's good to see you, Doc. We've missed you," Hugh said, pumping Ed's hand. "Are you coming to work tomorrow? We've got some problems with a couple of farmers and a breeder that won't be put off." Suddenly remembering his manners, Hugh said, "Hello, everyone, welcome to St. Charles. The town's been buzzing, wondering when the new Mrs. McDermott would be here. Let's go in. I'm sure Maisie's been dying to see all of you. That's all she's been talking about the past few days."

Chris had been standing next to Hugh, waiting. "Hi, Ed," Chris said, almost whispering. "I'd like us to go for a coke sometime, like we did when you used to visit us in Washington last year. Could we do it soon?"

Ed nodded and smiled at his stepson. "Sure, Chris, when I catch up with the farmers, I'll make time for us. I'd also like to take you over to the regional high school and check it out."

"Thanks, Ed," Chris said and walked away, his shoulders relaxed.

Amanda grabbed her brother's arm. "Where's Wiggles? Is she all right?"

"She's fine. Now let go of me, you little pest," he growled in a whisper. "I'll bring her over tomorrow after the movers leave. Otherwise, she might get stepped on or run away."

Maisie must have been watching for them, because, as soon as they walked in, she hurried across the room as quickly as her small, plump frame would allow. Taking Ed's arm, she led their party to one of her new private rooms that she had just added to the original structure. Like a mother duck with her ducklings, everyone followed obediently along behind her.

She opened the door into a lovely, cool room with an imposing polished wood table in the center and enough seats around it to serve as a boardroom table. "This room is for dinner meetings and big families," Maisie said proudly. "I have two more that are for kids' birthdays and anniversaries. I installed air conditioning units in here, as well as in the rest of the place. It cost me a pretty penny, but my customers love it. Make yourselves to home, and I'll get someone to take your orders."

"I knew you were building on this summer, but I never guessed it was this nice." Ed grinned and in a teasing manner asked, "Does it cost more to sit in here?"

Maisie waved off his comment. "You were so busy with building your new little house, patio, and pool, it's a wonder you were able to keep the clinic up and running, going to Washington all the time."

She smiled at Maria. "I guess congratulations are in order. Glad it was you who caught him. The whole town has been talking about you, missy." She turned to Ed. "What are you planning to do up there besides giving people more to talk about all summer?" She leaned over between Winston and Ruth. "Ed's been like a whirling dervish since he got married. I know you'll like your place. He had a good builder and put in the best of everything."

Ed grinned at Maisie. "I'm turning my place into a country club, and Maria's going to run it for me."

"Well, Doc, that idea has been mentioned by a few folks. Perhaps it's going to have a riding club too." It sounded like Maisie wouldn't be outdone. "The word is that you're planning to build a barn and track up there." She stood there with her eyebrows raised, looking pleased that she might have caught him off guard.

Quick as a wink, Ed countered with, "Yes, I'm going to give pony rides to all the country club guests, and Amanda is going to be in charge of it."

Amanda's ears perked up at the mention of her name and pony rides. She leaned across her mother and poked Ed. "Dad, do you really mean we're going to have a barn and give pony rides? That means I'll have a pony," she said, giving him a hopeful look.

"I was going to surprise you and your mother, but Maisie beat me to it. The builder will start as soon as he can—maybe next week—to put in the barn's foundation."

Amanda frowned. "Daddy, I don't want to give pony rides; I just want to ride." She sat quiet for a moment. "Daddy, I want to see where the barn is going to be."

"How would you like to go exploring when I have a minute? I bet we'll find all sorts of interesting things up there, including the spot for the barn. You won't have to give pony rides, Petunia. I was just joking with Maisie. Adults do that sometimes. She knows I didn't mean it."

"Whew, I was worried." Amanda took a breath. "I'm hungry! When do we eat?"

Maisie clasped her hands together. "I forgot my manners. Welcome all of you back to our town." She looked perplexed. "Forgive me, I see a new face among you," she said, looking directly at Briggie. "I guess I was too busy jawing with the two honeymooners to be neighborly."

Realizing that Maisie was singling her out, Briggie said in a loud voice, "Nice to be here! Me name is Bridget. I'm from Ireland, as you can guess from me talk. I cook for Maria and Ed." She paused, appearing to be at a loss for words. "I like your place," she said finally, smiling at Maisie.

"Perhaps we can compare recipes sometime," Maisie said. "Stop in anytime." As for Ed, I want you to know all the women love him, and all the men are jealous, but they know he's the best darn vet this town has ever seen.

"My customers have been driving me crazy all summer asking me if I had any news about you, when you were coming, and a lot of nonsense like that. Eat here all you can so I can pay my bills. Now, that I've had my say, I'd better get back to the rest of my customers. I'll send Stephen to wait on you. He's new, but very quick. He'll take good care of you." Maisie bustled out, and in a minute or two, a nervous young man appeared at the doorway.

He smiled, cleared his throat, and as he started to speak, he croaked. Turning red, he tried again. "My name is Steve, and I'll be your server this evening."

Maria watched him passing out menus and thought about the summer so long ago when she'd said those exact words to the hotel guests at King's Ridge, a resort only about an hour away from there. She'd worked there during the summer of her freshman year at Iowa State. She was as nervous then as she imagined he was now. His forehead had a fine sheen of sweat—from nerves, no doubt. How old was he? Perhaps he was the son of one of the waitresses. His hands were shaking slightly as he carefully poured everyone a glass of iced water. Retreating to the waiter's station, he sighed.

Ed nodded to him and Stephen immediately came over, took out his pad, and began writing down everyone's order. When he came to Amanda, he leaned over and smiled. "The fried chicken pieces and French fries are good."

She turned pink. "Whatever you say," she blurted out, then ducked her head to avoid looking at him.

As Maria observed Amanda watching Stephen making his way around the table, she couldn't deny that her daughter was beginning to grow up.

Ed leaned over and whispered in Maria's ear, "If we can get together tonight, I'll go easy on your workload at our country club."

She grinned. "You old charmer, negotiations are certainly in order for tonight."

He leaned over and said to Amanda, "I'm having a run put up for Wiggles, possibly tomorrow, so she won't get lost when you put her outside. Because she's a hound dog, she'll only need a day or so to know where she lives, but we may need to keep her in it once in a while when we're away."

"Daddy, you're so nice. I love you." She turned to Maria. "Mommy, when is my food coming?"

Maria laughed. "Daddy gets the love, and I get the serious questions. Steve is coming."

As if he heard his name, Stephen appeared at the door loaded down with a big tray of extras, compliments of Maisie, he announced. He placed several bowls of fresh shrimp and crackers, baskets of hot rolls with plates of butter, and two large bottles of wine—one white and one red—on the table. Returning with sparkling wine glasses, he carefully poured the adults a glass of their preference with studied concentration.

Not to be ignored, Amanda asked, "Daddy, can Chris and I have some Coke?"

Ed caught Stephen's eye and made a few simple gestures. Stephen got the message and brought Cokes for Amanda and Chris.

A satisfying meal soothed Maria's frayed edges and she felt renewed. She viewed the people around the big table. Everyone had a glazed look on their faces, except for Ed and Winston, who were having a little discussion about the bill. Moments later, they laughed and took out their wallets. It was time to go. They led their tired little band out the new convenient side entrance directly to their vehicles.

Chris got in Hugh's car after a quick good-bye to Maria with the promise that he would be home the following night. Briggie rode with Winston, and Ed drove his truck while Maria, her mother, and Amanda walked the two blocks to the hotel in the balmy, summer weather, enjoying their pretty town's main street.

Amanda skipped along and every few steps gazed up at the sky.

"Mommy, I can hardly see the stars because the trees' arms go right across the street."

"They've made a canopy, honey. I fell in love with these old trees when I was a teenager. I used to come out here with my dad and ride my horse while my dad puttered around on his little dry farm, in his garden, or with his bees."

"You had a horse, Mommy? You never told me about that. Where did you keep him?"

"*He* was a *she* named Jetty, because she was jet black and beautiful. My generous dad kept her at a stable out here for me." Those were happy memories. "I wonder if they're still in business."

"Mommy, what happened to her?" Amanda sounded enthralled with Maria's story.

"I don't know, but I do know Betty was jealous of my dad and our closeness. I think she insisted that my dad sell Jetty, but I can't prove it. In those days, I rarely asked questions. After he married Betty, he and I were never close again." Maria felt tears welling up in her eyes. She hadn't expected to have such tender feelings about her father and her horse after all those years.

"Mommy, don't cry. I'm going to ask Daddy to get you another Jetty when he gets my pony," she said, grabbing her mother's hand and swinging it back and forth, as she continued skipping along.

Her mother looked at Maria with tears in her eyes too. "I didn't realize that that was happening to you. I was drinking too much. I'm so sorry the way we both treated you."

"Grandma, don't you cry. I'll ask Daddy to get you a horse to ride, too."

Maria's mother wiped her eyes. "Sweetness, I don't want a horse. I haven't ridden in years."

"It's time to think about our move and our new life, not our old one," Maria said, her tone sounding upbeat.

"How do you like your place, Mom? I wanted to get over and see you this afternoon, but I was busy trying to make a little order out of chaos around my place."

Her mother reached over and gave her daughter a love pat. "We're delighted. It's just like Maisie said. Ed spared no expense. The place is beautiful, well-built, and I'm dying to show you. There's only one problem. It's still filled with building dust, and that's been making Winston and me sneeze all afternoon."

"That's too bad. I'll ask Ed if he knows some good cleaning people, and we'll both use them. But you go first. My place is a mess, but we're not sneezing."

"Wonderful, honey, I knew you could help us. Winston said we're going to stay at the St. Charles Hotel until we get our place cleaned and a cook lined up."

"Have your meals with us. Briggie loves you folks. She mentioned it to me again tonight when we were going in for dinner."

"I'll see what Winston thinks about that. He hates to overburden her with her sore feet."

As they were talking, Amanda detached herself from her mother and ran up to Briggie, who was getting out of Winston's car in front of the hotel.

"Mommy told me we're going to sleep together, Briggie, just like old times when I was little. Would you read to me before we go to sleep?" Before Briggie could answer, Amanda turned to her mother and grandmother and announced proudly, "We're going to our room alone."

Watching Amanda skipping and Briggie lumbering along to the elevator brought a pang of concern in Maria. "Before you and Winston go to your room, I need you to think about what we can do for Briggie's swollen feet. They're getting worse and nearly crippling her. This move has really made me notice. I'm ashamed to admit I've been too involved with work and Ed and have been ignoring her.

Her mother offered a tired smile. "Maybe we can talk over breakfast. If not, later in the day."

"Thanks, Mom." Maria gave her mom a kiss on the cheek. "We made it here, and it's wonderful."

"By Jove, we did, Maria," Winston said. "We're delighted with our place. I'll be negotiating with Ed about buying it, but I'll let the dust settle first, and believe me, there's certainly a lot of that." He laughed at his own joke, then turned to his wife. "Did you talk to Maria about help?"

"I did and we are."

"Mom, I was thinking, Maisie is the one to get us some cleaning help. I'll ask Ed to talk to her. She's madly in love with him, will do anything he wants, and knows everybody in town."

They rode up together in the elevator, then parted when the doors opened, happy to be winding down from a long day. Maria stopped at Briggie's door and knocked. She heard a little voice yell to come in. She tried the door, but it was locked. A minute later, Briggie was standing in her big nightgown, almost filling the doorway.

"I just wanted to say good night and let you know that we're right next door if you need us."

"Mommy, we're just fine aren't we, Briggie? Briggie promised to read two more chapters of *Black Beauty* to me. Didn't you, Briggie?"

"I did, me darlin'. Now hop into bed, and I'll get our book."

Maria left them snuggled together with Amanda holding her stuffed dog.

Maria paused at their hotel door. *Why do I feel like I'm waiting for a shoe to drop? I remember how happy I felt with George when we were newly married. I have that same feeling again.*

28. Learning to Adjust

Summer 1963

(Maria)

Ed was showering and singing a little off key at the top of his lungs when Maria walked in. She tossed the dusty clothes she'd been wearing into a pile, then rummaged around in her suitcase, looking for the flat box holding her diaphragm. A few seconds later, she opened the shower door. Putting one bare leg into the shower to tease, Ed's hand immediately slid all the way up her leg, taking her breath away.

He pulled her gently into the shower, lifted her onto the shower stool, and proceeded to kiss every part of her body. The combination of Ed working his way up her body with his lips and the warm water running down all over them made her so excited she choked out, "You may drown if you don't come up for air, and I can't stand one more second of this."

"Really?" he said, massaging one of her breasts with one hand, pulling her into him with the other, and giving her a hot French kiss, exploring the inside of her mouth with his tongue. Moments later, as the water fused together, she felt him as he began making love to her, slowly at first, but building rhythmically into an intensity they wanted and needed. Clinging to him tightly, waves of electricity kept shooting through her entire body until suddenly she went over the edge. It was over, and all that remained was a feeling of utter relief. He held her tightly for a minute, then murmured, "Thanks for giving your body to me." He kissed her gently. "Welcome home, Mrs. McDermott," he said softly. "How is your husband doing so far?"

"I love that when you love me, I feel like I'm part of you. and you're a part of me. You never leave me behind," she whispered. "How do you know I'm ready?"

"From all your body signals. I'd be stupid not to know."

Wrapping a towel around her protectively, he said, "Let's go to bed. I'm beat."

"I love you and this place," she said, as she jumped into their king-sized bed.

"Don't fall asleep just yet, please," she begged, as she heard his breathing slowing down. "I need your male thoughts on having good sex like we have."

"I'll give you another lesson tomorrow morning." He turned over and was out.

All her cares had melted away with Ed's loving attention. He'd soothed her broken heart, and it was healing, something she never thought would happen. She also knew now that her foolish desire to take George back would have been a mistake. It was amazing how her perspective had changed with his death and Ed returning and breathing life back into her life.

The next thing she knew it was early morning. Traffic outside had awakened her. Ed stirred, and she immediately moved closer, laid her head on his chest full of black curly hair, and listened to his strong heart pumping smoothly. He put his fingers in her tousled brown hair and began rolling her curls around his fingers. "Don't ever cut your hair or I'll divorce you," he whispered. "It's beautiful and very sexy."

"You're the only man who has ever been so complimentary about my hair."

"I can't help your poor choices in men in your youth—until you married me," he said and laughed. "What was your burning question you needed me to answer before my lights went out last night?"

"I've overheard a lot of complaints in the women's bathroom at work about their poor sex lives. I'm so naïve, I thought everyone had good sex. It seems so simple with you. You're so good at it." Maria hesitated, sounding embarrassed. "I never would have asked George, but I feel much more comfortable with you."

"Well, after that big build up, I'll tell you. If anyone asks you, tell 'em to make their male idiot friends go see a sex therapist so they know what makes women want sex. It's called women's sexual anatomy 101, and every guy I knew learned it as soon as he hit puberty." Ed's confident tone of voice sounded almost amused. "If they have overly active release problems, they'd better go for help, or they'll be in for a life of misery for them and their women. If they won't go on their own, drag 'em there or dump 'em.

"As for you, my wild and passionate woman, how about a repeat performance this morning? We're still honeymooners, aren't we?"

"I should be all a twitter, but the movers are coming." She tried to pry his arms away, but he held on to her tightly.

"Before we get up, I want to say, I've been thinking for months about something very important. I wanted to wait until we were married and back here before I discussed it with you."

"Fire away, handsome. I'm so happy we're here and together." Maria could forget household problems for the moment. He was trying hard to take care of everyone, run his clinic, keep his clientele happy, and most importantly, love her and be good to her kids.

He peered into her eyes. "First of all, I'll take you down to the bank tomorrow and set up an account, just in your name, for anything you need to fix our wreck of a house. If you run short, just tell me, and I'll slip an extra five in there."

"Five dollars?" she fired back, laughing. "That won't do a thing."

"I meant five hundred, or five thousand, if necessary. Just let me know first."

She relaxed. "I'm thrilled that you trust me to put our house in shape. You're one generous guy. When my house sells in Washington, I'm giving you half of it."

"No, there are better places to put that money—like in the bank for the kids. We'll talk about that later. As for now, I insist that you get enough help so you have something left over for me in the evenings. I know I said this before, but I can't work all day, knowing at the end of the day, my wife is so tired she isn't interested in me in bed." He leaned over and kissed her nose.

"I'll talk to Maisie and have her send up some help for you and your mother. Our house hasn't ever been cleaned properly. Your mother's place has building dust, and ours is plain dirty. Winston said they weren't going to stay there until it was well cleaned, and I don't blame him."

"Now, for the big agreement with you," Ed said, his voice faltering.

Maria felt slightly alarmed. "What agreement, handsome? We never talked about agreements. I'm pretty easy unless you tell me that you have a mistress or a case of gonorrhea." She was trying to be funny, but the idea of a mistress still hurt.

"Listen to me," he said, softly. "I don't want us to have any children."

"What—what did you say? No children?"

"Yes," he said, searching her face.

Maria could feel his heart beating. "Wow, I'm relieved. I thought you might be impotent, although I can hardly believe you only fire blanks."

"Let me explain, you little minx. Be serious. I've a lot of friends who've had some horrible experiences with their older wives getting pregnant, losing the baby or worse." Ed paused, then said quietly, "I don't want to lose you, now that I finally have you."

For the first time since she'd known Ed, she saw tears rimming his big brown eyes.

"Older, yes, but I'm only going to be thirty-three this summer. I'm not quite ready for the nursing home." She laughed. "But to tell the truth, the thought of another baby bothers me. That's why I used my diaphragm last night. I just wanted to be safe. We have two great kids, and that's plenty for me. I wanted my babies, but I hated being pregnant, sick the first few months, and then turning into Tubby Tuba. Let's have a life together without being tied down with a baby."

Ed's concerned face dissolved in relief, his lips burst into a smile, and his eyes danced. "I can't believe you baby proofed yourself last night. Thank God! Peter said I should trust your good judgment, and he was right."

"Speaking of Dr. Peter, we should call him and bring him up to date on how well we're doing." Maria kissed his nipples and began working her way down his chest.

Ed did a quick intake of breath. "That's why I'm crazy about you, you little devil. You're making love to me." He quickly got up, went into the bathroom, and came back wearing a condom. Leaping back into bed, he whispered, "I can't get enough of you," as he began a different style of foreplay, surprising her by massaging her naked body with his strong fingers, then lightly tickling her face and breasts with his fingertips until she grabbed him and said *enough*.

He took his time, helping to slowly lift her into him in a rhythm that brought her so much pleasure she groaned. As he picked up the tempo, nothing mattered except she wanted more. As she clung to his sweaty body, he brought her to that intense moment they needed and wanted, followed by a rush and release, and then an incredible feeling of peace.

"I feel so relieved that you're on board with me about kids," he said after a few minutes of rest. "I feel like a million dollars. But now back to reality. I have to check into the clinic after breakfast and put out some problems before they burst into flames. When I have a minute, I'll call you, then meet you at the bank to get you set up so you can spend my money."

"Ahem, you've got that wrong. It's our money. I contribute to this marriage too, in bed and out, just not monetarily right now. You refused my offer from my house sale, and I'm so busy redoing the house and helping everyone become adjusted, I don't want to go out to work."

"Oh Maria, what you do for me can't be measured in terms of money. I just wanted to tease you. I can't wait to come home to you, Mrs. McDermott. My business is booming and I want you to make our home beautiful. Then we'll fill it with friends, and I'll watch the guys wish you were their wife."

He jumped up, and she heard the water running in the shower. "Come join me if you dare."

"No, I know what would happen."

Maria waited until he left, then she quickly showered and dressed. Noting how late it was, she called her folks and Briggie to get them ready for a quick breakfast. They soon all met in the lobby.

"Let's go face our day and try to make calm out of confusion and peace out of chaos—not to mention clean up our place and meet the movers," Winston said in his most sonorous tone.

"Amen to that, buddy," Maria agreed emphatically. "Maisie will help us too. She'll know of some good help, and we need it as soon as possible. I'm feeling overwhelmed with that ark of a house on my mind."

They headed over to the café, where they found Maisie waiting for them.

"Your husband was here for all of ten minutes, but he took time to ask me to send a couple of gals up to your places to clean" Maisie said. "When would you like them? They're farm girls looking for some money to buy clothes for high school. I know both their families, and those girls will work hard for you."

"Send them today!" As far as Maria was concerned, help couldn't come fast enough. "You're a darling to help us. I'm glad school hasn't started. It will take a week or two for us to dig out up there." As Maria was talking to her, Maisie's eyes were on Winston.

"Right, I'll call them and send them up," she said, smiling at Winston. Maisie lowered her voice. "I know they'll be happy with whatever you want to pay them, but the going rate is a dollar an hour. Their names are Laura and Sarah."

"Do you suppose we could have Laura work for us?" Briggie asked. "Me sister's name is Laura and was me favorite. I'd like that."

"Sure, why not?" Maria caught her mother's eye. "Do you care, Mom?"

"Not at all."

"As long as our girl can push a broom and a vacuum cleaner, we'll be satisfied," Winston piped up. As if to send a little cautionary note to Maisie, he added, "If she can help my Ruth, that's the important thing."

Maisie became very business-like and seated them quickly.

Thirty minutes later, they all had finished breakfast and were getting ready to go. "The movers are probably on our doorstep. Let's get this day behind us," Maria said, shuddering slightly, wishing it was all over. "Sorry, Maisie, we have to meet the movers. Thanks for all your help," Maria called as they hurried to their car.

Afterward, when Ed told her that Maisie was informing all of her interested customers that Maria's father, Winston, was a very important man from Washington, Maria laughed. Let Maisie say anything she wanted about her stepfather. Winston had never sought any limelight about his past life in the State Department and had gone to great lengths to avoid giving any personal press interviews ever since she'd known him. As for letting Maisie think he was her father, she'd wait until the right time to tell Maisie the truth.

29. When Does It Get Easier?

Summer 1963

(Maria)

The movers' bright yellow trucks were waiting when Winston dropped Maria and her family off at her kitchen side door. The head man got out of his truck, obviously perturbed with the wait and placed his hands on his hips. "Where do you want this stuff?"

Quickly identifying her load, Maria sent the other truck around to the back of Winston's home. The rest of the morning was a blur to Maria with all the running up and down the stairs and directing the movers as to where to set up beds, where to put the boxes labeled clearly by Ed in large dark printing, and where to store the furniture until she could make sense of it all.

After a while, she gave up. "Stick the boxes anywhere," she said to the movers, wishing she could tell them where all of it could go in a much more vulgar way.

While Maria was directing traffic, frazzled beyond reason, Laura and Sarah, the cleaning girls, arrived with lunch bags in hand, smiling, calm, and happy to have a job. Glazed over from being forced to make too many quick decisions, Maria pushed Laura into the kitchen to talk to Briggie, then shooed Sarah across the patio to her mom's door.

At that moment, one of the movers called from upstairs for her help. As she leaped up the stairs for yet another time, she heard the comforting noise of vacuum cleaner buzzing downstairs, although its sound was barely distinguishable, drowned out by the movers' feet pounding like a herd of elephants.

Suddenly, Maria felt her daughter's delicate little hand slip into hers. Amanda peered up at her. "Mommy, when are they going to go away?"

Ready to scream, Maria merely sighed. "Not soon enough for me, honey."

"Where's Daddy? He needs to help us," Amanda yelled over the noise.

"He's working to pay for all of this, sweetheart." What had she gotten all of them in for? She wished she knew.

"He won't go away and leave us because we spend too much money, will he, like our other daddy did?" Amanda wailed and started to cry.

Maria closed Amanda's bedroom door, sat down on the bed, and pulled her slightly overwrought, sobbing girl onto her lap. "Daddy is very generous, he loves us, and he's just up to his neck in work right this minute. He likes to work and help the animals get well."

"Where is he? In a big lake? Can't he swim?" Amanda asked, with a twinkle in her eye.

"No, sweetie, I meant he has to see a lot of farmers today and take care of their sick animals. While Daddy helped us move here, the farm people who need him have been waiting for him to come back."

That explanation seemed to satisfy Amanda that everything was okay in her little world. "I met the new lady who came to help us clean," she said. "Her name is Laura and she's nice."

"She's going to high school this fall with Christopher. I believe she's a freshman, just like him," Maria explained to her now smiling little daughter.

"She's not a man, Mommy. Why did you call her a freshman?"

"That's what they call everyone who is starting high school," Maria said, wondering herself why women were lumped together with men in the English language, whether they liked it or not.

"Now, my sweet, Mommy has to go out into the dreaded hall and face the movers' questions again. Come with me and soon this will all be over."

Morning slipped into afternoon, the movers were just about finished, and Laura was vacuuming downstairs. Briggie was in the kitchen opening boxes, and everyone was hungry.

"Let's go see Grandma and Grandpa, Amanda. I need to talk to them about lunch and a couple of other things." Holding hands and skipping down the now even dirtier stairs, Maria and Amanda reached the first floor and ran out through the French doors of the living room, across the patio, and to the grandparents' door.

Winston was just coming out, and he greeted them with a big smile. "Can you hear the wonderful sounds of cleaning going on? Our Sarah is hard at it." He stuck his head back through the open door. "Ruth, where are you, dear? Maria is here with our darling Amanda. Come in, and I'll find her. I'm getting hungry; how about you?"

Ruth came out of their kitchen wiping her hands, her hairdo rumpled, probably from leaning over while unpacking their boxes. "I'm a mess, Maria, which I seem to be saying often lately."

"We're here to rescue us all from cleaning and stop for lunch. What about it?"

"Sounds wonderful to me. How about you, Winston?"

"Say no more, I'll settle up with all of the movers, and then we'll pick you up at your side door. Ed and I have a man's agreement," he said, sounding very paternal and secretive.

"What am I going to do with you?" Her mother shook her head. "This isn't a Russian spy novel."

"That's okay, Mom. He's fun to spar with, and he adds charm to my life. As for that husband of mine, I hope his brain doesn't burst. He works so hard and thinks so much."

As Maria and Amanda ran back across the patio, they were met by a tall, nice-looking young man who announced that he was the pool cleaner Doc had hired to take care of their pool. Again, Maria was astonished by her husband's interest in doing everything he could to make her life easier. Stunned by Ed's almost overconcern about their household, she stood there smiling at the young man.

"I'm Paul MacDonald, with an *a* in Mac. We're Scottish, you know."

"Glad you're here. I'm Mrs. McDermott without an *a*, and this is Amanda, my daughter."

Amanda started giggling and hopping around on the slate floor as she smiled at Paul.

"I'll pay you before I go for lunch."

"Thanks, but Doc has already taken care of that."

He's done it again. Maria felt a tiny bit of apprehension. *Is he for real?*

"Paul's cute, but not as cute as Stephen," Amanda said, making a new judgment.

"Let's concentrate on getting Briggie and going to lunch with Grandpa and Grandma," Maria said, suddenly realizing her tone with her daughter was sharper than necessary because of her uneasiness about Amanda's new interest in boys.

Soon, no one was thinking about anything except food as they went off in Winston's car to Maisie's for some well-deserved lunch.

Just as they were leaving the restaurant, Ed's truck pulled up, and out he came on the run. "Hi, everybody," he said, but his eyes remained on Maria. "Will you and Petunia come sit with me while I catch a bite? Then we'll go down to the bank and set up your account."

A look of dismay came over Amanda's face. "Daddy, I think I need to go home. I'm sort of tired. I'll ride with Grandma and Grandpa. You and Mommy go to the bank, and I'll see you later." She gave him a sickly smile and took her grandmother's hand.

"Sure, Amanda, I'll see you tonight. Come on, Maria, I'm starved." They found a table inside, and Ed soon had a juicy hamburger in front of him. "Is Amanda all right? She's never tired." His eyes were full of concern.

"I think Amanda has the Paul bug."

"The who bug?"

The bug for the cute guy who's cleaning our pool as we speak, thanks to you. In case you're interested, Amanda has discovered boys since you came into our lives."

Taking a swallow of coffee too fast, Ed coughed a little and looked at Maria. "What does her newfound boy interest have to do with me?"

"You, my unsuspecting hero, have been showing her without conscious effort how nice guys act around women and their daughters. You kiss and hug me in front of her, hug her, and tell her how special she is to you. Your attention has brought her out of that frightened shell she was in when she was around her father. She can admit she likes boys, thanks to you."

Ed beamed while listening to Maria's comments. A few minutes later, he'd finished his lunch. "Okay, light of my life, let's go to the bank and set you up to spend our money. Notice, I said *our* money." He took Maria's hand with one of his, then waved at Maisie with the other. "Put it on my tab, I'm good for it."

"Let's walk," she suggested. "It's only a block from here to the bank, and I love strolling and holding hands under these old, beautiful trees."

Robert, the bank manager, expertly filled out the forms for Maria to sign, giving her a private account. While Maria and Ed were on their way out of the bank, an office door opened and a gentleman stepped out, looking pleased to see them. "Hello, Doc. Congratulations are in order for the two of you," he said, eyeing Maria.

"Mr. Madden, I'd like you to meet my wife, Maria. We're back from Washington and in the process of moving in. I'm sure you'll meet Maria's mother and stepfather, Mr. and Mrs. Brooks, soon when they come to do their banking. He's just retired and bought the town-house next to us."

Shaking Maria's hand, Mr. Madden said, "Your husband has done a good job settling into the community. His clinic and the way he runs it are a credit to him and his skills. I'm delighted to meet you. I'm sure you will love our community, and they will love you. If there's anything I can do, let me know." He grinned and said, "I'm going to have lunch at Maisie's. I'm hungry!"

When they climbed into Ed's truck, Maria reached over, took Ed's face in her hands, and kissed him lightly, breathing out the words, "Thank you for being so generous."

Ed seemed so surprised at her thanks, that he stopped looking for his sunglasses and said, "It's the other way around, honey. You're a champ. Not one word out of you about the movers, the confusion, the fact that I couldn't get there, nothing. You are my darling wife and prove it to me every day—and hopefully every night," he said, his eyes sparkling with desire. He fended off her attempt to whack him, laughed, and kissed her on her cheek. "Hope the onions I had for lunch didn't ruin my kiss." He grinned at her, put on his sunglasses, then started his truck to take her home and run back to the clinic.

After he dropped her at the front door, she watched his truck bounce down their road out to the main highway, prolonging going in until it had disappeared around the bend. *How I love that man! I hope I wasn't too quick to agree to a no-children pact with him. He's so darling, he would make a wonderful dad.* She sighed. *Back to work. Ugh! How I wish I could lie down for a few minutes.*

Looking around at her cleaned entryway, her spirits notched up a bit, especially when she could faintly hear the vacuum working upstairs, somewhere, knowing her house was becoming more of a home.

Gosh, it's hot! Maria pulled her hair back into a ponytail with an old rubber band she found in her pocket.

Her daughter was sitting on the patio in one of her grandma's lawn chairs, her eyes glued on Paul, giggling while he cleaned the pool and talked to her. Maria stood by the French doors watching him as he carefully tested the water for its cleanliness with a chemical pool kit.

She joined Amanda on the patio. "So, what's the verdict? Can we swim here this afternoon, Paul?"

"Oh, hi, Mrs. McDermott. You can after about an hour or so. I'm going to add some chemicals right now. I cleaned out the filter and the lines, so I think the pool will be fine until next week when I come again." He gave her a gorgeous smile, showing some beautiful white teeth. A lady killer in the making with all that blond hair and sparkling blue eyes.

"Thanks, Paul, I'm so happy to be able to swim and cool off this afternoon. See you next week." Maria forced herself back into the living room, reluctantly, to try to arrange the area in some kind of order. Perspiration had collected on her upper lip and her forehead, which she wiped off with the edge of her shirt. Ignoring the furniture tightly pushed together in the middle of the room, she went to Ed's study to make a detailed, honey do list for herself. She also began to acquaint herself with the household accounts, but became frustrated trying to decipher Ed's methods of bill paying. Maria decided to call it quits and went into the kitchen to see what Briggie and Amanda were up to and heard Amanda's voice.

"Briggie, are these table and chairs our old ones?"

"Yes, me darlin'. Isn't it grand to sit here and look out at the lovely hill behind us?"

"I guess it's okay, but I want to ask you and mommy about love."

Maria smiled at the look on Briggie's face.

"My girl, are you in love? I am, too," Briggie said.

Amanda's eyes grew wide. "Who with?"

Briggie grinned and glanced at Maria. "I love your mother, new father, grandparents, being here, and life in general."

"I mean a boy or a man, the exciting kind." Amanda sounded disgusted.

Maria reached over and held Amanda's hand.

"Mommy, I love two boys, Stephen and Paul. Is it okay to like both?"

"Of course, you're just learning about boys. You'll love lots of them."

"Mommy, what time is it? We don't have any clocks around here. I miss our other house. It had lots of clocks."

"I don't know. I haven't unpacked any, yet."

Amanda made a sour face. "Our house is a mess, Mommy."

"I know. It will be less messy just as soon as we pitch in and change it. Let's go upstairs. I want to make our beds for tonight, and I want you to help me."

"Can't the nice cleaning girl help you?" Amanda asked, whining a little.

"All three of us working together will accomplish the job much faster."

Upstairs, Maria enlisted Laura's help, and with the promise of a swim, Amanda said she was pitching in like Mommy. They had the three bedrooms ready in no time. Looking in at the spare bedroom, Maria made a mental note to turn the room into a lovely guest room for Dr. Peter, who was visiting later that month, and for Elena, who planned to stay when she had her fall show in Chicago.

"Mommy, what can I swim in?"

Finding Amanda's bathing suit was easy—it had made her suitcase smell terrible. Picking it up with two fingers, Maria dropped it into the bucket with the cleaning supplies. "Ugh," Maria said, grinning at Amanda.

Amanda giggled at the face her mother had just made.

"Just swim in a clean pair of shorts and a top, Amanda." She opened a box labeled summer clothes and handed a set to Amanda. "I'll find your other suits later. Go down and wait by the pool. I'll be along shortly."

In her bedroom, Maria opened her suitcase, found her suit, and squeezed into it. She studied her bulging tummy in the mirror. Too many good meals, no worry, and plenty of sex., Running down the stairs, she saw Winston and her mother sitting in the shade on lawn chairs, enjoying a couple of delicious looking drinks.

"Mom, what are you going to pay Sarah?" Maria whispered. "I want to give Laura the same thing."

"We thought ten should do it. It's more than Maisie suggested."

"Fine. I'll see you in a little while. We may have to give the girls a ride to Maisie's."

"Capital, Maria," Winston boomed. "I'll be glad to run them down. That girl Sarah cleaned like a whirlwind. She's a strong young lady. I guess farm girls have to work hard, judging from our Sarah."

Paying Laura, Maria said, "Thanks, see you tomorrow. Mr. Brooks will be by in a minute to drive you. Wait here at the kitchen door."

"Gosh, thanks, Mrs. McDermott. It's more than I thought I'd get."

As Laura was talking, Maria heard the phone. Convinced it was Ed, she excused herself and ran into the study to answer the call. "Hi, there!" she said, waiting for his familiar voice to respond with some silly thing to her. But there was silence. Someone was on the other end of the phone. She could hear him breathing. A scary little premonition flitted through her mind. "Who is this?" she asked firmly, irritated that a pervert was playing a nasty game with her. Whoever it was clicked off, and she heard the dial tone droning in her ear.

Replacing the phone, she sat down on the scruffy sofa, shaken. Who was it, and what did they want?

30. Getting to Know Each Other

Summer 1963

(Maria)

"Mom, I've been waiting for you forever by the pool." Amanda sounded perturbed. "Come play with me. Grandma is there. She's having a grown-up drink. Briggie brought us some lemonade and is sitting on the pool stairs cooling her feet." Amanda began yanking at her mother. "What's wrong with you? You're so quiet."

"I'm just tired, sweetie. I'll be fine as soon as I get in our nice, clean pool. Forcing a laugh, Maria held Amanda's hand and jumped in with Amanda.

"She swam around her mother like a little fish until Maria splashed her.

Amanda screamed and paddled away in mock fear, turned, and splashed Maria."

Her grandmother watched from the umbrella's shade, content to be there, away from the broiling afternoon sun.

"Ed has certainly made this place beautiful," Maria's mother said. "He positioned the pool and our homes so our living rooms face the pool. And the best part—up here with the hedges hiding us from the road, the pool is secluded from view."

Piping up from the edge of the pool with her feet dangling in the water, Briggie said, "Missy deserves a good man. I'm especially proud he's an Irishman. He had good parents."

If you only knew the half of it. But I'll never tell.

Playing in the water with her darling girl, Maria's mind retreated back to the day she'd met Amanda's father, George, in Winston's pool in Miami, long ago. What a handsome, dashing, young man. It seemed almost like a dream now. She'd fallen in love with him, thinking he was too good to be true—and he was.

Winton's booming voice brought her back to the moment. "I dropped off our girls and now deserve a good, stiff drink. I'm exhausted after watching Sarah work all day."

The sun had disappeared behind the tree tops when Chris arrived holding Wiggles, who was struggling to get out of his arms. Amanda screamed. She jumped out of the pool soaking wet to squeeze her puppy. Their reunion didn't last long. Wiggles squirmed out of Amanda's arms, put her nose down, and began looking for a place to pee.

"Take her over to the bushes where there's some grass, Amanda," Chris said, sounding more and more like a man with his deepening voice.

Maria was proud of her son. He'd certainly changed. Working hard for Ed and her brother-in-law, he'd developed a muscular frame on his thirteen-year-old body. He'd also inherited George's intelligence and drive, but, for the most part, the resemblance to his father ended there. He had a softer look to his face and gentle, light brown eyes, and his coloring was deeper with rusty-brown hair. His disposition reminded her of her own father, not prone to flamboyancy or anger, but a thoughtful, somewhat serious demeanor. Like her father, Chris had a good sense of humor.

Chris strolled over to where Amanda was watching Wiggles roam, and he said something that made her laugh. Maria was glad he was enjoying his sister's company more than he had in the past. Maybe they'd become good friends.

Standing in his swimming shorts by the door, Winston asked, "Any adult who wants a beverage, please speak up now." A loud no from the group brought him out with his drink in hand and the evening newspaper tucked under his arm. "This is living. No more schedules to meet—freedom at last." He plunked himself down under the shade umbrella, looking very pleased. Seeing Chris pouring himself a glass of lemonade, Winston asked, "Hi, Chris! How did you get here?"

"Glen dropped me off on his way home. We've been up since five this morning. Doc had two early surgeries and an emergency delivery. Some champion pups whose mama was having a bad time having them. Doc said it's because the breeders aren't being careful weeding out bad characteristics of the breed and are breeding dogs for the money and that's all."

Maria was pleased with that small bit of information that Chris had delivered to his family about dog breeding, even though she doubted that anyone else was particularly interested. It was the first time in a long time that Chris had acted like he belonged to their family and had volunteered some information.

"Mom, when's dinner? I'm starved." Chris looked tired. "Amanda said that she helped you make up my bed. Thanks for that, 'cause I'm going to hit the hay early tonight. Doc wants to pick me up at seven tomorrow to help him, so I think I'll go see where I'm living and unpack some stuff." Chris walked over to his mother and smiled. "Thanks, Mom, for everything you've done for me."

With him standing so close to her, Maria realized he'd started to shave and it made her realize how precious the time with him at home would be from now on.

"Come on, squirt, show me my room," he said to his adoring sister, who would have followed him off the end of a bridge. Amanda jumped up and ran after him, talking nonstop.

Following Chris with his eyes, Winston waited until the kids were out of earshot. "Chris has grown up a lot since his father died. I'm proud of him working so hard for Dr. Glen." He took another sip of his drink. "Will you be able to sleep in this oven tonight, Maria? What about you, Briggie? Ruth and I are going to stay at the inn until we get a couple of fans and some air conditioning in our place."

Maria used a towel to wipe moisture from her arms. "Ed mentioned something about having installed whole house fans in the roofs of our houses when he built them. I'm not sure how they work, but he said they do a fairly good job of cooling off the place in the evening by drawing in the cool air."

"I guess we haven't discussed the fine points of our new place with him, but I'm not sure a fan will work. Anyway, during the day, the place is hot as hell. I'll talk to him over dinner, which I hope will be soon. I'm starving. What about the rest of you? Briggie, we want to treat you to another night in cooled bliss."

"Thanks for the wonderful invitation," still cooling her feet in the pool. "I'll be delighted to take you up on your offer, if you'll let me serve you dinner when I get me kitchen up and running."

"It's a deal, Briggie." Maria's mother replied. "My kitchen isn't very well stocked, and I'm not ready to make any meals. I've never liked to cook. I'd love to have Sarah cook for us once she gets our place cleaned up."

"Good thought, Mom. I'm going in to call the clinic and track down that hard-working doctor I married. I should feel guilty sitting here so comfy, but I don't," Maria said, laughing.

The phone rang only twice before Ed's receptionist picked up. "Gladys, this is Maria. I haven't met you yet, but I will soon. Is his 'nibs' around?"

"He just pulled in, all spattered with blood. Hold on, please. Doc," she yelled, "phone, line one, it's your wife, and she sounds mad." Gladys laughed. "That'll get him quicker than anything. Stop by anytime, and I'll tell you all the secrets I have about this clinic and the people who work here."

Maria laughed and waited for her darling husband to pick up. What a character Ed had hired since Hilda left. She liked Gladys.

"Hi, honey. Are you mad at your hardworking, blood-covered vet who loves you?"

Maria giggled. "Come home—right now—we're hungry."

"Your command doesn't match your giggles. I'll opt for your giggles, and I'm coming."

"Ed's on his way," she called to the pool crowd from the door. "We'll be leaving in a few minutes." Maria hurried upstairs and opened all the windows.

She heard her two kids convulsed with laughter in Chris's room. "Dad's coming home. Get ready for dinner." Chris had Wiggles jumping for treats standing on her hind legs.

"Isn't Wiggie fun, Mom?"

"Yes, but hurry. Open your windows, and take the dog out before we leave."

While changing into her jeans and a much too snugly fitted top, Maria heard Ed bounding up the stairs, and then he appeared in his briefs. "Well, it's a good thing we don't have any company around. Why the underwear?" Maria asked, laughing in spite of herself.

"I dropped my bloody whites in our soon-to-be working washer. That is, if you'll make the call to the plumber tomorrow." Ed leaned in and tried to kiss her.

"Ugh, into the shower with you. No kisses! You're all sweaty."

He moved in closer, held her, and kissed her anyway. "Sweat doesn't bother you when I'm making love to you."

"That's different," she said, trying to whack him as he ran off.

When it was time to leave, Maria looked for the truck in the driveway, but it was nowhere in sight.

The garage door opened and Ed drove out in George's little red sports car. "In the back, kids," he said, as she hopped in next to him. He turned and gave her a satisfied look.

Briggie lumbered out of the house and heaved herself into Winston's car that was parked right behind them.

Later, dining in cooled comfort, Maria said, "Darling, I'm dreading our hot house." She wrinkled up her face in a knot.

Ed said with a confident look, "Wait until you see how my whole house fan works. The place will be cool in a few seconds."

"Promise?"

"Absolutely."

At home, he flipped the switch on the wall, waited until he heard the soft whir of the fan in the attic, and gave her a satisfied grin.

Maria stood there only half believing him until she felt the outdoor breeze blowing through the windows. Within a few moments, Ed gave her another self-satisfied smile as the cooling effect of the fan had made the second floor bearable.

Amanda and Chris both were standing in the hall, and they asked what had happened.

He crowed, "What did I tell all of you? You have to have more trust in me."

I'll poke a hole in his balloon. "It sounds like a plane taking off," Maria teased. I don't know if I'll be able to sleep through all that noise."

"Mom, don't tease Daddy. It feels wonderful, doesn't it, Chris?" Amanda said, racing her brother back down the hall, the noise of their feet reverberating against the walls.

"You little devil, things are going too smoothly, aren't they? You want some excitement, don't you? I have the perfect prescription." He slipped his hand under her shirt and felt her breasts as they went into their bedroom.

Unhooking her bra, she laughed as she pulled it off in front of Ed. "Let's go swimming. It's a perfect night for it, and it's still early."

Ed's face fell, realizing what he had planned had to be put on hold for a while. "Okay, my little tease. I'll see if the kids want to swim too. By the way, the place looks fantastic," Ed said on his way out.

Later, standing in the open French doors, Maria felt awestruck marveling at the beautiful pool and patio Ed had built for her. With the underwater lights on, it reminded her of Winston's pools in Washington and Miami.

"Ah," she said, letting herself slip slowly into the pool, feeling the luxurious quality of the water on her skin. She was all alone for a second. Then Ed jumped in holding his nose, followed by Amanda screaming with delight, and family life returned.

"Where's Chris?" Maria asked Amanda.

"He's on the phone."

"Oh," Maria said, as Ed threw the beach ball to Amanda. "I wonder who he's talking to."

Ed turned to her. "Who do you think thirteen-year-old boys talk to? Your son has discovered girls." He continued tossing the ball back and forth with Amanda.

Maria began swimming lazy circles around the deep end, watching her little family play. Ed didn't seem very comfortable in the water, but he was making a valiant attempt to enjoy it with his new family. A long time ago he'd confided in her, almost grimly, that poor farm boys like him didn't have any time to go swimming.

Unlike George, who grew up around water and water sports, but she couldn't remember a single time when George had ever played with his kids in the water. He drove them to the country club for swimming lessons and playtime with their friends, but spent his time on the tennis courts or golf course.

After an hour, the three of them were tired. "Let's get out and dry off. I have a treat for us. I'll bring it right out." Maria hurried into the house. She returned in less than two minutes and pulled off the napkin hiding her surprise. "Compliments of Maisie. She insisted I have some of her special chocolate cake cookies that she makes from a secret unshared recipe."

As if by magic, Chris appeared and sat down by the cookies.

"Glad you could join us. You missed a lot of fun," Maria teased. "I'm glad something brought you down here."

Sitting in the dark, with only the pool lights casting a little glow on their picnic, Chris said quietly, "I like my room, folks. It looks really clean and nice." He picked up a cookie and swallowed it whole, then reached for more. Maria saw Ed look at Chris and smile.

"Glad you like Maisie's cookies, Chris," Ed said, taking the plate and handing it to Amanda, who refused to take one.

Ed raised his eyebrows. "No cookie? That's not like my Petunia."

Amanda looked pale to Maria, and she had a little whine in her voice. A tiny worry ran through Maria's mind. Surely, Amanda was just tired. She'd be fine after a good night's sleep. Maria couldn't stand one more thing to worry about."

Perhaps moving had been harder on Amanda than Maria wanted

to admit. Being so high strung, sensitive, and a worry wart, Amanda used up a lot of energy every day. *My daughter takes after me in the worry department.* She heard Amanda crying. The child was exhausted.

"Petunia, does your stomach hurt?" Ed asked as he scooped her up in his arms and carried her upstairs.

"No, Daddy, I'm just so tired, I feel like I can't walk."

"I'll tuck you in and tell you a story about a tiny pony that I saw today in a farmer's barn," Maria heard him say as they disappeared into Amanda's bedroom.

Silently thanking him for being so good to her little girl, Maria stripped off her bathing suit, showered off, and shampooed the chlorine out of her hair. She put a nightie on her nightstand in case she needed to get up and check on Amanda and crawled under the sheet. The fan had done its job, and the bed was invitingly cool.

She said a little prayer of thanks for the way things were going between her kids and Ed and asked for Amanda to be her old self in the morning. What a blessing. He actually talked to, teased, and played with the kids. She turned on her side to wait for Ed. The next thing she knew, it was morning.

Something was tickling her face. She put the pillow over her head, but the darn bug followed her there too. Maria tried to shoo it away, half-heartedly with her sleep leaden arm. The nibbling on her neck wasn't a bug. Turning back over, she opened one eye to see Ed's handsome face two inches from hers.

"Hi, cutie. I lost out on last night with you. We didn't get to christen our bed, but we'll do better tonight. You had a rough day yesterday, and I didn't have the heart to wake you when I came in. I gave Amanda a couple of aspirins and checked on her once in the middle of the night. and she was sound asleep. I think she'll be fine after a good sleep.

"Today should be much better for all of us."

Maria certainly hoped he was right.

31. Scary Moments

Summer 1963

(Maria)

The sound of a car driving up under her window brought Maria out of her sleep haze. The sound of voices outside, then moving inside, really woke her up. What time was it? She glanced at the clock by her bed. Thank goodness it was only eight o'clock. She lay back for a moment, trying to pull herself together and wake up. When did Ed leave? It must have been in the middle of the night. Hopefully, he'd slow down soon and not wear himself out. It worried Maria.

Her mind was a blur. It must be the girls. They were right on time. She should get down there and give Laura directions, but there was so much to do, she didn't know what to tell her. As Maria shifted into gear, got dressed and went downstairs, she expected to find Amanda talking to Briggie, but she wasn't there. Her little sleepy head was still upstairs catching a few more winks.

"We tried the door and it was open, so we came in. I hope you didn't mind," Laura said.

"No, of course not. I'm going to get myself a cup of coffee and sit here for a minute. My folks should be bringing Briggie back in a moment. Until they come, why don't you tackle the rest of the kitchen boxes for Briggie. I'll help you decide where to put the pots and pans."

While Maria sat sipping her coffee, gazing out the kitchen window, two men walked by. They peeked through the kitchen door window and knocked on the door.

"We're here to put in the dog run for your dog. Doc called us. Where do you want it?"

Maria went outside and made some quick decisions about the run and hoped she was right. She heard the men getting their materials out of their truck and she went back to finish her coffee. Laura met her at the door with the kitchen phone extension.

Expecting it to be Ed, she said, "Hi there, it's nice to talk to you." There was someone on the line, just waiting, not talking. Maria got that sick feeling again and hung up.

Briggie shuffled into the kitchen. "Who was it, me darlin'? You look upset," she said with a concerned yet puzzled expression on her face.

"I don't know, Briggie, but let's not talk about it now," glancing at the girls. "Laura, would you help Briggie any way you can today?" She smiled at Sarah, "My folks are home, so you can go over and work with them."

"I hear you, Wiggles," Maria said, as she opened the utility room's door.

She was greeted by a jumping, wiggling little dog who needed to go out. Giving Maria a wag of her tail, she scooted to the kitchen door waggling her body. As soon as the puppy got outside, Wiggles stopped, looked at the men for a moment, put her nose down, and found a place to relieve herself. She finished, then bounded up the side of the hill and looked back at Maria.,

"Wiggles, come back," Maria called, climbing as fast as she could to catch her.

Wiggles had picked up a scent. Her head was down and her tail stood up, waving back and forth waving like a flag. Wiggles led Maria to the top of the hill looking down into a lovely meadow. What a beautiful piece of property they owned. How many acres? As an added bonus, she could hear water running down there—somewhere.

"Wiggles! Wiggles, come back here," she called as she ran down the hill following that little flag of a tail. Wiggles had stopped at the little stream and was drinking noisily. When Wiggles finished, Maria grabbed her and started back to the house. The dog struggled to break free, but Maria held on. "Listen, missy, I'm not letting go of you until we're inside."

Amanda was sitting at the kitchen table drinking some juice. She seemed listless and hardly looked up when Wiggles came bounding into the room. Without her usual enthusiasm, Amanda picked up the puppy, then ambled down the hall with Wiggles in her arms trying to lick her and say hello. Amanda did nothing but put her in the utility room.

Maria felt Amanda's forehead. *What am I'm going to do? Amanda is burning up.* "Look at me, baby!" Amanda's eyes looked milky. "How do you feel?

"Mommy, help me! I don't know what's wrong."

Maria's stomach suddenly was in knots, her palms wet, and she prayed, "Help my little girl." She sat down and pulled Amanda into her lap, wrapped her arms around her and began to think. All kinds of ugly worries started crowding into her mind—flu, pneumonia, strep throat, and, the most frightening of all—polio. *Does she have polio? Please God, don't let it be that.*

As a family, we took our oral polio vaccines the minute we could. Didn't it work with Amanda?

"Back to bed with you, my sweet. My father, your real grandfather, is a doctor. He's told me ever since I was little that bed rest cures lots of things." Amanda didn't put up an argument, which frightened Maria. Her daughter had always been such an active child that even when she was coming down with something, she'd never rest without a fight.

After settling Amanda back in bed and laying several new comic books Ed had picked up for her on her night table, Maria rushed to call the office. How she wished she could talk to him, but that would be a miracle. He was never in the office, he spent the day driving from one farm to another to care for some animal.

"Hello, Gladys, I need help; my little girl is terribly sick." Suddenly breaking down, Maria started to cry and through her sobs she begged Gladys to call his short wave and have him come home or at least call her as soon as possible.

"I need the name of a doctor," choking back more sobs.

"I'll get Doc as soon as I can. I'm sorry, Maria."

Maria hung up the phone, already feeling worn out, and the day hadn't even begun. Worry did it every time.

One more peek at her little girl for reassurance before she went down to work with Laura. She slipped into the room and listened to Amanda's breathing. She was sleeping in a fitful pattern and moaned when Maria felt her heated forehead.

Maria, shaking, sat down in Chris's old rocking chair. "Oh, Lord, please help us."

The insistent ring of the phone made her run for it.

"Hello, Ed. I want the name of a good doctor," she blurted out, not thinking. Silence met her from the other end of the phone, but she thought she heard a slight, muffled cough. "Get off the phone this instant, you monster!" Maria slammed down the receiver and ran downstairs and across the yard to talk to Winston, telling Briggie as she whizzed by her friend to get her if Ed called.

Her parents' living room French doors were open and she burst in. "Winston, where are you? I need to talk to you!" She could hear some movement coming from their second floor, and she went to the bottom of the stairs., "Winston, please answer me." She felt her voice starting to break, and tears began welling up in her eyes.

Winston appeared at the top of their stairs in his underwear. "What is it, Maria?" He looked alarmed by her sudden appearance and obvious anxiety. "I'll be right down. Just let me put on my pants and T-shirt. Ruth, our girl is here and very upset. Come help me." He disappeared for a moment and then reappeared dressed. He headed down the stairs. "Now, what's happened? Are the children all right? Is Ed hurt? What's the matter?" He boomed one question after another, then waited for her to answer.

"I'm coming, Maria," her mother called from their bedroom.

"Amanda is sick, very sick," Maria blurted, "and I called Ed for a doctor, and Gladys said she'd have him call me with the name of a doctor, and I was waiting for his call in Amanda's room." Maria paused and cleared her throat. "I ran when I heard the phone ring, and I told Ed that Amanda was sick and I needed a doctor, but it wasn't him! It was that damnable silence again!" She stopped to take a breath and the dam broke. Tears cascaded down her face.

Ruth put her arms around her girl and held her close.

"Now, slow down, by Jove and let me try to understand what you just said," Winston spoke quietly. "Thank goodness for you, Ruth, so quiet and calm. As I understand you, Amanda's sick, you're worried, you need a doctor, you called Ed, and thinking it was him calling back, you talked to silence on the other end of the phone. Have I got it correct?"

"Yes," Maria wailed.

"Let's call Ed first and find a doctor for Amanda, then we can sort out the rest of this," Winston said, as he dialed the clinic's number. "Who am I speaking to? Gladys, good, have you heard from Ed? This is Winston. We haven't met. I'm Dr. McDermott's father-in-law."

"Glad to meet cha, Winston. Stop by any time. I just got a hold of Doc, and he said to tell Maria that Dr. Roger Schumacher is a good pediatrician who's had a practice here for the past four years. According to Maisie, he seems to be doing a good job."

"Thanks, Gladys, you've been a big help." Winston hung up the phone and immediately called the doctor's office. While waiting for the receptionist, he put his hand over the receiver. "Ed gave us this doctor's name and said he's well thought of. We might as well try him. Uncovering the phone, he said, "Yes, Doctor Schumacher, my granddaughter is sick, and we were hoping you could see her as soon as possible. Yes, I'll give you the address. She's Dr. McDermott's little girl. Oh, you know where he lives, do you? Thanks so much! We'll see you in an hour or so."

"I'm glad that Dr. Schumacher is coming. I've heard that a lot of the younger doctors are asking their patients to come to their offices instead of making house calls. Imagine having to move Amanda, her being so sick and all. What is this new world coming too?" Winston, looking disgusted, shook his head.

"Oh, thank you, Winston, I don't know why I fell apart so easily. I think the move is catching up with me and I'm slightly unstrung. I'm so glad you're both here," Maria said through another wave of tears.

"Now that we have that part of the problem solved, tell me what you know about this strange call," Winston said, smiling at Maria and ignoring her tears.

"I've had two calls today—one earlier this morning and then another a few minutes ago. The first call came yesterday. At first I thought they'd stop, but with two today, I'm scared."

Winston frowned. "Not a word was said to you?"

"Not to me, but when Laura took one call for me, the person knew Laura wasn't me." Maria wiped her face, still wet from tears. "They recognize my voice. Otherwise, how did they know it wasn't me when Laura answered?"

Winston put his hand on his chin, a sure sign his mind was evaluating what she'd said. "I'll give this some thought, Maria. Now, don't you worry. We'll get to the bottom of what's going on. Share this with Ed, and have him come and talk with me."

Even though Winston's position in the State Department seemed very open and routine, her stepfather had spent many years working quietly in undercover intelligence. The tip-off to Maria was his intricate knowledge of George's OSS assignments during World War II and his war on illegal drugs. If anyone could help her, Winston could.

Maria had been up to see Amanda twice since Winston had called Dr. Schumacher. Both times, she'd been asleep, moaning and rolling in bed. Where was that doctor?

Maria agreed to help Briggie with the grocery list, but she was so worried about Amanda, it was hard to concentrate on what they needed to fill their pantry. The pleasant tune of the front door chimes announced someone's arrival, and relief flowed through Maria's body. Expecting an older doctor, she was tongue-tied for a moment as she flung the front door open and was faced with such a handsome young man carrying a medical bag. "Hi, it's good to meet you, Dr. Schumacher. Thanks so much for coming on such short notice."

"No problem. Things are pretty quiet right now. A lot of my patients are either vacationing or sitting around a pool. The only people working are farmers and your husband." He laughed and his eyes twinkled. "So, where's my patient? I hope she's feeling better."

Amanda was awake and taking a sip of water when Maria and the doctor walked into her room. "Honey, this is Dr. Schumacher. He is a kid's doctor and will help you get better."

He caught Maria's attention. "Mrs. McDermott, where can I wash my hands?"

"Down the hall, first door on the left."

"Thank you." He smiled at Amanda. "I'll be right back and take a look at you, young lady." After he stepped back into the room, he proceeded with a careful examination of Amanda, asking questions as he teased her and made her laugh. He finished and told her he'd give her a shot and some pills that would make her feel better.

Amanda's eyes widened when she heard the word *shot*, but she bit her lip and nodded.

"I'll be right back after I see the doctor out, Amanda," Maria said as they walked out of the room. They moved downstairs. "So, what's wrong with her?"

"She has a bacterial infection caused by contact with impure water. She mentioned swimming every night in the motel pools on her way here. My guess is that's where she got it. Her throat, tonsils, and ears are badly infected. The shot will work wonders. Have her continue with the pills for seven more days. After that, she'll be fine. Call me if she hasn't improved."

"I was scared that she might have polio, even though she had the vaccine. What was in the shot you gave her and the pills I'll be giving her?"

"Penicillin—an antibiotic that fights bacterial infections better than anything doctors have ever had. It's safe and has been on the market for a while."

32. Impetuous Actions

Summer 1963
(Maria)

"Mom, let's get Grandma. I want to see my friend Lois. I haven't seen her since yesterday." Amanda sounded very impatient.

When did this new behavior start? She's growing up.

"I'm almost ready. I just have to ask Briggie if I can pick up anything for her on our shopping trip. Why don't you bring Grandma over here?" *Anything to get Amanda out of my hair, so I can think.* As Maria watched her healthy girl run across the patio, she thanked God.

She turned to Briggie. "Please be careful when you speak on the phone, and please caution Laura not to answer it. I think I've had ten calls in the past several weeks from our silent enemy. Don't mention I'm away. Just say I'm busy and don't want to be disturbed."

"Missy, you don't suspect that Laura has anything to do with this, do you?"

"I don't know, but Winston told me exactly what to do. Oh, and be sure Laura stays out by the pool the entire time the girls are swimming."

With a nod of agreement from Briggie, Maria checked her purse, making sure she had the grocery list and the window measurements for each window. She was confidant they were perfect. Ed had helped her measure. She loved his interest in every detail when she asked for his help. She was ready to shop!

Giving Wiggles a final pat and making sure she had water and food, she heard Amanda chattering to her grandmother as they walked in. "Hi, Mom, ready for our first shopping foray?"

Her mother laughed. "You know this is my cup of tea, Maria. After Oak Park, we'll tackle Chicago."

Amanda had disappeared into the garage, and when she returned, she rushed past Maria and her mother. "I'll be right back. I forgot something."

"Come out the kitchen door. We'll be waiting, Toots. Get going!" Maria turned to her mother. "She's been driving me crazy all morning with wanting to leave, and now that we're ready, she's forgotten something. Isn't that just like a kid?"

Jumping in the car, Amanda said, "I couldn't forget my cards. Lois and I love to play."

Pulling up in front of the well-designed Bellinger's home set back in the woods, Maria couldn't help but admire the dwelling. *That's what I wish we had.*

"Missy, don't forget the plan Lois's mom and I made for your day together. After lunch, she'll drive you two back to our house and you can swim when Laura is free to watch you—not before. It's very important you have an adult there in case anything happens. Understand?"

"I promise, Mommy. Now let me go so I can see my friend."

Maria watched her bundle of energy run up to the front door and ring the bell. When Lois's mother, Alicia, came to the door, she waved and ushered Amanda in, and Maria waved back and called, "Thank you."

"Whew, now we can think about where we want to go and what we want to accomplish," Maria said, shifting George's sports car into gear and settling into driving. After a moment or two, Maria said, "I'm thrilled Amanda snapped back quickly with the medicine Dr. Schumacher gave her. She gave me a scare. All I could think of was polio. I shouldn't be so impatient with her."

"You're only normal, Maria. You weren't harsh—you were just being a good mother. Her mother paused for a moment, then took a deep breath. "I hate to ask, but I must. Anymore phone calls?"

"Since my breakdown with you and Winston, I've been keeping track, and I think I've had about ten more. Sharing the scary stuff with you folks helped me."

"I've heard Winston on the phone to Washington several times, but he hasn't offered me any information, so I don't ask. I've found that Winston will tell me everything he thinks I need to know and nothing more. I've given up ever trying to question him. He's a master at spinning a yarn that is so farfetched it makes me laugh. I'm sure he'll tell us all something soon."

"I know, Mom. George was the same way. Those intelligence guys are all alike."

"Have you mentioned the calls to Ed?"

"No, I don't want to put one more thing on Ed's plate. He can't do anything about it—only Winston can."

Spotting Marshall Field's famous clock as they drove into the shopping district of Oak Park brought back lots of memories for Maria and her mother. They'd shared many shopping trips before the big breakup between her parents. When she was in junior high, she couldn't understand why her beloved daddy wanted to leave them and marry another woman. As an adult, she'd forgiven him, but what he did still hurt.

Maria turned into the familiar parking lot. "Mom, a penny for your thoughts."

"I thank God every day for Winston, Maria. I've never been so loved and so happy. I'm actually glad your father divorced me because out of that painful situation came a life with Winston.

"Good. I'll call Dad up and invite him right over. You can introduce him to Winston." She winked at her mother and said, "I was only teasing."

After spending an hour in the household department ordering all the window blinds, drapes, and curtains, they wandered into the clothing departments.

"We've got to leave before I buy any more clothes for the McDermotts. But we needed everything, especially for the kids."

"Shopping's hard work, I'm hungry. How about lunch, Maria?" As they headed for the tea room on Marshall Field's top floor, Maria said, "It's nice to have a day shopping and doing our girl stuff. I missed it when we lived in Washington."

"Me too, honey. The move was the right thing to do. A change for the better, I believe. Winston and Ed certainly get along, and the kids seem happy. So are we."

"I hate to mention this, but it looks like our lives are going to become more hectic. Ed wants to do something for my birthday. He also feels we need to have a party for all the breeders and a few local bigwigs this fall. Peter is coming to his shrink conference, as he calls it, in a couple of weeks and wants to see us. Elena has an art show in Chicago sometime this fall and wants to spend time with us, and we should get together with Ed's family and May's family, too."

"You know I'll help all I can, including calling May and asking them to visit."

"Now that I'm married to Ed, it feels like he wants me to present a good image to the community as his new bride and quell any gossip about us. It's not his fault. He's just knows small town folks.

"You know how little social life George and I had. If it wasn't for you and Winston, I wouldn't have ever gone anywhere. He did all his entertaining when he was traveling, so when he was home, he wanted peace and quiet. I would have liked to have had friends in, but he never encouraged me in any way. After a while, I gave up."

"George wasn't cut out to be a family man. Winston and I were heartsick with how he began treating you, and we were so glad to be there for you."

"Well, it's over, and I have a darling husband who is entirely different from George. He loves my kids. But guess what? We had a long talk about having more children, and he said he didn't want to risk losing me due to complicaitons. Isn't that adorable? I'm fine with that."

"That's music to my ears, Maria. I was worried about you, too."

Their waitress appeared with their salads and iced tea. "Perfect timing," her mother said. "I'm hungry."

"Having you and Winston across the patio from us makes me so happy. That rascal, Ed, was thinking about our arrangement when he started visiting me in Washington. Remember that night when he asked Winston out of the blue if he'd considered retiring?"

"I do, and I was surprised by his question, but I'm glad Ed planted the seed. Winston is very happy being here. After we visited you waitressing at the King's Resort those many years ago, he fell in love with the Midwest."

"This is my treat, Mom. Ed even mentioned it. We're so grateful to have you so close."

"All right, if you let me give you some of my Oriental rugs I brought from Washington. They belonged to Winston's first wife. With downsizing, I can't use all of them, and they'll look beautiful in your living and dining rooms."

"What a deal—a five-dollar lunch for your gorgeous rugs. Are you sure?"

"Absolutely! Now, let's go and give our table to some tired shoppers." Her mother stood, and holding her back, stretched. "Are you done for the day? I am." Walking out, arm in arm with her mother, Maria asked, "Is your back okay?"

"Don't worry. I've just been doing more physical things than I've done in a while."

"Good, because we still have to shop at the grocery store for Briggie on the way home. How do you like having your dinners with us?"

"It's fine, but I'm making progress with getting Sarah to do more cooking for me now that she has cleaned every inch of our little place. She says she likes to cook, but she's never had a chance to do much on her own." Her mother chuckled. "She says her mother runs her kitchen like an army sergeant."

They stepped into the elevator. "I need to do a little shopping on my own, so let me out on the second floor" her mother said. "I'll meet you in the cosmetic section in a few minutes. "She grinned at her perplexed daughter. "You'll find out all about this in a few days."

Maria stopped on the main floor to replenish her makeup supplies that she hadn't thought about for a year or so.

A smiling, well made-up cosmetician immediately appeared as if by magic and gave Maria a great big smile. "What can I show you today? We're having a special on foundation, eye cream, wrinkle cream, and blush."

"I need a few things. I want to look beautiful for my husband and hide the little lines creeping in around my eyes." The wily salesgirl had a look of dismay and acted as if Maria's skin was beyond repair. Maria stopped the salesgirl's automatic practiced routine to sell Maria many more products than she needed. "Please, just a new lipstick, some blush, and wrinkle cream for my eyes. My husband doesn't like any makeup on me."

"Hi, Maria. Good timing for both of us," her mother said, carrying several bags with her.

"Can I peek?"

"No," her mother said with a twinkle in her eyes. Let's go and get Briggie's groceries. "I'll buy them. That's the least I can do, eating with you every night."

"Besides making me happy, Ed really loves talking to Winston. He calls him his favorite uncle and makes reference to wishing his family was like mine. He said we have to bite the bullet and ask his mother and father to visit soon. We're going to need you and Winston to come for moral support. You'll understand when you meet them," Maria said, making a face.

As they loaded the groceries in the trunk of the car, Maria said, "It's late. We'll be home in about fifteen minutes. Hang onto your hat."

"You're a good driver. I'll just shut my eyes if I get scared," her mother said.

"Here we are, safe and sound," Maria said as she turned onto their road. A black car drove by her as fast as though the devil was chasing it. It flew down the road and disappeared. "Who was that? I'm sure glad we didn't run into him," Maria said as she pulled up to her house.

"Crazy people!" Her mother shook her head, then stepped out of the car. "I can't wait to see our windows after we get everything that we bought put up. We'll have the installers come and do both houses the same day." She grabbed her packages from the back seat. "See you, later. I'm anxious to see what Winston has been up to all afternoon."

"Don't go until you hear what I have to tell you both," Briggie said, running up to them. "Missy, something strange happened today," Briggie whispered.

"Are the girls all right?" Maria worried that one of them had been hurt.

"They're fine. The girls played beautifully together."

"Mr. Brooks came over this afternoon and asked me to take a rest and sit out on the patio for a while with Laura and the girls who were playing in the pool. I didn't mind, but when he said not to come in until he came and got us, I got suspicious. Laura and I saw a man moving around our house, upstairs and downstairs. He had just left when you came in. Did you see him?"

"Yes, he blew past us like a tornado."

"Something fishy is going on in me house," Briggie said, with a scowl on her face.

Her mother looked at Maria. "Why don't you come over in a few minutes and have a drink with us? I'd like to show you the rugs I want to give you."

"I'll tell Amanda I'm home, and that I'll be over in a minute or two," Maria said, nodding to her mother.

"Miss Amanda is up on the hill with Wiggles. I told her to stay close until you got home." Briggie's eyes narrowed. "Now, what's going on?"

"I don't know until I talk to Winston." Maria tried to give Briggie a reassuring smile. "Would you call Amanda back in a little while? We should put up a bell we can ring to bring our wanderers home. I'll ask Ed about that."

Maria was dying to find out what Winston had been up to, so she followed her mother across the patio. Winston was probably playing secret agent again. It was nice to have his protection.

Winston met them at the door with a drink in his hand. "So the weary shoppers have returned. I hope you were successful." After giving his wife a kiss, he said, quietly, "A friend of mine put in some bugs on your phones. Tell Ed what I did and why. He should know. I hope he won't feel I overstepped my bounds. My friend surprised me. I thought I'd have a chance to speak to Ed before he came."

"I'll tell him tonight. He'll probably be over here to talk to you," said Maria. "How does it work?"

"Every call will be picked up on tape. The device is hidden in your attic, and the phone number will register from every location that a call is made from. My friend will be back to read the tapes and decide what to do next."

Maria could hear Amanda calling her. "Thanks so much, Winston. I hope this scary thing is over with soon. Now, I've got to go. I'll see you folks for dinner. Mom bought the groceries today, so we're eating on her dime tonight." Maria laughed with relief. Something was being done to end the calls.

Maria met Amanda halfway back to the house, and they threw their arms around each other.

"Mommy, we have to go to school tomorrow and sign me up for fourth grade. Mrs. Bellinger told me so."

"On Saturday?" That seemed odd.

"Lois's mom said the school does it on Saturday when more dads are home. All the classrooms are open from one until four. The teachers are there, and there are games to play. It's like a big party." Amanda's bright eyes sparkled with anticipation.

"We'll go. I have all your school records for them. Now tell me, did you have fun with your new friend, Lois?"

"Yes, and Mommy, Lois is my best friend. She told me so today. We're going to be in fourth grade together."

Maria heard Chris talking to Briggie in the kitchen, making her laugh. He must have come home with Ed. She ran up the stairs and heard the shower running. She laid the cosmetics she'd bought on the bureau. Odd. Her special black boxes were lying out on the top. Ed must have been in her side of the bureau. *Why?*

33. Coming Clean

August 1963

(Maria)

"Hi, handsome, how's the shower?"

"It's wonderful! Want to join me?" Ed yelled out.

"Can't! Got to help Briggie! But I want to talk to you tonight," she said over her shoulder.

Thinking about those damnable calls, Maria realized they were never made in the evening when Ed was home, only during the day when he was gone. Briggie hadn't received a single call today while Maria was away. How did the caller know that much about them?

Dinner was a big hit. Maria had bought filet mignon, a favorite of the men and easy for Briggie to serve. Looking at the bare, scarred floor in the dining room, Maria made an observation. "Our new rug from Mom will look beautiful in here once the floors are redone."

Her remark didn't seem to register with Ed who was enjoying his steak. She'd better give him the bad news. "The men are coming tomorrow to do the floors. It will take one day to sand and one day to varnish and dry. The day they varnish, we'll eat at Maisie's. Okay, sweetie?"

"Anything you want, my little organizer. Between you and Ruth, this place is going to be a show place," Ed said, sounding pleased with everything and happy with the way his money was being spent.

Well, she thought, squeamishly, *I'll not mention the agent up in our attic. My darling is too happy.*

Ed passed a basket of bread to his father-in-law. "Winston, have you tried the whole house fan yet?"

"It's capital, Ed. We love it at night, and during the day, our air conditioning units and fans make our place delightful. You should invest in some air conditioners, too."

"Daddy, tomorrow Mommy's taking me to see my new school and register me," Amanda broke in, apparently not wanting to be left out of the conversation. "I'm going to be with my best friend, Lois."

"That's wonderful, Petunia. Chris and I are going to the high school tomorrow afternoon. Sorry, I can't be in two places at once. I guess the whole school system is doing open houses. We talked about it on the way home today."

Maria glanced at her son and saw a very pleased look on his face. He had partially accepted Ed. He needed Ed more than he wanted to admit for man-to-man advice to help him grow up. Every boy needed a good father figure. Winston had been a wonderful grandfather, especially when Chris was young, but now he needed someone younger. It was only natural. It had all started last summer with the help of her brother-in-law, who had taken Chris under his wing. And now with Ed, Chris was on his way.

"Everyone, carry your dishes out to the kitchen for Briggie," Maria said, watching her daughter squirm in her seat. "It's time to get ready for bed, Amanda. Take Wiggles out and then go up and get started. I'll be up in a few minutes."

Maria was anxious for the house to settle down for the night so she could talk to Ed.

When she opened their closed bedroom door and found her handsome husband lying naked on the bed, reading a murder mystery, she impetuously jumped on the bed.

"What's in your fertile mind, Rosebud?" He closed his book and attempted to kiss her, but she wiggled away. "You look like you're ready to burst. Out with it before you do," Ed said, grinning at her. "Guess what? Glen's on duty tomorrow so we can play hard tonight. I have a question or two for you, but you go first" He tried to pull her over to him.

She wiggled farther away. "I need to strip before I do anything else and let the cool air blow over me." She lay there trying to decide how to explain something that had truly gotten out of hand. "I want you to know that I'm thrilled with the way Winston has helped us with a worry that has been plaguing me since we moved in. Hopefully, he's solved it."

Ed's demeanor changed immediately. He sat up in bed. "I thought you were going to tell me about all the nice things you bought for our house today. What's the worry you haven't shared with me?" His tone had become sharp and demanding.

Maria's stomach fluttered. She instantly was on guard. It was a reflex left over from when she lived with George and he was angry, but there was a big difference. She wasn't afraid of Ed.

Maria cleared her throat. "I'm sorry for not including you from the beginning, but I thought I was sparing you. Since the day we moved in, I've been getting phone calls with no one talking on the other end. It has scared me and made me angry. I thought the calls would stop and I wouldn't have to bother you. They didn't—they kept coming. The day Amanda got sick, I felt like I couldn't take one more thing. Have you ever felt like that?" Maria waited for his answer.

He wouldn't or couldn't answer, so she continued. "I'd called the clinic and was frantic. I wanted to talk to you for comfort and needed the name of a doctor. It seems a little ridiculous now as I am telling you, but it wasn't then. When the phone rang, I thought it was you calling me back. It wasn't. It was another one of those calls, and I lost it," Maria wailed. She began choking up as she talked. "I hadn't mentioned anything to the folks, either, because I thought I was probably overreacting, but I was cooked, done, finished. I had to talk to somebody. I ran over to Winston and told him and Mom about it, crying and being silly. I'm sure he felt sorry for me. He said he'd take care of the problem. Right then he asked me if I had talked to you and when I said no, he gave me a surprised look."

Maria tried to touch Ed to reassure herself that he wasn't angry, but he pulled away and got up, put his swim trunks on, and left the room. She heard him splashing up and down the pool for at least half an hour before he got out and returned to their room.

"Remember when I asked you to include me, no matter what?" His voice kept rising as he talked.

Maria nodded soberly, holding back her tears. Damn, she didn't want to cry. She willed herself to stop, jutted out her chin, took a deep breath, and waited. She'd been sitting on their newly acquired sofa from her mother, idly paging through Ed's book while waiting for him, and trying to think of what more to say when he came back.

"The thing that makes me furious is that you went to Winston first—not me!" His eyes dark with hurt and rage. His voice continued to grow louder. "I'm your husband. I promised you that I would take care of you and your children when I asked you to marry me. Have I ever disappointed you?" His face was flushed with anger, and his eyes had grown cold.

She was glad the house fan was whirring away up in the attic, hopefully drowning out his voice, so the children didn't hear him. Thank God their bedroom was at the other end of the house. So, this was it. They were having their first big fight, and she didn't like it. Maria took a big breath and looked him squarely in his eyes. Peter had told her that when she got into an argument, she shouldn't turn away. Instead, she needed to look at her opponent. She stared at Ed, something she could never do with George.

"You've never disappointed me in any way since we've been married, and I love you. I apologize for going to Winston before you. I wasn't thinking clearly, and I ran for Daddy. That's what Winston has been to me since I met him." Overcome with emotion, she whispered, "You have no idea how much he's stood up for me and kept me from losing my mind with George. Winston has always been there for me." Maria started to sob as all the anguish from her past life began surfacing. "I'm sure George tempered his actions around me because of Winston," she said through tears.

Maria cleared her throat and wiped her eyes. "As I said before, Winston asked me if I'd spoken to you about the problem, and when I said no, he didn't say a word, but I could tell he wasn't pleased. He said he'd like to talk to you as soon as you knew."

Maria stopped talking and started shivering. Feeling suddenly cold and sick to her stomach, she took the little summer blanket lying on the sofa and put it around her shoulders, even though the temperature in the room was hot with the door closed.

Ed had sat down on the sofa, wet trunks and all. "How can I stay mad at you? But please, try to realize I'm there for you now. I'm not like George. At least, I hope I'm not."

He pulled her close to him, hugged her, and didn't say anything more for a few minutes. "You're trembling. I can't stand doing that to you. That's what happened to you with George, isn't it?" Ed's voice was hoarse with emotion. "My little Rosebud, I'm sorry."

She hated to, but she had to finish the story. "Ed, there's more," she said, feeling his muscles tensing up in his back. He dropped his arms and waited. "When I told Winston I wanted the phone calls to stop, all I meant was I wanted them to go away. Winston got a look on his face that was all business. It was the same look he gave me when I came to him, frightened out of my mind after George tried to beat me.

"Anyway, to get back to my story, I felt better having my secret revealed. I heard Amanda calling me and went home to see what she wanted. The tip-off that Winston had started something came when Mom and I were coming home from shopping earlier today. A black car was leaving, and it flew past us driving hell bent for election. I ran over to see Winston as soon as I could. He told me a friend of his had bugged our phones, and all calls would be recorded."

Ed sat there for a moment, looking stunned beyond belief. "This reminds me of the book I'm reading—only it's really happening to us." He sat there, perfectly quiet for a moment. "So that's it? No more surprises?" He smiled and put his arms around Maria. "Don't look so stricken, my little Tiger Lily. It's okay."

Seeing him smile, Maria kissed him in relief that their big fight was over. There were moments when she thought she'd really done some permanent damage to their relationship. But Ed was a very forgiving guy, and he loved her. That made the difference.

He returned her kiss with a much longer, hot kiss. "Let me make love to you," he whispered.

Maria held her arms out to him. Nothing like a little sex to calm him down. All he wanted was to show her how much he loved her and apologize.

He laughed, picked her up, then gently tossed her on their bed and crept in beside her. She could feel his breath as he slowly made his way up her body with his lips, his breath coming in gasps as it spread out all over her body. Looking down into her eyes, he whispered, "I love you, Maria."

She could feel his body trembling as he adjusted his position next to her skin. Their emotions, raw from all the anger, surged with the relief of making up.

"This is it, baby," he whispered, and within minutes they had catapulted into wild, mounting, rhythmic movements. She clung to him as he lifted them into their final moments of ecstasy before he whispered, "Here we go, baby." The incredible feelings that passed between them in the next few moments flung them headlong into nirvana and oblivion, finally giving them their agonizing, beautiful release.

Neither one moved for a second or two. "Oh, my God, Ed, if fighting produces this kind of a finish, maybe we'd better get out our boxing gloves more often," she breathed in his ear.

He rolled over and lifted her on top of his chest and closed his eyes, holding her in his arms. "I guess this is what it's all about, my beautiful, sexy wife. Truce?" Ed asked as he opened his eyes, her face just inches from his. "I have a surprise for you. I'm going to steal you away for a promised honeymoon. Glen reluctantly agreed to work one more weekend because it's also your birthday."

Thrilled by his invitation, she propped herself up so she could look into his eyes. "Wonderful! I'll alert the troops and off we'll go. You just tell me when, but not where. I love surprises." She lay her head back down on his chest to rest and to feel his closeness. Twisting his curly, black chest hair around her fingers, she lay there relaxed with her eyes closed. In a haze, she heard him ask her another question.

"There's just one more thing. What's in the little boxes that were in your lingerie drawer?"

Coming to, she sat up. "What were you doing in there? Am I married to a guy who has a secret fetish with women's underwear?" she asked, giggling.

He cracked up in laughter. "Shall I show you what kind of a fetish I really have?"

"Save it for our honeymoon," she said, before licking his lips with the tip of her tongue and jumping out of bed. "You're obviously interested. How did you find them?"

"I actually get confused over which drawers are yours and which are mine. I'm still not used to sharing your dresser."

"Are you sure you want to see what's in Pandora's box?" she teased.

"I'm interested in anything you feel is so important that you brought them with you."

She held up a small box holding George's medals. "These were George's. A Purple Heart and a Medal of Honor he received for gallantry behind enemy lines. I'm saving them for the children."

Ed took them and examined them carefully. "I give him a lot of credit for doing what he did for our country. I wish I'd gone instead of taking a deferment."

Maria didn't know what to say. "We all make mistakes, but sometimes they turn out to be what we really needed to do, even though we didn't understand it at the time."

"Thanks, Maria," he whispered, his solemn eyes holding hers.

"Anytime, buddy," she whispered back. Maria replaced the medals in her drawer. *Time to change the serious mood.* "Now for the next box," she said, and waved it under his nose. "Guess its contents."

"A wedding ring from George, and Bill's engagement ring from your wild past."

"Very good guess, but George also gave me his mother's engagement ring from his father and a gorgeous watch to go with it. They're in here. I tried to give them back to his father, but he said I earned them. I'll give them to Amanda. George was such a snob, he didn't like my Minnie Mouse watch." Ed grinned at her remark about George and glanced at the contents.

"Now for my big finale! You open it!"

Ed sat up and took the little box from her hand. "The College Jewelry Store, Ames, Iowa," he read out loud. He opened the box and broke into a big grin, but his eyes were soon misty. "You kept the Minnie Mouse watch I gave you all those years ago?" He seemed stunned.

"I could never part with Minnie. It was such a sweet thing for you to buy her for me that cold afternoon so long ago. I've tried to get her fixed several times but no luck," she said softly, leaning over and brushing his lips with hers.

"Oh, Maria, if only I'd asked you right then to marry me, things would have been so different for both of us. We would have had children of our own." He put his arms around her, pulled her down on him and held her tightly, breathing into her hair. "One more question. What was the letter tucked into the box with all the jewelry?"

"An apology letter from George, written the night before he flew out to Oshkosh to the air show, crashed his plane, and died."

"Do you want to talk about it?"

"Sure. He asked to come back to me and start over, promising he would never leave me again if I would forgive him and give him another chance. He said he was leaving his mistress. He also willed everything he owned to me. I'm a wealthy lady, in case you're wondering."

"You've never talked much about your finances to me. Suppose we do that soon and get all our cards out on the table," he said, with a trace of irritation.

"What's your problem?" she asked, sensing his attitude change. "You've never brought up what you pay for alimony or what kind of money you make, buster. So don't be so high and mighty with me," she snapped back, tired of another interrogation.

"I'm sorry. We've both been holding out on each other because we've been burned."

"The past is gone, Ed. We have each other, and hopefully we're much wiser than before. Both of us bring baggage to this marriage.

No one escapes their past, but maybe we can change. Let's just forgive and try to forget the bad things, but keep remembering the good things."

"I agree. Peter has pounded the idea into me to let go of the past. He calls it my negativity problem and beats me up about it all the time. He says it has to do with the way I was raised. What did you think of my mother? I bet you had a huge awakening about her from my tape."

"She scared me, and I wasn't even there in your memories."

34. Family Intrigue

August 1963

(Maria)

Sounds of people moving around downstairs filtered into Maria's sleep-filled brain. She opened an eye and closed it quickly. It was so bright in the bedroom, it must be late. Ed was sound asleep next to her. She heard Briggie and the kids downstairs, which always pleased her. She loved the way Briggie talked to her kids, filling them full of stories of Ireland. She thought about Ed, their first big fight the night before, and the results. She understood him a little better now, and they both trusted each other enough to talk about their finances.

"Mom," Amanda called softly from the doorway.

Maria grabbed her nightie, slipped it on under the sheet covering them, and got up quickly. "Shush! Daddy's asleep. I'll be right down, and we can plan our day. Be a good girl, and take Wiggles out. See you in a few minutes."

"Briggie sent me up here to tell you there's a truck parked out behind the house near our garage doors," Amanda whispered back with a look of concern.

"I'll go out and investigate as soon as I come down. Don't go near that truck. Stay inside and take Wiggles to the grass by the patio and let her pee there this morning, or put her in the run to take care of it."

Amanda didn't move. "But Mommy, Grandpa asked me to get Daddy," she whispered. "He wants to talk to him now!"

"Tell Grandpa that Daddy has the day off and is still sleeping. He'll see Grandpa in a little while. Now, scoot."

What was a truck doing in her driveway? That was so strange. She showered and dressed, then ran downstairs to find her folks. They were out on the patio having a cup of coffee. "There's a truck behind our house, Winston. Come investigate with me."

Winston was up and walking toward Maria's French doors almost before she'd finished her request. She hurried to catch up with him, and she gave Briggie a thankful wave for alerting her to the unfamiliar vehicle parked out back. While Winston strode toward the truck, Maria read ATTIC REPAIRS in bold lettering on the side of it. She stood back and waited, watching Winston talking to a man in the front seat. The man got out of the truck carrying a small tool box and headed toward Maria.

"Mrs. McDermott, Adam Kowalski reporting in to service your attic and check for leaks."

Winston nodded and smiled at her, allaying her fears about the man. *What a strange way to greet me—reporting in.* Now she knew why he was there. He was an agent and friend of Winston. It was reassuring to have an agent helping them with the mystery caller, but it gave her an eerie feeling, nonetheless. She'd neglected to tell either Ed or Winston that the last call she received had a new feature—earsplitting noise in place of silence.

As Agent Kowalski disappeared through the kitchen door, she felt her home—her sanctuary—had been breached. First by the anonymous calls, and now by a man, a complete stranger, who knew the inside of her house almost better than she did.

In the kitchen, Briggie's questioning face waited for her to speak. "I'll fill you in on what's going on when I can. I'm also expecting the floor men to arrive, and when they do, send them out to me on the patio. Ed's still asleep, and I want to keep things quiet a little longer." As she was talking, she glanced out the window. Amanda was playing on the hill with Wiggles. All seemed well, yet Maria couldn't help but feel that her life was moving out of control.

Maria caught up with Winston back out on the patio.

"Is Ed around?"

"You know he's asleep. Amanda told you." Why was Winston in such a hurry to speak to Ed?

"Is he getting up soon?" Winston looked a little concerned. "I would hate to have him run into Kowalski without understanding the circumstances. I don't want a good agent to hit the floor when Ed socks him."

"I told Ed last night about the whole thing, and he got mad that I hadn't told him right away, but I cleared your part in it."

"Capital, Maria. I was concerned that I'd really overstepped my boundaries, which I've always tried to avoid. You know that, Maria."

"He's not mad at either of us. We had it out last night, so you can relax. He'll be down, and I'll ask him to stop by your place so you two can talk." Maria had just turned to ask her mother a question when she was stopped by the tense expression on her mother's face.

Focusing on something behind Maria, her mother said, "Hi, Ed. It's nice to see you this morning."

Ignoring his mother-in-law's greeting, Ed roared, "Who in the hell is in our house, Winston? As I was coming out of my bedroom, some guy was pounding down the stairs ahead of me. I yelled at him, but he just kept going like the devil." Ed stood there, his arms folded across his chest, waiting for an answer.

Winston stood up slowly. "Agent Kowalski is the best in the business, and I'm sure he didn't want to have a discussion about why he was there and what he was doing," he said calmly. "He might have thought you were the culprit. That's why he took off."

"Agent who and what is he doing in our house?" Ed asked, slightly more relaxed in both his body and voice. "We can talk in my study or at your place, it makes no difference to me. I just want some answers."

Breathing a sigh of relief, Maria sat down next to her mother who was fascinated with the whole episode.

"Ed certainly loves his home, doesn't he?" Her mother put her arm around Maria and said, "Relax."

"I'm just finding out how intense his feelings are about home and hearth." With the men still in Ed's study, Maria sat back, and followed her mother's suggestion. "Mom, yesterday was fun, wasn't it? I can't believe all that we accomplished.

"Now that the fireworks are over, I must tell you. Ed asked me to go away for my birthday next weekend and I agreed. I should have checked with you first about taking care of Amanda Saturday and part of Sunday. I can back out if you don't feel you can do it." Maria waited for an answer. She shouldn't have been so quick to agree with Ed.

"Of course! I'll look forward to it. What about Chris?" Her mother sounded a little concerned.

"I don't think you'll see him. Between his work and his friends, he's a will-o'-the-wisp around here. Just concentrate on Amanda and call if you need to. I'll give you the hotel's phone number when I get there.

"Which brings me to the next question I was about to ask when my raging knight came charging in here this morning. Do you want to go with me and Amanda to see her school today? They're having an open house to meet the teachers before the first day of class. It's so civilized to do it this way. Oh, and Mom, do you want the floor men to look at your floors when they finish with mine?"

"Yes to both questions. Seeing where Amanda will be this year means a lot to me. I can pick her up easily then, if I have to. As for my floors, they got all scuffed up by the idiot movers walking around on the newly varnished floors and not covering them properly. Send your men over."

"I think I hear a truck now. I'll let them in." Maria jumped up and ran through her house to the kitchen door. "Come in, men, and get started. When you finish with mine, my mother wants to have you look at hers. You'll have plenty of business for a day or two with us."

"We'll do that, missus. Now, where do you want us to start?"

"Upstairs. Just one sleepy head's in bed, and I'll get him up." On her way out, Maria turned back. "The floors will be quite a challenge for you."

"Don't worry, missus. They'll be beautiful when we finish."

Climbing the stairs, she heard Ed and Winston coming out of the study, laughing. *I bet Ed told Winston an off-color joke or two. How he can remember them is beyond me.*

After alerting Chris to get up, she heard more guffaws coming from the kitchen. The floor men were doubled over in laughter, Winston was chuckling, and Ed was standing there enjoying himself immensely. *More jokes, no doubt.* How different Ed's home was from George's.

"Well, gentlemen, whenever you're ready," Maria said, looking at the floor men. "Start your machines."

"Daddy, you're home!" Amanda said, slightly out of breath, as she came in the kitchen door with her dog. Wiggles scooted around the congregation to get to her breakfast. "Where's Briggie, Mommy?"

"I'm right here. I was putting in a load of wash and getting some groceries from the pantry," Briggie said with her hands full. "What does me darlin' girl want?"

"I just wanted to know where you were," Amanda said, hugging her friend's big, round middle.

Now that everyone was there, and the workers were in place, it was a perfect time to move on with their day. "Ed, why don't we go out for lunch and dinner today to escape the noise and mess from the workers?"

"Fine with me. Briggie, Ruth, Winston, are you game?"

"We are," Winston quickly agreed. "Ruth hates to cook in a mess. She'll be delighted." Winston's expression made Maria wonder what he was up to. "What are your plans for this afternoon, Maria? Busy with shopping or something?"

"We're going to see Amanda's school, meet her teacher, and hopefully some other friendly parents." Maria was still looking at Winston. "Briggie, come with us for lunch, and we'll drop you back home afterward."

Winston immediately smiled. "I've got a great idea, Ed. Why don't I tag along with you and Chris, see his high school, and afterward, we can stop in at the country club and hit a few balls with Chris?"

Her mercurial-tempered husband had quickly rebounded from his outrage just minutes before. His swift recovery was refreshing. George would go for days after a fight, silent and unwavering in his misery.

From the very first, when Winston met Ed, they'd formed a mutual admiration society. Why else did Winston, astute in money matters, decide to back Ed's dream of a clinic with an investment of ten thousand dollars. As men, they looked to each other for support.

"Men, we're picking up Lois and her mom, so take your own vehicle. I'm driving the sports car." Maria saw Ed's face fall, and she laughed. "Just kidding! You can drive the red, hot one. We'll take Winston's boring family car."

"Let's get ready to go. I'm hungry; I'll alert Ruth," Winston said.

Ed and Winston felt so comfortable in Maisie's café that they immediately started pushing two tables together.

That brought Maisie over in a hurry. "Well, I never, the whole kit and caboodle has come for lunch. Have you quit yet, Bridget? Ed's a pain to work for, isn't he?" She put her arm around Ed's waist and grinned up at him, then looked at Alicia and Lois. "How did you nice folks get hooked up with this scallywag?"

"We're going to see my new school this afternoon, and Lois is my best friend," Amanda piped up.

"That's nice, you kids have fun," she said, her tone changing from teasing to more serious. "Are you wading through the dust and dirt up there, Maria? Ed's a great vet, but a terrible housekeeper." Maisie winked and handed them their menus. "I'll get a waitress over here pronto to take your orders. I recommend our delicious pork barbeque sandwich."

236

"Maisie, thanks for your help with finding floor men. They happen to be working on our floors as we speak."

"Glad to do it. How are those girls working out for you?"

Maria smiled. "Wonderful! What would this town do without you?"

Maisie's face flushed as she turned away to summon a young waitress, who hurried over and took their orders. Everyone ate in record time, anxious to move on to their exciting afternoon activities—visiting the kids' schools and the men golfing at the country club.

35. Cliques

August 1963
(Maria)

The school parking lot was full of trucks and cars, the trucks outnumbering the cars. "I like the idea that a lot of parents are here. It looks like a thriving community," Maria said, as she slipped into a space that someone had just vacated. "I'm also glad we're all here together. It makes me feel more like we belong."

"The girls certainly are excited," Alicia said, as they walked quickly to catch their daughters.

The school building, while old, was meticulously clean inside, well built, and all on one floor. Each classroom had a large bank of newly washed windows and an outside door that faced a sunny courtyard filled with picnic tables and benches. How charming to have the option to eat and have classes out there.

They found Amanda and Lois's classroom easily. Miss Hollister, their teacher, introduced herself and encouraged everyone to wear name tags to make socializing easier. Maria could immediately see the cliques of long-time friends forming in the room. They were laughing and catching up on what had happened in each other's lives over the summer. Miss Hollister made it a point to seek out the new children like Amanda and spend time with them. Maria had a good first impression of the teacher. She seemed to be a caring person, which was so important for teachers in the lower grades. Amanda would have a good experience in her classroom.

After a well-presented program of the subjects she planned to teach, Miss Hollister served cake, iced tea, and lemonade. It felt like a party. Food shared made a more relaxed atmosphere. Soon the kids were running around and talking with each other. Lois never left Amanda. Like a true friend, Lois took Amanda everywhere and introduced her to her last year's friends. They acted almost like twins.

The cliques dissolved after the initial excitement of seeing each other again had worn off, and the parents took their children and left. A few of the more extroverted parents came up to Maria and introduced themselves. She had the distinct feeling that several of the women seemed overly interested in meeting the new wife of Dr. McDermott. Maria spotted two well-dressed women moving in her direction. She stood a little taller and took a deep breath. Her still small voice of intuition whispered to her to present a solid front to the women who closed in on her.

Touching her mother's shoulder, Maria said softly, "Don't look now, but two society queens are bearing down on us."

Their stance in front of Maria was one of silent aggressiveness. Matching their posture, Maria waited. She'd stopped talking or gesturing with her hands, and she'd put her arms down by her sides. Uncomfortable silence lingered.

"Hello, Mrs. McDermott," one of the ladies said, finally initiating conversation. "I'm Babs Decker, and this is my friend, Lydia Farmingale," Babs said in a soft but pseudo-sophisticated manner. "We're looking forward to coming to your party this fall, and we're anxious to see how you've decorated that wreck of a house I used to live in. Do you have a fourth grader, or are you just visiting?" She was obviously probing for information, but Maria didn't respond to her questions. "Everyone was amazed when Ed announced at one of the parties last year that he was planning on getting married *again*." She laughed as though she'd just said something hilarious. "Ed's track record was five years with me, and he dumped his last one in just a couple of years. So watch out, your time clock is ticking." Her beautiful face convulsed in laughter.

A perfect comeback popped into Maria's head at that perfect moment. "Thanks for the warning. Now I'll share one with you, Babs," she said in a firm, crisp voice. "Always keep your words soft and sweet, just in case you have to eat them. They digest better."

The two women's jaws dropped, and their eyes looked like they were ready to pop out of their sockets. Maria forced a tiny smile on her face, then turned away without saying another word to the social queens. The two women clung to each other and melted in with the last few remaining adults on the room.

Her mother and Alicia had stood nearby, listening to the conversation.

Maria gave a slight nod toward the door. "Let's collect the girls and make our excuses." Beckoning Amanda and Lois, she waved good-bye to Miss Hollister. "It's time to go home," she said triumphantly to her little group.

While making her way to the car, Maria played back the last scene in her mind with delight. She'd been weaned on women like that in suburban La Grange, Illinois. They seemed to be everywhere—at parties she attended with George in Washington, DC, at the posh resort she worked at, and also prevalent in her children's private school in Maryland.

"Well done, my girl." Her mother practically beamed. "You handled them beautifully."

"I agree, Maria. I wish I could be so brave." Alicia's tone was one of amazement. "Babs Decker comes from a lot of money and usually intimidates everyone—but not you."

Her mother nodded. "My first husband always told me that no matter how much money you have, you still have to put your clothes on like everybody else."

Maria turned to her happy little group. "How about a swim and some lemonade, everyone?"

"Yes!" two very happy and red-faced little girls shouted together.

Maria grinned at her mother and drove out, a little faster than necessary.

"Mom, I love Miss Hollister. And besides, her cake was yummy," Amanda yelled to her mother as Maria speeded a little, reveling in her coup. The wind from the open windows swirled around the inside of the car, blowing their hair and cooling them all down.

Maria dropped off Lois and Alicia on their way home, and again invited them to take a dip in their pool when they were ready to come over. As soon as Maria, her mother, and Amanda arrived home themselves, Wiggles barked her greeting. Amanda bounded out of the back seat of the car, ran past Maria, and said she was going to rescue Wiggles from loneliness.

Still proud of herself, Maria felt charged for handling the sparring session with Babs. She ran upstairs, changed into her suit, challenged Amanda to play in the pool with her, and ran headlong downstairs, giddy with her win.

With a pitcher of lemonade in one hand and cups in the other, Maria laughed when she spotted Briggie sitting on the pool steps, her skirt above her knees, and her bare feet dangling in the water. "I see my cook is enjoying herself for a change. Good for you, Briggie."

Once again, Maria felt a little guilty over her neglect of Briggie's feet. Promising herself to call Dr. Bentley, her old boss's husband, for an orthopedic exam for Briggie, she dove into the deliciously cooling water that flowed over her body like silk and made her feel like she was twenty-one again.

Making its regular journey across the sky, the late afternoon sun had dropped behind the trees when Maria, her mother, and Alicia dragged themselves out of the water. The girls had stopped earlier, their need to talk with each other more important than pool play. Lying on their towels with drinks in hand, they were emitting gales of laughter.

As the women were drying off, Winston appeared in his doorway, dressed in swimming trunks and with a drink in his hand.

Maria smiled at him. "Where are the other men in my life?"

He ignored her and strode over to Alicia, then introduced himself. "Did you have a nice swim?"

"Yes, I did. I'm Alicia Berringer, Lois's mom. We live down the road."

"Where do you live, precisely? You see, I'm trying to learn my way around here, and I have yet to understand these back roads."

"We live about a half a mile on this road. Our name is on the mailbox, so you can't miss us. We're so glad to have such nice neighbors living here now. My little girl, Lois, really enjoys Amanda."

What had it been like when Ed's other wives lived there? If only she could ask Alicia. Maybe when they became better friends Alicia could offer some insight.

Winston turned his attention to Maria. "Your men, as you put it, are walking around on your property somewhere. Ed wanted to show Chris the lay of the land, so to speak."

Alicia got up, called to Lois, and waited. Lois ignored her and whispered something in Amanda's ear. "Lois, it's time to go and make dinner," Alicia said firmly, her tone making it clear that she was losing her patience.

Maria walked Alicia to the door, and Lois straggled behind.

"Thanks for such a great time today. Lois and I really enjoyed it." Alicia's voice caught, and she quickly wiped tears from her eyes. It's very lonely here for Lois and I. My husband travels a lot. I'm so happy you've moved in.

"We'll do lots more things together, Alicia." Maria offered a genuine smile. "I need friends, too."

"Mom, I wish we could stay with our friends tonight," Lois whined. "It's lonely without Daddy."

By Alicia's pained expression, Lois had struck a nerve "Come on, honey, we'll have fun. We'll play games, have our dinner on the coffee table, and watch a show on the new television set Daddy bought us."

What was Alicia's husband like? Hopefully, not like George. Though traveling on the weekend seemed odd.

36. Man to Man

August 1963

(Ed)

Up on the hill, Ed and Chris were standing together looking over the landscape.

"Ready to go?" Ed surveyed his meadow. "I want to show you where I'll put the barn."

They moved down the other side of the hill and across the meadow.

"Thanks for coming with me to the school today," Chris stammered. "It was a new experience."

"What was? Having me there or seeing your new school?"

"Both, but especially having an older guy with me."

"I was glad to be there and see the high school myself. I'd never been there in all the years I've lived here." Ed paused. "I have an idea what it feels like to be out there on your own. I was, for most of my young life, because of a well-meaning but alcoholic father who tried but couldn't make it."

Chris stopped in his tracks. "I thought you must have had a wonderful life being such a good vet and having this great place." Chris was quiet for a moment or two. "You also know how to talk to my mother and sister."

"Being a vet came fairly easy. I had to work hard, but I knew how to do that. If I worked, everything fell into place. Relationships with women are different. I've made plenty of mistakes with them, but the one thing I finally figured out was to marry your mother.

"Before we decided our marriage might work, she suggested I see Dr. Rudolph, a shrink in Washington. Thanks to her, I went every time I came out to visit you. At first, I didn't want to go, but little by little he helped me. He's coming to a big psychiatric conference in a couple of weeks, and he plans on staying with us part of the time. I think you'll like him. He's quite a guy."

"I remember Mom mentioning his name a few times. My dad went to see him because the war had messed him up so badly, and then my folks went to see him after they were married."

With their long legs and fast strides, they crossed the meadow quickly and ended up near a forest. "Here's where I want to put the barn, next to my forest. I thought your mother and I could ride there. She likes nature, flowers, and all that stuff. What do you think?"

"It's a long ways from the house."

"That's the idea. Less odor and flies. Although I'm going to have a farmer haul away the bedding from the stalls religiously. Remember those golf carts we saw with Winston today at the country club?" Ed chuckled thinking about his plan. "I'm going to get one to drive back and forth to the barn. You and Amanda can drive it because it's on our property."

"That's great, Ed. They looked like fun." Chris's eyes grew wide with interest. "How many acres do you have?"

"I started out with ten, but had a chance to buy about forty more, so I now own that forest behind you. It stretches way back there. The farmer who owned it needed some ready cash, so I made a deal. I'm going to fence it in when things quiet down, but life has been hectic lately. I'm sorry I haven't had a chance to talk with you sooner."

"That's okay. I never got to talk to my dad about anything important. He was always gone," Chris said bitterly. "I used to ask Mom if he liked me, and she said he showed his love by paying for everything for me, like my school tuition, food, and stuff like that. But you know, I didn't care a damn about those things." His eyes filled up with tears. "I just wanted to be with him and talk to him. You know, get to know him, just like we're doing, Ed," Chris quickly wiped his eyes with his hand.

"You're a great kid, Chris, and I'm glad you're part of my family." Ed put his arm around him for a moment. "Let's go sit by the stream. It's nice down there."

The little brook was barely trickling now, almost dried up because of the hot, dry August weather. Chris sat and watched a few blades of grass he tossed into it float away. Neither one of them said anything for a while.

Birds were calling, the stream was gurgling, and leaves on the trees fluttered in the early, evening breeze. Ed felt the peace of the meadow as the sun gave way to nightfall.

After a few minutes, Chris finally blurted out, "I always blamed my mother as the reason my dad stayed away. I wanted her to make a fuss over him the way I used to see some of the women at parties did. Mom seemed so quiet around him. I thought she must have hurt his feelings." Chris cleared his throat and looked at Ed. "She changed when you started coming out to Washington. She acted like a kid and was so happy. I used to ask myself why she was so nice to you and not to my dad. She began joking with all of us, hugging us at odd moments, and talking about things she hadn't ever mentioned before.

"Then I began watching you and realized you were nice to her, too—not like my dad. You hugged her, held her hand, kidded with her, and once in a while, I saw you kiss her when you thought we weren't around." Chris paused and took a deep breath. "I realized that was the difference—the way you treated *her*."

"It's called being in love with each other, Chris. That's the difference."

Chris looked away for a moment, then turned back. "How do I talk to a girl like you do? I want a girlfriend, but I freeze."

Ed studied Chris, delighted that his stepson wanted his advice. "How you feel about a girl is the most important thing. The rest will come later if the special girl you picked out gives you a look that says I'm interested. You'll know the instant it happens." Ed offered a smile in encouragement. "Is there anyone in particular that gives you that feeling?"

"Yah, Laura, the girl who works for my mom. I've seen her several times when she's leaving and I'm coming in. She smiled at me, once or twice. She's pretty, and Mom likes her. So does Amanda, so I figure she must be nice, and I get a feeling, like you said, when I see her."

"Have you met any other girls since working here this summer?"

"Lots. They bring their pets into Dr. Glen at the clinic all the time with their folks."

"So, for now, she's the one?" Ed waited for an answer.

"Right, she's the one," Chris said, but hesitated. His face turned the color of a ripe tomato. "When you were my age, did you ever feel like things were going on in your body that you couldn't control?"

"All the time—even now. Did you ever wonder why men wear tight jeans?" Ed laughed and tousled Chris's hair. "It helps take care of that part of the male anatomy."

"Gosh, Ed, sometimes I get embarrassed and have to walk away. I know the girls think I don't like them, but I like them too much."

Chris's serious expression broke into a big, relaxed grin. "Thanks, it's great to talk to you."

"Just remember . . . when you see her or any other girl you like, go up to them and say hi. You'll know immediately if they're interested in you by what they do. They might giggle and smile, say hi back, or ask you a question. If Laura does that, it's a sure sign she's interested. Take your time. If the chemistry is there, you'll know it, and so will the girl." Ed started to get up, then changed his mind and sat down. "I'm sure you know all about breeding, working in the clinic. Just remember, it only takes one time. Carry condoms with you in case you get lucky." He laughed and so did Chris.

"According to the locker room guys, it happens all the time, but I don't believe them."

"I was never in the locker rooms going to school, because I had to take care of the farm when my dad couldn't. Sports were out for me," Ed said with a note of bitterness in his voice. "But from what I could gather, guys do a lot of bragging about things they wish they really did."

37. The Success of a Reunion Hinges on the People Involved

August 1963
(Maria)

On Sunday morning, before the pressures of the day crowded in around her, Maria crept downstairs to their study, planning on making long overdue phone calls to family and friends. Her most pressing call was to Peter. Using the emergency number he'd given her long ago, she dialed. It rang and rang. She prayed for him to pick up.

"Hello, Dr. Rudolph here. This'd better be important," he said gruffly.

"Peter, it's Maria. I'm calling from St. Charles, Illinois." She found herself hurrying, as if what she had to say was boring and he wouldn't listen. "We made it safe and sound, and I'm sitting in Ed's study calling people to make amends for ignoring them. You happen to be my first call."

His voice tone changed immediately. "It's good to hear from you," he said slowly. "I was just thinking about my trip to the Windy City, and I was wondering how the big move affected everybody's nerves."

"We're making it, Peter—so far. I made one bad decision by reverting back to my behavior while living with George. I ran to Winston for help on a situation instead of talking to Ed about it first. Ed blew up. I realized my mistake and apologized. He cooled down, and we're learning how to live with each other and fit the kids in there, too. I'm trying, Peter."

"Any regrets? I keep waiting for you to run out of old boyfriends so I can make my move." He laughed and quickly asked about the kids.

"You've made that same comment before. I never know if you're kidding or not. For a psychiatrist, you're not very clear. As for the kids, Amanda adores Ed, and Chris is beginning to warm up little. Oh, and Peter, Chris actually likes me again, too."

"Let me guess. He's getting interested in girls."

"Yes, I think so. He and Ed spent a lot of time together yesterday, and I had a feeling they weren't just talking about sports all that time. But why does that affect the way he is with me?"

"Boys have to separate from their mothers, and it's hard, especially if the father is gone. When they find girls, they feel a lot of relief because they can relax around mom, have a girlfriend, and not worry about loving their mother incestuously."

"Peter, you always help me understand my life, my husband, and my kids. Thanks for the phone counseling."

"That bit of wisdom just paid for my room and board at the McDermott home when I come to visit. Which reminds me, I need your new phone number, address, and some directions." He took time to write down everything Maria thought would be helpful. "Don't file for divorce until after I go. I'm looking forward to seeing your family intact. Regards to the good doctor! See you in a couple of weeks."

After she hung up, Maria sat there smiling at Peter's truthful help with Chris. But it still felt a little unsettling that he'd never responded to her question about his interest in her. Penciling in Peter's visit on their big desk calendar, Maria congratulated herself for reaching the illusive Dr. Rudolph and having a fairly normal conversation with him.

Before she made any more calls, she'd brew some fresh coffee. Maria stood in the shadows of the kitchen, which still felt pleasantly cool while shrouded in darkness. The coffee maker began to gurgle, announcing to the household it was making coffee and sending out its intoxicating aroma. Impatient for it to finish, she fingered the new blinds. They were good looking and blocked the summer heat. Come winter, she'd welcome the sun's rays bursting through the kitchen's large window, but not now.

She sipped her first taste of coffee. *Yum.* Opening the kitchen door to watch the quiet day unfolding before her, she saw Wiggles in her run, sitting quietly. "What a dear little dog you are," she murmured. That brought Wiggles over to the fence, tail wagging. "Amanda will take you out in a little while," Maria said, laughing at herself for talking to a dog.

Cup in hand, and returning to the study, Maria anticipated talking to her dear Elena. It wasn't too early to call, but she waited, those precious, quiet moments she had would soon be lost in the clamor and demands of her husband and family.

"Hi," a male voice croaked.

Had she dialed the wrong number? "Is this Elena Avila's home?" she asked, haltingly.

"Yes, is this Maria?" The man's response was rather exuberant.

"Bill Morgan, is that you?"

"In person, or at least a phone person. Elena went out for coffee. I surprised her last night when I flew in from Heathrow."

"I'm calling to let her know that we made it to St. Charles with nary a bump or bruise."

"Was she supposed to call you? You know Elena. When she gets started on her next show, she loses track of everything else."

"Bill, I want you to know that when we left the East for good, the one thing that helped me leave Elena was you being with her."

"Thanks, Maria." He paused. "I wish things . . . I hear Elena coming in. I'd better help her with her bundles," Bill said, softly. "I'll have her call you, but I can't promise when. Give me your address and phone info for both of us. I may stop in sometime when I'm between flights in Chicago."

She waited for him to get something to write on, then filled him in. "We'd love to see you anytime. Just call to make sure we're here."

"Say hi to Doc, Maria." Bill was silent for a moment. "How is the old boy? He's a good guy. I'll never forget how nice he was after my accident. I was so distraught with my amnesia and headaches, I must have been a pretty sorry character."

"Do you have any effects from the accident?"

"No, nothing, thank goodness. You can't hurt big farm boys with hard heads."

"How are your folks? I'm going to give them a call and hope they can come see us. They're only about four or five hours from us on the new interstate."

"They'd love that." He seemed to hesitate for a moment. "You know, Maria, they've always wished we'd married," Bill said, in a tone that Maria couldn't discern.

Covering her unease, she quickly said, "Keep in touch, and so will I."

Maria could hear Briggie in the kitchen, moving around, singing along with the music on the radio Ed had bought her. Maria needed to hurry and make a quick call to her dad before the family discovered she was up.

Her father answered the phone, and Maria breathed a sigh of relief that she wouldn't have to spar with Betty in order to speak to him. Maria had finally given up trying to make friends with her father's wife. It didn't matter anymore. "Hi, Dad. It's me, Maria. How are you?"

"Trittie, is it you? Where are you?"

Smiling at her dad's nickname for her, she said, "I'm in St. Charles, Dad. Your old stomping ground. Did you get our wedding announcement last April?"

"No, I didn't, Trittie." He sounded disappointed.

Had Betty intercepted it and thrown it away? "Never mind, Dad, we're talking now. Ed, my husband, has a veterinarian practice here. He owns and runs a clinic and is doing well. We'd like to see you again. Perhaps you and Betty can come out and visit us."

"I don't think so. I don't drive very far anymore, and Betty never learned, so we rely on her brother and our two girls to take us shopping now," her father said, rather sadly.

"Then why don't we come and see you, Dad? It would be easy for us to do that."

"Well, I don't know," he said, haltingly. "I'll have to check with Betty."

Even after all those years, hearing her father rebuff her in favor of Betty hurt. His wife's hold on him had never loosened, and Betty didn't want to see Maria.

"I'll call again, Dad, in case you can see us." In one last attempt, Maria gave her frail-sounding father her phone number, hoping Betty wouldn't throw it away. "Have a nice day, Dad. I've gotta run."

Each call she'd made that morning to three important men in her life had brought up feelings she hadn't felt for a while. It was enough for one day. She'd sort it out another time. For now, she was looking forward to a swim. It was still early, and the pool was just waiting for her.

The phone ringing broke the silence and made her jump. She hadn't expected anyone to call so early. Pouncing on it, she held the phone as if it were alive and dangerous, hoping it wouldn't be one of those calls. A male voice asked to speak to Edward.

"Hello, I'm Mrs. Maria McDermott," she said exuberantly, delighted to have a real person on the line. "Who is this?"

"I'm Elmer, Edward's father," he said, sounding a bit hesitant. "You came to Edward's party before graduation, but you probably don't remember me."

Maria could hear an angry female voice in the background. "All right, Wilma," she heard Elmer say. "Hold your horses, I'll ask her. Maria, we were a wondering if'n we could come see you today? Edward's maw has really missed him and so have I."

38. A Few Words of Caution

August 1963

(Maria)

"Well, Elmer, I don't know if Ed is up yet. He has the day off from the clinic. I'll have him call you back as soon as I can," Maria said, speaking loudly and clearly into the phone.

"That will be just fine, Maria, I don't mean to be no bother," Elmer said, apologetically.

"You're not a bother, Elmer. Tell Wilma Ed will call back shortly." Somehow, Maria wanted to protect Elmer. She remembered him with kindness.

Now for her swim. She took the newly sanded stairs two at a time to find Ed and give him the message from his father. He was still in bed yawning and stretching when she ran in and gave him a big kiss.

"My gosh," he said, then kissed her back. "You're either in trouble or have done something you need to confess," he said, pulling her down on the bed and hugging her.

She was trying to sit up when Amanda appeared at the door. "Mommy, Daddy hugs you a lot. I want a hug, too." She hopped onto the bed on the other side of Ed and hugged him.

"This is quite a treat, both my girls hugging me." He put his arms around them. "What are we going to do today?"

"One thing for sure, you need to call your dad. I just spoke to him, and he said they want to come and visit us today."

Ed's entire body stiffened, and his demeanor saddened. "I'll call him. What shall I tell them about dinner?"

"I'll check with Briggie, but I think we should take them out this one time. I bet they would enjoy it immensely."

"Done. Now, ladies, let me get dressed. Scoot! I have some thinking to do."

Maria gave him another little peck. "I love you, Doc." She took Amanda's hand. "Let's go find Briggie."

"I'm hungry, and I want to see Lois today," Amanda said, completely uninterested in the fact that Ed's parents might visit them.

"Okay, go call her." So much for Maria trying to drum up some enthusiasm from her daughter.

Briggie was standing in the hall outside the door, her arms full of laundry, when Maria and Amanda stepped out of the bedroom. "I couldn't help overhearing," she said as she followed them downstairs. "Missy, stop pretending you're so happy to have Ed's parents come and relax. Your daughter knows you don't care a fig about seeing them. She can read you like a book and so can I, but Ed's a different story. I've seen that Irish husband of yours look at you with daft eyes, not knowing whether you'd be fooling him or not."

Maria sighed. "Am I that obvious? Briggie, I need your advice. Should we take Ed's folks out for dinner or should we feed them here?"

"Since his Nibs had the lovely air conditioners installed, it would be more family-like to have them here. Don't talk about not feeding two little old grandparents who have an hour or two drive. Just to make sure there will be plenty, I'll pop another chicken in the oven right now. I'm going to do my cooking for the day before it gets too hot. We'll be having a cold meal this evening—salads and sliced chicken sandwiches with me special sauce to shake up your taste buds."

While still wanting to swim, but having guilty thoughts about not helping Briggie, Maria heard a knock on the kitchen door. She pulled the door open. Standing there with two baskets in her hands was Sharon with Violet and Timmy. "For goodness sake, come in, everybody!" Maria was surprised to see her old college friend and her two children visiting so early in the morning.

Timmy dashed in and disappeared. "Quick, Amanda! Amanda, come here right now and help me!" Maria yelled, panicked Timmy might fall into the pool.

Amanda leaped into the kitchen and shrieked, "What's the matter?"

"Go find a little boy named Timmy. He's run off. Make sure he's not near the swimming pool first!" Maria shouted. Why did Sharon seem so unconcerned about her son? She and Briggie were much more interested in the fresh vegetables Sharon had brought.

"I tried to call you several times this morning to ask if we could come visit, but the phone was busy, so I just decided I'd do it. I picked the vegetables early this morning before it got hot and wanted you to have some. The flowers are from the garden, too."

"I was making some long overdue phone calls and tied up the phone. How about a cup of coffee? We can sit out on the patio and catch up." Maria smelled the fragrant blooms. "Thanks for coming and bringing all the goodies. I'm sorry I haven't been better about calling you," Maria said, realizing that Violet had been eavesdropping.

"Violet, Amanda is around here somewhere, keeping track of Timmy. Why don't you go find her?" Maria could really use a private, adult conversation with Sharon.

"How did you know my name?" Violet asked in a little voice.

"I met you last summer when we stopped by to see your mother. She showed us her wonderful gardens and seed buildings where she does her experiments. When you find Amanda, tell her you'd like to swim. You'd like that, wouldn't you?"

Violet smiled. "There was another girl who came with you when you visited us last summer. I'll wait for your girl to come and swim, too."

"Yes, that's my daughter, Amanda. We'll find her—she can't be far." Maria led the way to the patio with a tray of juice, paper cups, and coffee. "How about a glass of juice, gals?"

Suddenly, Ed appeared with Timmy on his shoulders. "Look who I found rolling his toy cars in our upstairs hallway."

"Let me . . ." The rest of Timmy's sentence was garbled as he twisted to get down.

Ed grunted as he tried to hold onto the squirming boy. "Can he swim, Sharon?"

"A little. He loves it and paddles around like a puppy. He has no fear, unfortunately. I'll watch him when you let him go."

"Okay, you little dynamo, here are your cars. You can run them all over the patio." Ed put the boy down.

But Timmy had other ideas and was quickly climbing up on a chair to get a cup of juice. In the process, he knocked over several paper cups full of juice, and the sweet liquid flew everywhere. Sharon jumped up, sat him down, and proceeded to give him another cupful.

"Sorry," she said, "he doesn't have temper tantrums like he did last summer now that he's three, but he's just too fast for his own good. Timmy, you sit there and drink your juice. I'll be right back."

Amanda came running out of the house. "Mommy, I didn't think

254

he'd run away so fast after I showed him Wiggles. I lost him, but I guess someone found him. Do little boys always run away?"

"When they're three, they do. Did you call Lois? Can she come over for a swim?" Maria poured more juice into several cups and handed them to Amanda and Ed.

"Yes, where's the lady who came? Oh, here she comes with a cloth."

"Her name is Sharon. You met her last summer when we went to her house."

Watching Sharon wipe everything clean on the table, Maria said, "I've forgotten how busy three-year-old boys can be. Chris was three once, but now he's thirteen, and he reminds me he's almost grown up. He's going on fourteen."

"I'd have another baby if I knew I'd have a girl, but one little boy is plenty," Sharon said, sitting back down. She poured a cup of juice, then helped Timmy down.

Soon Maria could hear Timmy making engine noises, running his cars all over the patio while Ed watched. He was probably relieved that Timmy was just visiting.

"Mommy, can we go in swimming? I'll find something for Violet to wear, but not Timmy. He can play with his cars," Amanda said, giving him a disgusted look.

Lois appeared at the door and Amanda squealed "Do you have your suit?"

Lois held it up.

"Fine. Go get changed," Maria suggested to three giggling girls as they ran across the patio.

Ed stood up. "I'm going to call Dad now. What's the deal with dinner?"

"Your Irish cook got her Irish up when I suggested we take your folks out for dinner. Briggie is preparing food as we speak. I bet she thinks your parents have a brogue."

As Ed was leaving, one of Timmy's cars came shooting across the patio floor. Ed got down on his knees, made all kinds of engine sounds, and sent the little car flying back across the floor to Timmy. Timmy squealed with pleasure and ran over to Ed, who picked him up and, holding him out away from him, twirled him around and around.

Timmy squeaked with delight and stuck out his arms. "More! More! I'm flying!"

"Enough, Timmy. Uncle Ed's dizzy. I'll give you another twirl later," he said, putting the boy down. "I've got to make a call." Timmy's expression was sad as he watched his friend leave.

"So, Sharon, how's life treating you?" Maria clasped her hands together and shook her head. "I can't believe it's been a whole year since we visited you. Still working for the seed companies, developing better strains of plants?"

"Yes, I just love my work, and since Glen installed heaters for the winter, I work all year round. Sometimes, I work at night. It's so peaceful with Timmy asleep. Violet will be starting kindergarten this year, half days, and the nursery will take Timmy now that he's trained, so my life will have some normalcy."

"I'll come visit you this fall when my kids are in school and try to understand what you're doing. Perhaps you can give me another tour. It sounds fascinating. All I've been doing is putting the house in order, but it's kept me hopping since I came." Maria leaned closer to Sharon and whispered, "Ed wants to have a party this fall for the horse breeders he does business with, and I know their wives will be judging me by how this place looks."

"I want to warn you." Sharon's face resembled a storm cloud. "That crowd is rough. I'm glad I don't have to deal with them—lots of wife swapping."

"Really? Wow, I never thought of that scenario. Ed makes a lot of money working for them, so I'm caught."

"Watch your step, a lot of those women are out for Ed. I know because of what Glen has told me. They aren't interested in marrying him; they just want to sleep with him."

"I ran into one or two of them at Amanda's open house yesterday. One named Babs, who was married to Ed and was particularly nasty."

"She was a nymphomaniac. She slept with so many guys, I'm amazed that she was able to attract any guy foolish enough to marry her. Of course, she has a trust fund and her parents are loaded. That might explain it. Poor Ed, he didn't know how wealthy she was when he married her, kept working through it all, but it really took a toll."

Amanda came running across the patio, holding Violet's hand. "Mommy, look what I found for Violet to wear." She stood there grinning, as if waiting to be complimented.

"Where did you ever find that little outfit? I thought we gave away everything."

"Not this one, and it's perfect for Violet." Amanda beamed with pride. "She can take it home."

Sharon eyed her naked son. "Timmy, where are your clothes?"

"I want to go swimming, too!"

"Okay, but first you need to pee." Sharon took him over to the grass and watched him make a little yellow stream.

Oh, dear . . . Well, we let Wiggles go there, I guess we can let a little boy go, too.

The girls were already in and splashing each other with great glee. Timmy jumped in over his head, submerged, and came up sputtering. "See me swim, see me, Mommy," he squealed, paddling as fast as he could, splashing wildly.

Maria joined Sharon at the side of the pool. "I've been dying to ask you about Ed's second wife, Jacqueline. Did you know her very well, and where is she now?"

"She was a nut case, if I ever saw one," she said out of the corner of her mouth, while still keeping her eyes on Timmy. "Glen said she would drive out to a farmer's place when Ed was out on an evening call and read him the riot act in front of God and the farmer. She was sure he was sleeping with the farmer's wife or any other stray female that happened by. She went in cycles, first paranoid over him being out in the evenings, then she'd leave and spend a month or two with her crazy mother. Your husband has been through hell and back with those two wives of his.

"When he told Glen that he was seeing you, we were so thrilled, we could hardly stand it. We had our fingers crossed hoping you'd marry him, and when he casually mentioned to Glen that you'd said yes, we jumped around the house like a couple of idiots."

The noise of her folks' French door opening stopped their conversation, and her mother appeared in the doorway.

"Mom, come out. Sharon's here and her kids, Violet and Timmy."

Winston was right behind her mother. "Hello! Any coffee left?" he boomed

"No, but I'll be glad to make another pot for my favorite stepfather."

"Thanks, but we've really had enough. We went over to the country club brunch this morning." Her mother grinned at her husband. "Winston thinks he's interested in getting on a golf committee, but I think he really wants to run the place." She smiled at Sharon. "I'm so glad you stopped over. Please come whenever you can. I know how busy you must be, but Maria loves company, and so do I."

Sharon returned the smile. "Nice to see you again. Ed has worked hard to make this home into what it is. You wouldn't believe what a mess this place was until Ed began seeing Maria. He shifted into gear and hasn't stopped since." She began drying Timmy off with a towel Amanda had brought out. "I'd better get going. Glen will be home for lunch, and no one will be there. Violet! Come on, honey. Time to go."

Maria walked Sharon and the children out to the car. "Thanks, girl, for filling me in on the 'exes.' I'll call, and we'll gossip some more, especially after you and Glen come to the big party for all the big socialites of St. Charles." Maria paused, then grinned. "At least *they* think so."

39. You Can Pick Your Friends, Not Your Relatives

August 1963
(Maria/Ed)

Maria

Maria wrapped her arm around Amanda. "We need to eat brunch. I loved having Sharon and her family over, but now it's late. Time to get organized. Thanks for helping with the kids, especially Violet."

Maria joined Ed, sitting under the umbrella with her parents. She stuffed her cold cereal down as fast as she could. She was ravenous. "Did you get your folks on the phone?" she asked, wiping a dribble of milk off her chin.

"Yes," he said, in a tone she didn't like. He sounded so angry.

"When are they coming?"

"Around two. I was just inviting your unsuspecting folks to join us. It will help to take the edge off. How do you all like being guinea pigs?"

"If you mean like victims being thrown into the ring, we've been there before, haven't we Ruth?" Winston gave her a sly grin and a wink. "I'll get Wilma to laugh this afternoon or know the reason why."

Ed sat up in his chair. "Shall we make a little wager, my friend?"

"I've tamed far worse, haven't I, my dear?"

Maria's mother laughed. "When Winston gets going, there's no stopping him."

After brunch, Ed took Amanda for a long walk with Wiggles to have some "Dad time" with her. He showed her where the barn was going to be built and promised he'd get her a pony. Maria helped

259

Briggie prepare for the forced reunion dinner, and Chris went with his new friends. When Maria asked him where he was going, he always answered he was going to the town's park, but she wondered if he was just putting her off.

It was almost two when Maria ran to her bedroom to shower and change. She was just brushing her hair when she heard the car pull up in front of the house. Looking out her window, she saw Ed helping his mother out and his father coming around the side of the car. Wilma was heavier than the last time Maria had seen her, and Elmer was even more lean, just like the nursery rhyme, Jack Spratt and his wife.

Almost catapulting down the stairs, Maria quickly laid some clean throw rugs down over the newly sanded floor in an attempt to make the place look more inviting before they came through the door.

Pushing her hair out of her eyes and plastering a smile on her face, she said, "So nice to see you again, Wilma and Elmer. It's been a long time since Ed's graduation party, hasn't it? Come and sit in the living room and cool off," and led the way.

Everyone except Wilma sat down. She began slowly walking around the room, touching the backs of chairs and clucking like a chicken to her captive audience. "Land sakes, a body don't know where to sit, there are so many places" she said in a loud voice. "Did you buy all this furniture, Ed? My, my, I guess when you're a fancy veterinarian you can afford all this, but it looks like a waste to me."

Finally picking out a large sofa, she sat down stiffly on the edge, but slowly her big body began sinking down into its softness. "My, this is comfortable," she murmured, sounding almost embarrassed for enjoying herself.

With his mother finally firmly planted, Ed asked, "How about some lemonade?"

"I'll get it, Ed, darling," Maria replied, purposely emphasizing "darling." Wilma certainly had a nasty tongue. She'd fired off remarks like bullets aimed to hurt. But Elmer had just sat quietly across the room. He'd been wounded by his wife too many times.

In the kitchen, Maria rolled her eyes at Briggie. "Ed's parents are here, and we need some lemonade. I'm putting out an SOS for my folks to come soon and help break the tension. Ed's standing there so taut, he looks like he might break in half."

"I don't believe Ed's good Irish folks are that upsetting. I'll bring in me drinks while you call. You've probably misjudged them."

Maria gave Briggie a wry look and picked up the phone. *Great, Briggie, wait until you run into Wilma, the pit bull. I'm alerting Amanda and Lois to stay away.*

Ed

Ed was relieved to see Briggie slowly enter the room with drinks—he didn't feel quite so alone.

Briggie smiled at Wilma and set her tray down. "Have some of me cooling lemonade on such a hot day?"

"Now, who is this?" Wilma gawked at Briggie. "Do you mean to tell me you have a maid in your house? Well, I never, Elmer! What do you think of these carryings on? You must be made of money, Ed. That's why your wife called you darling?" she scowled. "She ain't so dumb!"

"Saints preserve us," Briggie said, raising her voice. "Me name is Bridget. I'm from the old sod, like your parents, no doubt, and I'm not a maid. I'm a cook, nanny, and trusted friend. I've known Maria since she lived in Washington, DC," Briggie fired back, red-faced.

"What does your fancy wife do, if'n she don't cook?" Wilma asked peevishly, ignoring Briggie's reference to her background and heritage.

"I'm not going to respond to that remark," Ed said, his cheek muscles twitching as he clenched and unclenched his jaw.

"Hmm, idle hands are the devil's workshop. Must have plenty of time to spend your money by the looks of things."

Ed's white knuckles gripped his mother's glass of lemonade firmly as he glared at her and handed her the drink. "Briggie, where is Maria?" he asked, sounding like he needed to be rescued.

"Me girl's inviting her mother and stepfather to come over. She'll be right back."

Ed turned back to his mother. "The very couch you're sitting on is part of the furniture Maria and her mother generously gave me for this house," he said through clenched teeth.

"Son, there's some'un peering in. Should I let him in?" his father asked, sounding hesitant.

Ed looked toward the window. What a relief. "Come in, Winston, we're having drinks."

Winston walked in with a flourish with Ruth by his side. He spotted Wilma, walked over to her, took her hand, and kissed it. "Mother

McDermott, I presume. It's so nice to meet you and your husband, Elmer. I'm Winston, and dear lady, this is my wife, Ruth, Maria's mother. Ed has told me all about you," he said, giving her a charming smile.

Maria

Maria stood in the doorway watching the show, her hand over her mouth to stifle her giggles. Her mother sat next to Elmer across the room, and when Maria caught her eye, she seemed to struggle with maintaining a calm exterior.

For a moment, Wilma appeared to be at a loss for words. She kept looking at her kissed hand and making little clucking noises. Winston sat down next to her on the sofa, showering her with attention. Had Wilma ever received that kind of male attention in her life? She seemed to be at odds with herself. Gradually, her stern face melted and took on an absolutely glazed look of fascination for Winston. When he took her limp hand and told her how beautiful it was, her eyes fluttered, and she began making an odd little humming sound.

Maria gradually eased herself into the room and sat down quietly observing the continuing play. Winston was outdoing himself. *Just like years ago, you old ham. What a job you did for me as MC at George's and my engagement party. Perhaps you missed your calling.*

Since Winston's arrival, Ed had relaxed, now that he was off his mother's hook. He stood behind Wilma's sofa with gratitude on his face as he watched Winston hypnotize his mother. Ed's eyes met Maria's across the room, and he gave her a silent *thank you* with them.

"Tell me, Winston," Wilma asked, "are you an actor? Were you in the movies?"

"Ah, my dear lady, you have found me out. How clever of you. I toured all over the world as an actor and producer of fine plays. My dear wife, Ruth, starred with me on Broadway in many theatrical productions." He glanced over at Ruth, who responded by rolling her eyes at him.

"Hmm," Wilma said. "I knowed it! You was in show business. You cain't pull the wool over old Wilma's eyes. You talk like them people."

Maria couldn't keep her eyes off of Ed, who was doubled over in silent laughter behind his mother's couch.

"And now, dear madam, I would like to show you the humble

abode that your son built for us to live in during our reclining years. We're right next door to him and his dear wife." Winston stood up, and towering over little chubby Wilma, took her hand, helped her up, and led her out through the French doors like the Pied Piper.

Maria darted into the kitchen with Briggie struggling behind her to put the finishing touches on dinner. "I'm so glad we have a chance to have everything ready when they come back so we can eat and send them on their way. It was a stroke of genius for Winston to take Wilma on a little tour."

Briggie fumed as she was cooking. "I niver heard the likes of that evil woman talking about you like that, my darlin' girl. "She's a divil, that one is. How does me darlin' Ed stand her?"

"He doesn't. That's why they haven't been here until today."

"Where is she now? I'd like to poison her food."

"Winston is probably giving the performance of his life. Let's get the food on the table." *I'm so relieved to have Winston make this day bearable.*

As they finished their work, Briggie asked, "Where's that poor little husband of hers? I was so busy answering her, I niver laid me eyes on him."

"He sat next to Mom. He just doesn't talk much around his wife. He's learned to be silent."

Maria stood back and surveyed the dining room. "Everything looks and smells delicious, Briggie. Thanks, my friend. I'll call the girls to wash up, and then we'll be ready."

Maria was filling the water glasses when she heard Winston's melodic voice out on the patio. He was extolling Ed's wisdom about the placement of the pool, going into great detail. "I've bored all of you long enough, including myself," Winston remarked. He popped his head in the door. "Maria, are you ready for us?"

"Yes, come and eat."

The girls came thumping down the stairs, taking two steps at a time, as the adults streamed into the dining room. Looking over the table quickly, Winston took Wilma's hand. "Sit next to me, dear lady, so we can enjoy this bountiful repast together." Pulling out her chair for her, he motioned for her to sit down. She actually tittered, and with enchantment in her eyes, she meekly obeyed, smiling shyly at him as he sat down next to her. It was as if Winston were the snake charmer and Wilma the snake.

Maria's first and only impression of Wilma had been at Ed's college graduation. The image of an angry woman had been imprinted in Maria's mind until today when Winston had melted her crustiness away with his thoughtfulness.

Had Wilma ever dreamed of a love-filled life when she married Elmer? She must have—she'd been young once. When had she given up and turned into such an irate, controlling woman? Or had she always been one?

Outwardly, Maria fulfilled her obligation as hostess, passing platters of food, smiling, and nodding during her first family reunion in her new home. But inwardly, Maria's thoughts compared her own once romantic dreams with George to Wilma's possible hopes with Elmer.

No one could have ever convinced Maria that her marriage to George would gradually dissolve into the nightmare it became. But it did. When did she give up? No one date jumped out at her. The destruction had come from a slow, methodical wearing down of her spirit, little by little, as George's distant behavior ripped the fabric of their marriage apart.

"Maria! Maria! Hey down there!" Ed grinned from the other end of the table and gave her a look that said he enjoyed catching her daydreaming. "What's for dessert?"

She shivered, slightly embarrassed she'd been caught so far away. "Briggie made a surprise. Amanda, Lois, would you please clear the table while I help Briggie?"

As she bolted from her chair, Maria knocked over her water glass, spilling the contents all over. That hadn't happened to her since George continually unnerved her at the infrequent dinner meetings with him while he pretended to play the role of dutiful husband and father.

Moments later, Maria walked into the dining room with a magnificent cake and a single candle burning brightly. Amanda was right behind her, bubbling with excitement. All eyes followed as she placed the dessert in front of Ed.

"Daddy, isn't it pretty? Read the words that Briggie put on it." Amanda wrapped her arms around his neck from behind.

"Happy First Reunion," he read out loud.

"Now blow out the candle and cut us all a piece," she said, kissing him on his cheek.

"Listen, Petunia, your mother is much better at this," then blew out the candle. "Run get the ice cream from Briggie."

Maria began cutting the cake, mentioning how pretty and important the cake was and its message to keep their families together, which she didn't believe at that moment. As she spoke, she passed plates of dessert to everyone, intrigued with Wilma and Elmer's reactions. Beaten down, Elmer gave her a slight smile, but Wilma didn't look up. She was too busy stuffing bites of cake and ice cream into her mouth. Too bad Wilma hadn't heard the message. Was Wilma a lost cause? Would she ever change? Maria had a sinking feeling just thinking about it.

40. Yippee, the Reunion Is Over

August 1963
(Maria/Ed)

Maria

Glancing around the table, Maria could feel the urgency in some of the conversations being carried on as the final moments of their first reunion drew to a close. Ed and Elmer had their heads together, engaged in a long overdue enjoyable exchange. Amanda was chattering nonstop to her grandmother, making her laugh continuously, and Wilma and Winston acted like life-long friends catching up with each other.

As Maria watched, she absentmindedly touched the smooth, burnished surface of the beautiful table inherited from her folks. If only it could talk. How many memories were stored in that table?

Ed held up his wrist and looked at his watch. "I'm sure you folks would love to stay longer, but I know Dad is worried about getting home before dark."

"Right, we'd better git while the gitting is good, son. Thanks for having us."

From the way father and son looked at each other, it was clear that they shared a common bond. Elmer tried to solve his problems with alcohol, but he loved his son. He'd saved Ed from a life filled only with anger and criticism and made it possible for him to grow up with a love of animals, storytelling, and a quiet sense of determination.

Although relatively happy, Wilma was also tired and drawn. Her weight was her worst enemy. She'd denied her problems all her life by drowning herself in food. Now it was an ingrained habit. She'd overeaten again.

Wilma struggled to get up from the table, and Winston immediately stood up, pulled her up, and steadied her as the two of them followed Ed out to the car. Maria watched from the front window as Winston helped Wilma into the car, then closed the door on a contented woman who would probably never forget him.

Ed

Ed stood next to Winston as they watched his parents drive away.

"How about some sipping whiskey to celebrate our achievements today?" Winston asked as he and Ed watched the car finally disappear.

"Thanks for saving the day and keeping my blood pressure from going through the roof dealing with my mother. What a performance! Where did you learn to act?"

"Through necessity, dealing with members of Congress, State Department officials, and especially their wives. Actually, I enjoyed today, and your mother is such a needy old lady, I felt sorry for her."

Winston turned back toward the house. "Where are our women? We need to congratulate them on their work. "Maria, Ruth, Briggie, come out and join us! Briggie, you can put your tired feet in the pool to cool off, " he called into the kitchen as they strode by. When there was no answer, he asked, "Have they left us, Ed? I wouldn't blame them.

"It's cooling down a bit. Let's sit on the patio you built for us, have a scotch and soda, and contemplate our next move now that the reunion of sorts is behind us."

"Is this bar a new addition to the recreational area?" Ed asked, as he ran his hand over its smooth, steel surface.

"Yes, I finally unpacked it and set it up in case we needed it today, but we had a lemonade crowd instead. I miss Dean. He used to replenish my stock, and now I have to do it." Winston pulled out several glasses. "How about a scotch and soda, Ed? We've earned it."

"Bring them on, I'm ready," Ed said, taking off his shoes and socks and sitting down.

"I wonder where the ladies are? It so quiet, it's rather unnerving." Winston's question was barely out of his mouth when Maria, Ruth, and Amanda appeared.

María

"How are the men in the family?" Maria gave them a salute. "Relaxed I see. Winston, you were so good. What a performance! I never knew an actor lurked inside of you! I wish Chris could have been here to witness his grandfather give the performance of his life, but I'm sure he was happy with his friends," ruffling Ed's hair with her fingers.

"We just took Lois home, and now we're ready for some fun." Maria put her arm around Ed's neck and smiled at him. "How about a swim? I feel jubilant!"

"Ugh, I'd probably drown after this scotch and soda." Ed glanced around. "Where's Briggie?"

Ruth chuckled. "She's lying down, watching a football game, of all things."

"Please, Daddy, Grandpa, Grandma, come on," Amanda said, jumping up and down.

Ed clapped his hands together. "Okay, I'll come in if we can play water polo."

"I want to be on your team, Dad."

Maria joined her reluctant stepfather in the water to play against her mother, Ed, and Amanda. Ed was serving when Maria heard her son calling them from the French doors.

"Come out and play with Grandpa and Mommy," Amanda yelled. "They need you." At first Chris declined, saying he was tired and would see Ed bright and early in the morning for work. But when Ed weighed in on the invitation, Chris agreed. Moments later, he came out on the run in his gym shorts and leaped into the pool, splashing water all over Winston.

Reacting quickly, Winston tried to duck Chris, but he twisted away, took the beach ball, and hurled it over the net right at Amanda. She screamed and the game was on. Ed grabbed the ball, smashed it over the net at Chris, and scored a point. The two of them seemed to be testing each other as they became the dominant opposing players in the game. Watching Chris match Ed in speed and outdo him in agility, Maria knew her boy was growing up, moving into the new world he was making, and was growing away from her.

Having so much fun, they played longer than Maria had anticipated. The water had such an enervating and relaxing effect on all of them, they acted like kids. The final score was blurred, but no one lost that day, they all were winners.

Basking in the afterglow of their boisterous and sometimes hilarious game, they sat in the warm quiet of the early evening, completely relaxed in their bathing suits. No one moved, not even the kids. But that momentary pause didn't last. Chris left first, followed quickly by Amanda, who asked her mother on the way out if she could shower in her bathroom and then have another piece of cake. Pleased with the success of the day, Maria couldn't say no. Maria's eyes were closed, enjoying a quiet moment when she heard Winston clearing his throat. He was obviously getting ready to say something he thought important, so she opened her eyes.

He took a sip of whiskey. "Agent Adam Kowalski called with the first results from the phone tap," he said quietly. "Pull your chairs closer. I don't want the kids to hear any of this." He waited for them to move. "The calls are coming from the Naperville area, but they're dispersed. The caller doesn't use the same phone twice. Although the caller hasn't spoken, the rate and intensity of breathing indicates a woman or a slightly built man. Now, as for the ear splitting high intensity static, it sounds like a tape of noise from a factory that produces some kind of metal machinery. The workers probably have to wear protective head gear when they're working. Adam said he was going to Chicago to investigate those kinds of companies."

Winston took another sip of his whiskey. "We're just getting started, so don't be discouraged. It might take a while until we begin to see a pattern. I'm putting up a map in our study with pins in every place a call has been made from. Sooner or later, he or she will make a mistake. They always do."

Maria shivered with his last comment, then glanced at Ed and saw an incredulous look on his face. He was being baptized into the world of FBI agents, something completely foreign to him. She'd been just like him, naïve about intelligence and counterintelligence when she met George. As she'd learned more about George's involvement in the whole nefarious world, it had caused her many sleepless nights and had lingered in her subconscious ever since.

"God, Winston, what a mess," Ed said. "This whole thing doesn't seem real to me." He wiped his forehead. "Thanks for helping us. Also, thank Mr. Kowalski. I must admit that I got a little excited when I saw him upstairs the other day." He took a sip of his drink. "What kind of money are we talking about?"

"Don't worry about that, my boy. Agent Kowalski owes me a lot of favors. Let's catch our man or woman—or both—first." Winston leaned a bit closer to Ed. "Do you have any idea who might have it in for you? Enough to do this to Maria? The calls only come when you aren't here. Who knows that much about your comings and goings?"

"The only one who comes to mind is my ex-wife, Jackie. She's got the motive, although I don't think she has the guts or the brains to plan such a thing, and she wouldn't know my exact comings and goings." Ed waited for a moment, then looked at Maria. "She probably hates Maria," his said, his voice catching. "God knows I tried, but Jackie's certifiable. I was at my wit's end before Maria came back into my life. I thought of pulling up stakes and disappearing."

"And leaving your practice? That would have been a mistake." Winston was quiet, thinking for a moment. "Old man, do you send Jackie alimony?"

"Of course, doesn't every man pay alimony after a divorce? I give her a lot. It was that, or we would have been in court for years. My accountant takes care of it every month without fail. At first, I was so relieved that she was out of my life, the money didn't matter. And now, my business is booming and I have no trouble covering it."

"Where does he send the check?"

"To a PO box in Chicago, I think. I've never really wanted to know."

Winston rubbed his jaw. "So, anyone with a key can get into the box and get the check?"

"I guess so. I've never really thought about it until now."

"Thanks, Ed. I'll fill Adam in on this, plus your accountant's name and address."

Ed drained the last drop of his whiskey, got up, stretched, and said in a tone that worried Maria, "It's time for me to try to make some sense out of our reunion with my parents. It's the first time they've ever come to see me." He picked up his towel and flung it over his shoulder. "I need to think, and I'm also tired, so I'm going to head up to bed. Tomorrow will come soon enough." He gave a big sigh and walked off of the patio alone.

"I'll see you tomorrow, folks," Maria said as she hurried after him.

"Go on up, honey. I'll lock up," he said, dejectedly.

Why was he so unhappy? Winston had handled his mom all day. Perhaps Ed had too many bad memories from his past still plaguing him, or maybe he was worried about the phone calls and if they were coming from his ex-wife or her friends.

41. Making the House a Home

August 1963
(Maria)

Maria was still thinking about Ed after she'd showered and slipped into bed, naked. She loved to sleep in the buff and feel the smooth sheets over and under her. No night clothes to twist around her body and wake her up, especially in the summer.

She was riding her horse, Jetty, again and they were flying like the wind with Jetty's mane tickling Maria face. She kept pushing it away, but it kept bothering her. "Oh, stop it," she mumbled and opened her eyes. Ed was tickling her forehead quietly with a cosmetic brush and giving her a devilish smile.

"You must feel better. You smell good with your clean, damp hair, and sexy body. What do you want?" she asked half awake.

"You know what I want."

Ignoring his comment, she rolled over, lay on her stomach, and put her head on his chest. "I can hear your heart pumping nicely. I pronounce you perfect inside and out, including your nipples." She turned her head and sucked them so fast it surprised him. He grabbed her in a bear hug and roared, "You little devil, I never know what you're going to do."

"So, you don't think I'm a dried up, sex-starved woman?"

"No, but just in case, I volunteer to remedy that problem."

"Show me," she squealed. Maria threw her arms around him and gave him a hot kiss. He immediately responded so passionately, she'd accomplished what she wanted. He wasn't thinking about his mother or Jackie when she whispered, "Let the games begin."

Early the next morning, with the room still dark in shadows, Maria felt Ed's breath as he whispered in her ear that he'd call her later in the day, and then he was gone. Still in that haze between being awake and asleep, she went over their delicious love making the night before. The banging of a truck door stopped her licentious thoughts and jolted her awake.

She wondered who it was for a second, then became convinced it was the floor guys. Hopefully, they'd finish their work by the end of the day. But what was she going to do while the floors dried? Of course! She, her mother, and Amanda would go shopping. Chris would appreciate anything she bought for him as long as he didn't have to go himself. It would also give Briggie some time off to watch television and soak her feet in the pool.

Then she heard their hired girls being dropped off. How could Maria have forgotten they were coming? She quickly threw on her jean shorts and a top. Downstairs, the men were bringing in their supplies, and Laura was waiting for her in the kitchen.

"Hi, Laura," Maria said weakly. "I forgot to call you last night and tell you not to come today because the men are staining the floors." Suddenly, she was looking into a teenager's crestfallen face. Maria needed to make amends. "Amanda and Chris need clothes. Would you like to come and shop, too? We're going into the Windy City," she said, hoping Laura would turn her down.

Her face brightened. "Why, Mrs. McDermott, I'd love to go. Could Sarah come, too?"

Maria gulped. Now she was faced with two teenage girls going on her impetuous shopping spree. But it made perfect sense. With Maria's mother gone for the day, Sarah wouldn't have anything to do.

"Help Briggie by putting all the good china and silver away from last night's party. I have something I need to do." Maria ran across the patio and knocked lightly on her mother's door.

Moments later, her mother opened her door. "Not more phone calls?"

"No, thank goodness, but I have a great proposal for you." Maria smiled her most convincing smile and launched into her decision for a shopping trip.

"Couldn't come at a better time." Her mother's face lit up. "Winston is into this phone call mystery, and he's meeting Adam for a strategy session. You know Winston, when he gets his teeth into something, he doesn't let go. And frankly, I'm glad for a little less togetherness now that he's retired. Besides, Amanda will love going with Laura and Sarah and soaking up their teenage charm."

"So, it's a go for us. And to sweeten the pot, with the floors drying, we'll certainly have to go out for dinner again. Isn't that a shame?" Maria grinned and rubbed her hands together. "I'll tell Briggie. She'll love it and be able to rest those tired feet of hers. See you in an hour. We'll swing by the girls' homes so they can get their spending money and tell their folks what they're up to."

It didn't take Maria long to circle around out into the country where the girls lived and be on her way to suburban Oak Park's "L" station to Chicago. Hearing gales of laughter coming from the back seat, Maria glanced in her rearview mirror and saw a happy Amanda sitting between Laura and Sarah, completely mesmerized. Maria appreciated their kindness to her daughter. They seemed to have an unending amount of patience, and Maria attributed that quality to being raised in big families with many little brothers and sisters testing them every day.

Riding on the "L" to Chicago's Loop took Maria back to her childhood when she was about Amanda's age. Going shopping in the big downtown store of Marshall Field's with her mother had always been a special occasion. Her mother had always made their trips fun, bribing May and Maria with the promise of a wonderful lunch and a movie at the magnificent Chicago Theatre. Maria had adored the thundering organ concert that preceded every movie. Those were treasured memories for her when their family was intact, and her mother and father still loved each other.

As she grew older, she sensed trouble, but she didn't understand that her parents' marriage was beginning to unravel. Although her beloved dad still took them on trips, there was always a subtle change in his behavior and attitude when they returned.

On the evening of her eighth-grade graduation, he took her into his study where they'd spent many evenings together reading Oz books, and he finally admitted to Maria that he loved his secretary, Betty. As Betty gained more sexual appeal to her father, he slowly bowed out of the marriage. But even toward the end, her dad still took her places. Their visit to her mother's family in Wyoming had remained as one of his favorite trips because he was able to fish with his brothers-in-law and recuperate from the stress of his medical practice. It was if he was struggling to stay with her mom, but was being drawn to a younger, more exciting woman. In his way, he wanted to make her mother happy, if only for a few precious days.

Her reverie about her dad fishing in mountain streams was suddenly broken when she felt her mother's touch on her arm and heard the conductor calling, "Next stop, Marshall Field's."

The teenagers each held one of Amanda's hands, and they hurried off the train together. Maria nudged her mother. "I was lost in memory lane. It was fun to remember our trips."

"I was thinking about our good times, too. And what's even better, we now have wonderful husbands and three generations here together for a great day."

"I know, Mom. It makes it all worthwhile, doesn't it? But now, we'd better set the rules. Girls, the store's directory is right by the elevators. Use the directory. It will be a great help. We'll split off and meet you for lunch in the Walnut Room around one o'clock. It's my treat, and I don't want any arguments about it."

After a successful morning of shopping, Maria, her mother, and Amanda saw the girls standing in front of the Walnut Room, waiting patiently, clutching their precious bags of clothes. Maria led her little group through the entrance of the beautiful dining room, stepped to the desk, and asked the hostess to seat them near the windows overlooking the city.

"Mommy won't care what you order," Amanda announced, trying in her small way to be hospitable to her teenage idols.

With so many school shoppers crowding the store, the service was slow, but the food was excellent once it finally arrived at their table. But by the time they were finished eating, it was time to head home.

"It looks like your trip was successful," Maria said, observing them carefully gathering up their loot while dropping both girls off at Laura's at the end of the day.

"Oh, Mrs. McDermott, we had so much fun and found some really pretty things for school," Laura said with a smile. "Didn't we, Sarah?"

"No one will be wearing the stuff we bought," Sarah said, gleefully.

"Good, I'm so glad we all could go today. We'll do it again sometime." Maria felt good about including the girls. They were wonderful kids. "See you tomorrow, bright and early. We've got our work cut out for us, Laura," Maria called as she turned her car around and pulled out of Laura's farmyard.

"Mom" Amanda yelled from the back seat, sounding like she could hardly contain herself. "Laura likes Chris, and Chris likes Laura. When you and Grandma went to the ladies' room after lunch, I heard Laura whispering to Sarah about him."

"Thanks for the information," Maria said, laughing with her mother. "Nothing like a little sister to keep us informed."

"I knew you'd like to know. Are you going to ask Chris about Laura?"

"No, and neither are you, if you want to remain Chris's friend."

"Oh, Mom, you're no fun," Amanda said, peevishly.

When did Amanda stop calling her mommy? And when did she start being so impatient?

To change the subject, Maria said, "We're going out for dinner tonight at Maisie's. Maybe you'll see Stephen."

"I don't like him anymore. I met a boy at school the other day that I like better. And besides, this boy is in my class, and I can see him every day," she said, matter-of-factly, then picked up the new comic book Maria had bought for her and began to read.

Amanda would be occupied for a while. Maria and her mother could now focus on household problems. "Mom, I'd like to talk to you about some decorating ideas I have for the two upstairs guest rooms, but I need to have the whole house painted first. Maisie will know some good painters. Are you interested in doing anything in your place?"

"Oh my, yes, but I have to do my floors first so we can get our rugs down. Winston hates the bare floors and complains every day about them. He hired your floor men to do ours tomorrow, I think. I hope I can stay with you while they work."

"Of course. Let's go exploring at paint stores for swatches of paint samples. No need to wait at home when we can shop," Maria said, giggling as she drove into their driveway.

"You're such fun. I'm so lucky to have you as a daughter, but it makes me feel a little guilty spending so much more time with you than with May. I've never been as close to her as you. That's an awful thing for a mother to say, but I think we all have favorites. May has always seemed so organized, even as a child. And then, she made a good marriage. Don's been so solid all of their lives together."

"Not like me and George," Maria said, grinning at her mom.

"True, but you must admit you've had a much more exciting life, even with all its troubles. And now you're married to a stable, generous, loving husband. So things work out the way they're supposed to." Her mother's face reflected concern. "Let's think about a reunion with your sister and Don before too much time goes by."

Maria nodded in agreement to her mother's suggestion, but secretly wished it hadn't come up. Goodness—another reunion! Nothing like feeling overloaded.

"Help us with your packages, Amanda," Maria said, as she parked in the garage.

Amanda struggled with her bundles and shrieked as soon as she stepped inside the door. "What's the awful smell in this house?"

It only took a second for Maria to take a whiff. "The floors, but hopefully, the stench will go away soon."

Maria turned to her mother. "I'm going to need help laying down our rugs, especially the beautiful Orientals you gave us. I'm sure Chris and a couple of his buddies could do it sometime this week. He can also do yours when you're ready. I'll ask him tonight. I don't want to bother Ed or Winston when I have all this young manpower looking for money."

After Chris enlisted his friends, they couldn't get there fast enough to use show off their muscles and get paid besides. At the last minute, Chris had to work, but his four friends showed up the next afternoon in an old car. While Maria directed, Amanda shadowed her mother, ogling the boys. The fellows went from one room to another, following orders and easily completing all the muscle tasks asked of them. Maria marveled at how coordinated and strong they were. It somehow made her feel old.

When the boys thanked her exuberantly for the cash she handed them, she told them to save it. But Maria knew her words had fallen on deaf ears when she overheard their plans for a trip to play pool in Naperville.

She couldn't wait for Ed to come home and see the combination of beautiful floors and rugs. While sitting in the shade on the patio and enjoying some lemonade, Maria heard Ed's voice yelling his approval.

Bursting out onto the patio, he gave her a big noisy kiss of gratitude. "You little rascal, you didn't tell me you were putting the house together today. I'm glad you didn't ask me. Who helped you?"

Before Maria could answer, Amanda piped up and said, "Chris's friends. They were fun to watch, and they were strong."

"Well, Petunia, I'm glad you were there observing the muscular activities of the boys," he said, reaching over and hugging her. "Are they stronger than your daddy?"

"Oh no, Daddy, you're the strongest and the nicest," Amanda said, hopping up and down with excitement at the attention he was showing her.

"Here, me Irish lad, have a drink of me homemade lemonade, freshly squeezed," Briggie said, handing him a glass. "We're going to have a lovely summer meal after me big rest yesterday. You would have been proud of your little wife getting those boys to do a good job."

"Briggie, she's scary when she's on a mission, I know." Ed put his hands up to fend off Maria's attempt to whack him, his eyes dancing. "Thanks for taking care of this. I love you for it." He downed his glass of lemonade and stood up. "I'm sure you'll all approve of my showering. I reek from all the dirty barns I was in today."

Their household's tempo notched up a bit the rest of the week because of Maria and Ed's impending trip. Maria worked hard filling the pantry, washing clothes, and paying bills in her efforts to provide smooth sailing for the family. Ed came home late all week, working extra hours with Chris's help to give Glen time off in exchange for the weekend.

The earsplitting phone calls kept coming, sometimes two and three times a day. But it had stopped bothering Maria because she knew Agent Kowalski was on the case.

Early Friday morning, Ed called from the clinic. "I'm dying to get out of here. I feel like a kid and want a change. Would you ask your mom and Briggie to watch the kids for us?"

"Of course, my darling," she replied, laughing at his last-minute attempt to help her. She'd set the dates with both Briggie and her mother as soon as he'd asked her.

Ready to go with her bag packed, she was sitting quietly in their cool living room with her eyes closed when Ed bounded into the house calling her name.

"Aren't you ready?" He asked, peeking into the room.

"Of course, I am." She'd given emergency phone numbers to Briggie, her mother, and Alicia, and had left Amanda playing happily with Lois.

"You look good enough to eat. Come on, gorgeous." His eyes were sparkling as he grabbed their bags and ran to the Rocket.

He leaned over his bucket seat, gave her a hot kiss, shoved the car in gear, backed out, and shot out of there. "I've been thinking about you all morning. God, I love you, Maria. And besides, you smell nice."

She reached over and lightly touched his face with her fingertips, tickling him slightly.

"It's been so long since you've done that to me. It brings back some pretty wild memories with you, years ago at college."

"We heated up the Tucked Inn a time or two, didn't we, handsome?"

"Did we ever, only I was too stupid to realize how precious those times with you were."

"Well, we do now, and that's all that matters," Maria said as she reached over to the dash board and turned on the radio. "I'll find some good music from Chicago to put us in the mood."

"If I get any more in the mood than I already am, I'll have to pull over and take you right here," he said, flashing her a sexy look.

She giggled. "It's certainly nice to be wanted. I love you, Doc, with my whole heart, but it will be much more fun in a nice big bed at the hotel."

"I know, Rosebud," Ed said, sounding resigned. He gripped the wheel, settled back, and listened to the music as he drove them into the heart of downtown Chicago.

42. While the Cat's Away

August 1963
(Winston/Chris)

Winston

Back at the compound, Ruth sat with Winston on the patio. They finished their drinks as the sun dropped down behind the trees, signaling the end of the day.

"Have the calls still been coming, Ruth?"

"Yes, but Maria just hangs up now."

"I think our man is making some progress. He's contacted the office in Chicago for more manpower to cover all the factories in a planned effort. The men have fanned out over the city and are making tapes of the noises they find. We'll get a match. It's just a matter of time." Winston's brow furrowed with concern. "Adam is concerned seeing this new type of technological harassment against American citizens. It could be the beginning of a new type of crime, and the Bureau is taking it seriously."

"That's good news, honey. We'll all feel better when we get to the bottom of this."

"I haven't mentioned my fear that the intensity of the attack may increase. In these kinds of cases, the aggressor gets tired of the same thing and wants more satisfaction from his victim. I'm thinking of putting a surveillance team on to watch the property," Winston said, looking at Ruth with a serious frown.

"Oh, Winston, you don't mean—" Ruth's question caught in her throat as she saw Amanda skipping across the patio with Lois, full of smiles.

"Grandma and Grandpa, we're getting hungry. Can we go and eat soon?"

"Sure," Ruth said, "go get Briggie and Chris. We'll meet you all in five minutes."

Seated at Maisie's, Winston surveyed his little group. "It's fun to be retired and here with our family," he said proudly, reaching over and giving Ruth a peck on the cheek.

"It has its compensations," Ruth said. "But being completely in charge is harder than I realized. Now, where is our waitress? We need to order."

Apologetically, Maisie handed them their menus. "Sorry folks, my new waitress is learning the ropes. Feast your eyes on all our new entrees. We're now serving the best pizza in the area. Try it, kids, you'll like it."

Winston gave her a sly grin. "Is that your answer to the new pizza parlor in town?"

"Yes, the town is growing, and we have a lot more young people with money to spend because of the industries coming into the area."

"I'm sure your pizzas are better. We'll have two of your best."

"I want one with pepperoni—no vegetables. I hate them," Chris said.

"Briggie, you can order something else if you like," Ruth offered.

"Pizza's fine, folks, I've niver had it before. It's a whole new world."

"Well, that makes it easy," Ruth said, as Winston hailed their young waitress.

"We better have three pizzas. One for the adults, one for the kids, and one for anyone who doesn't like what's on the first two," Winston said firmly. "And three cups of coffee for the adults and three Cokes for the kids."

"I need to be awake tonight," Winston's face was serious. "I recommend that you, Ruth, have a cup to keep me company later, and you, Briggie, have a cup to make sure we both stay awake! Chris wants to stay downtown after dinner and meet his friends at the park. I've agreed, but with conditions."

Amanda and Lois's eyes widened with Winston's last remark. "I wonder what they are," Amanda whispered to Lois, and both of them started giggling.

After dinner, as everyone left the restaurant, Winston took Chris aside. "I'm counting on you to call on time so I can come get you."

"Okay, Grandpa, I won't disappoint you," Chris said, calling over his shoulder.

Winston drove the rest of the group home, pleased there was so little traffic.

"We adults need to band together," Winston said. "Why don't you women become a team of necessity, taking turns making sure the girls don't stay up all night talking. I'll take Wiggles out for a little walk, and we can all meet out on the patio and keep each other company until Chris calls. When that happens, I'll go get him, and you two can go to bed." Winston folded his arms across his chest, looking pleased with his plan. "For now, let's sit here and watch the stars come out."

"I'll check on me girls first, and you two can look at the stars while I look at me telly."

Winston and Ruth sat in darkness with only the sliver moon keeping them company, listening to the evening insects playing their discordant but rhythmic summer tunes. Winston occasionally checked the time on his watch. He gave it another look. "Chris is late calling me. I told him no later than nine, and it's already ten. What's he up to?"

"Don't you remember how you lost all track of time at that age, especially if any young ladies were involved?" Ruth gave him an encouraging hug.

"Just the same, I think I'll call the police and let them know I'm concerned. I feel so responsible for him with his folks away."

"Give him a few more minutes, then I'll go with you to find him. Briggie is here for the girls, and we won't be gone long. Don't call the police yet."

Chris

After Chris had left his family, he loped along, covering a lot of ground with his long legs. His objective—the city park. While crossing the street, he'd heard an unmistakable sound—Dewain's old clunker roaring toward him.

"So, where are you going, mister-too-good-for-your-old-buddies?" Dewain asked, leering out of his car window.

"None of your beeswax," Chris snapped back, instantly on guard.

"Get in," Dewain demanded

"No, I'm walking."

As Dewain's car roared away, he saw several fists shaking out the windows at him.

Chris's stride lengthened as he covered the ground quickly, unconcerned by Dewain. When he saw Laura swinging on the park equipment with Sarah and three of her friends, his hormones kicked into gear. Wonders of wonders, she'd come, just like she'd promised when he'd called her. His spirits soared. *She likes me.*

It hadn't taken Chris long to figure out that Dewain was a bully. After watching him swagger around his cronies, taunting and demeaning them if they didn't give him complete obeisance, Chris dropped him. As a new guy in town, he'd welcomed Dewain's friendship at first, but no more. Chris wanted no part of him.

Chris had quickly made friends with young men he'd met in the summer sports program the school sponsored in the evenings for boys who wanted to compete in fall school sports.

Laura beamed when she saw him, hopped off the swing, and waited to introduce him to her friends. Moments later, Dewain's rowdy gang's yelling and laughter signaled their arrival in the park, and immediately Laura's face filled with disgust.

One girl said, "Oh, my gosh, here comes the goon squad. They'll ruin everything."

Dewain swaggered up to Laura, Chris, and the other girls. "Introduce us to your friends, Laura, or do you think you're too good?"

"Get lost," Sarah said grimly. "You're so dumb, you probably will get lost."

"Gee, I'm really worried," Dewain hooted in her face, waving his hands in mock fear.

Behind Dewain, several of Chris's new athletic friends were crossing the field. They hailed him and yelled they wanted introductions to all the girls around him.

"Not on your life," Chris yelled back, delighted his friends were coming. Dewain was getting ugly, and he had his gang with him.

As the newcomers ran up to Chris, some of the girls smiled and started talking to them. Showing off, several of the more coordinated fellows took off their sneakers, ran up the slide, turned around, and slid back down. With his gang encouraging him, Dewain tried to do it, lost his footing and fell off, sending waves of laughter from the kids.

Red-faced and looking murderous, he walked up to one of the guys who had been laughing the hardest and shoved him hard, surprising him. Down he went.

He got up like a bull and rammed into Dewain. Before Chris knew it, a full-fledge fight had started. Dewain's two sidekicks waded into the fray, but were quickly knocked down by two big football hopefuls. When Dewain tried to come to his friends' rescue, one of the players landed a punch on Dewain's chin that knocked him down with a thud. His opponent was young, but hard as rock from summer football league. Dewain lay there, dazed for a minute or so, then he picked himself up, swore at everyone there, including Chris, and walked away with his henchmen following.

For the next couple of hours, everyone in the park had a wild and outrageous time reverting back to games they'd all played as children. Having the girls there made the men's testosterone levels skyrocket, putting the thrill of the chase into the games. Hide and seek quickly became their favorite. Many guys had the excuse and momentary thrill of grabbing and holding a gal as she ran for home base.

After one particularly sensual game in which Chris caught Laura, she said, breathlessly, "It's almost nine thirty, Chris. My mom or dad will be picking me up at the entrance of the park soon. Do you want to walk me there? I'm a mess after all that running, but it was fun, wasn't it?" She smiled shyly at him.

"You never look a mess to me." Good thing it was dark and they weren't facing each other, because he was aroused. "Thanks for coming, Laura. I'd like to call and see you tomorrow night."

"You can call me, but I don't know if my dad will let me go out again so soon."

"I'll call you anyway," he said, smiling at her. Then he waited with her at the corner for her parents.

"Just one more week and school starts," Laura said, looking into his eyes.

It was just the way Ed had described to him. Chris knew she was interested by the way she looked at him. At that moment, Chris felt he could almost fly over the treetops.

"That's my dad's car," she said as the car stopped.

Her dad leaned toward the open passenger window. "Get in, young lady."

"Dad, I want you to meet my friend, Chris Fuller. He's Doc McDermott's stepson."

While Laura got into the car, Chris stepped around to the driver's side. "Hi, nice to meet you."

Laura's dad grunted a short hello and drove off.

Chris stood there for a moment, enjoying his first success with a girl, but he returned to reality and looked at his watch. He was late calling his grandpa. Chris began jogging to Maisie's to call, and he'd just crossed the street when a couple of guys grabbed him from behind near some dense underbrush.

They were part of Dewain's gang—Chris's only enemies. He fought furiously. Chris was stronger and in better shape from working and playing summer sports than they were, but when a third guy joined them, they finally dragged him into the underbrush away from the street. He broke free momentarily, and was about to run, when he felt Dewain's arms grab him from behind.

"I've been waiting for you, you little bastard," Dewain growled. "Think you can make a fool out of me? I thought you were my friend after all the work we did for your mother the other day, but you think you're too good for us."

Chris opened his mouth to reply, but a punch to his gut by one of Dewain's henchmen knocked the wind out of him. He doubled over. Barney and Gopher grabbed him, then held him upright and pinned his arms behind him.

This time, Dewain swore at him and hit him full force in the face, and then again in the stomach over and over until Chris slumped. Everything went black.

Chris opened his eyes. Dewain's goons were gone. What time was it? He looked at his watch—almost ten thirty. He slowly stood up and struggled out to the sidewalk. Dried blood covered his shirt, his stomach hurt, and so did his head. Chris stood holding onto a lamp post, trying to get his balance. He had to get to Maisie's and call before she closed.

As his eyes refocused, he saw a car moving slowly down the street. The car stopped right by him. Through his haze, he heard Winston's voice. Thank God, he was saved. Chris felt Winston's big strong arm holding him up and helping him into the car seat. Then he passed out again.

When Chris woke up, he was lying in his bed. Everything hurt, and he couldn't breathe through his nose. He carefully felt his stomach and face. Voices could be heard from the other side of his bedroom door—Winston and another man were talking.

His door opened. "So, we meet under sad circumstances, Chris. I'm Dr. Schumacher." He pulled up a chair and sat down. "Tell me, what wall did you run into?"

Chris tried to smile, but his face was stiff and sore. "Is my nose broken, Doctor?"

"We'll see. I'll examine you, and I may ask your grandfather to take you to the hospital and have some x-rays." After going over Chris carefully, Dr. Schumacher smiled at him. "You're going to live. There's nothing broken or dislocated, just bruised. I think your nose is fine. We'll have to wait a few days until the swelling goes down. The rest of you is fine; there's nothing like being young. I'll tell your granddad. He's fuming at whoever roughed you up." The doctor raised his eyebrows. "Do you know them?"

"Yah, I thought I did, but evidently, I didn't. One thing for sure, I'm going to go out for the wrestling team this winter, and no one is ever going to do this to me again."

"That's the spirit. I'll probably be at some of your matches. I volunteer my time at the high school sporting events. Call me if anything hurts for too long," he said as he left the room.

Chris lay there trying to put the pieces together about that night when he heard Winston's heavy tread on the floor. One thing for sure, he was going to see Laura tomorrow, no matter what. The doctor said aspirin for his aches and pains would do the trick.

"Hi, Grandpa, what have you got there?"

"An ice pack for your nose and some aspirin for everything else," Winston said, with a worried expression on his face.

"Don't feel bad, Grandpa. I'm fine, just a little beat up. I'm going to get up after I stick the ice on my nose for a while and take plenty of aspirin. I want it to look good. I'm going to see Laura tomorrow, and I don't want to look like a beat-up prize fighter."

"Do you want to talk about what happened?"

"No, I'll take care of it myself in my own way," Chris said, adamantly.

"I know you will, Chris. Let me know if you need anything." Winston's voice was full of concern. "You remind me of your father. I wish he could see you right now. He'd be proud of you."

"Do you think so, Grandpa? I wonder. He never seemed happy with me."

The following morning, stiff and sore, Chris made his way to the shower to ease the pain with hot water and steam. At noon, he was dressed and sitting at the breakfast table, physically hurting, but emotionally on top of the world. His girl had said yes for another date, and Dr. Glen was picking him up after lunch for work.

"You eat up now, me boy. That skinny body of yours has got to be fed."

"No more pancakes, Briggie. I'm stuffed."

"We'll eat them, Briggie," Amanda said, plopping down on a chair across from Chris with Lois slipping in beside her. "What happened to you?" his sister asked in a blunt style she reserved for her brother. "You're a mess."

"I walked into a tree," Chris said, getting up slowly to escape his sister's annoying questions and wait outside for Dr. Glen's car.

"That's a big lie," Amanda yelled after him.

43. Surprising Honeymoon Revelations

August 1963
(Maria)

Maria lay for a minute wondering where she was, then got up quietly and pulled the chiffon-like drapes back and opened the door to their balcony. She'd missed the ocean since moving to Illinois but had to admit that although Lake Michigan wasn't the ocean, it was big and beautiful. Out on her balcony, the small but adequate man-made beach below seemed smaller than the night before when she and Ed had strolled there. Beaches and walks in the moonlight with both George and Bill had never ended in a good way. She hoped her luck with Ed would change and their lives would be full of love.

Ed had certainly showed courage and perseverance dating her the past year, and he'd never complained that they were continually surrounded by her children. When was the last time, other than their wedding night, they had been alone together? Maria remembered only a few stolen nights in college. Why had Ed been so insistent on getting married? Did he have a dark, ulterior motive? Peter hadn't found any during all of his sessions with Ed, or he would have cautioned her.

Maria stood there looking at him, still out like a light. Poor guy, he'd worked from six the previous morning to the moment before he picked her up, drove them into Chicago, wined and dined her, and even walked on the beach in the moonlight, humoring her.

How he had the energy to make love after all that amazed her. What drove him so hard? He continually surprised her with his passion, but it was almost too good to be true.

The elegant hotel he'd chosen for them was right on the water, because he knew she loved the ocean. To fill that wish and make her birthday and their first and only honeymoon something to remember, he'd chosen the Beach Hotel. Survivors of bad marriages, they hoped this one would be a winner, and she knew she'd never be thirty-three again.

As she stood there, heat poured into the room through the open door. She'd forgotten how extreme the weather was in the Midwest— too hot in the summer and too cold in the winter. Thank God for air conditioning. They'd spend the day inside the cooled Museum of Science and Technology building. It was full of machines, experiments, and scientific studies he'd love to explore.

She hated to close them off from the water, but she pulled the sliders and shut the drapes. The cool air blowing into the room from the vents began changing the temperature immediately. How did she ever grow up without air conditioning?

Maria slipped off her nightie and stood naked while she picked out the coolest outfit she had for weather that generated as much heat as a broiler. Instinctively, she felt Ed's eyes on her and she turned. "You caught me."

"I always know when there's a naked beauty in my room. Come back to bed."

"If you promise to be good."

"I'll be as good or better than I was last night." He gave her a teasing smile. "At least you thought I was good, as I remember."

She jumped into bed and hugged his sleepy body. Playing with the curly hair on his chest she said, "We can't spend our whole weekend in bed, as much as you would like to—"

Ed kissed her into silence, then said softly, "Just an hour or so in the morning and a little more in the evening. That's what a honeymoon is all about. Admit it, you love it."

When room service came with their breakfasts, they were starving. "Nothing like sex to give one an appetite," Ed said, jumping out of bed with a towel wrapped around his waist to answer the door. She watched the bellhop go through the delivery motions with a stone face. When he left, they burst out laughing.

It was true, as Ed had quickly pointed out, that this was their only chance for love in the morning. At home, he was gone by six every working day, and it was iffy with Amanda around on the weekends. Amanda had the unnerving propensity to pop in for unscheduled visits to see her beloved daddy, making Maria too nervous to even think about sex.

Ed sat propped up in bed, eating. "I like this place except for one thing, it doesn't have a big bathtub. Remember the one at the Berkmar Hotel in Des Moines? That was the night I knew in my gut you were the one, but I didn't do anything about it."

"You told me you loved me, which clearly you hadn't been able to choke out until then. You didn't make any promises. That was honest, Ed. You were trying to be up front with me."

"And stupid. What was I afraid of? You'd have worked and helped me."

"Handsome, we've been all over this. Forget it, it's over. We're married now." She reached over her tray and stuffed a piece of muffin in his mouth. "Eat up and let's think about spending time inside Chicago's nice, cool museums."

"Maybe, but first I've got other plans for us this morning. Don't ask. Just wait and be surprised." After he put their tray outside the door, he ran for the shower.

Maria joined him in the bathroom. "I wonder where all those sailboats and yachts are going that I saw this morning. I'd love to be on one of them," she said, dreamily.

"We'll go to wherever you want to go. I'll look into it." Ed's voice didn't sound very encouraging. "I'd like to see some of the ships up close. Let's go down to the wharves and see what we can find."

"Will they be all fishy smelling with lots of fish being loaded onto trucks?"

"I don't know, but it should be interesting."

"For whom? Not me."

"Trust me," he said and kissed her nose.

"Ed, did you pick out this place? It's lovely." She whirled around the room.

"I did. Veterinarians do talk about something other than animals at the vet meetings. They actually travel, dress, and act like normal intelligent people."

He wouldn't tell her where he was taking her when they left the hotel. All he would say was to trust him. Glancing at a slip of paper from his pocket, he drove slowly down into the heart of the city, looking for an address. Finally, he parked. "We can walk from here. Let's go." He took her hand and sauntered along at an easy pace.

Maria glanced around, trying to get a clue as to where they were going. "What happened to the boats, yachts, and fishing fleet? I thought that was on your mind. You're a man of mystery. It's fun. How about doing this every weekend?"

"Great, but unfortunately my partner wouldn't like it. Which reminds me, I need to call the clinic sometime, but not now." He stopped in front of a set of gleaming double doors. "After you, Mrs. McDermott."

Maria looked questioningly at her handsome husband. "What do you have in mind?"

"Trust me, I should have done this a year ago, but was too busy to think. I'm still rough around the edges, but I'm learning."

Inside the luxurious, cool, and quiet interior, Maria wrinkled up her nose and whispered, "I smell something."

"What?" he whispered back with a frown.

"Money."

He grinned. "Yeah, you're right. It's not the Ames Jewelry Store." He guided her over to a well-dressed, smiling older man who'd been watching them.

"Good morning, what can I show you this fine day?" the gentleman asked, smiling and looking hopeful.

"First, can you repair this little watch?" Ed pulled out Maria's old Minnie watch, and smiling, dangled it in front of the salesman.

The look on the salesman's face was priceless. He stopped smiling and gingerly accepted the watch as if it were a dead mouse. "I'll take it to our man," he said, disappearing.

Maria started giggling. "You're such a tease. Was that the only thing you wanted in this store? At least let me buy you a tie clasp."

Ed had a stoic look on his face as he waited.

"Good news, sir. Our man can repair it, although he is backed up. Could you pick it up later today, or should we mail it to you? That requires you to prepay the charges and costs." The gentleman glanced at Maria, then focused his attention on Ed again. "Are you from out of town? Are you staying here?"

"We are indeed vacationing here, and we're staying at the Continental Beach Hotel for the weekend." Ed handed him a business card. "My name is Dr. McDermott, and this is my wife. I practice in St. Charles, Illinois. Now, show us new watches, dressy ones for my wife."

Hearing they were staying at a fancy hotel, the magic word *doctor*, and the chance for a big sale, the salesman's demeanor changed into a smiling person, nearly tripping as he rushed across the store to another locked cabinet. "If you'll step over here, I'll show you some lovely watches."

"You're a bad boy, teasing that poor man," Maria whispered.

Ed's brown eyes twinkled. "And you like bad boys."

"This is a complete surprise," she said to the salesman.

"It's her birthday, and she's always late, so I hope this will help."

Ignoring Ed's smart remark, she was in a quandary. Why did Ed want her to have a new watch? She didn't need one, now that Minnie Mouse could be repaired. Perhaps he wanted to match the watch George had given her. "I like this one," she said, picking out a small, gold watch with a delicate design etched into the edges of it. "Do you like it?"

"Yes," Ed said, sounding not too interested. "As long as you like it, that's all that counts."

The salesman smiled. "Will that be all?"

"Yes, thanks," Maria said, picking up her purse. "Wrap it up, and I'll take it."

"No, we're not finished." Ed had a determined look on his face. "I'd like you to show us engagement rings."

Maria took Ed's hand, and they walked over to a small alcove to talk. "Now, really, I don't need an engagement ring. I love our matching gold bands."

Ed put his hands on her shoulders and looked her straight in the eyes. "An engagement ring is a promise from a guy that says he values his lady love so much he wants the whole world to know—especially other men—that he wants to marry her. She's off limits. I didn't do that, but after seeing the ring George gave you, I want to make it right. Please let me do this."

"Okay, whatever you want," she said weakly. Maria shivered thinking how little her engagement ring mattered to George when he started cheating on her, but she knew it meant a lot to Ed. Searching through the maze of rings sparkling in their trays, as if they were saying *choose me, choose me*, she thought deciding was impossible. She closed her eyes for a moment. "Ed, maybe we should come back again. This is hard for me to decide."

Disappointment registered on his face as she was talking. "Okay, I'll try again." She said a little prayer, closed her eyes, and when she opened them, her eyes rested on a delicate little ring she hadn't noticed before. Set with three diamonds, one large and a small one on each side, it was perfect.

"Try it on. It may need to be sized," Ed said.

"Can you believe it? It fits perfectly." Maria raised her hand for him to see. "The big stone is for you and the two little ones are for the kids."

Ed smiled, looking pleased. "I want a box for both the ring and the watch, please. Wrap them up." Ed took out his checkbook.

"Yes, sir, and you can forget about the watch repair charges and mailing fee. We'll have your watch delivered to the hotel," he said, giving them an ecstatic smile. "Please come back again, anytime."

Ed carefully put the boxes in the glove compartment of the car, opened his window, and glanced at that little slip of paper again and drove. As he worked his way through the traffic, he said, "I want to put your ring on your finger tonight."

"Okay, handsome, and I suppose it wouldn't do me any good to ask where we're going."

"Trust me," he said, emphatically.

Actually, Maria loved the treatment she was getting. There was no need to make any decisions, drive, or try to convince the family to go along with her plans. She felt free.

He stopped in the business section of Chicago and parked in a lot with an attendant. Locking the car, he said, "Come on, I want to get you some dresses for the parties we'll give and go to this fall. When was the last time you bought any clothes?"

"I've always bought my own work clothes. George never bought me anything, except for my wedding dress in St. Croix where we were married."

"I'm different, remember?" They stopped in front of a fancy boutique. He squeezed her hand. "That's for the courage you'll need to shop," he said, smiling at her.

Inside the boutique, Ed turned on his charm. "I'm here with my wife and want you to take care of her," he said to the lady obviously in charge. "You look like you know exactly what to do, and I don't know anything about this. I just want her to be happy and look nice."

"Of course, sir, I'll do my best. As a little thank you, we serve our gentlemen friends fresh coffee, snacks, or drinks from our bar—whatever you prefer." She took him across the room, gave him the morning newspaper, and waited until he was seated to serve him his beverage.

"It's too early for a drink, but I'll have some coffee," Ed said, smiling broadly at her.

As Maria stood waiting, the manager, all smiles, hurried over to her. "Your charming husband said to help you and make you happy. I'm going to do that. Is there anything in particular you would like?"

"Well, I'm not sure. My husband surprised me by bringing me here today, and I really haven't thought about clothes recently. *Why am I apologizing to a perfect stranger?* "Perhaps I should look at some dresses and suits for fall. According to my husband, I also need some evening dresses," glancing at him hidden behind the newspaper.

An hour later, Maria was moderately pleased, but also irritated trying to guess at the different kinds of outfits she would need for future parties and gatherings that she'd never been to before. Ed was no help. He liked everything she modeled for him. Where was her mother with her critical eye when she needed her? Maria agonized and reversed her decisions a dozen times, ending up with some outfits she hoped would be appropriate.

Sitting down next to her relaxed, happy husband, she whispered, "Ed, some of these things are terribly expensive. I don't know what to do."

"I do. Buy them. You're going to be by a lot of women who are used to having everything they want, and I want you to look like a knockout and show them what a great woman you are. In a couple of months, I'm going to bring you back again for more clothes. Now finish up, it's time for lunch." He grinned and picked up a magazine.

When they left with the blessings of the manager, Ed put her boxes and bags in the trunk of their car. "I'm hungry, how about you?" He opened her door, then tried to kiss her before she got in. "What's the matter?"

"Get in. I have a question for you. Am I a trophy wife for you to show off? Is this why all the clothes?" Maria was beginning to feel a slow burn the more she thought about it.

Ed had a sheepish look on his face. "I won't deny I want you to make a good impression. There are also some other things I should have told you, but my male ego has held me back. It's like it's not masculine to say too much. It's stupid, I know. Now that you have put me on the hot seat, I'll come clean to save our weekend." He sounded sincere.

"I'm proud of you, how you handle yourself, how smart you are, and how you can talk to men and women alike. Wealthy people don't bother you, you're pretty, and full of fun. You are everything I've ever wanted in a wife." Ed sat looking at her, not moving, just waiting.

How was Maria supposed to respond to that? "I'm trying to be mad at you, but it's impossible because you're so darn convincing. Did you really mean all those things?"

"I'll let you in on a little secret about me. I don't spend money easily, but I can't resist you in or out of bed, my wild passionate woman. I love you, always have, always will."

"Well, I can't resist you, my charming, handsome husband. Where to for lunch?"

"Maisie said there are some good places for fresh fish near the fishing docks."

"After all the money you spent on me, I'm not sure we can afford it."

"I've said enough about money. Now, let's have fun the rest of the day." He leaned over, closed his eyes, and slowly brushed her lips with his. "I'll collect more tonight," he whispered.

It was getting hotter and hotter. Maria didn't like the idea of eating at a smelly restaurant near the docks, even if the fish were fresh. As Ed drove slowly down to the wharves, he called to a fisherman and asked him about a good place to eat. The guy pointed to a rundown place across the street and gave him a thumbs up.

"Is this it, Ed? It looks terrible from the outside." Maria could just make out a faded sign that said, "Fish House."

"The guy said all the dock workers come here. Come on, let's try it." Taking her hand, he pulled her into a raucous place full of loud-mouthed fishermen, eating and drinking beer. The food smelled delicious, but it was so hot, and she thought she might be sick. All of a sudden, a hush fell over the crowd. She was the only woman in the place, and she didn't like it.

"Don't mind us, fellows," Ed said. "We're vacationers and will be out of here in a few minutes." Smiling at everyone, he started to sit down on a long bench, then turned to help Maria, but she bolted out of the place.

44. Getting Things Straight

August 1963
(Maria)

Maria stood outside, away from the building, trying to catch her breath.

Ed had followed her. "Why did you leave?" Ed's face was a mass of confusion.

"I'm not eating in there. One thing you'd better learn about me. I like to be asked my opinion on questionable places, especially restaurants."

"I just thought it would be an experience for you," he said, looking frustrated.

"You just thought, you didn't ask. I'm not used to having twenty men ogling me, plus the place was filthy and the temperature unbearable."

"You're so fussy. I thought it looked like a great place!"

"You come back when you're in town with some male friends and eat here. I'm going to wait in the car. Give me the keys so I can lock myself in."

"I guess I'm used to dirt and manure. I've been around it all of my life. Maybe I'm too rough around the edges for you," he said, sounding dejected as he walked her to their car.

"I just want to be included in a decision as to where we eat and not be belittled for not enjoying having a bunch of rough workers leering at me. Maybe you need to smooth off some of those rough edges and think about protecting me," she said as she opened her own door and sat down.

"Well, where do you want to eat, now that you've won? Some tearoom, I suppose."

"I'm not hungry. Take me to an air-conditioned museum where

I can cool off." She turned and stared out the side window so she didn't have to look at him.

Ed drove, but not in the direction Maria expected. "We're leaving the city. Aren't we going to a museum this afternoon, where it's cool?"

"No, I wanted to surprise you with something else. You'll love it."

"Like I loved your choice of restaurants. It's so hot in here, please roll down your window. I may get a windburn from the hot air pouring in here, but I can't stand the heat. I never needed air conditioning in the East, but out here, I want it in my car."

"The next car I get for you will be a station wagon with air conditioning, like all the married women drive, not this hot little item."

"I'll never get rid of this car until it falls apart. I'm a woman first and a mother second. This car represents freedom for me, and I intend to keep it."

"You intend to keep your freedom, your car, or both?"

"Both," she snapped, giving Ed a defiant look. They rode for miles in silence. Maria looked at the fast-changing landscape. "We're in the suburbs. Are we going to Cicero?" She'd been reading the city signs.

"Yes, we're going to a place I've wanted to go to for a long time, but I never had the time or didn't have anyone I wanted to take with me, until now."

The cars were streaming in from the highway, following the signs to the Cicero racetrack. Maria was pleased, but held back her enthusiasm. She was still angry.

"How do you feel about coming here?" Ed gave her a quick glance and then a smile. "Think of all the horses you'll see."

"I haven't been to a track since Winston took Mom and me to one in Maryland."

Ed parked and opened her door. "Come with me to lunch in an air-conditioned dining room before the races. Then we'll walk around and observe the horses and decide which ones look best to win. If you don't like my ideas, tell me what you want to do."

"When you put it that way, I can't refuse. It's hard to stay mad at you," she said, slipping her hand into his strong one. "Lead the way, but answer me one thing. Doesn't this heat get to you?"

"I'm like a cactus, my little Rosebud. I grew up on a farm, remember, and I'm in barns every day that feel like ovens."

"How awful. I forget how hard your work is because you never complain."

296

"Good, I've got you fooled," he said, laughing. "I like my woman to feel sorry for me."

That afternoon she followed him all over the racing park where they discussed the merits of the horses by watching them as they were walked around an enclosure by their trainers before each race. Ed's knowledge of horse flesh helped them pick out winners. He also talked to trainers, owners, and several race vets who were hired by the racetrack to examine each horse entered in a race, making sure they were healthy and not on any drugs.

Maria's face looked sunburned as the afternoon wore on, prompting Ed to say, "Let's get a beer and sit in the stands in the shade. You didn't bring a hat. I'm sorry about that."

"I'm pretty tough and more like a tiger lily than a rosebud. I'm just thirsty and hot. Let's bet on some more races, drink copious amounts of water, and clean up. I have an unfair advantage because I brought a ringer with me."

"The cashiers are beginning to wonder about me picking so many winning horses." Ed grinned. "Let's go soon before the place empties out. I've had enough, how about you?"

On the way out, he gave her an envelope full of their winnings. "Put it in that bag of yours and count it after we get on the road."

"Yippee," she said, "We made out pretty well this afternoon. I told you I had a hunch about "Promise Me." She was a fast little girl out there with all those boys."

"She was running for her life. That's why she did so well. How about all those boys I picked who also won this afternoon? We can buy another trip to the big city with today's winnings."

Back at their hotel, Ed stopped at the desk to see if there were any calls or a package for them.

"Yes, Dr. McDermott, there's a package, but no calls." The man behind the desk smiled. "Is there anything else I can do for you?"

"Send up some good champagne in about a half an hour."

Ed's engine was heating up again, and Maria's body tingled with the look he gave her in the elevator. As soon as they closed the door to their room, Ed's hands were all over her, and his lips were kissing her hungrily.

"Down tiger," Maria said. "I need a shower, and the bell boy will be here in a little while." He laughed and started to undress her. "You've got to keep it under control," she said as she twisted away from him. She ran into the bathroom and locked the door. "I don't trust you or myself in the shower, my wild man. I'll let you in when I come out."

While toweling off and drying her hair, she heard the bell boy come and go. Maria peeped out of the bathroom. "You can come in now," she said softly.

"Don't put any clothes on." He walked in stark naked. "I'll be out in a minute or two," he said, looking at her like he could eat her.

Ignoring him because of the coolness of their bedroom, she slipped on a see-through bathing suit cover-up and waited for his approval. When he came out from his shower, she gave him a look as she poured two glasses of champagne.

Stark naked, he came up behind her, and nuzzled her neck. "You're really pushing my control button pretty hard," he whispered. "Where did you get that lacy little number?"

"My mother bought it for me for our trip," Maria said, delighted that he was pleased.

"Now I know how she keeps Winston so interested." He took a glass and also gave her one. "Here's to you, my darling. Am I forgiven for being so rough?" He took a sip, looking at her over the top of his glass, and waiting for an answer.

"I can't explain why I'm no longer bothered by anything you did today. Between your sexiness and this glass of bubbly, I'm going to end up flat on my back."

"One way or another, that's the general idea. Sit down and help me eat this bag of peanuts I bought today at the racetrack. Drink and see what happens. I'll also give you your birthday presents."

He took a box out of his suitcase and sat down. "I'd like you to sit in my lap, but I know that won't work the way I'm feeling. Here, open this box first."

She read the label on the gift. "When did you have time to go to Marshall Field's?"

"No questions, just open it," he said, before sipping his wine and tossing a few nuts into his mouth.

She opened the box and pulled out several pieces of gorgeous black lingerie. Holding them up to her body, she did a little dance, then took a sip of her wine.

"I want you to model them later," he said, his eyes full of excitement.

"Now, for the best part," he said, taking her left hand. He slipped on her new engagement ring. "There now, that's more like it," he said, holding her hand out in front of him, turning it this way and that. "The women at the parties are going to be examining your rings, and I wanted you to have something nice to show them. And now, Mrs. McDermott, come dance with me." Quickly finding a local Chicago station, he took her in his arms. "I don't know how long I'll last, but here goes."

They didn't last at all with both of them almost naked. He was trembling as they ran for the bed. With half a bottle of champagne in them, there were no preliminaries. After a furious few minutes, she felt herself going over the edge with him in a paroxysm of ecstasy. Holding onto him for dear life, she felt his orgasm taking her with him.

Lying in each other's arms, sweaty, hot, and loving it, she said, "Well, how does my big stud feel now? That was pretty sensational. We have to take more vacations."

Ed turned on his back and put her up on his sticky body. Do you have any idea how much of what you say and do affects me? It's what makes me want to give you the world. And what I like is the fact you really mean it. I love you so much, Maria, it scares me. I want to protect you and keep anyone from hurting you. I'm almost obsessed."

Lying a few inches from his face, she said softly, "Thank you for what you said today about me. I'll never forget it. I love you so much this minute, I could scream. No one can buy what we have. It is that intangible love that everyone wants, but is impossible to capture.

"And, guess what, I love what you do for a living. It's such a down-to-earth profession, caring for animals. It brings you home to me every night. I love hearing that truck of yours come roaring up the driveway. It means you want to be with me, not flying around somewhere else."

"You do? Let me tell you after coming home countless times to an empty house with both of my previous wives, knowing you're there gives me such a rush, I can't wait to walk through my door. I haven't had that feeling for the last ten years." Choked with emotion, he kissed her, his eyes cherishing her. When she kissed him back, her hands gently held his face to hold the kiss, and he turned her on her back. Pushing the tendrils of hair from her face, he said, "I love your scent. It makes me crazy."

She wiggled under his weight, and he moved into position. The next rational moment they had later, they looked at each other and laughed.

"I'm amazed at us. You'd think we were twenty-one again," Maria whispered.

"All it took was for us to be alone without any immediate problems and bingo, we hit the jackpot several times." He slowly sat up. "I'm hungry. We forgot dinner."

"Let's eat on our little balcony now that it's in the shade. I don't want to break the mood."

"Are you sure? I was planning on taking you to the Palmer House to bring back old memories for you with your dad."

"That's sweet, but the hotel has good food. Let's save the Palmer House for another time."

"Are you going to eat in your see-through cover-up?" Ed asked, his eyes dancing.

"No, silly, we're only on the second floor. No peep shows on this balcony tonight."

"True, I don't want to fight off any aggressive males in my weakened condition. Let's order room service and take a shower. By the time they bring the food, we'll be ready. And after dinner, let's walk on the beach. You've converted me.

"Better yet, let's swim in the lake afterward." Maria gave him a gentle shove. "Don't give me that look. It'll be fun."

They loved dining on their small balcony and watching the lights from the boats and the ships as they moved out into Lake Michigan. Some were tiny images out there, and others seemed to be hugging the coastline. Ed was unusually quiet. Perhaps her suggestion of swimming had turned him off.

"Let's take a harbor cruise tomorrow morning before we set sail for St. Charles." Ed offered, hesitantly. I know you'd love that. "We can save the museums for a winter visit."

"Okay," Maria said, delighted with his plan. "Your suggestion reminds me of another idea running around in my head."

"When I hear that tone, I know that fertile mind of yours is hatching something big. Shoot."

"It needs the water as a backdrop. Let's go down and walk on the beach."

"Now I'm really curious."

She giggled, ran inside, and put on her water shoes. "Come on my big, handsome, lovemaking machine."

"Okay, okay, give a guy a break. I'm coming." Ed took her hand and down they went on the outside stairs like a couple of kids.

"Gosh, this is beautiful, Ed. Look at all the people out on the beach. It's a perfect time to go swimming with the sun almost setting and the air not so hot. I love that it stays light so late in the summer."

"So, out with this idea that needed to be shared on the beach. I'm interested."

"Before I tell you, I want you to enjoy the beach and the water. Let's walk and get our feet wet," she said, taking his hand and pulling him along with her.

"You know I'm not the biggest fan of the water. I'm interested in sailing and navigation, but swimming isn't a big thing with me."

"I know, my Midwestern hunk who grew up on a farm and never had time or money to go swimming. What if I tell you about a place that's free, the weather is usually balmy, and you could learn to sail. What would you say to a Christmas vacation there?"

"Sounds too good to be true. Where is this Nirvana?"

Maria swished her feet in the watery sand at the edge of Lake Michigan as she walked along. "No fair answering a question with a question."

"Okay, my persuasive, clever little Rosebud. I might be interested if I could give Glen a week or more off this fall. He's taken up the slack for me many times over this past year while I chased you to the altar."

Ed picked up a piece of driftwood and threw it in the water. "I'm having personnel problems in the office right now. Gladys is out a lot, claiming sickness, but I doubt it's true. When she's there, she spends way too much time talking on the phone to God knows who. Hugh is wracked with arthritis and has a terrible time getting around, has to cover for her, and can't keep up with the drug ordering and keeping his books because of it."

"I didn't know things were so bad in the office." Maria stopped and stared at him. "Why didn't you tell me? Remember what you said about me not shutting you out? Well, you've done that to me, haven't you?"

"Ah, well, you've had your hands full, getting the kids and Briggie settled in their new surroundings, plus getting that wreck of a house in shape. I didn't want you to have to deal with my problems, too."

Maria stopped dead in her tracks again and looked up at her dear, worried husband's face. "Guess what, that's what being married means. You've got to trust me enough to confide in me. I'll come work for you. You can't afford me, so I'll work for free until you fire

Gladys and replace her. Ask Winston to help Hugh out for a while until he's caught up. He'll love it. And, when you can, you need to advertise for another junior partner."

Ed raised her hand to his lips and kissed her knuckles. "It's not that quick or simple."

"I know that," she said, standing on her tiptoes, trying to look taller and see into his eyes. "But you have to start somewhere."

"I'll think about hiring another man to help us. Our business is expanding all the time."

They quietly walked along the shoreline for a long while. Ed's silence indicated to Maria that he was mulling over what she'd said.

"I'm so hot, I'm going to get wet," she said, breaking their silence. "Sit on one of the hotel's lounges and watch me in case I get a cramp and you have to save me."

Twenty minutes later, she came back to him dripping water all over him and laughing.

"Hey! No fair!" He pulled her onto his lap and gave her a big kiss.

"What's that for? I just got you soaking wet."

"Thanks for the straight talk. I knew there would be big dividends going away with you for a couple of days. It really is pretty simple to fix things. I just need to do it. But what you said about me trusting you is harder to fix. I was raised by a mother who silenced me and would have cut out my tongue rather than let me tell her anything. She could twist everything I said into a knot, and I'd end up feeling so guilty I'd think about it for days." Ed shifted his body. "I'll try to do what I expect from you—that's only fair.

"I'll ask Winston to help out when I see him tomorrow, and I'd love to have you working your magic around the clinic for a while. As for another partner, I'll call some of my vet friends and see if they have any prospects for me. That may take a while, but I'll get started." He looked relieved with his decision. "Want to take another swim with me? I feel like it now." He pushed her out of his lap and ran for the water.

When they came out laughing, Ed asked, "Where is this Nirvana you mentioned?"

"Miami. Winston has owned a place there for years. It's really nice. You'd love it."

"It sounds like a winner. We'll go. Part of me wants to go so badly, but part of me—" Ed was obviously trying to sound confident, but Maria heard the catch in his voice from emotion.

"Let's walk and dry off," Maria said, holding onto him with her arm around his waist, hoping it would give him time to be able to say what was really bothering him. They walked quite a distance, but Ed never finished his sentence.

Returning to their room, happy with each other, they quietly slipped into bed and fell asleep, hugging each other. The day and evening had extracted its emotional toll from them. Getting used to being married was hard work.

Ed's attitude in the morning was puzzling to Maria. He said all the right things while signing them out of the hotel and driving to the harbor, but he wasn't completely there. On board the boat, Ed said, "Maria, you seem so distant this morning. What's the matter?"

"You're the matter. I wasn't the one who got up this morning, not saying a word or even letting me kiss you. Believe me, I'm a pro being around a guy who can hardly stand to be near me. I had years of it." Maria looked at him, tears falling and sparks flying.

"God, Maria, don't shut me out, even if I act like an ass. That's when I need you the most."

She stared out into the harbor. "I don't feel I deserve the angry, silent treatment this morning. All I said last night was that I'd like to show you another part of the world—Miami and all the fun it holds. What was so bad about that?" She felt tears running down her face, hot and wet, and she turned away quickly, wiping her face with her sleeve.

"Are you crying? God, Maria, I'm a shit. I'm so confused, I need to talk to Peter."

"Fine," she hissed, as the passengers were crowding up to the rails to enjoy the view. "Don't talk to me. Don't confide in me. What do I know? Yesterday, you couldn't do enough for me, buying me a ring, a watch, and expensive clothes, and when I mentioned giving yourself some time off at Christmas, it evidently sounded like I was sentencing you to hell."

"Let's go find someplace where we can talk privately."

"In this boat, stuffed with people out to have a nice tour, where would that be?"

"Maybe in a lifeboat. I don't know," Ed said, returning her anger with his own.

The bar wasn't crowded. It was too early for most people to drink. They found a little table off to one side and sat down facing each other. He took her hands and held onto them as he cleared his throat.

"I hate to admit this to anyone, especially you," he said, keeping his voice low. He paused and cleared his throat again. "But I felt—panicky." He held her gaze, as though watching for her reaction.

"So?" Maria was confused. What would cause him to feel that way?

"I find it awfully hard to admit that I'm not always in control and can't handle my emotions. The scary part is that I don't know why I feel this way." He leaned across the table. "I had a couple of nightmares last night. In one of them, I was a little boy terrified of a black, enveloping cloud that threatened to suck me up and never let me go."

"Oh, Ed, I wish you'd wakened me."

"Don't you understand, Maria? I didn't want you to see me like that. I'm supposed to be the one who takes care of you, not the other way around."

"That's crazy thinking, Ed," she whispered. "We're married for better or for worse. Either partner might need help, it doesn't matter." Something about Ed's confession reminded her of George and she shivered. She saw the bartender watching them. He was probably wondering what they were talking about so seriously inside when they should have been outside, enjoying the view.

"I guess so, but I was raised that way."

"I'm sorry that you felt upset when I mentioned a vacation. For your information, it would be for all of us, not just you, if that helps any," Maria said, smiling and squeezing his hands.

"It does. Rationally, I think it's a great idea, but there's something in me that can't handle not having an important purpose for very long. Just having fun makes me feel guilty."

"It would be very good for you to talk to Peter. He's coming next weekend and may suggest another hypnotic regression. He'll know what to do." A tear escaped and slid down Maria's cheek. She wiped it away with the back of her hand. "I'm sorry to be so emotional, but I'm gun-shy when I think we might be slipping into the type of life I had with George. I get panicky, speaking of panic. I react irrationally too."

"I love you, Maria, and I'm not George. I'll figure this out with your and Peter's help." Ed stood and reached for her hand. "Come on. Let's get our money's worth with this cruise." He kissed her, and they saw the bartender give them the thumbs up sign.

"I love you, Doc. We'll make it, as long as we keep talking or fighting. Silence is the kiss of death, so please don't shut me out."

45. Circling the Wagons

August 1963
(Maria)

They drove home slowly from the harbor cruise. Anxious to hold onto the good feelings and memories of their weekend, and ignore their worries for a moment more, they stopped at their favorite root beer stand for a float before they gave in to their responsibilities and turned toward home.

About a half-mile away from their house, Ed slowed and then stopped by a truck that was parked off of the road. Maria waited while he got out, peered into the locked cab, then shook his head as though puzzled.

"What's the matter?" By his expression, something didn't make sense. "What was in there?"

"An active shortwave radio set, complete with antenna, just like mine."

"Mention it to Winston when you see him. It sounds strange."

"I'll also alert the police."

As they pulled into the garage, Maria reached for the door handle, but something made her look at Ed.

He took her hand and smiled. "There's no place like home as long as you're in it, Mrs. McDermott."

She leaned over, kissed him, and breathing into his ear said, "Sometimes, Doc, you are so eloquent. Thanks for a wonderful birthday and honeymoon. I'll never forget it."

Walking from the garage into the hallway, Maria felt the beautiful runner under her feet stretching all the way down the hallway. "Oh, Ed, thanks for your generosity in letting me make this place into a home. This rug is so soft, I can't wait to walk barefoot on it. They must have put it in yesterday."

Ed beamed. "That's why I married to you. You appreciate every-thing."

The house was quiet, except for Wiggles, who was scratching at the utility door to get out. "Briggie must be resting, so let's be quiet until she gets up," Maria whispered.

Ed nodded, let Wiggles out, scratched behind her ears, and started for the study. Wiggles followed quietly right behind them.

"I'm going to try and reach Elena," Maria said. "I see Briggie left me a message in her perfect handwriting that both Elena and my sister, May, called while we were gone. Probably to wish me a happy birthday. Do you have a lot of messages?"

"Yes, but no emergencies. I think I'll take our luggage up, change, and take care of everything early tomorrow at the clinic."

Sitting at her desk, Maria dialed Elena's number. After a dozen rings, Maria decided to hang up and try later.

But suddenly Elena came on the line and said, "Hi," in her soft voice.

"You sound breathless. You must have just come in." Maria was delighted to hear Elena's voice. She so seldom had a chance to talk with her.

"We did. Bill talked me into taking some time off and going to the Maryland Eastern Shore for swimming and some seafood. We had a wonderful time. Bill called it a blast, but I don't know why he used that word. Now I'm still faced with so much work to do for my exhibit in Chicago in a couple of weeks, I'm crazy."

Maria heard Bill say in the background, "She's crazy like a fox, Maria. She's got me doing all her household chores while she works. Can you imagine me, spoiled flyboy, cleaning?" he yelled into the phone.

"Bill exaggerates, but he has a wonderful heart," Elena said in her gentle way with just a hint of her Spanish accent. "I called before to wish you a happy birthday, and Briggie said that you were away in Chicago celebrating it with Ed."

"We were there for two days, and it was wonderful. I just got in and saw your message."

"Maria, I remember your first birthday with me when George and I had just escaped from our captors in Puerto Rico. You were so beau-tiful, and George was so in love with you. And I was so jealous of you, I acted like a brat. I'd decided in my fifteen-year-old brain that George was going to marry me someday. Do you remember that?"

Maria did, but she didn't want to bring up any unpleasantness.

She loved Elena like the younger sister she had never had, being the baby of the family, herself. "I'm dying to see you and your wonderful exhibit. Tell me when you're coming and where the exhibit will be. We're all going to Chicago to see it." Maria repeated everything back to Elena as she wrote it down to make sure she had the information correct. "I feel so much better now that I've talked to you."

"Maria, is it all right if Bill comes out with me to visit you?"

"Of course, you're both so welcome. I've fixed up two guest rooms." Maria giggled. "But I doubt Bill will use his. Come and enjoy the family. It will be like old times."

"Thank you so much, my dear Maria," Elena said, in her soft voice. "I love you and am looking forward to being with you. Your kindness over the years has meant so much to me."

After they hung up, Maria sat there in the study, thinking about Bill and Elena. They'd reached a balance in their relationship. Her first love had met his match with Elena. She kept him hopping and he loved it, otherwise, he would never have stayed around. Not handsome Bill, the darling of the stewardesses.

The scales of love were definitely tipped in Elena's favor, but Maria doubted that Elena even realized it. Elena's primary passion was her work. Her sculptures and paintings were magnificent. Maria smiled as she thought about Bill being domesticated by a sensitive, gentle artist like Elena.

Getting a drink of water in the kitchen, she heard Briggie calling, "Who's in me kitchen dirtying up everything?"

Maria flung her arms around her best friend in the world. "Did you miss me?"

"Aye, I did that, me little darlin' and that big bloke of an Irishman, too."

"Look what he got me while we were there." Maria lifted up her left hand and chuckled.

"May the saints preserve us, that is a beautiful ring, and you deserve it. Did you have a grand time? You've waited a long time, me girl." Briggie's eyes filled up, and she turned and opened the refrigerator to escape Maria's observation. "Look what I made for our dinner tonight. Doesn't everything look grand?"

"Oh, Briggie, it does. I'm hungry. We actually didn't have any lunch, but we had a big breakfast. I loved being away, but I love coming home to you." Maria gave Briggie a big kiss on her chubby cheek. "Now tell me, where is the rest of my family hiding?"

"Winston and Ruth took Amanda and her little shadow, Lois, to the Fox River to walk on the trails near the water. They should be back soon, and Chris is working with Dr. Glen."

"Can anyone else get into this love fest?" Ed asked, standing in the doorway.

"Begora, you're a sight for sore eyes, you old Irishman. You can kiss me anytime."

Ed quickly crossed the room and gave her a peck on the cheek, making her blush. "I'm hungry, but I need to check with my accountant. I'll be in the study. Don't forget to call me."

Briggie touched her cheek and turned toward the window that looked out on the hill behind the house. "Saints above, I forgot to mention some peculiar goings on up on that hill. I was in me bedroom to have a lay-down after all me cooking yesterday, and I looked out me window. Someone or something was up there and then vanished before me very eyes. I would say I was daft, but Wiggles had started barking to beat the band about the same time out in her dog run. She kept it up for over fifteen minutes afore she stopped."

Maria needed to tell Winston. No—she needed to tell Ed first. He could tell Winston.

"Briggie, we'll get to the bottom of it. I'm sure it was a deer or some other animal." Maria tried to offer a reassuring smile. "Thanks for leaving such clear phone messages for me. I love your handwriting."

"The holy nuns made sure we all had good handwriting. Many a ruler was used on my knuckles to produce those words," she boasted, then went back to preparing dinner.

Walking silently down the hall on the thick, soft runner, Maria found Ed in the study where he appeared lost in thought. Instead of sitting at her desk and risking disturbing him, she'd make the rest of her phone calls from their bedroom.

She stole out, went upstairs, admiring their new stair rugs as she climbed, and silently said a prayer. She dialed May's number by rote, having memorized it years ago. May answered in a whiney voice, and Maria's sensors went up. It was going to be a downer. Was May chronically depressed, or just bored and spoiled, making her continual complaints about Don? She seemed obsessed with him and hated the fact he loved to play horseshoes with the boys every chance he could.

Maria would chance an argument. "You've got to wise up, May. Think about something besides Don. Get that part-time job—anything! It's a big world out there."

"That's easy for you to say with a new, handsome husband. Anyway, happy birthday, sis. I didn't have time to get you a card, but decided to call and found out you were in Chicago on a belated honeymoon and birthday celebration. My, Ed certainly spoils you."

"Thanks for thinking of—"

"We were wondering when you were going to invite us over to see you and your new home. Don mentioned it just the other day. I told him it was typical of you not to think of it. As I remember, you've always thought about yourself all your life. Not that I mean to say you're selfish."

May began to hum softly—a habit when she said something hurtful.

Desperate to stop May's incessant humming, Maria impetuously interrupted and invited them to visit in a couple of weeks. She explained that the next two weekends were busy, but the following weekend, they were entertaining the local horse breeders and a few other friends. She was sure Don and May would love the party. Maria was babbling, the result of being nervous—and May made her nervous.

What was she doing? Why was she including them in her party plans? Maybe she'd be so busy with party prep, she could ignore May. Besides, Don would be a welcome addition, impressing the breeders with his vet knowledge.

"Would I need a gown?" Her sister sounded excited about the prospect.

"Not exactly a gown, but a late summer to early fall number with a little jacket would be perfect. It's hard to tell what the weather will be like, but I'm sure you have something."

"I've put on a few pounds," she tittered. "I'll just have to buy a new outfit for it. Sounds like an exciting weekend for a change," she said in a much more pleasant tone. "I'll have Don call Ed when he gets in tonight, *whenever that is,*" she snapped, an angry tone returning to her voice. "He always stops and has a few drinks with those miserable friends of his."

Maria ignored May's parting shot at Don. "Good, May, we'll look forward to having you. Invite June, too, if you'd like. I'm sure Amanda would love to see her big cousin again. There's room for all three of you."

Running down her thickly carpeted stairs in her bare feet, Maria laughed. The positive outcome from her call to her sister, coupled with the delicious feel of the rugs as she ran downstairs, made her interrupt Ed from his work. "Hi," she said, as she nipped at his ear.

"What's with you?" he asked, feeling his ear and laughing. "You're wild! Tell me before you choke." He pushed his chair away from his desk and sat her in his lap.

"I just added two more people to our party, and I hope they'll make it better. I've invited Don and May to our bash with the gentry of St. Charles. It also solves a big problem I have."

"Okay, I'll bite. What's the problem?"

"May drives me crazy when I'm alone with her, always complaining about Don. With the party to think of, she'll be out of my hair. And, after it's all over, we'll have fulfilled our obligation to them."

"Ed smiled and gave Maria a little kiss. "You're a fox, you know. It will be great to have Don here, telling his stories and jokes nonstop. May can help you, if she will, and then you're home free."

"Thanks for your approval. Oh, before I go, I wanted to tell you what Briggie told me. Maria quickly recounted Briggie's tale about a stranger up on the hill.

Ed frowned. "I'll call the police and report what Briggie saw, talk to Winston about it, and also mention the truck down in the gully with the shortwave equipment." He looked up, and Maria followed his gaze. Amanda and Lois were standing in the doorway.

Ed shifted Maria on his lap. "Hi, girls. Did you have fun while we were away?"

Remaining in the doorway, Amanda asked, "I'm fine. Did you bring me anything?"

"We did. I think your daddy put your presents on your bed." Maria watched Amanda and Lois run toward the stairs. "I guess presents outweigh hugs right now."

"She's a typical kid, Maria. Let's go see the folks. I want to talk to Winston." Ed lifted Maria off his lap, then taking her hand, led her toward her mother's home.

Ed and Maria knocked on her folks' patio door and heard a summons from within.

"What about an adult afternoon beverage?" Winston asked as soon as they entered. He licked his lips as though he were anticipating Ed's answer.

Maria smiled at them. "How about grilling some marinated chicken breasts while you indulge? Briggie has the chicken all ready."

"Trapped by the fairer sex, Ed. They get us every time."

"Winston and I'll be out after we clean up. It was a hot afternoon on the trails," her mother said, pushing her windblown hair out of her eyes.

Within minutes, everyone had gravitated to the patio. Briggie gave the chicken breasts to Winston. Amanda held a toy sailboat, and Lois hugged a statue of a horse. Both girls were in their swimming suits.

"Dad, thanks for the beautiful horse statue, but who is Whirlaway?" Amanda asked, sounding excited to have a gift from her dad.

"He was a famous racehorse, born and raised on a big farm around here. And the sailboat is a replica of all the little boats sailing around the harbor of Lake Michigan."

Amanda gave Ed a big hug. "Thanks for thinking of me, Dad. I never got any presents from my other dad. Is it all right to share them with Lois?"

"They're yours to do with as you please, Petunia."

Maria's heart missed a beat when she heard Amanda's honest comment about George. Memories were the only legacies that might have a chance to last forever, and Amanda's memories of her father weren't very nice.

Amanda touched Maria's arm. "Mom, can Lois stay for dinner?"

"Of course." Maria turned her attention to Lois. "Sweetie, just call your mother and make sure it's okay."

Briggie stopped the girls on their way inside. "Amanda, please bring enough lemonade outside for everyone. You'll find it in the fridge."

After the girls disappeared, Maria's mother let out a large sigh. "I think we should let you know about Chris.

"What about him?" Maria's immediate concern was obvious on her face.

"While you were away, Chris was beaten up by the same four fellows who helped you lay your rugs. As I understand it, they were bothering the girls at the park and several football friends of Chris really worked those bullies over. Their leader, Dewain, was furious and embarrassed.

"To get even, they waited for Chris in the bushes and jumped him when he was walking to Maisie's to call Winston. They held him while Dewain punched him until he passed out. Winston found him holding up a streetlight post when he was driving around looking for him."

"Oh, my heavens, was he badly hurt? I wish we had been home when this happened. Why didn't you call us?"

"I called Dr. Schumacher. He came out, checked Chris over, and said he was fine. He was just bruised, and his ego was hurt. Chris went to work the next day and went out that night again to see his girl. I didn't want to bother you while you were away, but just wanted you to know how well Chris handled it," her mother said.

"Wow, that kid has guts," Ed said. "Maybe I'll say something to him, but probably not, unless he brings it up."

"Well, *I'm* going to talk to him. This can't happen again to my boy." Maria pounded her fists together and gave Ed an irritated glance.

Amanda and Lois came bouncing out of the house with the pitcher of lemonade and some glasses. They put them on the table and jumped into the pool. Winston was grilling the chicken with Ed's encouragement, and the two men were talking quietly. Their serious faces were dead giveaways as to what they were discussing, but the minute Chris came out and joined them, they began joking with him. Maria stole a peek or two at her son, standing taller and stronger, acting as if nothing had ever happened to him. Maybe Ed knew best letting the incident drop.

46. Closing in on the Phone Stalker

Late August 1963
(Maria)

The next morning, when Ed kissed her good-bye, Maria croaked out, "When do you want me to come to work?"

"I left you a note on your desk before I came to bed late last night. Winston and I had a long talk about what our family could be facing," Ed said. Then he strode out of their room.

Maria's body responded quickly, remembering her routine in Washington, DC, when she had had a job. She jumped up, showered, and dressed for work in a soft summer skirt and blouse. She'd always received compliments on them when she'd worn them in Washington, and she wanted to make a good first impression in her new role. She brushed her hair longer than usual, making it shine, and decided on a little makeup. Even though Ed didn't like it, she did.

Laura and Sarah were coming in when she was making her way down the stairs.

"Mrs. McDermott, you look like a movie star," Laura said with a grin. Sarah nodded. "Did you buy that outfit when we went shopping?"

"No, it's something I had. You're just used to seeing me in jeans." Pleased with their reaction, Maria almost skipped down the rest of the stairs. "Come on, girls. I'll get you started washing windows. Just start at one end of the house and work your way around. By the time you finish, it will be time to do them again," Maria said, then laughed.

She found her note propped up against her picture of Ed that she'd framed when she was a freshman in college and he was a senior. It had taken a lot of coaxing to get him to send her his picture from the University of Kentucky that spring. His future had been a priority at that time—not pictures.

Looking back, he'd made wise decisions concerning his career. Maria had had no idea at the time of how important it would be for him to spend those three months studying their horse breeding program, but he had. It was the basis for what he did now. All she had known was that she had missed him. Why hadn't she been thinking about her future then? Maybe it was too late for her, but not for Amanda. Maria would raise her daughter differently.

Maria opened and read the note.

Come under the pretext of bringing me my wallet and stay a while. Winston will come on his own. Winston's suspicious. We'll take it one day at a time.

She laughed and shook her head. No heading, no closure—that was it.

Had Ed ever written her a letter or note before? Not that she could remember. Maria read it one more time. It matched his style, the way he worked—quick and to the point.

Next to the note was a box from a printer in town. She opened it, pulled out a card, and read the invitation inside.

Dr. and Mrs. McDermott invite you to spend an informal afternoon and evening with them at their home.
34 Hill Top Ridge Road
Sept. 21, 1963
Come any time after 3:00 PM.

The message was plain and to the point, just like Ed. There was a little enclosure to be returned to them with a simple statement of regrets.

Underneath the box was another shorter note, simply asking Maria to help him out with the invitations. Attached was a long list of breeders, farmers, and townspeople that Ed wanted to invite. It must have been why he was up so late the night before.

The phone rang and she grabbed it quickly. "Hi," she said.

"Hi, yourself. You sound efficient this morning," Alicia said. "Can Amanda go with us to the Chicago's Museum of Science and Industry today? I hope so. Lois's dad is taking off a few days before school starts, and we're going to do some family outings this week. If Amanda can come, it will make it more fun for Lois. We'll pick her up around ten o'clock."

Maria sighed with relief. That would be the perfect solution to keeping Amanda entertained for the day. "That's fine with me, and I'm sure Amanda will love it. I'll have her ready when you swing by."

Maria ran upstairs and into Amanda's bedroom. "Wake up, sweetie. Guess what? You've been invited to go to a big museum in Chicago today with Lois and her parents. Won't that be fun?"

Amanda bolted upright in her bed. "When do I go?"

"They're going to be by in about a half an hour, so shake a leg, and I'll see you downstairs. Wear one of your new school outfits. They don't have any spots on them." Maria hugged Amanda and went back to her bedroom to get Ed's wallet and her purse.

As soon as Amanda went out the front door, Maria jumped into the Rocket and was on her way to the clinic. She didn't feel nervous, just wary. *Watch your step. Ed doesn't need any more problems.*

Ed's truck was gone when she pulled into the parking yard next to Hugh's car. No sign of Gladys, at least no other car was there. Dr. Glen was just leaving with Chris. Her son gave her a surprise wave as she got out. Maria laughed and gave him a thumbs-up salute.

Glen opened his window. "Why the visit?"

"I stopped by to bring Ed his wallet."

"I'm surprised. Doc rarely forgets anything. As for us, we're on our way to make a house call. A lady's dog got his head stuck in a fence, and she wants us to get him out."

"Do vets do that?"

"I do. We do kindness rescues, occasionally, free of charge if it doesn't require a lot of time. Wish us luck and stay a while. You can help us clean cages," Glen said, laughing as they drove away.

Maria opened the clinic front door, heard Hugh talking on the shortwave, and walked over to the receptionist's desk. He brightened and waved. Sitting down in the swivel chair behind Gladys's desk, her spirits rose. The desktop was spotless with only a calendar on it. Congratulating Gladys prematurely, Maria opened the first drawer looking for business files, but found it stuffed with all kinds of bills in Ed and Glen's handwriting for services rendered. She quickly opened the lower drawer, and it held more of the same. Some of the bills were dated months ago.

If bills weren't being sent out, the clients had no reason to pay them, and that hurt business. A slow burn had ignited within Maria. Her poor husband had been treading water, ignoring problems at the office.

Ed's accountant and CPA received all the payments and handled his business affairs, but he had to have money to do it. If Maria didn't know better, she'd say Gladys was trying to ruin them. Maria felt her cheeks getting hot with anger at what Gladys's indifference to her job was costing them. If it were up to Maria, she'd fire Gladys that morning the minute she walked through the door.

"Nice to see you, Maria," Hugh said, interrupting her investigation. He laid his ear phones down. "I hope you're here to help us."

She'd felt his eyes on her when he was on the short wave with Ed. Offering a lame explanation, she said, "Ed forgot his wallet, and I said I'd bring it to him."

Hugh grinned at her—he wasn't fooled for a moment. "Now tell me why you're really here. Not that I'm not complaining. After all, I get to see the prettiest girl in town."

"You old flirt, you know just what to say to get a girl to help. Let's say I'm here to make a little order out of chaos."

Hugh walked across the room, leaned over her desk, and looked at her with his blue-grey eyes. "Good. Gladys is either dumber than mud or smarter than all of us because she's never here half the time, and when she is, she's always on the phone. At first I thought she was booking appointments, especially for Glen who does most of the small animal surgery. But one day, I caught her going through Ed's desk. Luckily, his accountant keeps all of Ed's financial records in his own office. But lately, he's been calling Ed."

As Hugh was confiding in her, the phone rang. Maria picked up. "McDermott-Woods Clinic, how can I help you?"

"Who's this?"

Maria recognized the voice. "This is Mrs. McDermott, Gladys." She wanted to read her the riot act, but choked back her anger. "I'm here to work," she said firmly, hearing an edge to her own voice.

Silence hung in the air for a moment. "I'll be there in about an hour, give or take a little," Gladys finally stammered. "I had to make an emergency visit to my sick, old mother in Chicago."

"I see from the look of things, I'll have plenty to do. We need to talk when you get here. I'll expect you in half an hour."

"Oh, *you* don't need to stay. I'll get it all done when I get there."

"I plan on working with you every day from now on, regular office hours, nine to five." Maria, smiling to herself, hung up. "Hugh, where is the typewriter around here?" she asked hotly after her irritating talk with Gladys. "I need it for these statements."

Hugh looked at her like she'd asked for a new car. "Gladys never uses a typewriter. I think our last gal left one in the back. I'll go see."

He came back with a dusty machine and plunked it down on her desk. "I never thought you could type, Maria."

"How do you think I got through school and worked in the publishing business in Washington, DC, for years?" Maria shouldn't have sounded so insulted. It was unfair to take her irritation out on Hugh.

"Doc sure got himself a smart gal when he got you. If I can help you in any way, just holler. I can work on the drug orders now that you're here. I'll come back if either doc calls me on the shortwave." He grinned. "Am I ever glad to see you."

I could use a few things first, Hugh. A brush to clean the dust out of this baby, some new typewriter ribbon, and a ream of office paper with the clinic's letterhead on it.

"That's easy. I know right where the office stuff is. Gladys never uses it."

Maria had stacks of opened and unopened letters, invoices, old newspaper articles, drug orders, surgeries performed for the last few years, and two or three months of movie magazines spread all over her desk and a table Hugh had found in the back room. She'd filled the wastebasket with old gum and candy wrappers and bottles of nail polish. Her head was in the back of the bottom drawer cleaning out the last of old candy wrappers when Ed breezed in.

"Hi, down there," she heard him say as she straightened up and felt him nuzzling her neck.

Pushing her hair out of her eyes, she said, "No heavy fraternization with the help, Doc."

"I don't know what fraternization means," Ed said, as he nuzzled her neck some more.

"I'm in no mood for this," Maria said, stretching and pushing him away. "I need to go to the ladies' room. Trying to make sense out of this mess has put me in a bad mood. Maybe when I get back, you'll be gone."

"Not on your life. I need my wallet so I can take you out to lunch in an hour or so. My wife will never know."

She grinned at him. He was so darn cute, she couldn't stay angry. "You're as bad as you were chasing me for a date in college." Maria tossed him his wallet.

Ed's truck was gone, but Winston was there when she returned.

"The boss said to tell you to be ready for your date with him, and then he ducked out," Hugh called to her.

Winston's laughter filled the room. "Is the good doctor planning on cheating on his wife with the new good-looking office help?"

Hugh guffawed. "I'm sure glad to have both of you here. I've drug orders waiting to be put on the shelves from boxes stacked over there, plus all the paperwork to go with each order. Where do you want to start?"

The clinic was quiet, except for the occasional call for an appointment for either of the vets. Maria worked all morning to develop a spreadsheet of clients to make sense out of all their bills. Just when she thought she couldn't sit still a moment longer, Ed's truck came roaring in, and she heard the door slam.

He popped his head inside the room. "Ready, woman? Let's go in your car."

She grabbed her purse. "I'll be back soon, men! Maria hopped into her car and tossed him the keys. "So, why the car? Where are we going? I thought we could walk to Maisie's."

"I want more privacy. There are too many ears listening at Maisie's. We're going to my favorite root beer stand and eat under that big, old tree. Besides, if we ate at Maisie's, she'd tell my wife."

Maria ginned. "You like that line, don't you?"

Ed ignored her and drove to the stand, then jumped out. "How about a hotdog and a root beer float?" With her nod, he gave a quick clap. "You got it. Save us a place under the tree while I order."

Sitting down next to her at the weather-beaten picnic table, he took a big bite of his hotdog covered in every condiment they offered. He wiped his lips, leaned over, and nuzzled her neck. "You'll have to put up with me. I have the keys to the car."

"With all of that stuff burying it, how can you taste the hotdog, my frisky fellow?" she asked, pushing him away.

"I like it hot and spicy, just like my women," he said, his eyes sparkling.

She smiled at him. "Doc, *what* do you want to talk about?"

Ed wiped ketchup off his mouth, then seemed to give thought to what he wanted to say. "Last night, after you went to bed, I had a long talk with Winston. He laid out what he knew so far about the phone calls. Adam's FBI friend found the company in Chicago on the South Side that produces the noise that matches the tape noises on the phone calls.

"The agent flashed his badge to the production boss who didn't have a clue about any suspicious guy, but he let the agent nose around until he found a workman who told him about a man who'd come around and used some kind of equipment in the building. After a cup or two of coffee with the workman, the agent had a fairly good description of the man. The Bureau is trying to identify him and have alerted the Chicago police. They may have a rap sheet on him.

"Winston also told me that when he took Wiggles out for an early morning stroll Saturday, Wiggles took off like a bat out of hell, baying at the top of her lungs. When Winston finally caught up with her on the top of the hill, she was barking to beat the band at someone who was running across the meadow and into the woods.

"When I mentioned Briggie's sighting on the hill and the truck with the shortwave equipment to Winston, he seemed convinced our quarry is getting nervous, and that we'll get them."

"So, what's next?" Maria couldn't help but worry that whoever they were, the culprits might be closing in on them. Suddenly she started to shiver. "Oh, no," she groaned.

"For God sakes," Ed said, grabbing her. "Are you having a heart attack?"

She wrapped her arms around him. "I had a big premonition a moment ago," she said quietly, almost afraid to mention her terror.

"A what?" Ed asked, hugging her.

"I know this sounds weird, but hear me out. Years ago, before Bill had his terrible car accident, I'd been having awful feelings of impending trouble. They scared me to death. When George was kidnapped, I just knew beforehand that something was going to happen to him. And now . . ." Maria choked up and started to cry. "I just had that same feeling again," she whispered, sobbing." She buried her head in his shoulder to muffle her liquid anguish. "If something happens to you, I'll die. I'll just die."

47. Making Sense Out of Chaos

Late August 1963

(Maria)

Ed held her until she quieted down. "I'll be fine," he finally said, just loud enough for her to hear. "I'm big and tough. We're going to get them soon, Maria. I'll speak to Winston about having a surveillance team around our place all the time from now on until we catch them. That will make you feel better, won't it?"

She raised her head so she could look him in the eyes. "Yes, that will help a lot."

"I'm leaving the whole case to the FBI. If they want to, they can alert Chief Broderick. Now, can I let go of you before the whole place notices us under this tree?"

Maria straightened up, wiped her eyes on his shirt, and smiled at him. Her eyes were still blurry from emotion. "I'm sorry for falling apart. I'm okay now."

"So how's it going receptionist/secretary?" asked Ed. "I like your outfit, especially that swishy skirt. Are you making head and tails out of all that stuff in your desk? Is Gladys coming in?"

"She called and was surprised I was there. She gave some half-assed apology for not coming in and said she'd be here in an hour or so. I told her I'd expect her in half an hour, but she wasn't there when we left. I want you to start advertising for a new secretary. I may kill her. In the meantime, I'm going to get that place up and running if it's the last thing I do."

"That's my brave, little Tiger Lily. I need your help." Ed flashed her a loving smile. "What did you do with Amanda? "

"She's having a day in Chicago with the Bellingers on a family out-ing. They're going to the Museum of Science and Industry."

"Speaking of industry, we've got to move along. I have a one o'clock appointment with a breeder."

The rest of the day was confusing for Maria. Gladys never showed up. The waiting room was filled all afternoon with owners and their animals scheduled for surgery with Dr. Glen. Every time Maria looked up from her work, she saw Chris out of the corner of her eye helping owners with their stubborn patients. He was doing a good job and even waved at her once or twice. Taking a break during the afternoon for a minute or two to stretch her back, she went into the back room where Winston and Hugh were opening one box after another.

"You're having entirely too much fun back here. What will the patients think?"

They looked at each other and Winston said, "My dear girl, the animals don't care, and their worried owners aren't listening."

Maria laughed. "I'm going to be leaving in a little while. It's almost five, and I need to drop these bills in the post office on my way home. See you tonight, Winston."

Maria arrived home and found Briggie in the kitchen. "Did Laura and Sarah go home, and did I get one of my special calls?" The first was of casual concern, and the second, a dreaded one.

"Your mother paid the girls and took them home," said Briggie, holding a dish towel, leaned against a counter. "No, not one call, missy. It seems odd, doesn't it, that there weren't any?"

"It does, Briggie. Did you see any suspicious movement outside?"

"No, but Wiggles set up a clamor several times today."

"I'm going to check with Mom. Amanda should be home soon. The women in this family will be all accounted for, but I can't speak for the men." Maria's face was taut with concern. "When's dinner?"

"Whenever you say. It's so hot, we're having club sandwiches and fruit salad tonight. Invite your mother."

"Briggie, it's so wonderful to come home to you." Maria threw her arms around her friend for a quick thank you.

Her mother was making her way slowly out onto their shared patio with a library book and a drink when Maria ran out.

"How was your first day on the job?" Her mother settled into one of the patio chairs. "Come sit with me and fill me in. Do you want a lemonade? I just made a pitcher full." She sipped her own drink. "I've been waiting for the sun to drop behind the trees to come out here. I love air conditioning, but I find myself wanting fresh air."

As her mother chattered on, Maria thought about how much she loved living next to each other and being able to share their days and moments like this one.

"Mom, it was a shock to look into Gladys's messy drawers and see how many bills were in there. What has she been doing? I think she's trying to ruin Ed's business."

"But Maria, what good would that do? She'd lose her job if he couldn't pay her."

"I know, but something is really wrong. I have to work for the foreseeable future until Ed can hire my replacement." Maria held her hands together in the prayer position. "I have a proposition for you. Would you help me out with Amanda and Lois until school starts? I suggest you call Alicia and work out a deal with her. There's a good family movie playing in Naperville. Maybe you could take them there tomorrow."

"Certainly, honey, anything to help. I know this isn't fun, but it must be done." Her mother's eyebrows raised. "There's something else, isn't there? I know that look on your face."

"Yes, Ed gave me a list of guests and a box of printed invitations he wants me to send to everyone for a dreaded party, and now I don't have the time. Would you help me out?" Maria tried to convey an apology by her tone.

Her mother's eyes lit with interest. "With both Winston and you working at the clinic, I need a project. Besides the invitations, let me plan the party. We'll show St. Charles racing society a real party, just like the ones I did in Washington, DC, for all the State Department bigwigs. Just leave it up to me. It will be like old times. Winston will be in charge of the bar, which he loves to do, and I'll hire Laura and Sarah to serve for us. Remember your engagement party we had in Washington before you and George were married?"

"I do! Thanks, Mom, I'm thrilled. Briggie will be there for you, too. Speaking of Briggie, come for dinner. She said to invite you, and you don't want to cross Briggie!"

Their moment of shared excitement stopped when Amanda burst through the French doors and ran to see them. "Mom, Grandma, I had so much fun today," she yelled at the top of her lungs. "I just loved everything! Going to the museum and seeing the dinosaurs. Afterward, we went to a big restaurant called a cafeteria and picked out our food ourselves."

"That's wonderful," Maria said. "Are you going to sit down with us?"

"No, I'm going to take Wiggles for a walk to the meadow. We love that little stream. Then I'm going to go swimming. Mom, can Lois come over tomorrow?"

"Your mind is going nonstop, isn't it?" Maria grinned. "Your grandma has a surprise for you girls."

"What is it, Grandma?" Amanda asked, hopping from one foot to the other.

"We're going to the movies on the big screen tomorrow!"

Amanda's face lit up. "What are we going to see?"

"It's a movie your mother recommended." Opening the newspaper, Maria's mother searched the entertainment page. "*Flipper.*"

"Groovy, Grandma, I'll call Lois and ask her."

"Groovy, what does that mean?" Her mother laughed. "This world and our kids are changing."

Maria smiled and shook her head. "One whirlwind taken care of, soon two or three more will be here."

Two minutes later, Winston appeared in his doorway. "Who needs or wants a drink? I know I do. Working is hard when one does it all day."

"None for me, stepdaddy. I've got work to finish on household papers, so I need a clear head. I'll leave you two alone."

The following morning, Maria was on her way to the clinic before the household woke up. She'd left notes behind that would help everyone keep their little world operating.

She and her husband had an intimate moment when she pulled in beside his truck. He threw her a kiss and was gone. A few muffled doggie barks from the back greeted her as she walked in. Buried in invoices and so immersed in making sense out of chaos, she barely looked up when Hugh came in. Even Chris didn't appear on her radar screen until his questions broke her concentration.

"Hi, Mom. How come you're here again?" He stopped by her desk. "Do you like it? Working, I mean."

"Yes, and I get to see you once in a while." She stood up and stretched.

Maria watched him walk into the surgery room to get things ready for Dr. Glen's operations. Chris had changed and grown up a lot since they'd moved.

The tempo of the office was faster than yesterday. She made more phone appointments for both Glen and Ed, bringing in business.

Now for streamlining the office billing operational system so we'll have our money more quickly. When she stood up and got a drink of water, it was almost noon. Where had the morning gone, and where was Gladys? She saw her darling for a hurried lunch at Maisie's, got a quick kiss, and then he was gone for the afternoon. How he could work in that heat all day worried her a little.

By three o'clock, Maria was ready to go home. She was tired because of her early start—almost as early as Ed's. Gladys wasn't coming. It was too late in the day. Maria had amazed herself with the speed she'd completed cleaning up the back bills. Her drawers were clean, and she was ready to start reorganizing the files on Wednesday.

Turning off the main highway onto the long country road to her home, she saw a truck waiting on a side road for her to pass. As she passed, the truck pulled out right behind her, then moved alongside of her, crowding her car over farther and farther on the narrow road.

"You idiot," she screamed at him. Before she knew it, he'd run her off the road into the ditch where she sat precariously, her car tipped, poised to roll over. She caught a glimpse of a ghoulish Halloween mask over the driver's face as the huge truck roared away. She assumed it was a guy, but it could have been a woman.

Maria began to shake uncontrollably. She was scared to death that her car was going to roll over, trapping her inside. *Take deep breaths, calm down, and get out carefully,* she said to herself over and over as she pulled herself out on the passenger's side.

As the shaking subsided, uncontrollable tears started. After sobbing for a couple of minutes, Maria began to feel better and started walking home. She'd never realized the road was so desolate. She could have been trapped or bled to death in her own car, and no one would have noticed.

Wiping her eyes, she walked and walked to the first house on her road, hoping to use their phone. No luck, no one was home. The next neighbor was nearly a mile away. Stumbling along, she heard a car and darted off the road out of fear.

"Are you all right?" a friendly woman called out. "Would you like a ride?"

"Would I ever. I'm so glad you came along. I had a little accident back there, and my car is in the ditch. I live down this road about five miles," Maria said, tearing up again as she scurried into the car. "Thanks so much," she said as her savior stopped in front of her house. As the lady pulled away, Maria realized she hadn't even asked her neighbor's name.

The house was terribly quiet. Her mother had taken the girls and Bridget to the movies as promised and probably had stopped for some grocery items on the way home. But why did it seem quieter than usual? What was it? Wiggles wasn't barking her usual *hello.*

Maria opened the utility door looking for Wiggles, but she wasn't there. Maria opened the kitchen door and looked out at the run. Her scream could have been heard for miles as she rushed to her poor little dog. Wiggles was lying on her side in the run with blood caked on her head.

A terrible feeling—a premonition—ran through Maria as she held her dear pet in her arms. Wiggles wasn't moving. She had to be dead, but Maria desperately didn't want to believe it. *Oh, my dear God, I must hide her from Amanda. I want Ed. I'm scared.*

Carrying limp little Wiggles, her lifeless body draped over Maria's arms, her tears fell on Wiggles's fur. Maria wrapped the sweet dog in her little special bed blanket that Ed had brought her in to Amanda over a year ago. She gently laid Wiggles on the floor of Briggie's closet to hide her.

When Maria picked up the phone in the kitchen and then replaced it, she had a terrible feeling in the pit of her stomach. She had no way of reaching Ed. She had no idea how to use his shortwave radio receiver, and there was no other way to reach him.

Dear Lord, help me get through this. Tears rolled down her cheeks. Quietly, the door opened, and Chris was standing there. Her prayer had been answered.

"Mom, what's the matter? You're crying. Is Ed okay?"

"It's Wiggles. She's been shot, and she's dead! Oh, Chris, I'm so glad you're here. I hid her in Briggie's closet because I didn't know what else to do. Help me tell Amanda," she wailed.

Chris was gone like a shot, then he came back, looking ruthless. "Who would do such a thing?" he yelled, looking at Maria and wiping his eyes.

"Talk to Ed and Winston. They'll fill you in on what has been going on around here. I'm too upset to be rational."

Suddenly, Maria froze. She heard her mother, Briggie, and two giggling girls coming in. Maria quickly pulled herself together. Everyone had a bag of groceries in their arms, and the girls dropped theirs on the table.

"Mom, we had so much fun at the movies." Amanda glowed with excitement. "We're going upstairs to get our suits on, and then we're going swimming. We're so hot, we can't wait to get in the water." Off she went with Lois.

Maria waited until they were gone, then she called a wrecker to pull her car out of the ditch. Once that was settled, she went upstairs to change her clothes and then went to find her mother. Together, they would wait for the men to come home, and when they did, Maria wanted a war council meeting.

48. The Ultimate Price of Abuse

Late August 1963
(Angelina)

"Rocco, where the hell are you?" Angelina yelled up the stairs, wiping the sweat off her face with her apron. *That no good kid of mine is never around when I want him.*

She sat on the front cement steps of her three-story walk-up, her black skirt covering her doughy legs splayed out in front of her. *What do I care how I look?* She lifted her arms. Rings of dried sweat on her blouse added to the sickening smell from her arm pits. *Phew, I smell like garlic!* She laughed. Sweat was trickling down the middle of her back, over rolls of fat, soaking the underwear and black stockings she was wearing.

Rocco came out and perched on the stone railing. "Did you want me, Ma?" he asked, looking down at her, a cigarette hanging loosely from his thin lips.

"Yeah, I wanted you to know Jackie and Gladys went to the bank with her ex's alimony check. That bastard is going to pay for what he done to Jackie."

Rocco took a deep drag on his cigarette and flipped it out into the street. "I don't care about no lousy check. I'm going down to the bar for a drink and a hand or two of poker. See youse later."

"You are, like hell. I need you to go upstairs and put the arm on that bastard, Mickey, who hasn't paid me a cent of rent in two weeks."

"But Ma," he whined, his thin body wasted, the product of too much drinking, smoking, and long hours playing cards with the local mafioso.

"You heard me! Get that skinny ass of yours upstairs, and don't come down until you have some rent money from that guy."

Muttering under his breath, Rocco slowly eased himself off of the stone railing and climbed the old dilapidated stairs. A few minutes later, she smiled as she heard sounds of scuffling and swearing at the top of the stairs. A scream pierced the air, and then it was quiet.

Rocco appeared and handed her some bills. "There! Satisfied? Now I'm going to play cards."

"Did you kill him or what?" Angelina asked as she heaved herself up to go start dinner.

"No, I just gave him a bloody nose and a headache," Rocco said, starting down the stairs. He stopped at the bottom, watching Gladys pull her old, dented car into the space in front of the tenement.

Jackie was with her, and they both got out of the car.

"Hi, Mrs. O'Brien. It's hot, isn't it?" Gladys asked, ignoring Rocco's leering smile.

"Is the money in the bank?" Angelina scratched her protruding belly and laughed like the devil, himself. "We're going to ruin Dr. High-and-Mighty McDermott. Leaving my little girl . . . we'll fix him. Nobody does that to one of my family."

"It's in there, Ma," Jackie said. "You can pay your bills now. We're going out to celebrate, but we'll be back later on tonight. Don't wait up for us. I have my key."

Angelina lumbered down the hall on the cracked and broken linoleum floor to the kitchen. She glanced at the framed, barely perceptible, ancient images of her mother and father on their wedding day in Sicily. It hung on the food spattered wall, behind her old sink, discolored from age.

Her mother had always boasted that she'd married the handsomest man in Sicily on the first of January in the first year of the new century. They looked so young. Her mother, pretty, and her father, nice-looking, both hoping for a better life.

Angelina sighed when she thought about the fact that both of them were gone, leaving her with ugly remembrances of her life in Sicily. *Except for the goats, my life was rotten. How I loved those goats. But I also remember how poor Sicily was. We were always hungry and never had no money. My sainted mother promised me she would fatten me up when we went to America.*

The trip over in the boat's steerage had been a nightmare with everyone seasick and throwing up. And the smell that clung to their clothing even when they washed them without soap in salt water. Ellis Island was another hurdle to jump through, and luckily, they had

328

all been well. Otherwise, they would have been sent back. But New York City was the scariest. People everywhere, speaking in languages she couldn't understand. At least when they were on board ship, and even on Ellis Island, they could talk with many of the immigrants. But there in New York City, they were on their own and knew no one.

Papa kept patting his pocket, making sure he had his precious paper. She remembered the day when he saw a policeman and decided to trust him enough to get directions. Her father carefully took out the paper, and still holding it tightly, showed the policeman. It was written in English from Uncle Anthony, introducing them and asking for help to get them to the bus station in New York City. That paper was their only chance to find him.

At that moment, Angelina had promised herself that she was going to learn how to speak English. Never again was she going to feel so helpless. When the policeman pointed them in the right direction, Papa was jubilant. It was raining and cold as they walked to the bus station. Her parents didn't notice, but she did. They were going to Chicago to meet Uncle Tony.

The trip from New York City to Chicago was long, their money was almost gone, and they were hungry when they arrived.

She remembered her first impression of Uncle Tony in the bus terminal. He was dressed in a fancy suit, but they were in rags. He had a big fat face and broke out into a big smile when he saw them. One of his front teeth was gold. They were skin and bones, and he was the fattest man she'd ever seen. No one in Sicily was fat.

Holding her mama's hand tightly, they struggled across the bus terminal building with Papa carrying their tattered bags to meet Uncle Tony. When they got close, he leaned down and patted her head and smelled good.

Riding in Uncle Tony's car was an experience Angelina remembered to this day. It was the first time she had ever been near a car, let alone been able to ride in one. In his back seat, she secretly felt the soft, velvet material. She thought her uncle was as rich as a king. Then she closed her eyes and pretended the car was hers. She made herself a promise. She was going to have a car someday.

There were lots of people in America. They were everywhere, on the streets, in the apartment building, in the parks and stores. Coming from a desolate part of Sicily and living out in the country, she'd always wished she could see and talk to more people, and she finally had her wish.

Crammed into a third-floor walk-up in the South Side of Chicago, Angelina had felt rich. The roof didn't leak, there were no holes in the walls letting in the cold, and best of all, there was running water.

She'd been intrigued with the sights and sounds of the city. At night, sitting on the iron bars of the fire escape outside her window, she could hear the freight trains rumbling on their way to a distant city, the police sirens ripping through the air, sometimes so close she thought they were outside on her street, and on foggy nights, the distant, continuous drone of the fog horns. It was so different from living in the country where the nights were so still. The city, vibrating with the energy of thousands of people, thrilled her.

It took only a few months until they moved to their new three-story house on the South Side. Her mother had kept asking her father how they could afford such a grand place. Papa never answered her other than to say that he belonged to a powerful group that took care of their own. She learned much later that he'd joined the union, and with Uncle Tony's help, belonged to the mafioso. By day, Papa was a tile setter for all the new construction going on in the city. By night, he did things for the Mafia that he never talked about.

Angelina had gone to school for the first time in her life, and within a month or two could understand and speak English. When her teacher said that she was smart, Angelina was proud.

One day, some men came and told Mama they were going to turn the back of the house into a special room where men could spend the afternoon and evening playing cards, drinking, and having a good time.

Mama couldn't understand what they'd said in English and asked Angelina to translate. Then she asked them in for coffee. They smiled, shook their heads, then began to work.

They made an outside entrance near the back of the house so no one needed to go through their living space. Telephone trucks, workmen's trucks. and lots of men began going to and from the back throughout the day and sometimes into the night. Papa would come home from work, go back there for a while, then join the family for supper. Angelina always begged him to let her see too, but he wouldn't.

When the pounding and sawing finally stopped and there were no more workmen, a new class of men began walking past the side of their house. Those men drove new cars, wore nice clothes, and looked like business people to Angelina, who would huddle in the corner of her porch and watch them until her mother made her go inside.

Papa put up a fence around their tiny front yard, and Mama began softening the soil, like in the old county. She buried all her vegetable peelings every day, digging them into the hard, barren soil. By the end of the first year, a few hardy flowers popped up in that unforgiving dirt. By the end of the second year, Mama had managed to grow some spindly tomato vines and a few cucumbers. Each year, her garden grew more and more food for them as she nourished the soil and turned it into fluffy compost.

By the time Angelina went to high school, a first in her family, her brother Anthony was just four. Named after their savior and benefactor, Uncle Tony, Anthony was the boy her papa had always wanted. Angelina loved her little brother, but he was treated like a prince and was spoiled rotten by her mother and father. She chafed at the way she was ignored and Tony was adored.

Studying harder and harder, she was rewarded by becoming the valedictorian of her senior class. Her father didn't come to graduation, he was too busy. Hurt beyond measure, she decided she'd punish her father by telling him and her mother exactly what Uncle Tony had done to her while growing up. When she tried to explain that he had been sexually molesting her from the time she was eleven until she went to high school, her father had disowned her and thrown her out of the house.

Her girlfriend, Victoria, had taken pity on her and let her stay with her family that fateful summer when she had met her husband, Private Dennis O'Brien. She and Victoria had lied to Vicki's family and said they were going to a movie, but they really went to the USO headquarters to dance with the servicemen before they were shipped out to either Europe or the South Pacific during the forties. The war was raging in Italy, and the United States was fighting the Japanese in the Pacific.

It was a wartime romance in every sense of the word. Dennis O'Brian's big pitch to her was that they only had a few days together before he had to go off and face the enemy. He told her he didn't want to die never knowing her sweet body, and she had believed him. After a week of his pleading, they ran off and were married by a justice of the peace in the Chicago courthouse. When he left, promising his undying love, she believed him. She went to work in the big public library in Chicago. She landed the position because of her outstanding high school record.

She knew she was pregnant six weeks after he left. She called him and said she was coming to stay with him. Jacqueline was born in March 1942, in an army hospital in Fort Worth, Texas, where Angelina lived with her husband. He was training new recruits as a newly appointed sergeant.

Angelina had called her mother to tell her the good news about her baby girl's arrival, and her mother had countered by telling her that her father had been gunned down in a battle with a rival gang of the Mafia in the streets of Chicago. Her mother begged Angelina to leave her husband and return to Chicago with the baby. It had been tempting—he'd occasionally hit her after drinking too much.

When Dennis was shipped overseas a year later, Angelina and Jacqueline did go home to stay with her mother, gratefully. When he returned from overseas after the war, Dennis would periodically appear on their doorstep, begging her to return to him and promising to never touch her again. Her mother begged her not to go, but Angelina was lonely and wanted to be loved. She decided to give him another chance and was bitterly disappointed when he ignored her more and more, and then began turning his attentions toward their daughter as she grew older.

Jacqueline was a well-developed girl for her age. Angelina knew something was going on, but was so afraid of her husband, she pretended it was all in her mind. She no longer was his target. When Jackie tried to tell her that her father made her feel weird, and he was always trying to hold her hand and kiss her cheek, Angelina lied to herself and accused Jackie of lying. But in her heart, Angelina knew. It was only a matter of time before his inappropriate touching would turn into something more intense sexually.

Angelina kept promising herself she would leave Dennis for good and take her daughter away to save her, but Angelina also secretly kept hoping Dennis would love her again. By the time she finally gave up and decided to leave, the damage had been done. Her husband had raped her daughter. Frantic to escape, thirteen-year-old Jacqueline had run away to her aging grandmother's.

After Jacqueline left, Angelina was devastated. She asked for a divorce and fled to her mother's. Desperate for an income, Angelina took a chance and restarted the bookie joint that her papa had developed in the back room years before. She put in new telephone equipment, new tables, a shortwave radio set, and a bathroom to keep the men from going outside and peeing in the alley.

Her father's old friends started returning out of respect to his memory and to help and encourage her. The word on the street was to go bet on the races at Angelina's. Soon her business was booming, and she made plans to have Jacqueline see a doctor who could help her with her problems. Because of the guilt Angelina carried for what she'd allowed Dennis to do to their little girl, she made a promise to herself to take care of Jacqueline. She'd never allow anyone to hurt her daughter again.

49. Strategy Planning Gone Awry

Late August 1963
(Angelina/Rocco)

Angelina

Angelina looked at the kitchen clock. She'd been sitting there for nearly an hour. She wasn't hungry. No one was home to eat supper with her, anyway. She laboriously stood up, turned, and slowly climbed the old familiar stairs to her second-floor bedroom and living room. The place was quiet, her roomers on the third floor had all gone to bed, and Mickey was probably drunk after his beating from Rocco.

Beatings didn't bother Angelina at all. She almost liked them. Having been exposed to every type of violence on the streets of Chicago where members of opposing gangs beat and killed each other on a regular basis, she didn't care. Even the death of her husband only added another layer of armor to her already toughened personality. The only crack in her shell was her daughter, Jacqueline.

Tomorrow, she'd call a meeting with the family, Gladys, Tommy, and a couple of his friends. They needed to step up pressure on Doc's damned new wife. It enraged Angelina that from Rocco's and Tommy's observations on the hill behind his house, Ed was crazy about his wife. Evidently, damnable Ed and his trophy wife had been away for the weekend, and they came back hugging and kissing each other.

An evil grin crossed her fat face. His wife was the reason he left Jacqueline. She was one of those women who ruined perfectly good marriages by tantalizing husbands into cheating on their poor wives. After they got rid of her, Ed would come to his senses, go back to Jacqueline, beg her forgiveness, and make her happy again. All Angelina wanted was to make Jacqueline happy.

It took some doing, getting everyone around her kitchen table the following morning. Everyone but Angelina had hangovers. "Drink my hot coffee. It will chase the headaches away," she said, pouring them all a cup while they groaned and moaned.

"Today, I want you, Tommy, to take the truck, wear your Halloween mask and your cap, and push the bitch off the road on her way home from work. Don't hurt her, just scare her. Cover your license plates. Even though we get our plates through the mob, it's such a pain changing them.

"Gladys, you'll be late for work tomorrow morning because of your sick mother. I want you to make a note. Make it say, *Get out before it's too late.* Slip it into the bitch's car without anyone seeing you. I *repeat*, without anyone seeing you. Don't write it, take the words and letters from magazines." She wagged her finger to make the point. "Don't you write anythin'." When Angelina was particularly pleased with herself, she had a laugh that terrified people, and she knew it. Today that laugh ricocheted around her greasy walls.

"Okay, report back to me tonight." Angelina waved them off. "Now, go and see what we can do to her today."

Rocco

"I'm sick of this game," Rocco whined. "All I get to do is watch that damned house. Tommy gets to run the broad off the road. I'm taking my rifle with me today. Maybe I'll kill something," he said, liking the way he sounded so tough. "And if I'm hungry, I'm going into that hick town and get somethin' to eat. You can't stop me, Maw."

"Don't youse go into no town. You stay away and keep your nose clean, youse hear me?"

Rocco parked a mile or two off the road from his stakeout and closed his eyes, sleepy from a big breakfast. When he woke up, the car was broiling. He checked his watch. Nearly two in the afternoon. He'd slept for three hours.

He circled around behind Doc's property, approaching through the woods on his usual route to the hill behind their house. As he made his way to the edge of the forest, he heard loud noises. A big, powerful machine was digging out a road, and it was just stopping short of the forest. He had to hide for over an hour before it finished. Quickly, he ran for his observation post in the little stand of woods on top of the hill.

"Whew," he muttered. "Doc must be planning on building something back there." He carefully laid his rifle against a tree and trained his binoculars on the house and then slowly swept them around the property. A car was in the yard, and he watched two girls get in and then leave. That damned dog in the run started to bark. He picked up his rifle and aimed, getting the dog's head in his crosshairs. *Bang!* The animal dropped. He'd gotten the mutt with one shot. *Wait 'till I tell the boys.*

Rocco was ready to leave. *One last look around before I go.* He raised his binoculars again. Two guys in a black car got out and were standing by the house. He saw one of them looking up at him with a set of binoculars.

Damn, they see me and are running up here! They're not supposed to do that. He grabbed his rifle and ran as fast as he'd ever run, twisting his ankle but finally reaching the forest and disappearing. Catching his breath and rubbing his ankle, he ran limping for another mile or so before he cut to the road, jumped in his car, and drove like the devil was after him.

Out of his rearview mirror, he suddenly saw that same black car that was parked in the doc's driveway come into view behind him. "God damn it!" he shouted as he pushed the accelerator down to the floor. "If they catch me, it's all over."

They pulled up close to him once or twice. He'd have to get new plates now. His only chance was to lose them in traffic. Rocco floored it.

He heard the train coming as he crossed the tracks, breaking the traffic barriers, just before the train crossed behind him. He raised his fist and yelled, "You'll never get me now, you damned pigs. I hope it has a hundred cars!" Rocco made the sign of the cross on his chest.

After pulling his car into the alley behind the house, Rocco opened his trunk and dug around until he found a screwdriver to take off his plates. He entered the side door that led to his mother's bookie operation. The place was quiet. He picked up the phone and dialed a friend in the mob. "Joey, I need a favor. I need a new set of plates. Mine are hot." He listened for a moment. "Thanks! Now I owe you one."

As he walked into the front of the house, he called, "Ah, Maw, it smells so good. What's for dinner?" Rocco gave his mother a hug, and she gave him a suspicious look.

"What have you done now? I can always tell when you've screwed up."

"Nothing, Maw, I swear." He wanted to eat before he got her mad and she threw him out. "What about some lasagna? I'm starving."

She couldn't resist feeding her son, even if he didn't use his head. "Okay, first you eat, and then you tell me. I'll find out sooner or later."

Gladys came in with Jacqueline, laughing about something. "Maw, we had a great time, spending some of the bastard's money."

"Did you make the note, Gladys?"

"Yeah, here it is," she said, giving it to Angelina, who studied it and nodded.

Rocco had stuffed the last of the lasagna down while his mother was distracted. He headed toward the door.

She grabbed him. "Sit back down, boy," she said, shoving him down. "I want to know what happened today." His mother, leaning over the table not more than four inches from his face, gave him a hard look.

"Maw, you know how I hate to have your face so close to mine. Your breath is bad, and I hate the big black mole on your cheek. Why don't you go to the doctor and have it off?"

His mother gave him a hateful look. "Watch your mouth, you ungrateful kid."

"Hi, everybody," Tommy said.

Angelina

"Have some of my lasagna, Tommy." Angelina dished up a big plate of food for Tommy. "You look like you did a good job. Tell us all about it."

Jackie gave her mother a sour look. "You didn't offer us any, Maw. Don't we count?"

"You're only women." Angelina put her hands on her hips. "You can get your own."

When she turned her back, Rocco started to sneak out, but Angelina caught him. "Sit down, Rocco," she said sharply. Her boy was weak, he made poor decisions, and he had a hot temper, but he was her son, and she would protect him as long as she could. How she wished he was like her husband or her brother, Anthony. Both of them gone now, gunned down in their prime.

Tommy was gleefully eating and talking at the same time. "You should have seen the bitch's face when I pushed her down into the gulley in her snappy little sports car. She thought she could get away from me, but not Tommy, the race car driver."

"Did her car turn over?" If only Angelina could have seen it for herself. "I hope she was hurt, or better yet, burned."

"Naw, she was tipped way over, but it didn't fall, damn it. I tried, but no such luck."

Angelina patted his shoulder. "Good work, Tommy. Want some more lasagna?"

"Naw, I'm full." He patted his stomach. "So, what's next?"

"I want to hear from my cringing son before I say anything else," Angelina said harshly.

"Well, I staked out the house like I always do, but after a while, I got sick of hearing their dog barking. He must have barked for an hour, and I got worried that someone would decide to come on the hill and investigate. For the good of our family's plan, I decided that I should silence the dog."

"What do you mean? *Silence* the dog? Did you kill it?" Anger began to boil within Angelina.

"Yeah, Maw, I killed it. I got it with one shot with my new high-powered rifle the boys gave me." Rocco lifted his chin and grinned at Tommy.

"So now, big shot, they'll know someone out there has a high-powered gun from the bullet they'll take out of the dog," Tommy said. "Thanks to you, I think we'd better lie low for a while until things cool down. They'll get the local police involved now, and maybe the feds."

Angelina wasn't completely satisfied with what Rocco had told them. He still seemed jittery, tapping his fingers and smoking one cigarette after another.

"I agree with Tommy. I want to slap some sense into you, idiot." Angelina gave the back of his head a little shove. "So, why are you so nervous, boy? Spit it out before I knock you on your ass," she growled.

Rocco

"It wasn't my fault," Rocco whined. "I was minding my business watching the house, when a black car drove into the bitch's driveway and two guys got out. I thought they'd go into the house, but they didn't. I was watching them with my binoculars, and all of a sudden, I saw they had a pair trained on me. I grabbed my gun and ran down the other side of the hill making for the forest. When I hit the woods, I thought I'd lost them, but they'd put the make on my car parked on the side of the road. When I ran out to get in, no one was around, but all of a sudden, they came roaring up after me. I lost them by getting over a train crossing before a freight train cut them off." Rocco looked at his mother and took a deep drag on his cigarette.

She narrowed her eyes. "Whose car was it that you were driving?"

"It don't have no home. Different guys drive it for errands the big boys want them to do."

Tommy leaned across the table. "So, the feds can't trace it to your house?"

"Naw, besides, I took the plates off just now and called Joey, the plate man. He'll get me another set, and I can put them on tonight after I meet him at the club."

"I don't intend to let things cool down," Jackie said, ominously. "I want the bitch taken out of the picture as soon as possible so Ed will come back to me. I miss him something terrible, and I know he misses me. She's the only thing separating us. He was so good to me, and I intend to be better to him." Her words didn't match her cold eyes.

"Jackie, we're going to scare her so bad, she'll leave." Their mother gave her a sly grin. "Give us a little more time. That's right, isn't it, boys?"

Rocco gave her a couple of weak waves, blowing her off. He was done with this. "Yah, sure, Maw, whatever you say." He pushed back his chair. "Can I go? I want to meet Joey and get the plates." Rocco stood and pressed his palms to the table. "Hey, Tommy, come play a little cards with the boys." He tried to act casual.

"Sure, Rocco, I'll see youse all later. Thanks for the meal, Mrs. O'Brian." He strolled out with Rocco and said quietly when they were outside, "Pardon me for speaking against your family, but I think Jackie and your mother are a little nuts."

"I know so, and I'm tired of the whole operation. Those guys acted like feds, Tommy, and I don't want to end up in the slammer because of my crazy mother and sister."

"I'm going out of town for a while, Rocco. I need a vacation, if you catch my drift."

"Can I go, too? I've got to get away from them."

"I'll see what I can work out for youse. Now let's go play cards and have some fun."

50. Terror

Late August 1963
(Jaqueline/Maria)

Jaqueline

After Rocco and Tommy left, Jackie sat on the front porch with Gladys. "Tomorrow, when you go to work, I want you to call me like you're calling a farmer and tell me if the bitch comes to work or not. I have a plan to take care of things. I also want to know where Ed is when you call. Get his work schedule for the day for me."

"Sure, Jackie, only I don't want to be involved with anything personal like running her off the road," Gladys said, with a worried look on her face. "What are you planning?"

Jackie clammed up and didn't say another word.

"If you're just going to sit there and stew, I'm going home," Gladys said. "I'm a working girl for at least a little while longer, and I need to get up early tomorrow. You're no fun when you're in one of your moods." As she stood up to go, Jackie grabbed her hand. "You're hurting me, Jackie."

"Don't forget. I need Ed's schedule," Jackie said firmly.

"I'll do it! I promise. As soon I can," Gladys said, wrenching her hand from Jackie's iron grasp.

Jackie sat in the dark for a while, then she got up and called her therapist, Dr. Tolliver. "Hello, this is Jacqueline McDermott, and I want to talk to the doctor. He isn't in? Why not? I need to talk to him," she said, angrily. "Things are piling up in my head, and I have a lot of questions for him."

She ignored the pounding in her head, but the voices wouldn't let her think. *I've got to reach him.* She tried the emergency number the secretary gave her, but was disappointed to hear a woman on the line who said she was covering for Dr. Tolliver while he was away on vacation.

"Are you a head doctor, too?" Jackie started to cry and said that she needed some pills to help her feel good before she saw her darling husband. "Things are going on in my head," she said. "No, I don't want to wait until tomorrow," she moaned. "The biggest problem I have are the voices that keep telling me what to do and make me feel so mixed up. I try to stop them, but they won't go away. I need some pills like Dr. Tolliver gives me to make them go away."

"Have you heard the voices for a long time?"

"After my dad started to get weird with me, if you know what I mean. Every time my dad got too close to me, they came. One afternoon when I was having my birthday party with my friends, he came home early. He embarrassed me by saying in front of everyone that I was pretty. I could smell alcohol on his breath.

"That night he came into my room late. I remember because I was listening to some music from a hotel in Fort Worth, Texas. I was wearing my new birthday pajamas from my mom. He came over and sat next to me, then surprised me by touching one of my buds through my pajamas and saying, 'They're growing now. Soon you'll fill out all over.' When I jumped away, he made fun of me by saying, 'My, you're jumpy around your old man. Just relax, I'm not going to hurt you.' But he did.

"I was scared and started screaming for my mom as he held me down. The voices were yelling at me to fight and get away, but I couldn't.

"At first, every time my mother was out, either working at her part-time job or shopping, my father would come find me, sit close to me, sometimes stroke my hair or rub my back and eventually," Jackie paused and whispered, "my breasts. After a month or so, he did it to me, and the voices were so loud, I couldn't hear myself think when he was doing it.

"After he went to bed, I packed my bag and ran away to Chicago to my gramma's. Are you still listening to me?"

"Yes, I am. Don't hang up, keep talking," the woman doctor said softly.

"When my mother showed up the following week with a black eye, bruises on her arms and legs, I knew the beatings had started again after I left. Mom was glad I was safe and was there with Grandma. She promised to love and take care of me for as long as she lived. But you know what, Doctor? I didn't believe her, and I sort of hated her for letting my dad act the way he did with me. I'd tried to tell her, but she always said I was being silly. He was only being fatherly. She mixed me up, too. We settled into a more normal kind of living, if one could call having a bookie joint in the back of the house normal.

"My voices disappeared as long as I didn't have any contact with the opposite sex. I couldn't date any men or the voices drove me crazy. Mom kept asking me when I was going to bring a nice young man home for her to meet. As far as I was concerned, I never would, and she knew why, but wouldn't admit it.

"My mom found out about Dr. Tolliver and took me to see him when I was in high school. He encouraged me to look for a job, and I did after I graduated, in the little town of St. Charles. I could type and read well. He showed me how I could take the train and work there in the newspaper's office. I wanted to get away from the dirty streets of Chicago, my mother, and the bookie joint. She couldn't understand, but I did it anyway. I liked riding back and forth on the train. All the voices stopped, and I felt fine.

"I met my husband there. He's the veterinarian and is an important man. I met him first in the newspaper office when he'd just moved to town. Later, I saw him at the local restaurant where I used to go for lunch every day. He was older and treated me nice. I know I'll be all right when I get back with my husband, Doctor. I never heard any voices around him as long as he didn't ask me for any sex. I know I need to change that, so I'd like to make an appointment and see you once I'm remarried.

"Tomorrow, I plan on telling him how much I love him. Wish me luck, Doctor. I'll call you soon." As Jackie hung up the phone, she could hear the doctor asking her to meet her that evening, but Jackie ignored her.

She raced up the stairs to shower and get ready to see her darling the next day. Jackie stole into Rocco's room, found what she was looking for, ran back to her room, and jumped into bed. She was so excited with her plans, she could hardly sleep all night.

When Gladys called in the morning and gave her Ed's schedule and directions to get there, Jackie was thrilled. Taking pains to look as nice as possible, she slipped past the kitchen where Maw was cooking and got in her car.

According to Gladys, Ed was at the Hollister's farm. Jackie drove right to it from memory and soon spotted Ed's truck parked next to the barn. Slipping into the truck, she hid in the space behind the front seats on the floor. Getting awfully cramped after an hour, she longed to get out and stretch her legs, but didn't. He was coming. She could hear him laughing and talking. When he got into his truck, she watched him make a few notes and pick up his shortwave microphone. "KSB 2291, calling home base."

"Home base KSB 2291."

She recognized Hugh's voice on the other end of the conversation.

Ed clicked the response button. "Leaving Hollister's, going to Meadow Brook Acres. Any calls?"

"KSB 2291 home base, no farm calls as of this moment."

"Okay, over and out, KSB2291." Ed replaced his receiver, started his truck, and drove slowly out of the farm gate. Picking up speed, he turned on the radio to the weather station.

Jackie couldn't wait a second longer. Climbing over the seat into the front, she slipped down next to Ed. "Hi, darling, it's been a long time, hasn't it?"

For a moment or two, Ed sat speechless. "Jackie. What do you want? How did you get here? What's going on?"

"I want you, Ed. I've been the biggest fool there ever was, letting my mother dictate my life with you. I promise to be a good wife to you. I'm going to a shrink now, and he's been helping me with the sex thing." The minute she said *sex*, one of her voices started to talk to her, but she ignored it. "I'm so much better, and I want to show you. She quickly slipped out of her blouse and bra, then pulled off her shorts and underpants. As he drove, she put her arms around his neck, and began kissing his face and neck. The voices immediately clamored so loudly she couldn't think.

Driving awkwardly off the road, Ed stopped his truck. "Listen, Jackie," he said quietly, trying to talk to her as she kissed his lips. "You're a very beautiful young woman, and I'm glad—"

She covered his mouth with her lips to stop him talking, then pulled slightly away. "Make love to me right here, right now. I want to prove how much better I am." She tried to pull him over on top of her.

Ed resisted. "Please don't embarrass yourself, Jackie," he said gently. "Let me help you put your clothes back on, and I'll drive you back to your car. It's at the Hollister's place, isn't it?" He turned the truck around, then waited for her to dress, but she crossed her arms and sat there, not moving.

343

Her mood had changed in a blink of an eye. "She has you scared to death to act like a man," she hissed. "What has she done? Has she threatened you? I know she has. Things would be different between us if she hadn't gotten her claws in you, and they will be different again."

"Let me help you get dressed. If a car or truck came by, you'd be embarrassed."

"I could say you were trying to rape me! Maybe I will. It'd serve you right." She sat there, her face heating up. Ed was talking to her, but she couldn't decipher what he was saying because of so much noise in her head.

"I'm glad you're getting help, Jackie," he said, slipping her bra on her as he talked quietly. "Please understand. I'm married now." He reached down on the floor and pulled her panties up to her hips. "Come on, Jackie, help me." She offered no resistance as he pulled her shorts up. "Now for your top." He slipped that over her head. After he drove her back to her car, he went around and helped her out, holding her hand a moment. "Keep going to your doctor, Jackie. Things will get better for you if you do."

Suddenly the voices stopped as he was talking. "You were always a gentleman, Ed. Not like the thugs I grew up with. See you soon." Jackie gave him a little smile. She glanced in the rearview mirror and saw him watching as she drove away in her own car.

Jackie turned off on a side road and waited until she saw him fly by in his truck. As soon as he'd disappeared, she drove to a shortcut that led to Hill Top Ridge Road. She knew those roads by heart. How many times had she driven all over to find Ed when he was late coming home?

She hurtled along, coming dangerously close to the ditches at times, not thinking about how fast she was going. She had a mission. She was going to kill Maria so Ed would come back to her. He was so sweet to her today. He wanted to make love to her, she just knew it. He held back because he was such a gentleman.

Another glance into the rearview mirror showed a demonic smile and piercing eyes that reflected her desperation. That bitch didn't deserve him. Jackie would save him. She felt for her purse under the seat. It was still there.

After pulling into the driveway, Jackie drove around to the back. Taking out her set of keys, she let herself in through the garage door between the bays. Some men up on the hill were watching her. *They're fools. They think I'm a friend of the family.*

As Jackie crept toward the hall door, it opened. *Who opened it?* She ducked down behind a car and waited. A car door opened and closed. Jackie peeked out and saw the bitch with some bundles. She knew it was Maria from the pictures Tommy had taken of her with his telescopic lens on his camera.

When the hall door closed, Jackie moved quietly, pausing in the hallway to listen to the bitch talking to a woman. She crept into the living room behind a big couch and heard them say good-bye. The bitch walked right by her and went upstairs, not suspecting anything. *I'm glad Rocco killed the pooch. It would have warned the bitch. That was a good omen.*

Because of the soft stair rugs, she was able to creep soundlessly up the stairs. An insistent shrill of the phone cut the silence. Jackie shrank against the wall and waited. The voices were hammering away at her, talking incessantly. *Shut up! Go away, I can't think. I'm doing this for Ed and me. You want me to be happy, don't you?*

Jackie couldn't hear what the bitch was saying because of the voices, and soon she heard the sound of running water in the bathroom upstairs. *Perfect, she's in the shower. I've got her cornered. I'll open the curtain, shoot her in her face and chest before she knows what hit her, and she'll die.* Jackie laughed hysterically at the thought of eliminating the only thing standing between her and Ed.

Maria

Maria heard a laugh and froze for an instant. She was naked, but not trapped. Ed's call and her intuition had warned her not to get in that shower, and she hadn't. She quickly tried to lock the bathroom door, but someone was pushing from the other side. Maria let go, stepped back, and grabbed a towel and a loose roll of toilet paper as the door flew open. A woman holding a gun hurtled across the bathroom, hitting her head on the shower door.

Maria bolted out of the bathroom, wrapping the towel around her as she ran. She started down the stairs, then turned and saw a woman she assumed was Jackie, hurled her well-aimed roll of toilet paper at the woman's gun, and almost knocked it out of her hand. It diverted Jackie's first shot, sending it into the wall instead of Maria. That gave Maria an instant or two to leap down the stairs. Jackie fired at her from the top of the stairs, and all but one of several bullets whizzed by her. One hit its mark.

Sharp pain shot through her arm, and Maria let out a cry as she stumbled on the last step. *Oh, my God, I've been hit!*

She struggled down the hall, heading for the kitchen to escape. Pulling frantically on the door before it registered that she had to unlock it, she finally did and started out the door. One last bullet thudded into the wall next to her head.

"Help me, help me," she screamed, starting up the hill in blind terror with her towel still clutched in one hand. The men came on the run, guns drawn. With blood running down her arm and stark naked, she ran toward the agents. Somewhere she could hear someone screaming, then everything was dark and quiet.

51. Surrounded by Love

Late August 1963
(Maria)

When Maria awoke after surgery on her left arm, the events of the last twenty-four hours seemed unreal to her until she tried to move. Everything hurt, but Ed's light, comforting touch on her face as her eyes fluttered open gave her hope that everything would be all right.

"Hi, my darling little Tiger Lily. You certainly lived up to your name this time." His smile reached both ears. He leaned over and gently kissed her lips. "I can kiss them, they didn't take a bullet," he said, his eyes full of the dickens.

"So, what happened to Jackie?" Maria croaked.

"She's in Chief Broderick's jail, awaiting transfer to a state psychiatric facility to see if she's sane enough to stand trial. I doubt she is."

"You're telling me!" Maria said, her voice cracking. "I'll never forget that laugh."

"Listen, Tiger Lily, just get well and come home to me. I'll answer all your questions this weekend, and what I don't know, Winston does."

"I need to go home now. Peter is coming Saturday night and—" Maria stopped and looked at Ed. "Tell me about Briggie. When did she get sick? I'm confused about everything. When the nurse came in to check on me this morning, she said another member of our household with a distinct Irish accent had been admitted to the hospital for some tests."

"She's fine. I spoke to the doctor about her condition. He thought she might have had a gallstone stuck in a duct, but he thinks she passed it because she isn't in any pain. He warned me about her weight and wants her to see an orthopedic man about her feet."

"Poor Briggie, she loves to cook and eat. Will she be going home soon?"

"She's home and raring to go, or so she says. She and your mom are planning the menu for when Peter comes, so relax."

"How's Amanda doing? Thank goodness for the Bellingers taking her with them to the circus yesterday. Can you imagine what would have happened if she had been home when the shooting started?"

"So confident you could take care of yourself, you didn't listen to me, did you?"

"I know, Ed, but when I moved here, I thought all the spy stuff was behind me with George's passing. I was ready to spend a safe and pleasant life in America's heartland with my new husband and family. But I learned people can have the same crazy emotions everywhere, no matter where one lives, and things can happen. Yesterday certainly proved that point."

"It's all behind us now. We can enjoy our lives with our past settled once and for all."

"Don't count on it, handsome. Just when the boat stops rocking, a new wave comes by and sets it off again." She gave him a hopeful look. "Ask the doctor when I can go home. I hate hospitals. And how is Mom? I hope she didn't faint when she heard the shooting."

"She'd gone to the store for a few groceries and didn't know a thing about your narrow escape until she came home and saw the men driving out of the yard with you. Someone evidently told her at the same time they called me. I was here last night, remember?"

Maria smiled. "Vaguely. I think I remember you saying I'd be fine."

"Get some rest. I'm going to the clinic, but I'll be back this afternoon to see you, my love." He bent over and gave her a light kiss on her lips. "You have such kissable lips."

She planned on calling home after he left, but fell asleep and didn't wake up until later that afternoon when the nurse came in to take her blood pressure. She'd slept through lunch, and the hospital staff hadn't wakened her. The doctor had given them strict orders to let her sleep.

Ed brought her home Friday morning to a joyous reunion with Amanda, her mother, and Briggie. He left for the clinic as soon as she was settled, promising to call her during the day.

Thinking back, she'd never considered changing the locks. What a simple thing it would have been to switch them. Would it have saved her? Maybe or maybe not.

Maria hadn't slept well the night before. Her frightening premonition had been flitting in and out of her mind, keeping her off balance for several days. Before the "Jackie Incident," she'd planned on spending most of the day with Amanda to console her about dear Wiggles's death. Somehow, Maria would make it up to her. Thank goodness that despite her failures, Amanda still loved her.

By afternoon, Maria was tired. She'd spent the morning answering Amanda's and Briggie's questions about the "shoot-out" as Amanda called it. Her mother had noticed that Maria was feeling a bit worn out and made her go back upstairs to take a nap.

She felt his warm breath on her neck before she was fully awake, and then his arms wrapped her in his embrace. Maria turned on her side and looked at him. Ed was searching her face, probably seeking any signs of trouble. He put his hand on her forehead and took her pulse.

"I'm fine, just a little over done. My arm starts to throb when I move around too much."

"I'll change your dressing tonight." Ed popped a thermometer into her mouth. "Just lay still for a minute or two."

"Anything you say, Doctor—" She felt his fingers on her lips to keep her quiet.

"Close your eyes while I rub your back," he whispered. "When you feel better, I want a blow by blow as to what happened Wednesday."

She looked at him, and for some reason . . . maybe because he was being so darned attentive, tears filled her eyes. She'd never felt more loved by him than she did at that moment.

"Okay, my little crybaby, let's see that thermometer." He slipped it out of the mouth and held it up in front of him. "Good, I pronounce you fit to get up and talk again. That will make you happy." Ed grinned, his big brown eyes smiling at her.

She pushed herself up with her right arm. "If I had to be shot, I'm glad I got it in my arm and not my leg. I don't have to walk on my arm," she said, remembering the ugly scar on Elena's leg where she'd been shot by a drunk while she and George were escaping from Puerto Rico.

"I'll be down for a cocktail with your folks after I take a shower," Ed said. Winston's bursting to talk about the whole thing with us."

Maria looked in her mirror and shuddered. *I look ancient. Nothing like a bullet wound and a trip to the hospital to add a few wrinkles.* While making her way carefully down the stairs, hair brush in hand, she noted the bullet holes in the wall as she went and thanked God for letting her live.

The sun had gone down, and the cooler temperature out on the patio made it feel superb to be there at dusk. "Mom, would you brush my hair and put a clip in it? It's so hard to do with one hand." She heard Winston calling from his French door, asking for her drink order. "Just ginger ale," she answered, sitting down a bit shaky.

"Ooh, that feels so good, Mom. Nothing like getting my hair brushed. It's so soothing. Sometimes, I want to cut it all off because it's so much work, but Ed would hate that. If he has anything to say about it, I'll someday be an old woman looking like a witch with long gray hair, pretending I'm still in my twenties."

"It looks beautiful for now. When the time comes, as you get older and older, your hair will get shorter and shorter," her mother said, laughing as she brushed Maria's shiny, brown wavy hair.

Winston handed Maria a ginger ale. "How's that arm feeling?"

"I have some pain, but it's getting better. I wish it had never happened." Maria still couldn't believe it *had* happened. "Thanks, Winston, for all you did. Tell me what you can. I know you were the brains behind capturing Jackie."

"Nonsense, Adam was the main man of the hour. I invited him out here for a drink, but he declined. He said he needed to get back to Washington."

Ed and Amanda strolled out on the patio, hand in hand. "Guess who was waiting for me, upstairs?" Ed winked at Amanda. "My other girlfriend. She wanted to know about the road that's going in behind our house."

Seeing them together sent a wave of happiness through Maria. Ed's genuine interest in her daughter was a blessing that Maria had only hoped for, but hadn't planned on. She also marveled at Amanda's resiliency. She'd lost her dog and had been afraid for her mother, but she was still looking forward to a new, more exciting world of her own.

Amanda's eyes widened. "Does this mean our barn is next after the road is ready?"

"That's right, Cupcake."

"I like Petunia better than Cupcake, Daddy," she said, getting up and pouring herself a lemonade from the pitcher on the table. "It's more grown-up."

"Then Petunia it is, my dear." Ed dropped into a chair. "Where's Chris?"

"Probably downtown where he usually is on Friday nights, talking to Laura. He gets a bite at Maisie's and then goes to the park afterward. That seems to be where all the kids congregate," Maria said, surprised that Ed hadn't been aware of Chris's new behavior pattern.

"Here's a man's drink for you, Ed." Winston handed him a glass. "We men need to stick together."

Ed took a sip and coughed. "How much water did you put in this scotch, two drops?"

Winston laughed and sat down. "I may have been a little heavy-handed." He took a sip. "Ah, perfect." He looked at Maria. "So, wonder girl, give us the lowdown on the afternoon of the shootout, as Amanda calls it."

"If I'd had a gun, it would have been more of a fight, but it was pretty one-sided. She was shooting, and I was running naked, trying to keep my towel around me."

"Mommy, why were you naked?"

"I was about to take a shower when I heard an odd laugh. I knew someone was out there, and I didn't have time to put my clothes back on."

"So, what did you do?" Amanda's eyes grew as large as a full moon.

"I ran like the devil was behind me, and then I threw a roll of toilet paper at Jackie to try to deflect her gun's position."

Everyone started to laugh, Winston in particular. His face turned red, his eyes were watering, and he was guffawing until Maria was afraid he'd choke.

Every time they quieted down, someone would say something about the naked Maria and the toilet paper incident, and it would send everyone back into gales of laughter. It was their hooting that brought Briggie out from the kitchen onto the patio.

"Saint's preserve us, what's all the merriment about?"

When Winston told Maria's story with a few embellishments, Briggie's face contorted as she tried to avoid chuckling and setting everyone off again.

Amanda pulled a chair next to Maria's and plopped down. "Finish the story, Mom. How did you get a bullet in your arm?"

"With my towel around me, I ran for the stairs. Jackie started shooting wildly, and I felt a hot pain in my left arm. I ran outside looking for protection from the men on the hill watching the house. They ran down, I lost my towel, and that's the last I remember."

"Mom, the men on the hill saw you naked?" Amanda covered her eyes. "How embarrassing."

"I don't remember, but I'm sure I didn't care."

After dinner, when Amanda had gone to her room, Winston volunteered the news that Jacqueline's mother had been brought up on charges along with her son and his friend. The FBI had caught the men just before they left town. "You may have to testify, Maria, but I'm sure it won't take place for a few months. The court system is overloaded with Chicago crime."

The household was quiet and settled for the night when Maria heard a car stop and Chris saying thanks to some of his friends. *Good, now I can get some sleep.*

Ed came in moments later as she lay almost asleep. She felt his body slip in next to her, and then he nuzzled her neck. "I've been telling Amanda a bedtime story about the little colt that nobody wanted, and Amanda wouldn't let me go until I made up a good ending."

"Mr. Imagination, someday I'm publishing your stories for children," Maria uttered.

He began rubbing her forehead lightly and stroking her hair. "What a sight you must have been to those FBI guys, running out of the house, trying to hold your towel, naked with a bleeding arm. You have to admit it's movie material. It'll be cold showers and lots of work for me for a while. But I don't care. You're safe and your arm will heal. He paused before he whispered, "If I'd lost you, my life would have been over."

52. Desires

Labor Day Weekend 1963
(Maria)

"Mom! Wake up, Mom! I want to get in bed with you," Amanda said, "but I'm afraid I'll hurt your arm."

"You won't. Lie down and talk to me. We haven't had a good talk in days."

Amanda snuggled in next to her mother. "Mom, can I go with Grandma and Grandpa to their club and take Lois?"

So, this is what talks with a daughter who's growing up too fast are like. Maria kissed the top of her daughter's head. "Sure, just wait until they're up on the patio having coffee before you go over."

"Thanks, Mom," Amanda said, popping up and skipping to the door. She stopped and thought for a minute. "I'm glad you're home. I missed you."

"Ditto, my sweet," Maria said, lying there wondering where her little girl had gone. Amanda had crossed over from being a child to prepubescent in a matter of months.

Motherhood had its shocks and rewards. Just when she got used to being needed 24/7, that dependency disappeared and was replaced by the buds of independence. But Amanda was different from Chris leaving her. Chris had never looked back. He understood he needed to be on his own and seemed to relish it, but Amanda was a girl who still needed her approval.

Sitting up gingerly, Maria felt her arm and the surrounding area. She didn't feel as sore today. She encased her arm in a plastic bag, took a carefully orchestrated shower, then pulled her shorts and top on without her bra. It had taken a bullet to make her realize how important both arms and hands were. In fact, she'd never thought about her health. Instead, she'd taken it pretty much for granted.

She carefully made her way down the stairs, then found her mother on the patio reading the morning paper. "Mom, I need your help," she said, holding up her arm sling, bra, and hair brush.

Her mother laughed. "It's been a long time since I was needed to dress you. Come on." She led her daughter into her bedroom.

"Thanks, Mom." Maria handed over the brush. "Would you give my hair a few more brushes?"

"Certainly, I know it feels good." Her mother took her time, moving through Maria's hair with gentle strokes. "There now," she said, surveying her handiwork. "Let's have a cup of coffee together. We're all set to take Amanda and her little chum, Lois, with us this afternoon. While we're gone, you rest so you'll feel good when Peter comes."

While working all morning helping Briggie, Maria really understood what the word handicapped meant. Almost every cooking task required two hands. Luckily, she'd be out of her sling in a few days, but for now, it forced her to bend forward to use her hand because of the sling's constriction.

"Saints be praised, we're all set for tonight, me girl. Now up you go for a little lay down. Your mother is going to help me in the dining room later, and I'm going to rest me feet now."

Briggie's kindness made Maria feel a little guilty about being irritated with her incessant comments about her new diet, but it didn't keep her from falling asleep almost immediately. She heard the phone off in the distance, and for a split second worried it was one of those calls. She reminded herself that they were over, and she felt an instant peace. Fumbling for the phone, she said, "Hi, Maria here."

"You sound sleepy. Sorry to wake you." Ed's deep male voice gave her goose bumps in her weakened condition. "How are things going? Has Peter called? I'll be finishing up here at the clinic in a few minutes and guess what? I'm bringing that never present son of yours home for a visit before he takes off for the evening," Ed said, laughing.

"I just woke up from a nap, if you can believe that. I don't understand why I'm so tired."

"As soon as that arm of yours starts to mend, you'll feel better. Just be happy the bullet didn't break a bone."

"No solace from you, I see. I haven't heard from Peter yet. I thought this call might be him. See you when I see you."

As she hung up, she heard Ed say, "I'm glad you're home."

With her outfit for the evening over her arm, Maria padded down the stairs, enjoying the soft fibers under her bare toes. Hearing female voices in the dining room, she peeked in. "Hi, Mom, I see you have the girls learning the art of setting a table." She grinned at Amanda. "You aren't too happy, but I see you're resigned, because you know you'll be rewarded for your cooperation with trips to the club and possibly the movies. Right, girls?"

Amanda gave her mother a pained look.

"This is what it means to get ready for company, girls," her mother chimed in. "Whatever you say, Grandma," Amanda whined. "When can we go? We're tired."

As soon as her mother released them, their energy level miraculously soared and they went shrieking outside, heading for the road to the barn site. *Let them go, no one is out there that shouldn't be.*

For an instant, Maria wondered what Ed had done with poor little Wiggles, but remembered that while she was in the hospital, he, Chris, and Amanda had buried her on top of the hill where Wiggles had loved to sit and watch the world. Maria turned to her mother to ask her help to dress, but stopped when she heard the front door bell chimes playing their melody.

She opened the door to see Peter standing there, sweating from the heat and smiling from ear to ear. "Come in and get cool. I can't believe you're here."

"What's that big bandage and sling? Don't tell me a jealous woman shot you for enchanting her husband like you do me?" he asked, his eyes holding hers a split second too long.

"You almost hit the nail on the head, my psychic friend."

"No, I'm just a student of human nature."

Peter followed Maria into the dining room. Her mother was standing there looking over her work when he said, "I'm glad to meet the woman who raised Maria. You did a good job, Mom. Maria's a special person."

Her mother smiled, but seemed a little surprised by his complimentary remarks. She shook his outstretched hand. "Come and have a cool drink in the living room. It's too hot outside right now. I hope September will be cooler."

Maria heard Ed's truck drive by, and a minute later, Ed called from the kitchen, "It must be Peter's car outside. Glad you could make it. I'm bringing out a tray of Briggie's lemonade. Do you want something stronger in it?"

"No, man, with this heat, I'd never utter another sensible word the rest of the afternoon."

"Is Chris with you?" Maria yelled.

"Yes, and trying to disappear, but he'll come out with me and meet the man who has been a good friend to your family for a long time," Ed yelled again from the kitchen.

When they came out, Chris walked up to Peter and stuck out his hand. "I'm Chris, George's son."

"I see a definite resemblance to that handsome father of yours, but your eyes are different." He shook Chris's hand vigorously. "You have the grip of a veterinarian. I'm pleased to meet you after all these years."

Opening their French door, Winston boomed out, "Peter, glad to meet you. I'm Winston, the lucky fellow who married Maria's mother."

"Winston," Peter said, looking up at the tall, white-haired giant of a man standing there pumping his hand, "I'm happy to meet the gentleman who was a good friend to Maria and George. Maria has told me a lot about you. I've already met your lovely wife. You're a lucky man, indeed."

"Briggie," Ed called, "come out of the kitchen and meet the guy who's drinking your lemonade. A man whom I call a real friend and am indebted to."

She came to the door, complaining she was cooking and her food needed watching. Ed took her hand, pulled her in, and said, "Meet Bridget Coyle, the best cook in the world, who also gives advice whether we want it or not."

"As an old batch, I've been jealous when Maria bragged about your culinary abilities," Peter said.

Briggie just stood there, embarrassed. Her face reddened, and after an awkward pause, she said, "It'll be dinner I'll be serving after a little while," in her lilting brogue.

Winston made a gesture toward the door. "I think the sun is sufficiently down so we can sit on the patio."

With the men and Chris following Winston outside, Maria and her mother ducked into the downstairs guest bathroom. Carefully helping her daughter into a soft, summery dress, she teased, "You look marvelous, my dear. Let's go give the men trouble."

Their entrance was not unobserved. Winston immediately handed them frozen daiquiris.

356

Maria accepted the drink. "What happened to the lemonade?"

"We drank it all," Ed said, sheepishly.

She eyed her son. "I see you've quickly moved on to stronger liquids."

"It's just a beer, Mom!"

Not wanting to embarrass her cocky son further, she shot him a concerned look.

Still sipping the last of his lemonade, Peter asked, "Where's your little girl?"

"You mean Amanda. She's growing up and is upstairs with her friend, Lois, probably giggling over boys."

"Well, the evening air feels slightly cooler now. Doesn't it feel good?" her mother asked

"Yes, my dear, it certainly does." Winston smiled. "I want to announce my official work in the drug department of the clinic is complete. Everything is up to date and a sight to behold. Not a stray box around and every drug in its proper place. Now my boss wants me to reorganize the surgery, which I will do with proper guidance. And since our wonderful fill-in secretary has literally been shot down, I will endeavor to answer the phone and direct Ed to his calls via his shortwave radio. With Hugh's help, of course, until Maria can work, or we replace her."

"Winston," Ed said, chuckling at Winston's description of his work, "you are way over qualified for the work I have you doing, but if you're willing to help me for a little longer, I promise to make the clinic better for the community and still be able to pay my bills."

Peter looked at Maria and her arm. "Maria, do you care to fill me in on Winston's reference to you?"

"You already guessed why it happened, only the specifics haven't been addressed. Ed's ex was the jealous one. I enchanted Ed, and he was toast. He chased me until I let him catch me. Jackie just chased *me*. Everyone started to laugh, except Chris and Peter.

"Will everyone stop being so coy and bring Chris and me in on this joke?" Peter asked.

Amused, Ed said, "I'm proud to tell you that your mother was a champ, but I'm also glad you weren't home to witness it. She was about to take a shower when I called her. I knew that Jackie was headed to our home and was going to get Maria when she flew by me in her car. I stopped at the office to alert Maria before I drove home like a maniac.

"Maria thought fast when she heard Jackie's maniacal laugh outside the bathroom. She tried to lock Jackie out, but Jackie was too strong. She pushed the door, so your mother let go of it. Jackie hurtled in, hitting her head on the other side of the bathroom. Your mom ran past her, down the stairs, and Jackie went after her and shot her in the arm."

"I must add, because Ed is too polite to say, I was running so fast to get away that I almost lost the towel I had around me. I might as well tell the whole story. After she shot me, I completely lost it, mentally and physically. I was running for my life. I didn't know how many more bullets she had in her gun."

"Completely naked, I fainted into the arms of the FBI agents. You probably think the mental image of me doing that is pretty funny, don't you?"

"I don't." Chris surveyed his mother's face.

"Chris, this story stays here. I'm sure you understand. This isn't locker room material," Ed said.

Chris nodded. "But it's tempting."

"So, life in the peaceful Midwest is fraught with danger," Peter said, grinning at Maria. "You thought you left all that cloak and dagger stuff back in Washington, didn't you?"

With the beer loosening his tongue, Chris said, "If you're referring to my father, he was a hero. Don't make fun of what he did," he said, his voice shaking a little.

Winston jumped into the discussion. "Chris, I'd known your father since he was a young man of twenty or so, and he was one of the bravest men I've ever met. That's why he was awarded the Medal of Honor by the president."

"That's another thing. Mom, I'd like to keep Dad's medals in my room. It's the only thing I have of his. He never let anyone take any pictures of him in uniform. Why?"

"He was trained to keep as low a profile as possible because of his work. After being an army intelligence spy for the U.S. in the Second World War, he continued trying to protect the U.S. by conducting sting operations against the huge drug cartel in the late forties and early fifties that threatened our way of life and maintained that same attitude. It saved his life."

"But I can't remember what he looked like anymore," Chris said, his voice breaking.

"Just go to a mirror and look into it. You'll see your father staring back at you," Winston said quietly. "With a few minor changes, mostly in the eyes, you could be his twin."

Chris stood up. "I need to make a call. I'll see you all at dinner."

"There goes a young man who will be a very good veterinarian," Ed volunteered.

"Your boy is quite a young man, Maria," Peter said. "Is it the first time Chris has ever said how he felt about his dad and really learned what he did for the country?"

"I believe it is, isn't it Maria?" Her mother's eyes filled with concern. "We should all talk to him more about his father whenever it's appropriate. He has a lot of feelings about his dad."

"I'll do my part. I was in close contact with George during the war and afterward," Winston offered solemnly.

"Dinner everyone," Briggie called from the French door. "Ruth, can you help me with the serving?"

"Certainly, and I'm going to get my helpers to lend a hand too," she said, walking toward the stairs. A few moments later, Amanda and Lois came chattering into the kitchen with Amanda's grandmother right behind them.

"Gosh, this looks good," Lois said to Amanda as they carried platters of food to the table.

Ed excused himself to change into more comfortable clothes, and Winston wandered into the kitchen to help Ruth with serving, leaving Peter and Maria on the patio.

"Ah, alone at last," Peter said, grinning as he said it. "So, how are you really, Maria?" His eyes searched hers for an answer. "Do you or Ed need a tune-up? I've got to pay for my room and board someway while I'm here."

For a second, she felt something indefinable between Peter and her, but ignored it. "I do have a concern, although it's probably silly. It happened when we were away for my birthday," she murmured under her breath. "I think he needs your help, more than he's willing to admit to me. He has nightmares, but promised he'd talk to you about them." Maria's eyes became misty.

"As for me, I have this awful feeling that after a couple of years, our marriage will start to dissolve the way George's and my marriage did. What do you think of me now, feeling that unsure of myself?"

"Ed isn't George. Remember that. He's stable and doesn't have the wanderlust that George had. He loves to come home every night."

"At first, so did George, Peter," Maria choked out in a whisper. "But after Chris was born, our marriage fell apart."

Peter leaned forward in his chair. "Do you two plan on having any kids?"

"No, and that's a relief. Ed is afraid that because of my age, if I were to get pregnant, I might not make it. Maybe he just doesn't want the responsibility. As soon as he can, he's going to get a vasectomy. He'll probably mention it to you." Maria stood. "It's time to eat. We'd better go in. They'll all be wondering why we're still out here."

53. Peter's Surprise for Maria

Labor Day Weekend 1963
(Maria)

The dinner table looked lovely, thanks to her mother. Peter exclaimed to Ed how lucky he was and insisted on sitting next to Amanda like a long-lost uncle who had come to visit. With glass in hand, he said, "May I propose a toast?"

Everyone stopped passing food and waited. "Thank you for including me in your family and making me feel so welcome. May we all have a good year and meet again next year, if I can wangle another invitation." He started the toast around the table with a click against Ed's glass, then he took a sip of wine and said, "Pass the food."

With each dish that was passed to Peter, he grunted with pleasure. Amanda and Lois giggled every time, which didn't escape his notice. "Do I sound like a piggy?"

"Yes," Amanda said, "and I love it. Do you have kids?"

"No, can I adopt you and be your uncle?"

Amanda giggled again. "Are you going to be here tomorrow?"

"Yes, all day and some of Labor Day too."

"Good, you can go swimming with us."

"He's going to have the pleasure of riding with me, aren't you, Peter? Tomorrow for part of the day, because someone around here has to work," Ed announced, "Don't worry, girls, I'll squeeze in a swim with you. We'll play Duck, Duck, Goose, and I'm great at it."

"Who's going to be goosed?" Peter asked with a devilish look in his eyes.

Amanda squealed with delight. "Not me! I can't wait. Maybe Chris will play, too."

Something in Peter brought out a wilder side in her daughter that was new to Maria. Amanda was growing up with a bit of her real father's personality showing.

"We'll also have a game of water polo, Doc," Ed said, "so get ready. The first time I ever played it was in Winston's pool. I got thrashed and decided I needed a pool to practice in."

Peter chuckled. "Well, you have a great pool to play in, as well as a lovely home to live in. You like being home, don't you?"

"Yeah, now that Maria and the kids are here with me."

A car honked its horn in the front of the house and Chris hopped up, waved, and left.

"Chris never stays home. He has a girlfriend and lots of boy-friends." Amanda sounded eager to share her brother's life with the others. "I wish I had a boyfriend, too."

For a second, Maria felt old. Her son was growing up too fast. In another three years, he'd be leaving for college. Where had the time gone?

"Girls, please clear the table for Briggie," her mother said. "Lois, would you also call your mother and see if it's all right for you to stay over?"

Maria leaned over to Amanda. "Don't look so bothered having to help. I need you, especially with my sore arm. You're important to me."

Amanda suddenly gave her mother a kiss. She lightly touched her mother's bandage, picked up some dishes, and headed for the kitchen. Following her with a light serving dish, Maria said, "You need some spending money, so I think it's time to discuss giving you an allowance. But first, I need to talk to your daddy. Now, do a good job for me. This won't be forever. My arm will be out of its sling in a week or so. When you finish, you and Lois can go upstairs, listen to your radio, and talk about boys. I'm sure you'd like that."

Maria returned to the patio where the rest of the adults, minus Briggie, had landed. "Ed, let's start having some family meetings once in a while, the way you wanted. It's time," she said, fully aware of Peter's presence.

"You're turning into quite a family man, aren't you? I'm glad you took my suggestion." Peter glanced at Maria as if to say, Ed's really different from George.

Winston pushed back his chair. "Now that we have family matters taken care of, who wants some of my sipping whiskey while we enjoy the rest of the evening?"

"You're in for a treat, Peter, if you can swallow it," Ed said, enthusiastically.

Winston raised his eyebrows. "Ladies, anything for you?"

Maria shook her head. "No, my stomach hasn't recovered yet."

"I think a ginger ale will suit me fine," her mother added. "I feel a little like Maria."

As the men sipped their drinks, Winston rubbed his hands in anticipation. "Would you like to hear the latest on the gang?"

"What gang? It's all new to me," Peter said. "I thought I was going to have to tell jokes and do a dance to keep the party rolling, but you all have been leading exciting lives." He took a sip and smiled. "I hope your information is as good as your liquor, Winston."

"Peter, after Maria arrived here, she was first subjected to phone calls that greeted her with only silence. They were aggravating, but not necessarily scary. Then a new twist was added. Ear splitting noise assaulted her when she picked up the phone. It went on for weeks while my man, Adam, began investigating with the help of his FBI friends here in Chicago. While looking for the perpetrator, they located the industrial company where the calls were coming from. A foreman went with them to police headquarters and identified a small-time gopher for the Mafia, Tommy Agano, from police photos as the man who had taped the noise.

"From there it was easy to trace Tommy and find out where he lived, who he hung out with, and guess what? He was friends with Rocco O'Brien, Jacqueline's brother. Adam quickly found where Rocco lived because he was a momma's boy, and he lived with his mother, Angelina Perrelli O'Brien and his sister, Jacqueline. The old lady was the brains behind the whole thing, besides running a bookie joint in the back of her house.

"The problem was that Rocco had a violent temper and was hard to control. He probably shot Wiggles. Tommy was amoral, but not crazy. After doing Angelina's bidding by running Maria off the road, he decided that he wanted out and was planning to leave town and get away from insane Mama Perrelli O'Brien.

"No one, including Gladys, Jacqueline's longtime friend, could predict that Jackie would go crazy and take matters into her own hands. But she did. Jackie was tired of trying to run Maria off, so to speak. She decided to kill her, and in her crazy mind, thought that once she got rid of Maria, Ed would go back to her. Truth is stranger than fiction, and both mother and daughter are being evaluated at the state hospital for the criminally insane." Winston sat back and took a sip of his whiskey.

After a few moments of recovery, Ed said, "The person who was the central player in this operation is sitting over there, sipping his whiskey. Thanks, Winston, for all you did for us. I hope I can repay you someday. It's an honor to know you," Ed lifted his glass and took a sip.

Looking first at her husband and then at Winston, Maria was silently awed by Ed's heartfelt compliment to Winston. She could see Winston was at a loss for words.

"One question, Winston. Was Gladys the spy who let Jackie know when I was home so she could make those calls to me?"

"Yes, Jackie talked Gladys into applying for the secretarial job after Ed's previous secretary left. In the future, I know you'll screen your applicants more thoroughly. Maisie inadvertently let Jackie know about the opening when she was having lunch at her cafe."

That information led to another question Maria wanted answered. "What was Gladys's game, not sending out bills to Ed's clientele?"

"That was just laziness. Gladys has a history of doing everything possible not to work. She was only at the clinic to help her friend, Jackie."

The party began winding down and Maria was glad. Her arm was beginning to throb like crazy, so she turned her attention to Peter. "For goodness sakes, I never showed you to your room." Embarrassed, she stood to rectify her negligence. "Come on, follow me. Your bag is probably still in the entry way where you dropped it when you arrived."

Walking down the hall, she felt his body closer to hers than normal. He said softly, "I'm overwhelmed, more than I care to admit, about being here with you and your family."

He gave her a look that was slightly unsettling. *What is he trying to say?* She switched on the light in the guest room, and pleasure filled her at how inviting the space felt. Her mother's decorating skills were outstanding.

Peter paused for a moment at the bedroom door. "Ed is one lucky fellow."

"I'm lucky, too, having you with all of us. You're a part of our family now. Amanda has declared that you're her uncle. And what would I have done without you all those years, Peter?"

"After George died, I'd hoped that we could have spent more time together."

"Peter, I didn't know." She risked looking into his eyes. "You never called." I've always thought of you as my special shrink, but off limits. You always seemed so busy, and you had a girlfriend. At least that's what you told me."

"I did date a lot, but I'm mad at myself for never taking the chance to ask you for a date after George was killed." After his confession, Peter's face had a resigned look. "Go find Ed, I'm sure he's waiting for you."

Ed *was* waiting for her, naked, and reading a medical journal on their bed. "Are all the chickens present and accounted for, my little caretaker? Come to me and let me rub your back." He opened his arms wide, simultaneously dropping the journal on the floor and giving her a look she knew so well. "How about it, my darling?" he whispered in her hair as he rubbed her back. "I'll be very careful not to hurt your arm."

"Are you kidding, you big lug? My arm is throbbing, I've been entertaining all day, and all you can think about is sex. I bet if your arm was in a sling, you wouldn't be so sexy. Help me take off my sling, get undressed, put my nightie on, and get into bed," she fired back at him.

Silently, he got up and followed her instructions. As he did, tears of trauma fell down her cheeks.

"I'm sorry I'm so crude. I don't know why I'm so oblivious sometimes." He carefully wiped her cheeks, gathered her up in his arms, laid her gently in their bed, and hugged her. "Please forgive me, Rosebud. You're the best thing in my life," he whispered.

"After that wonderful tribute you paid Winston, why do you act like you do around me?"

"I'm going to have a long session with Peter, and I'll ask him. Now, let me give you some pain pills so you can sleep, and tomorrow I'll talk to Peter."

54. Good News

Labor Day Weekend 1963
(Maria)

In the morning, the sun was streaming into their bedroom when Maria awoke. She could faintly hear some noise coming from outside as she carefully got up, put on her sling, and threw a robe over her shoulders. After making her way downstairs, she ventured out to the patio to see what was going on.

"Okay, Peter, this is war. Get ready to lose the next point. Ready!" Ed yelled across the pool to Peter, who was shaking his fist at Ed.

"Do your damage, I'm ready. Serve the ball and stop talking. Get ready, team, let's show him what we're made of," Peter said, laughing at his obvious pretense. Winston was standing next to Peter with his arms up in the air, ready to whack the ball back to Ed's team.

Chris, caught up in the moment, was screaming at Ed, "Serve it! Serve it, man! Stuff it down their throats!"

Good grief! The men were almost playing as though their lives depended on winning. It was just a game of water polo, for gosh sakes. Not war of the worlds.

Amanda and Lois came running out and joined her. "Is everything all right, Mom? We heard all the yelling down here and came to see."

"Everything is fine. The men are just having fun."

"It doesn't sound like fun to me. Lois, let's go see where the barn is going to be." She grabbed her friend's hand and left the patio.

"Go have fun! There's just one more day before school starts. You'll be big sixth graders," Maria called as they hurried off.

Her thoughts were interrupted with a wild cry from the pool. She laughed as she watched Ed and Chris dive under the net, come up, and try to duck Peter and Winston with a lot of wrestling, pushing, and shoving. A good-natured physical water fight had begun.

"Come on, you guys! Come out and have some breakfast," Maria teased.

Her comment helped dampen their enthusiastic rough housing, and they came crawling out of the pool out of breath, laughing, and pushing their hair out of their eyes—except for Peter, who had very little on top to push. Maria watched all their muscles flexing as they toweled off, then began flipping their towels at each other, just like they were back in high school.

Maria shook her head. "You guys never grow up, do you?"

"I guess not." Ed was grinning from ear to ear, apparently happy with his win. "Only, I never did the locker room stuff. It's sort of new to me."

Chris got Ed's attention and said something, Ed nodded, and Chris disappeared. Where was her son going now? Maria needed to relax. If Ed thought Chris's leaving was okay, she was fine with it, too. The two of them seemed to be becoming friends and less adversarial, especially since working together during the summer.

Her mother appeared at her doorway, and Maria waved to get her attention. "Mom, now that the big match is over, let's help Briggie with breakfast."

"I'm coming," her mother called back. "With your wounded wing, you need my help."

The phone rang while Maria was in the kitchen, and she casually picked it up from the kitchen wall, knowing that she wasn't going to be frightened or shocked anymore. "Hello, Mrs. McDermott here."

"I'm delighted to find you home, Mrs. McDermott. Good news, you have a buyer."

"Hang on a minute." Maria handed the phone to Briggie and ran to the study. "Hi, would you repeat what you just said?"

"Wonderful news, Mrs. McDermott. Your home has a buyer who is willing to pay what you're asking. His name is Lieutenant Colonel Fisher, he's attached to the Pentagon, and he has a young family to move from Texas. He wants to get them started in school as soon as possible. I'll send you the purchase and sales agreement by special delivery. Please send it back to me ASAP, if you don't mind. He's anxious to know he has a home for them."

Why did she feel like crying? This was great news! Maria sighed. Probably because it was the last remaining tie she had with George. He'd poured his heart into making their home beautiful when they were newly married and crazy in love.

Maria cleared her throat and said in a businesslike voice, "That's wonderful. I'll sign as soon as my lawyer gives me the go ahead."

"Colonel Fisher has given me a retainer for ten thousand dollars that he'll lose if he backs out, so I'm positive we have a buyer."

Thanking her real estate agent, Maria replaced the phone and sat in the study, her feelings raw and open again. How many times would she go over her part in their failed marriage? *Oh, dear God, please let me put this to rest.* She sat in the shadows, her head pressed against the back of her chair with her eyes closed, until she felt Ed's hand on her forehead.

He swiveled her chair around, leaned over, put his lips gently on hers, and kissed her, the moments ticking past. When he let her up for air he asked, "What's wrong, Rosebud? Why are you hiding in here?" He sat down on the sofa and opened his arms to her.

As she lay curled up next to him, she knew she had to lie. She couldn't open that can of worms with him again. "My real estate agent just called and told me that a mutual friend of ours was killed in a car crash. But she also had good news. She has a buyer for my house. When the agreement comes, would you ask your lawyer to read it over before I sign it?"

"Sure," Ed said, with a dubious tone to his voice. "I trust Earl Markham with my money. He'll do a good job for you. Is that all there is to this?"

Maria shrugged off his question. "I guess the market is hot in Washington, DC, and my place was in perfect condition, as you know. It sold for one hundred and sixty thousand. I plan on putting that in our joint account, my sweet. We're in this together."

"No, that money is going to be put in your account and saved for the kids' education. I can take care of us, especially now that Jackie will no longer be getting alimony." Ed's tone of voice indicated he was very much in charge. "No way will I change my mind on this one, my little Tiger Lily."

"We'll talk about it again. Now, I must leave your comforting arms and go see about feeding our band of hungry Indians." Maria slowly pulled away. "Where did Chris go? Will he be home tonight for dinner?"

"Maybe, but he's got a pick-up baseball game down at the park's diamond. At least that was his excuse. I imagine the girls will be in the stands watching. What do you think?"

"You're so good for Chris. You know how boys think. I don't know if his father would have been as understanding."

"I'm sure he would have. But thanks for your vote of confidence, cutie."

After a late breakfast, Ed said, "We've got to go, Peter. Now you'll see how I work."

"So, working for you is the price of earning my board and keep around here," Peter said, pushing his chair back from the table. "At least your clients won't require therapy like mine. Although, they may bite or step on you, something my clients haven't done to me, yet!" he said, then chuckled as he followed Ed to his truck. With all his joking, Maria hoped Peter would get time to talk to Ed about his demons.

Lois was spending the day and night with Amanda again. Alicia had called and asked if Lois could stay so she and Dirk could have a little getaway in Chicago. The upside was that Amanda wouldn't be lonely without Wiggles, and they could have school jitters together. Maria readily agreed.

Maria drifted out on the patio where her folks were having more coffee, put a smile on her face, and gave them the good news about her house sale.

One look at Maria and her mother stood up and hugged her. "It's all over, now, honey. It may be hard, but you can finally put George to rest," her mother said softly.

"I can't fool you, can I? Why do I still want to ask George what went wrong between us? I love Ed, but I just want to know. I know George left me a letter before he flew to Oshkosh, begging me to take him back. But I keep wondering why. Did his mistress gave him the boot, or did he really decide he wanted to be with me again?"

"I went through the same thing with your father. I thought I'd die when he left, but look how it's turned out for Winston and me. You'll have the same thing happen, little by little with Ed. It just takes time." Her mother held Maria and locked eyes with her.

"Sit down and have some coffee with us," Winston said, "and tell us more about the deal, Maria."

"The man who bought the place is a lieutenant colonel. He's attached to the Pentagon, the same as George, and his name is Colonel Fisher. Isn't it amazing, of all the names out there, he had to have the name of Fisher. It's almost like Fuller. And George was a lieutenant colonel too." Maria couldn't control the slight wavering in her voice.

"Bad memories will fade with time, Maria." Winston offered a sympathetic smile. "Ed's a good man. He'll help you get on with your life, and old George will be just a memory, just like your mother said."

"Ed is wonderful, and I know that. I just want closure. George died so abruptly, we never got to say good-bye. On a better note, Ed wants the money from the sale of my house to be saved for the children's education."

"Capital, that just proves what I said. You've got a winner there, girl." Winston turned to her mother and took her hand. "Now for our news," he said with excitement. "Your mother and I have been making plans for when our place sells. Do you want to tell her, Ruth, or do you want me to?"

"You start out, and I'll fill in the blanks," her mother said, encouragingly.

"When our place in Washington sells, we're going to take the money and buy a big boat. I've always wanted to have a boat. Your mother says it sounds like a yacht, but whatever it is, that's our plan. Then we're going to Miami and work with a real estate agent, sell our place in Miami, and buy a place where we can moor our boat. It all sounds very complicated, but it isn't. All one needs is money." Winston was practically beaming. "I was talking with one of Ed's breeder clients in the clinic, and he suggested we look in Ft. Lauderdale. He called it the Venice of the east coast." Winston settled back, looking pleased with his plans.

"As long as there's room for us, more power to you. It will be great fun riding around on a big boat." Maria was thrilled. She began thinking about visiting distant ports with them. "When are you going to Miami?"

"Probably in November," Winston said. Our joint real estate agent called us a couple of days ago and said she had a general who was interested in our Washington home. The Pentagon must be ramping up as the US is getting more involved in Vietnam and surrounding countries."

"No, it can't be. The government isn't thinking of another war, is it?" Maria immediately thought of her son. "I won't let Chris go. After what George suffered in WWII, it can't happen to Chris! Winston, why did you say that?"

"I'm afraid our leaders are succumbing to the god of war again, Maria. In 1961, President Kennedy sent Special Forces to help the South Vietnamese fight the communists in North Vietnam. That was the beginning of the war machine getting ready to eat all our brave young men and nothing stops it. Besides having an aircraft carrier stationed in the south, they now have five thousand troops in Thailand. I've seen it all before during the Korean conflict." Winston shook his head. "When will it stop, all this killing of our best and our brightest?"

"Perhaps it will be all over by the time Chris is of age," Maria said, softly.

"I hope so, my dear Maria." Winston's sad tone revealed how he felt about the conversation, "But I wouldn't count on it."

55. Confronting Demons from the Past

Labor Day Weekend 1963
(Peter/Maria)

Peter

The clinic was quiet because of Labor Day Weekend. Dr. Glen was on duty, but only taking calls from home for any emergency with clients' small animals. Hugh was helping Maisie in their café with the hordes of celebrators looking for a good meal, and Ed and Peter spent the better part of their day on large animal emergencies out at farms and stables.

Riding back to the office, Peter congratulated Ed for his skill as a veterinarian, but said he was glad he worked with people. He repeated himself several times saying he liked clients who didn't step on his toes or try to bite him. By five, they'd stopped for a quick bite at Maisie's and were back in the clinic.

"Okay, it's my turn to play doctor," Peter said, once they were inside the quiet office. "Let's get down to what ails you. We know each other well enough not to spend any time with preliminaries. From what I gathered when we were riding around in the country today, you're hurting big time. You had a panic attack when Maria suggested the family take a Christmas vacation. Am I right?"

"Right," Ed said, tapping his fingers on the old couch he'd brought from the house.

"We'll tape this so you can go over it tomorrow and get back to me before I leave. Maria gave me your recorder before we left." Peter pushed the record button. "You remember how hypnosis works. I'll give you a prehypnotic suggestion that you won't be able to lift your little finger when you're under, even though you'll want to."

Peter got comfortable in his chair. "Ready? Now look at an object on the far wall, and as I count backward, on each count, you'll open and close your eyes slowly. Here we go." Peter started counting, and within a couple of minutes, Ed's eyes were closed, and he couldn't lift his little finger. Satisfied, Peter asked Ed to go back into his childhood to the event or events that caused the anxiety he needed to discuss. "I'll count backward until you reach the year when the problem started. Twenty, nineteen . . ."

When Peter reached Ed's eighth year, Ed spoke in the high tones of an eight-year-old boy. "I'm so excited. I was just awarded a free week at the YMCA summer camp for my school marks and good citizenship. I get off the school bus, and I run to the house holding my paper. I give my mother the paper from school explaining the whole thing. I tell her it won't cost anything for me to go. She angrily grabs the paper, glares at me, and reads it for herself. Why is she so mad? I don't understand it.

"She says that's the week the corn needs to be picked, and our fruit and vegetable stand needs me there to sell the produce. She calls me Sonny and sounds angry. She says I have to learn to help around here. Money is tight, and if I want to eat every day, I need to work. She says she's tied to this miserable land and so am I and not to forget it.

"She says I need to learn to be a good farmer and not go lollygagging around some rich boy's summer camp. She says if I were to go away for a week, we would lose too much money at the stand and all my help in the fields. We all might end up starving this winter! She says, 'I'm counting on you to stay here and take care of us when we get old so that doesn't happen.'

"I beg her not to tear up my form and say maybe I can find a friend who will tend the stand and maybe Dad will help more in the fields.

"She says I'm a dreamer, just like my no-good father. He won't help me more. He hardly works now, he drinks so much. 'Sonny, you and I are on our own. There's no one to help us. I'm tearing up this paper of yours, right before your eyes. Then you'll know for sure that you can't go and have to stay here. You need to learn how to work hard, something your no-good father never learned. You can never leave. You have to stay here! And stop that sniveling! Act like a man, not a baby. Men don't cry, they just work.'"

Ed lay on the old couch crying like a little boy, trying to stop bawling but bursting into tears over and over again. Ed's sobs finally subsided, and he lay quiet with his eyes closed.

Peter turned off the tape recorder and waited until he knew Ed would be able to go on. He felt Ed's forehead, took his pulse, and asked him if he wanted to continue and talk about the monster nightmare that haunted Ed. He nodded slightly, and Peter pushed record.

"Think of a time when you first remember having the monster nightmare," Peter said. Ed's eyes remained closed, and Peter counted back slowly. When he reached fourteen, Ed broke in and said in the deeper voice of a teenager, "This is the year I started high school. I remember staying after school and talking to some girls who stayed after school, too. We were all interested in the same things and finding out about each other, and it was fun. I knew I would catch hell when I got home, but I was beginning to not care and rebel against my mother. In fact, I hated her most of the time.

"When I walked into the kitchen, she was standing there holding a big broom in her hands. She flew across the room and attempted to hit me, screaming at the top of her voice that I was late again, and she was going to teach me a lesson I'd never forget. I was so mad, I wrenched the broom away from her and broke it in two. She stood rubbing her arms from the wrenching, amazed and furious. Her eyes looked all crazy-like, and she stopped screaming. She talked in a low and scary voice, promising me that she would get even when I least expected it.

"I pretended it didn't bother me as I changed my clothes for my evening farm chores, but it did. We stopped speaking to each other, except for the absolute necessities, and I pretended I didn't care. Part of me liked it. We were at war. The nightmares started, and I installed a chain lock on my bedroom door."

Peter brought Ed out of the hypnosis. "Play these tapes early tomorrow before I have to leave to catch my plane back to Washington. I want to go over the material with you. Have Maria listen, too. She needs to know you better and what happened to you as a little kid."

Ed sat on the couch, not moving, exhausted by the session. Peter swiveled slightly in Ed's desk chair, touching the tips of his fingers together.

Before they left the office, Ed put the tape in his pocket and picked up the tape recorder. "Thanks, Peter."

But Peter didn't answer. He just walked slowly out to Ed's truck, his head down, deep in thought.

They arrived back at Ed's and found a note on the kitchen table telling them to help themselves to the food in the refrigerator. The family would be back later. They'd gone out for ice cream. The men separated—Peter went to his room, and Ed left for a walk around his property.

María

The family came home, and Maria read Ed's terse note saying he was walking and taking some time to think. She shouldn't wait up for him. She went upstairs to bed. She hurt for him, but knew he had to work it out on his own. He'd come to her when he was ready.

Maria was just coming out of the bathroom the following morning, her arm still bandaged, when he came into the bedroom. "You caught me naked, except for my arm," she said, attempting a little humor. He didn't smile. "Your meeting with Peter must have been a lulu," and handed him her brassiere. "Help me get dressed, and we'll talk if you want. I also want you to look at my wound, rebandage it, and kiss me."

Ed quietly attended her wound, helped her get dressed, and held her in his arms. "I feel better now. You're my shield. Help me through the pain in my tape," he whispered, holding her tightly.

"For what it's worth, I used to feel strangely better and strangely worse after a session with Peter," she murmured, searching his eyes.

"I couldn't sleep up here last night. I ended up out on the patio. I felt like I was choking and needed more air."

"Well, we're together now, and I'll help in any way I can." She held up her brush. "Please brush my hair out of my eyes."

He began gently pulling the brush through her hair. "You know, I've never brushed your hair, or any other woman's in my life," he said in a astounded voice. "I guess I thought it was off limits somehow."

"George said almost the same thing to me when we were dating," she said, giving him an incredulous look. "Neither one of you had sisters or mothers who let you touch them, did you?"

"Women are sort of mysterious to me, even you, Maria." They sat down on the couch, and Ed continued to work through her tangles. "I love the way your hair feels and smells. I love the way it curls around my fingers. Your hair is like you—soft, but strong and resilient. Brushing it makes me feel closer to you." He looked surprised at that revelation. "But before we listen to the tape, I need to shower." He returned appearing refreshed, but still not happy.

Maria locked the bedroom door and started the tape as Ed dressed. Then sitting on the sofa, holding his hand, she heard and felt the agony of her dear husband living through several more awful experiences with his mother. He had a vice-like hold on her hand as each heart-rending episode reached climax. The muscles in Ed's cheeks moved as he gritted his teeth from time to time. His face remained grim and his body, rigid.

When it was all over, he lay back on the pillows on the end of the sofa and gently asked her to lay on top of him. "As I said before, you are my shield." They lay there for a long time—he stroking her hair; she with her eyes closed, her body soothing his.

An irritating knock on their door brought her off of the couch and to her feet. "Mom, let me in. Why do you have the door locked?"

"Daddy and I were having a grown-up discussion and didn't want to be disturbed."

A wide-eyed Amanda stood there as Maria opened their door. "Were you and Daddy fighting?" she asked in hushed tones.

"No, sweetie, we're finished. Come in and tell us what's on your mind."

Seeing her dad on the couch, Amanda asked, "Are you sick? You never lay down on the couch. You aren't going away, are you?" Her face took on a worried frown as her old insecurities surfaced with any modification in his behavior.

"No, Petunia, I've got a barn to build and fill full of horses. No time to leave, too much to do," Ed said, forcing a grin and holding his arms out to give her a hug.

Pleased with his answer, Amanda's eyes lit up. "Do you want another dog, Daddy? I miss Wiggles so much. Could we get another one, Mom?"

Ed took out a little notebook from his breast pocket and wrote *a puppy for Amanda*, then showed it to her, and they laughed. They were so good for each other. In her childlike adoration for him, she raised his spirits with her love.

"Daddy, you're wonderful. I love you." Her quick little mind often changed directions. "Would you walk to our barn place and show us where everything is going to be? Lois and I saw stakes in the ground when we went there yesterday."

"After Peter leaves, we'll do lots of things. Now scoot and find your friend. Mom and I need to talk a little more, Petunia."

Maria sat down again studying his tanned face. A few more lines were appearing around his beautiful eyes, and his dimple in his left cheek seemed a little deeper, but his slight overbite and cleft chin remained the same. A sucker for his handsome, but slightly irregular features had turned her heart inside out from the very first time she saw him and still did.

He stared straight ahead and began speaking in low tones. "What hurts the most was how much my mother must have hated me. Every one of the regressions shakes me down to my toes," he said grimly.

Maria lightly touched the side of his face. "You couldn't be as kind and caring as you are without your mother having done some good mothering once in a while. Peter told me that our minds tend to hide all the bad stuff, but they keep the good stuff up where we can reach it. Tell me about some of the nice things you can remember that your mother did for you."

Ed sat and thought for a minute. "My mom always kept my clothes clean, patched, and mended so I looked as good as I could going to school." He smiled at Maria. "When I was ten, she even bought me my very own hair brush and comb for my birthday. She said I must wash my hair, and she made me take showers all the time until I started to notice girls. Then she didn't have to say anything to me again.

"In the summer, she cooked, canned, and made food for the second-hand freezer a friend of mine gave us. Mom wasn't a good cook, but she put something on the table most every day, unless she was really mad at my father." Ed paused. "She made sure our dogs and cats had something to eat every day and were warm in the barn."

"You see, Ed, your mother was there trying to do the best she could. She just had a violent temper that she couldn't control. Maybe she needed medication. For your sake, my sweet, I want you to remember the good things about your mother. You were loved by her in odd ways, but you were loved."

Maria tickled his cheek and opened her arms. "Your homework is to remember more things that your mother did for you growing up. Now kiss me, and let's go have breakfast."

He gave her a tender little kiss. "God put you on this earth to show me the way. I love you, Rosebud."

"You've never mentioned God before. I'm glad. You're very special, just like all of us, and God loves you as much as any other person. As I've said before, we're in this together."

Energized by their talk, as they went downstairs, Ed stopped and said, "I like the rugs on the stairs and in the halls, Maria. You've made this house a home."

His compliments warmed Maria's heart. "I couldn't have done it without the money you gave me, my generous benefactor."

They strolled into the kitchen. While pouring them each a cup of coffee, Maria spotted a pot of Irish oatmeal on the stove, but Briggie was nowhere to be found.

Peter poked his head around the door as she was serving the cereal. "Hi, folks, is there enough for me?"

"Of course!" Maria waved him in. "I'll fill a tray with our breakfasts, then one of you fellows can carry it out to the patio for me."

"I haven't had oatmeal since I was a kid!" Peter took another bite. "It's good." They sipped their coffee silently, enjoying the fresh, cool, fall air. "Did you listen to Ed's tape?" Peter asked, initiating conversation.

"We did," Maria said. "It always amazes me how the mind goes right to the place that deals with the problem."

"The mind is so complex, I'm astounded every day what I learn about it from patients. Did you know there are hypnotherapists who can regress people back before they were born in this life to a past life? I may take some seminars to learn the technique and try it on willing subjects. Would either of you be interested in learning if you've had more than one life?"

"No, I'm having enough trouble with this one. Actually, I don't believe it," Ed said. "They must be charlatans."

"No, I don't agree with you." Although he disagreed with Ed, Peter didn't seem offended by Ed's comments. "How about you Maria?"

"It's an interesting idea." Maria wanted to know more. "Imagine having lived more than one life."

"It's called reincarnation, and in some areas of the world, it's part of people's religion. They say their souls never die, they go on forever," Peter said, smiling at his hosts' perplexed expressions.

"Anyway, I digress." Peter took another sip of his coffee. "Any thoughts about what you heard on the tape, Ed? Can you see a connection with your current anxiety about vacationing and what your mother said to you at a very impressionable age?"

"Absolutely. After listening to that tape, I'm sure she pounded in the idea that I was tied to the farm and the land, forever and ever, but I don't remember it." Ed massaged the back of his neck. "Doc, with me just knowing what happened back then . . . Will that make the panicky feelings go away?"

"Every time you feel strange about taking time off just to play, listen to your tape again. I think your adult mind will wrap itself around the fact that you're now in full control of your life. You have a place in the community, you're well respected, you have money in the bank, and you have the right to a vacation. It's all about changing the tape in your head and giving yourself permission to enjoy yourself because you're worthy and deserve it. Knowledge of where pain comes from usually helps dissolve anxiety and nightmares. But please call me if it doesn't happen."

Peter pushed his chair away from the table, then focused his attention on Ed. "When you and Maria went to Chicago, how much time did you spend doing something just for yourself that was completely fun?"

"It was Maria's birthday, not mine." Ed sounded defensive. "But we did go to the racetrack because I wanted to, and Maria liked it. Didn't you, honey?"

"Okay, may I make a suggestion?" Peter hesitated, as though waiting for Ed to give him the go-ahead, which he did with a nod. "I want you to go away for a weekend and do exactly what *you* want to do. t can't have anything to do with work, Maria, or the family in any way. I'd like you to run this test to see if you're ready to spend ten days relaxing in Florida." Ed's face looked stricken. "I don't have any hobbies," he said quietly. "All I know is how to work. I guess all my dreams were knocked out of me when I was little."

"Well," Peter said, gently, "as I remember from one of our conversations, Maria's brother-in-law used to make you play horseshoes and cribbage with him from time to time. Go with him for a weekend to one of his horseshoe contests and play horseshoes. Or go to a cribbage tournament and play cribbage. You remember how to play, don't you?"

"Yes, I had to learn to play cribbage and horseshoes in self-defense." Ed turned to Maria. "When they come in a couple of weeks, I'll set it up with Don. He's been trying to get me to go with him ever since I started working for him."

"Great!" Peter stood, and looking pleased, shook Ed's hand. "Now

I've got to get ready and go, or I'll miss my plane back to Washington. Call me and let me know how the weekend turns out for you."

"Thanks, Peter, for coming and all the help you've given us," Maria said.

Surprising her, he hugged her a little tighter and longer than necessary.

56. Family Togetherness

Labor Day Weekend 1963
(Maria)

After Peter left, Maria and Ed settled back on the patio. "I wonder where everybody is?" "I've been so caught up in our discussions this morning, I've lost the kids." Maria barely had the words out of her mouth before Briggie came to the door, smiled, and came out.

"Briggie, where are the kids?"

"Saints above, me darlin', Amanda and Lois left with your folks an hour ago. Winston saw some puppies advertised in the Sunday paper and called for directions and an appointment. It was easy to eavesdrop. His booming voice was clear as a bell. I told them I'd tell you both when you were finished with your meeting with Dr. Peter." Briggie's cheeks pinked, and she gave them a slight smile. "He's a fine broth of a man, even though he isn't Irish."

"You noticed him, Briggie. Peter is single and available in case you're wondering," Maria teased, looking at her friend who seemed different. It suddenly hit Maria. Briggie had lost some weight.

Maria turned to her husband. "I need your help, Ed. Would you come upstairs and move the guest bed so Laura can clean behind it before we have any more company? We can also strip it for you, Briggie."

Ed stared at her like she was crazy until he saw a message in her eyes. They were saying make love to me. She grinned, grabbed his hand, and they ran back upstairs.

They didn't speak. They'd talked enough that morning to last them all day. What they wanted was each other. The physical release they felt matched the mental and emotional release that Peter's work had brought them.

"How do you feel now, handsome?"

"I liked moving the bed in the guest bedroom with you," Ed said softly in Maria's ear.

"Before we embark on our busy day, I have something to share with you. Mom and Winston are going to buy a boat and a waterfront apartment in posh Ft. Lauderdale after they sell their big home in Miami. They're going to ask if you will come with the family and visit them at Christmas."

"I'm going to have to test my ability to take a vacation," Ed said, uneasily.

"Why was it easy for you to visit us last year? You were doing it for yourself."

"It wasn't all that easy, but I had a purpose. I needed to find out if you were the right woman to help me with my life and work. I spent a lot of time with Peter, if you remember, which was a huge form of work."

Maria stretched, smiled, and sat up, completely happy physically and emotionally. "You are one great lover, and now you'll be one great bed maker. Come help me so I don't have to think about it again before Elena and Bill come next weekend."

"You weren't kidding about working in the guest room," Ed said. "I think I hear Winston's voice. They're back. It's perfect timing for me to escape any more domestic chores."

"Not on your life, friend," she said. "Help me dress and fix the guest room."

When Ed and Maria appeared, Amanda was in the kitchen giving Briggie a glowing report on the puppies they had seen. She squealed and ran to Ed, talking a mile a minute. "We just have to get one of those puppies, Daddy. They're adorable." She began describing the puppies, each one more adorable than the rest. Ed looked at Winston with a wry expression on his face.

"So Winston, old boy, what kind of dogs were they?"

"They were pugs, I believe. Yes, that's it, they were pugs."

"They're nice house dogs, but I was thinking along the lines of a border collie, an outdoor dog, maybe a pair, a spayed female and a male. That seems to be a good combination."

"What's a spayed female, Daddy?" Apparently, Amanda's ears had picked up on the conversation between the two men.

"It's a female dog who can't have any babies."

"Oh." Soft lines formed in her forehead as she stood there thinking for a moment. "Daddy, can we go look at the barn place? Grandma and Grandpa, you can come, too."

382

"Are we welcome, Ed?" Winston raised his eyebrows, as though uncertain if he was in trouble for taking Amanda dog hunting.

Ed chuckled. "Of course, clinic assistant, I don't want to lose my free help."

As their little band was nearing the top of the hill, Maria heard Chris calling, "Wait up, I'm coming, too." Maria watched her son take the hill in long bounds. She was happy to see him again. He was always gone or asleep these days.

The two girls and Chris ran ahead for the sheer joy of being outside. The weather held a tinge of fall, and the sun, while still warm, was not the intense, hot orb it had been in August.

After explaining the general layout of the barn, the kids started off into the woods behind that area. "Chris," Ed called, "just go to the fence. That's where our property ends."

"Sure, Ed, we'll be fine."

Maria knew Chris liked and respected Ed, but it ended there. Ed wasn't Chris's dad. Although Ed had formally adopted the children, Chris had asked to retain his father's name. Amanda, on the other hand wanted Ed's name. She was now Amanda McDermott.

For Chris to actually take a walk with his sister and her girlfriend was an unexpected pleasure for Maria. With Chris going to high school, they seemed to have grown closer since moving to St. Charles. Having a family meeting would add to the family solidarity.

Maria hurried to catch up with Ed. He was striding along with Winston, who was telling Ed about his plans in Florida.

"Later today, before everyone scatters, I'd like a family meeting," Maria said. "What about it, honey? We haven't taken the time to hold one before, but we need to start."

Ed looped his arm around his wife's neck and laughed. "Will we need a typed agenda, Miss Efficiency?"

Maria gave him a push and ran down the hill, shuddering a little as she thought about her experience a week ago on the hill. Somehow, it seemed like eons ago.

During their midafternoon dinner for Labor Day, Briggie announced that they were on their own for any more food the rest of the day.

Before anyone could escape, Ed said, "You two, clear the table for Briggie and wash and dry the dishes. That's going to be part of the new plan around here that we want to discuss with you as soon as you finish in the kitchen."

With Chris washing and the girls drying and putting away the dishes, they were done in short order. Maria drove Lois home while Ed went over the ground rules for their family meetings around the kitchen table with Amanda and Chris.

"Who would like to begin when Mom gets back?"

"I think you should start, Ed, and help us with this whole thing. We never had meetings with Dad." Chris dropped his head and murmured quietly, "He never seemed that interested in what we were doing."

Maria heard Chris's comment as she came in from the garage, and she quietly thanked God for Ed. "I'm here, everyone. Let the meeting begin."

"Let's hold hands and be thankful we're all together," Ed said, taking Chris and Amanda's hands. Maria took their hands too, and the circle was formed.

After a moment or two, Chris dropped his hands and looked at Ed. "Shoot, Doc, I've got things to do."

"First of all, you both did a good job in the kitchen, and it sounded like you had some fun. I hope that will continue because from here on, you'll clean up every night after dinner." Ed caught Maria's eye, and she gave him a sign to continue. "You both deserve some allowance because you won't be able to work like you did this summer, and it will give you some incentive for helping around the house."

Chris and Amanda grinned at each other at hearing they'd have money in their pockets.

"You'll both be starting school tomorrow, and I want you to do a good job with your studies," Ed said. "You're smart kids; now show us. Amanda, your mom told me you want to join 4-H. You have to let Mom know if you need rides home from your sports and club activities." Ed leaned back in his chair. "I guess that's all I have to say for now."

"Can I go out during the week?" Chris asked.

Ed shrugged his shoulders. "That depends on what the reason is, how long you'll be gone, whether you have your homework done and so on. Talk to one of us before the actual moment that you want to go. Give us some warning." Ed turned toward Maria. "How about you, Maria. Any thoughts?

She nodded. "I guess I just want to say that I know we'll have a good year here, and I want all of us to tell each other things that are important for us to know at the meetings and pull together as a family. If something bothers any of us, let's discuss it and clear it up."

"I like this meeting," Amanda piped up. "It makes me feel good."

"I forgot one thing," Maria said, "Grandma and Grandpa are going to buy a boat and keep it near their home in Florida. They'll be going in November to look for an apartment that has a dock for their boat, and then they'll sell their big place in Miami."

The joy in Amanda's face quickly turned to worry. "But they'll live here the rest of the time?"

"Oh, yes, they love being here with us. They just want a smaller place in Florida. And they've invited us to visit them during Christmas vacation and take rides on their boat."

Chris's eyes lit up at her words. "Gosh, that would be cool to ride out into the ocean on a boat."

"As long as Daddy and I can see the shore, it will be all right," Amanda said.

"I agree, Petunia. I'm rooted to the ground, but I'm trying to change that. You and I are going to be good sailors." Ed gave her a wink. I have one more thing to surprise you with before we end this meeting. I'm going to ask Mom to help me make that big empty room at the end of the hall across from the garage door into a rec room for us to enjoy this winter."

"Ed, can I have some parties in there?" Chris asked, suddenly interested in the conversation again.

"You bet! That's why we're going to fix it up with a pool table, hi-fi sound system, tables for cards and games, and comfortable, kid-proof furniture."

"Gee, thanks, folks," Chris said with a wide smile on his face.

He's probably planning his first party. Maria hadn't seen Chris so animated in a long time. Little by little, Ed was filling a place in Chris's life as an adult support system he'd never had before. She breathed a silent prayer in thanks.

Ed looked at his little family. "Are we done, here?" When no one spoke, he started to move.

Chris cleared his throat. "I'm going out for track and field this fall."

It was a big thing for Chris to share his plans with the family, taking the chance of criticism instead of choosing the easier path of silence. Everyone sat waiting for him to tell them more. "The coach suggested that I should run," he said quietly. "He thought I might be good at it."

Amanda sat up straight. "I want to be a good rider and have a pony that I can love. Lois wants one, too." She took a deep breath. "Daddy, can we go looking for a pony sometime?" Her heartfelt request resonated around the table.

Ed reached over and covered her little hand with his big one. "We'll do it soon, Petunia. You can count on it."

57. Perceptions

September 1963
(Maria)

"Get ready, everybody, we need to leave right away," Maria called, as she ran to her children's bedrooms. Amanda popped out of her doorway, dressed and smiling at her mother, holding her new little purse her grandma had given her.

"Take it easy, we'll get there, Mom," Chris said, looking very grown up in his new slacks and jacket.

"What a wonderful day, to be seeing me Elena, and her having a show," Briggie said to Ed, while she waited for Maria, Amanda, and Chris to squeeze in the back of the little sports car. As soon as they were settled, Ed helped Briggie into the front seat.

"No protests, Briggie," Maria said, "unless you want to ride with Winston."

"Well, I'll ride over with you and home with Winston," she offered in compromise.

"Do you have the directions, Ed?" Maria asked.

He turned around, nodded to her, and started the car. "As soon as the folks appear, we'll be on our way to Elena's first show in Chicago. Hang onto your hats, everyone."

"I don't have a hat, Mom, and neither do you," Amanda whispered, looking concerned.

"He just means we're going to go fast, Shrimp," Chris said, sounding slightly irritated.

Maria could smell Ed's aftershave lotion, and the aroma triggered a memory of sitting behind him in his new car back when they were in college. What a silly little freshman she was that day. She was one of five girls he was giving a ride home at Thanksgiving. However, what happened between them that fateful weekend changed her forever.

It had started innocently, but a few kisses had awakened in both of them a sexual passion for each other that blossomed, then retreated into dormancy, but never died. Reawakened after changes in both of their lives, the memory was always there and one of the reasons they'd married.

As she rode quietly through the countryside, she wondered how Elena and Bill's relationship was working. But why was she so interested? She really loved Elena—they were sisters. She truly wanted the best for Elena, so why was Maria feeling anxious about seeing Bill again? Was it possible to still be attracted to him and be in love with Ed? Did other people struggle with similar feelings for two people? Did Ed ever think about his first wife, Babs?

Maria felt a tugging on her arm. "Mommy, is Elena coming out tonight after?"

"I don't know, honey. I hope so. Daddy and I cleaned the guest room after Dr. Peter left. It's all ready for her."

"Is Bill with her, Mom?" Chris asked, his voice sounding more and more adult.

Maria smiled. Her son was a normal teenager. He was probably wondering about their sleeping arrangements. "Yes, I believe he'll be there."

After riding along in silence for a while, Ed checked on Winston's car behind them. "We're almost there. I'll let you all off and meet you inside once I park."

Quickly surveying the building from the outside, Maria liked what she saw. Elena's agent had chosen wisely. Elena's show was in a posh art shop located near the theater district complete with many quaint restaurants catering to the wealthy artsy crowd.

As soon as they stepped inside, a charming young man came scurrying over to them and introduced himself as Raphael, the manager of the shop. He was wearing a tux with a white, slightly ruffled shirt that had sleeves showing even more ruffles. Effusive in his greeting, he waved his hands and arms around as he pointed Elena out to them, describing her as the famous artist showing her work that day.

Amanda blurted out that Elena was her aunt, and he became more enthusiastic in his praise of her work. He led the way to Elena on his toes, dancing across the room to her. She was surrounded by a group of well-dressed people, all talking to her at once.

Catching sight of her family, Elena moved toward them with long,

388

graceful strides, her silky, red dress swirling around her legs. She hugged Briggie first, then each one of them. Elena looked radiant. Her cheeks were flushed with excitement, and her eyes danced with joy. She'd grown into a lovely young woman.

Bill had seen them, too, and he made his way across the crowded room, looking directly at Maria all the way. He smiled and shook both Winston's and Ed's hands. "Hello, everyone. Glad you could make it. Quite a party, wouldn't you say? Your girl has outdone herself, hasn't she?"

What a pair they made—Bill was more dashing than ever, and Elena was a Latin beauty. A warm, mysterious presence surrounded her, and he emitted a high-volt energy.

"All of my favorite people in the world are here now," Elena said.

Amanda clung to Elena, and looking up at her, asked, "Did you paint all these pictures and make all these things?"

"I did, and I want you to notice the painting over on that far wall, Amanda. I turned the sketch that I did of you and Wiggles into that picture. How is she, anyway?"

"A very awful man shot and killed her," Amanda said, looking forlorn for a minute.

Elena stood there quietly for a moment, then she placed her arms around Amanda, leaned over, and whispered something in Amanda's ear. She broke into a big grin and hugged Elena.

Raphael came dancing over to the group with Elena's manager, Kathy Gibbs, in tow. She was as tall as Elena, severely dressed in a black suit, her short dark hair was combed back from her thin, beautiful, angular face, and she appeared all business. Her dark eyes were alert—not inviting—and they were constantly moving around the room surveying everyone and everything.

Raphael took Elena's arm. "I must spirit this gorgeous creature over to some very important people," he whispered loudly to the group, winking at Ed and waving his free hand around in a dainty motion.

"I think you have a boyfriend if you want one," Bill said, grinning at Ed and imitating Raphael's arm movements.

Ed didn't seem at all amused. "He's more your type, Bill."

"While you two decide who's going to date Raphael, let's find something to drink." Winston glanced around the room. "I think I saw a waiter somewhere with some bubbly on his tray. Let's find sodas for the kids."

"Grandpa, not soda; the kids call it pop out here. They didn't know what I was talking about when I asked for a soda," Amanda said.

"Well, whatever it's called, we'll find some," Winston said, emphatically. The four men went off on their mission, leaving the women standing there.

Maria could hear strains of a romantic melody being played on a piano by a woman in an alcove on the other side of the room. "Ladies, let's go over and listen to the piano player. It will put us in an artistic mood, if that's possible."

The choice of songs and the ability of the woman playing reminded Maria of Diana, her English friend who had played at the party that George had given for Maria before they married. Sometimes, at the oddest moments, she had so many bittersweet memories bubbling up inside of her about both Bill and George, she wondered if she was different from other women.

"Mommy, look at the picture Elena painted of Wiggles and me," Amanda squeaked, running over to it. "It's so good. Mommy, it makes me cry. Wiggles looks like she could jump out of the picture."

"I know, sweetie, it's hard to lose someone or a pet you've loved. But I must say, Elena has made you look so real, too. It is a beautiful picture and a wonderful remembrance of Wiggles. I'm going to buy it for you." *For me too.*

"You don't have to, Mommy. Elena whispered that she's going to give me that picture after the exhibit. Isn't that nice of her?"

Maria laid her hand on her daughter's shoulder and walked her over to the piano. "Elena understands how young girls feel, Amanda. She was little once, too."

Watching the young woman playing, Maria was fascinated by how her long fingers flew over the keys. Occasionally, she played with her eyes closed. When she stopped for a minute, Maria took the opportunity to tell her how good she was and put ten dollars in her vase.

"Gee, thanks! You're very generous. I play to help with my tuition at the Chicago Academy of Music. Raphael teaches ballet there, and he got me this job today." She sipped water from a glass, closed her eyes, and began to play a haunting melody of love and betrayal.

Maria felt Ed's lips on her neck and turned to face him. "So, did I win out over Raphael?"

"Not by much. It was a hard decision. He's cute, but you're cuter. Here, have a glass of bubbly." He touched her glass with his. "The best is yet to come, Rosebud."

"Promise?" Maria peered at him over the glass as she took a sip.

"Come look at Elena's work with me, now we've had some juice to spur us on."

The place was really filling up, and Elena was continually surrounded by interested buyers who wanted to talk to the show's artist. Raphael was hovering about, suggesting various sculptures and paintings to prospective buyers.

By the time the afternoon had faded, the walls were increasingly bare, and customers were carrying away their precious artwork, wrapped and boxed. Kathy handled the sales of Elena's work, and Bill oversaw the two young men who made sure the delicate pieces were protected.

Ed bought a picture of a stately sailing ship being lashed by an enormous storm—the crew, half drowned, hanging on for their lives. It told a powerful story that Ed couldn't resist. Together, he and Maria had chosen a large landscape for their living room of the sun breaking through the clouds, producing a magnificent rainbow.

Maria bought several smaller pictures—one for Briggie, who immediately said it was a picture of Ireland, and three small flowery garden scenes that almost burst out of their canvases for the dining room. Maria was sure, if she closed her eyes, she could smell their scents. When she'd shown Ed her choices, he'd smiled and teased that he'd have to mortgage the farm.

Winston and her mother had also been buying, and because of the amount of their loot, Ed and Winston decided to stow them in Winston's station wagon.

"I'll make sure the boys do a good job protecting them so you can carry them safely home," Bill assured them. "I've got it down to a science, having done this a number of times." He grinned. "Elena is pretty amazing, isn't she?"

"Bill, I need to talk to you privately," Maria said, knowing that her request wouldn't sit lightly with Ed. She saw him frown, but he stood there, tight lipped.

"How about right now?" Bill turned to Ed. "Do you mind if I steal your wife for a minute or two?" His electric blue eyes were dancing with mischief.

"Just for a minute or two, and no stealing. Just talking, fella," Ed said, not smiling.

As Bill took her arm and walked her away, Maria said, "You don't need to hold my arm, you flirt. I can feel my husband's eyes boring down on us."

"I should give you a big, long kiss and see what he does," Bill said, his eyes laughing.

"You would, wouldn't you?" Maria's tone of voice was playful. "Don't you dare. He'll come across that floor like a tornado. I want you two to get along."

"So, what can I do for you, besides make love to you?"

"You *are* a bad boy, but you need to marry Elena—and soon."

"I've been trying to get her to say yes, but she's tough."

"I know you'll work on it, any way you can," she said, laughing with her insinuation. "Seriously, I need your help. I want to buy that sculpture of the magnificent horse over there for Ed's study. No one has bought him. Ed loves horses, and Elena has captured the wild spirit of a horse in that piece, but I don't want Ed to see me giving you money."

Maria had seen Ed eyeing the horse, and she was already imagining his delight at seeing the sculpture in their home. "Will you buy it and bring it when you and Elena come out? I'll give you the money later. I have two guest rooms all ready, but you may only need one." She laughed, but questioned why she was so interested in their personal life.

"It'll make Elena happy to be with her family. It's been a long time. I'll bring it out with me." Bill looked over at Ed and made a slight movement of putting his arms around Maria, but stopped and laughed.

"Business concluded?" Ed glanced at Bill, then locked eyes with Maria. "You two were having too much fun, for my taste."

"You're safe for now, Ed," Bill said, laughing.

Chris shot an angry look at Bill, which surprised Maria. Why was he mad? Was he afraid Bill was going to disrupt their new little family unit? She'd have to let him know, somehow, that she and Ed were solidly together for the rest of their lives. It touched her heart that Chris felt so protective of their family.

Ed headed out of town as fast as he could. He drove swiftly and silently. He was miffed, and Maria knew it. She'd have to do some repairs later that night. The kids were quiet too. Being with all those strangers milling around them all afternoon, the noise and atmosphere had sucked the energy out of them.

Hopefully, Briggie had been all right while at the event. Maria had encouraged her to sit on a comfortable couch she'd found for her. It was better that Briggie had ridden home with Winston and her mom. Ed was in no mood to talk to her.

In their bedroom, Ed stripped off his clothes and went into the bathroom to shower, cool off, and presumably calm down. Maria found her diaphragm and made sure it was in place before following him. She was brushing her teeth, naked and happy to be home, when he leaned out of the shower, covered with soap.

"Why is it whenever you see Bill, you flirt with him? Haven't you gotten over him yet?" The pained expression on his face grew darker. "What do I have to do to make you happy? Haven't I given you everything you've wanted since we got married?" He leaned against the side of the shower opening. "What were you two talking about, anyway?" Ed's voice was filled with anger.

Dropping her toothbrush, she turned, and looked into his eyes. Then she moved up to him, hugged his slippery body, and kissed his chest, despite the soap bubbles getting in her mouth. He stood stock still as she continued kissing him until he couldn't stand it one more moment. He swept her into his arms and began kissing her soapy lips, first lightly, and then ending with a French kiss that showed his anguish and desperation.

She stepped into the shower with him, silently. Maria rinsed off his soap with her hands, and then gently, softly, rubbed his body over and over, until she felt his heat rising. Taking his hand, she led him out of the shower, dripping wet into their bed. She climbed on top of him and slowly began kissing his neck and licking the water off of his chest. Her lips moved down to his stomach, kissing every inch of it.

His breathing changed sharply. Ed began to tremble, and he was so aroused, he stopped her. "I know what you're doing, and I like it, but you don't have to treat me like someone who has to be taken care of. I know I was acting ridiculously. It's just that I let Bill get under my skin, and I shouldn't. He's flirting with you in front of me and doing it in fun. He's not sneaking around behind my back."

She smiled and took his face in her hands. "Let's go, tiger."

He eagerly followed her command, devouring her, and driving them to a place so agonizingly close to the edge she cried out as they finally went over together. The rest of the evening melted into a long sexual adventure for them. Ed seemed possessed as he made love to her over and over, each time with an increasing amount tenderness that touched her heart.

He finally lay back, pulled her on top of him, and breathed the words, "God, I love you, Maria." She was about three inches from his face as he continued, "Forgive me for all I said to you tonight. I'm just so scared I'm going to lose you, I went a little crazy. I have so many demons inside me. I'm going to call Peter and ask for more help.

"When you came to me, telling me with your eyes that you loved me, and started kissing me after I'd yelled at you, I knew I was crazy. You soothed me, and by your actions let me know I was the most important person in your life. Letting me make love to you was the only way I could show you how much you mean to me. God, Maria, I don't know why I was so lucky to find you, but I did. Please forgive me, my darling."

"Ed, I thought you knew that I would never cheat on you or leave you. I promised when I married you that I would honor my vows to you. Bill is just an old friend." Lying, she continued. "He and I talked about Elena and how much he wants to marry her. She's the one who is holding out, and I think it's because of the terrible time she had in Puerto Rico when she was kidnapped by that drug lord. She was only fourteen. Just think, she was only four years older than Amanda and was subjected to sexual abuse by a thug twenty years older. I'm going to suggest to Bill that he contact Peter and take Elena to see him."

"God, Maria, I bet she's scared of men. I never realized she was so young. It makes me sick. I didn't know what you were talking about, and now I feel ashamed of what I was thinking. My problem, which Peter reminds me of as often as he can, is that I don't trust women because of the bad experiences I had with my mother. It spills over onto you at the wrong times."

"I know you don't mean to hurt me, and I appreciate that you're trying to heal wounds from your past." Maria kissed him. "We'd better go to sleep. It's almost two o'clock in the morning, handsome." She gave him another quick kiss. "I hope Bill and Elena came. Thanks for giving Bill a key and instructions on how to find their rooms." Maria grinned at him. "I was too busy to notice whether they came in or not." She cuddled up next to him. "Sleep well, my big stud muffin."

When Maria rolled over and looked at the clock it was ten o'clock. She hadn't slept that late since she was recovering from her bullet wound. Ed was inert, on his stomach and breathing softly. She showered, dressed, and went downstairs to see if her guests had arrived Briggie was in the kitchen making a big brunch for everyone.

"Briggie, did Elena and Bill come in last night?"

"Yes, I heard them, although they were quiet as mice."

"Good, I'm so glad. I'm sure Elena is exhausted from the show. She was spectacular."

"She was that and more. I've niver seen such pictures. I love me picture of Ireland. Just think, to have a painting that me darlin' painted is such a wonderful gift."

"Ed and I bought some incredible paintings, too, for the rest of the house."

"I'll put mine where I can see it from me bed."

Maria poured herself a cup of coffee, and smelling the enticing aroma, she sat down to enjoy her first cup of the day. She closed her eyes and shivered as she sipped her coffee, thinking about last night with Ed. Bill's cheerful voice broke the silence, making her jump in surprise.

"How about a cup of coffee for a tired worker? I brought your sculpture, Maria. Where do you want to hide it?"

"Can we put it in your bedroom, Briggie? It's a Christmas present for Ed."

"Saints preserve us, are you sure you don't have a wee drop of Irish blood in those veins of yours, Bill?" Briggie gave him a broad smile. "Bring that box to me room, and we'll hide it away proper."

Bill put his arm around Briggie. "You're looking good, woman. What have you been doing to yourself?"

Another smiled filled Briggie's face and she blushed. "Why, you old charmer, I've taken off a pound or two."

"Maria, you're going to have to watch her now. The men will be flocking to your doors."

"Go on with your blarney. Bring that box before you say another word about me," Briggie said, trying to act outraged, but Maria knew she was secretly delighted by Bill's attention.

When the two of them returned, Bill got Maria's attention. "Let's take a walk. Okay?"

58. A Cry for Help

September 1963
(Maria)

Maria nodded and opened the door. "Come on, Bill. I'll show you our new barn. It's a pretty walk there."

Climbing the hill, she laughed to herself, remembering running up there, naked, trying to hold her towel. "Wait up, you big lug. You always walked fast. Remember how I used to almost have to run to keep up with you when we were dating?"

"I'd take your hand and pull you up this hill, but Ed's probably looking out the window with his shotgun aimed at my head."

When they reached the top of the hill, Bill stopped. "Come on, you old lady, stretch those legs."

"My, you're fresh this morning. What's going on?"

"Oh, I don't know. I guess I'm just glad to be here and see you again. I've got some things on my mind I've been thinking about for a long time, and I'm hoping for some help."

As they walked down the hill into the meadow, he took her hand. "I feel closer to you and can talk better," Bill said, grinning, his eyes dancing.

Maria didn't pull her hand away. She liked how it felt.

He stopped when they got to the little stream, and they stood mesmerized by the moving water for a moment. "Do you have any idea why Elena is so reticent to marry me?" His expression had suddenly become serious.

"Whew, that's a big question, my friend. Let's see, how do I answer that?" Maria's face scrunched up in a quizzical expression. "How much do you know about her background?"

"Not much, she won't talk about it."

"Maybe she doesn't remember. People's minds protect them by hiding the bad stuff."

"Elena's twenty-seven. It's been fourteen years at least since she left Puerto Rico. When is she going to get over it?"

"Bill, she had a terrible time down there. Did you know George saved her life by bringing her with him when he escaped? If he hadn't, she probably would have killed herself."

"I know she gets a look in her eyes when she talks about George—like he was her savior."

"He was, although he didn't elaborate about the whole experience. I gathered that a thug kidnapped her when she was working in a hotel as a housekeeper and took her to his hide-a-away in the mountains and kept her there. He was twenty years older than her, and need I say more about what happened to her sexually? Bill, she was only four or five years older than Amanda when he kidnapped her."

"So how do I help her? I don't know anything about shrink stuff."

The person who can help you two is Dr. Peter Rudolph. He worked with George for years. We saw him as a couple while trying to make our marriage work. I saw him when our marriage was in ruins. Peter helped Ed work out some things in his life before we were married, and I had several sessions with him about Ed too. So you see, he knows a lot about our lives and would be able to help you two."

"But if she can't remember, what good is it all, anyway?"

"Peter works by using regression therapy. He'll hypnotize Elena and take her back to the time that she can't remember and tape the session. He'll give her the tape afterward to find out what was bothering her. And I recommend that you listen, too, unless Elena won't let you."

"Will one session do it?"

"No, she might have to see him for a year to make real progress. It takes the mind a long time to process the stuff and make changes."

"A year?" Bill squeezed his eyes shut, then opened them and sighed. "Do I really have to wait a year?"

"If you want a marriage that will last, you've got to be patient. A miserable marriage is just that—miserable. I know, and George and I did everything we could to make ours work."

"Weren't you happy, Maria? I always thought things were great between you."

"The first five years were okay, but even then, George slipped a few times with affairs. He always came back to me emotionally, and we went on again. But when Amanda was five and Chris was eight, George met someone who captured his whole being. He never left physically, he paid the bills and tried to act like a husband, but I knew George and our marriage were slipping away, and I didn't know how to stop it. He'd evidently met the woman of his dreams. When he was killed suddenly, all thoughts of divorce left my head. I didn't need to follow through. He was dead."

"So, we both made big mistakes with our marriage partners." Maria sat down. "Do you see Gerrie much?"

"I'm glad to sit with you, Maria. It's more comfortable, and I like looking at you when we talk because your face is so expressive. Sometimes I can tell what you're thinking. I always did when we were dating in college." His face saddened, but only for a moment. "As far as my ex-wife is concerned, I see her when I pick up Rosemary to spend the weekend with me, but I dread it because I can't stand the way she treats our daughter."

"How old is Rosemary now?"

"She's almost eleven."

"I wish she and Amanda could get to know each other. They're about the same age."

"I'll try to bring her by sometime when I have a long weekend."

"That would be nice. Now, ready to see the new partially finished barn?" Maria shifted her body, anticipating getting back on the move.

"No, I have to bring up something. But I don't know quite how to say it. I hope you won't take offense, but we have quite a history, and I trust you."

"Perhaps you should ask Peter. He's very good at getting to the bottom of things," she said uncomfortably, feeling a bit like a voyeur.

"I don't know Peter from Adam's apple, but I know you." There was an urgency in Bill's tone. He looked into Maria's eyes, paused, then cleared his throat. "No matter what I do, Elena isn't very interested in sex. I know her first love is her work, but Maria, there's some barrier there. She has a million excuses. And yet, she doesn't say much. She's very sweet."

"Peter is your man for this. My guess is that it's all tied up with that thug who sexually abused her. I know he'll be able to help you both with this."

"Okay, I'll call him, but there's something else, Maria. I just don't understand."

"Come on, let's look at the barn, and I'll give you Peter's phone number when we get back. I know he'll be able to straighten this out for you two." Maria smiled at her old friend, took his hand, and pulled him up.

"I've seen enough barns in my day to know what they look like. Let's skip that and go back. I've got a lot of thinking to do." From the look on his face, Bill wasn't too happy with how their talk had turned out.

She was sorry she couldn't wave a magic wand and make things be the way he wanted, but she couldn't. She had all she could do to keep her marriage working. She didn't want to open any more cans of worms.

Briggie had a message for her when they got back. Ed and Chris had to help Glen with a couple of emergencies and would be home later.

Briggie handed Bill a plate. "Eat up, my boy, you look like you could use it."

"I wish I could take you home with me. I love a woman who can cook," Bill said, heaping his plate with Briggie's specialties.

"Why don't you join us, Briggie?" Maria asked as she scooped up some eggs and toast.

"I believe I will. I want to hear what Elena has been up to since we left."

"In a nutshell, Briggie, she's been working day and night. At least she does when I'm there," Bill said, glancing briefly at Maria and then at Briggie.

A little feeling of desperation was being flashed from Bill to whomever wanted to accept it. He'd been seeing Elena for over a year and wasn't happy. Maria understood that, loud and clear.

On the patio, Winston was regaling everyone with Maria's story about the shooting. When he saw Bill walk out, he stopped in the middle of the tale. "I've been telling Elena the story about our brave Maria. I must catch Bill up. Sit down my boy and let me tell you about the fateful day."

When he'd finished, everyone was either giggling or laughing, including Maria. Winston had made the story both exciting and laughable. What a storyteller. Winston laughed so hard at his own rendition, he had to wipe his eyes.

Looking at Maria, Bill said, "I wish I could have seen the expression on the faces of those FBI men when you dropped your towel and kept running toward them."

"You bad boy," Maria said, and gave him a little poke in his ribs.

For an instant, he looked at her with such longing in his eyes, she had to pick up her cup and sip her coffee. She hoped no one had seen it. Maria looked at her mother—she'd caught it.

Amanda was completely oblivious to anything except sitting next to Elena and talking to her about Wiggles and her picture.

"What are your plans for the future, Elena?" Winston's face held a fatherly expression. "When is your next show?"

"My wonderful agent, Kathy Gibbs, is getting together with me when we return to schedule a series of shows for the coming year," she said her eyes sparkling. "Kathy has encouraged me at times when I felt I couldn't accomplish what I needed to in order to have a good exhibit. I owe her a lot."

Maria watched the body language between Elena and Bill, and it wasn't good. Not once had she looked at him, touched him, given him any credit, or in any way acknowledged him. Bill got up abruptly and took his plate to the kitchen. When he returned, he announced that he needed to get back to Chicago that afternoon because he was scheduled to fly to Seattle that night. He was filling in for a pilot who had called in sick that morning.

Maria questioned his story. Perhaps there was some truth in it, but she knew in her heart, Bill was ready to bolt. Unless Elena made a move to change things, it wouldn't be long before *he* would change them. Maria had known him too long.

"Elena, we'll have to leave in a couple of hours. Why don't you try to get your things together on time for once," he said in a disparaging tone.

There was an awkward silence for a moment or two. "Winston and Ruth, how about showing me your new country club?" Bill asked, breaking the tension. "I'll bring my golf clubs next time I'm in town, and we'll have a round or two."

Winston looked surprised at first, but smiled at Bill's suggestion. "Yes, of course, Bill. Anyone who wants to come with us is welcome. Bring your suits and have a swim."

Amanda jumped up and asked if she could call and invite Lois, Briggie begged off, and Elena said she needed to pack and call Kathy. Elena's face was flushed. Obviously, she was upset, but Maria didn't know what to do about it.

"How about you, Maria?" Bill asked.

"No thanks, I need to help Briggie," she said, dodging another encounter with him.

400

After Winston, her mother, Bill, and the girls left for the club, Maria went into the kitchen to see what needed to be done for dinner that evening. Bill and Elena wouldn't be joining them, but Ed and Chris would definitely be hungry.

After about an hour, Maria and Briggie felt they had dinner preparations underway. Beside planning and taking care of the preliminaries, they'd talked in low tones about what had just transpired on the patio.

"Missy, I thought we might be planning a wedding for the two of them, but after today, I think we will be planning a wake."

"I know, Briggie. I'm completely surprised at how things have deteriorated between them. Elena has never even hinted that they might be unhappy when we've talked. I wonder if she really knows how miserable Bill is?"

"What's to be done?"

"I talked to Bill about Peter, and I'll give him Peter's phone number before he goes. I'm also going up to have a little girl talk with Elena."

As she knocked gently on the guest room door, she noticed the extra guest room's door was open and the bed was rumpled. Bill had evidently slept in there last night.

"Come in," she heard Elena's soft voice say as Maria opened the door. Elena was standing with the phone receiver to her ear, listening to whomever was on the other end, shifting back and forth from one foot to the other. "All right, we'll settle it when I get back. Bill will be gone when you come."

Maria sat down in the bedroom chair her mother had given her and caressed the soft material with her fingertips. "Elena, I wanted to have a chat with you. I'm sorry I interrupted your call."

"It's all right," she said, but her tone said something different. She didn't sound happy. "It was my agent, and we had a lot to talk about, but we're going to see each other when I get back to Washington."

"I know I'm venturing into territory that probably might offend you, but as your big sister, I need to talk about Bill. It's obvious that Bill is miserable. Did you notice?" How far could Maria push her sister? "How are you two doing? Do you want to talk about it, or am I intruding?"

"I'm glad to talk, perhaps a relief. He's always unhappy. He doesn't seem to realize that my work comes first. I've tried to tell him over and over, but he always sulks, and he doesn't like my agent, Kathy. She, in turn, says he's too possessive." Elena rubbed her eyes, as though weary of the whole thing. "I'm always in the middle."

"Elena, I gave Bill the name of a good psychiatrist, Peter Rudolph, who lives in Washington. George and I used to see him. He helped me a lot, and he might be able to help you, if you feel the need to see someone."

"Thank you, Maria. Maybe I will. I'm pretty mixed up, these days." Elena tucked some loose strands of hair behind her ear. "Things used to be so simple, and then I grew up. My personal feelings for Bill are not very strong. They never were, but that seemed to make him pursue me all the more. He's been a wonderful help to me, but he wants to be paid in sexual favors, and I don't feel like that. Once in a while I have feelings for him, but not often. I can't explain it. It is just the way I am.

"I love my work. When I get started on a new painting or sculpture, I can't stop. My work is my lover," Elena said with conviction.

"If you're happy, fine. But I think you and Bill should try some therapy for his sake and see Peter." Maria paused and searched for the right words. "Otherwise, I don't know if Bill is going to stick around much longer."

"I know, and I would miss him a little, but I'd also feel relief. I don't want to hurt him, because I know he loves me far more than I love him."

"It's up to you, Elena. Let me know how things go when you go back. I've been bad about calling, too. I'll try to keep in touch more now." Maria got up and hugged Elena. "You're my kid sister, and I'll always love you, no matter what you decide."

Bill and Elena left an hour later, quietly and sadly. Maria ached for them both, but it was out of her hands. They were adults and had to make their own decisions.

59. Patience, Love, and Endurance

September 1963
(María)

Amanda's second week in school was not as pleasant as her first. Cliques were forming, and sixth grade girls, notorious for gossiping and hurting each other's feelings, were no different in Amanda's class. Lois and Amanda stuck together like glue, however, with a few fringe friends. The clique that ruled the social order in her class was the wealthy girls from the big breeding farms. Their families had been there the longest, some of them tracing their roots back three generations.

Maria knew that Amanda chafed at the way they treated most of the other girls. She felt they were the most aggressive, vocal, manipulative, and hurtful of all the girls, and she called them the "breeder girls" behind their backs. Maria suspected that while Amanda proclaimed her dislike for them, she secretly wanted to be accepted by them, but being a new girl in the class, it was a bittersweet situation for her.

Maria encouraged Amanda to be independent and not to worry about those girls, but it mattered. Amanda found solace in after-school sports, particularly softball. Her other driving desire was to own and ride her own pony. Four-H meetings were the place to learn all about horses, and Amanda knew it. She insisted that Lois go, too. She wanted a friend with her. Amanda said the breeder girls laughed at girls who joined 4-H.

After the kids left for school on Monday morning, Maria drove to work thinking about her heartfelt talk with Amanda the night before.

They needed to have another family meeting as soon as possible to pull the family together again. Thank goodness for her mother and Briggie. How would Maria get through the week without them? Her arm still ached when she typed too long, but Ed hadn't found a replacement for her at the office yet.

The minute she got home on Monday afternoon, Maria gathered her mother and Briggie for a conference over coffee to discuss menus for the coming week and weekend. With her sister and brother-in-law coming as weekend guests and hosting her first big party since arriving in St. Charles, there was a lot to talk about. Planning the food was paramount. Everything else took second place.

Maria was tired of having company. She looked forward to a breather. September had been filled with the special people in her life, but each person brought their own agenda, all requiring a lot of energy from her. Added to that was her new increasing concern with Ed's mood swings. It was a bit overwhelming to her, not being able to understand what set him off at times.

She'd be glad when the weekend was over. It had seemed like such a good idea at the time when she invited her sister and brother-in-law to come, stay, and meet Ed's big clients, but now she was dreading all the emotions her sister usually generated. One thing would be easier than the last visit from family—she wouldn't have to worry about Bill. He was gone, trying to love and live with Elena. Maria secretly missed Bill's easy manner, but she reminded herself, the grass is always greener in the other backyard, and Bill had made his choice to be with Elena instead of her after George had died.

When Friday afternoon came, Maria couldn't get out of work quickly enough. It had been a busy day. Driving home, she thought about the coming weekend. Thank goodness her mother had taken over all the party details while Maria and Winston worked at the clinic. The freezers were bulging with party foods that Briggie and her mother had prepared during the week, and Laura and Sarah were coming to work all weekend as waitresses.

Hoping she'd see more of Chris with Laura working for them, she wondered how Chris was coping with his classes, sports, and the other students, but as usual, he was very closed mouthed about everything. He was his father's child. George had bottled everything up. It worried Maria, but Chris had Ed, who perhaps was his confidant. She made a mental note to ask Ed about Chris.

As she drove into their yard, Don and May pulled in right behind her. Maria swore under her breath. She still needed a shower and time to dress. Don was his friendly self, tooting his horn and waving out of his window just like a kid. She showed him where to park out of the line of traffic.

Don's expression was so welcoming. As for her sister, it was a different story. Her face looked pinched and red. She immediately began recounting all the things that had gone wrong before they'd left, blaming Don. Hearing his wife's litany, Don scooted into the house.

"Come in and relax, May. I want you to meet my friend, Briggie," Maria said, hoping to shift May's mood. "I don't know what I'd do without her."

Briggie was standing in the kitchen and gave May a welcoming smile. "I'm pleased to meet the sister of me best friend," she said, pumping May's hand.

May looked surprised and just stood there. She began to hum, like she usually did to cover her embarrassment, and drew her hand back. "I didn't know you had a cook, Maria. When did you get her? I'm surprised you need a cook with two, almost grown children."

"Briggie's been with me since the children were small. You were sick and couldn't come to George's funeral, otherwise you would have met her. And over the years, things have been pretty cool between us. We rarely called each other, but all that is in the past."

It irritated Maria that May had ignored Briggie's kind welcome and then talked about her as if she weren't standing there.

"Well, I didn't mean to ruffle your feathers, sister, dear."

"Years ago, I gave another woman a piece of advice I'll pass on to you, sister, dear. Be sure you keep your words soft and sweet, in case you have to eat them." She gave May a look that she hoped would be seen as a warning. "Come out on the patio and have a pleasant visit with Mom and Winston. Judging by the voices, I think Don has already found them." Maria turned to her friend. "Briggie, as part of our family, I insist you come out and join the party, too."

"Me darlin' girl, thanks, but no thanks. I've got to watch me cookin' for your dinner."

May stopped at the French doors, surveyed the situation, and made a beeline to a chair next to Don. "So this is where you are. I don't suppose you brought in our bags? You were so busy getting out here." She eyed his drink. "It didn't take you long to get a drink in your hand, did it?" she snapped.

Her mother smiled and started to say something to May, but

Winston broke in and asked, "What can I serve you, May? Nothing like a good drink after a long drive to chase away one's troubles."

"I don't drink. It's bad for the liver, isn't it, Don?" Of course, May was Miss Perfection herself.

Don ignored his wife and continued sipping his drink. He asked about Ed.

"He'll be along as soon as he can. You know how hard vets work." Maria caught a glimpse of her mother's strawberry drink. *I'm going to drink a cocktail for my pleasure and May's discomfort.* "Winston, I'll have what Mom is having, it looks yummy." *Someone, please cast a spell over May and hide her away until the party is over and it's time to go home.*

Her mother grinned at Maria. "It's a daiquiri, you'll love it."

"My, it must be nice not having to worry about dinner and just sit out here and drink," May said, her words barbed in venom.

"I guess we know how to live, don't we folks?" Maria returned her mother's grin.

Winston, ever the gracious host, offered May a soft drink, which she took hesitantly. Maria had promised herself she would ignore May, but her sister reminded her of Ed's mother, Wilma, so strongly, she found herself wondering how and why women acted like that. As the first numbing hint from her drink began to soften her edges, Maria stole glances at her smug, older sister. Each time they got together, Maria had hopes that May would loosen up in a new situation, but she never did. Perhaps she was feeling insecure being there. She had been much more pleasant when they visited her because she was on her own turf.

Some talking in the kitchen alerted everyone that Ed was home, his voice ringing from the rafters calling for Don.

Standing up, Don yelled back, "Out here, old buddy." He grabbed Ed's hand and began shaking it so hard, they looked like they were wrestling.

"You old dog, you. It's good to see you again," Don said. "Do I see any white hairs in that black thatch of yours? You're getting up there near forty, aren't you?"

"Yeah, but I still have my hair. Your dome is getting shinier every time I see you," Ed said, grinning from ear to ear. "What are you drinking? I'll have one too, Winston."

After Ed sat down and apologized for his dirty work clothes, he took a sip of his drink. "Did you folks just get here?"

"We did. We made good time on that new road," Don said. "We

have President Eisenhower to thank for new roads all over the country. I floored it a time or two."

Ed leaned over to May. "Did you bring June? And are you still cooking those great meals I used to eat every day at your place?"

May pursed her lips. "She didn't want to come, so we didn't make her. I think she has a boyfriend she wanted to see. As for the meals, I'm still cooking, unlike someone I know," she said, looking at Maria and then smiling at Ed.

Ed winked at Maria. "Maria's been laid up with a gunshot wound, and she also works for me in the clinic every day."

"For heaven's sake, what happened to you? How in the world did you shoot yourself?" Maria looked at Winston and knew he'd been waiting for a cue to recount the story of crazy Jacqueline, and he launched into it with great glee.

"You're a bad boy, mentioning my wound," Maria whispered in Ed's ear.

He looked at her with a twinkle in his eyes. "It's a great story."

As Winston whipped into the narrative, Maria slipped away to take a shower and have a quiet moment. She didn't want to hear everyone laugh about her nakedness one more time.

With the warm water soothing her body, her mind quieted, too. *Nothing like a shower to help my sanity.* The door opened, and her naked husband stepped in beside her. *Darn, I can't even have five minutes to myself.* He began nuzzling her neck, and she pushed him away. "Wasn't my naked story funny when I wasn't there to laugh at?"

"I've heard it enough. I was hoping to catch you in the shower."

"There's no time for any games," she said, with an edge to her voice. "I have to help Briggie. Just because you fell asleep early last night, you may have to take a cold shower tonight." She didn't smile and stepped out of the shower.

"Why so touchy? I was just having a little drink. Blame Winston, too. He told the story."

"I will, and in the future, please don't bring it up again unless I do. I have feelings, too, although I wonder if you realize that sometimes."

Maria was setting herself up for trouble, but having her sister there had touched a nerve, and she felt cranky. She dressed, brushed her hair, and put it up in a clip, leaving a few ringlets loose, giving her a more sophisticated look than usual. One last check in the mirror and down she went to her guests.

Don had Winston locked into a cribbage game. Amanda was

watching them while her mother was looking strained talking with May. She heard laughter and saw Laura and Sarah standing in the hall with Chris. She hadn't seen him all week except to exchange a short comment or two, but with the girls there, so was he. Like all young teenage straight guys, Chris was on the hunt, and the girls loved being his prey.

On the way to the kitchen, Maria checked the dining room. Her mother had outdone herself. A huge bouquet of garden flowers filled the center of the table, and crystal goblets, silver, and china were present at each place setting. Candles added the finishing touch.

"Shall I call everyone, Briggie?"

"Yes, me darlin', and make sure Laura and Sarah come to serve."

Ed was sitting with Winston and Don, watching them finish up their game, when she called from the doorway. He looked up at her with an angry glance. She was in for it. *Bring it on, my moody husband. It's time to stop walking on egg shells and stand up for myself.*

At the table, Winston held up a bottle of chardonnay. "I have it on good authority that we're having baked stuffed trout, and that's why I chose a white wine for this evening."

What a ham. Maria blessed him for it. Winston made a difficult party much more pleasant. Ignoring May's protest of not having any wine, he poured everyone a glass, including her. Not to be left out, Chris got both him and Amanda a bottle of soda pop to drink, leaving the bottles on the table, much to Maria's chagrin.

When Laura brought in the huge platter of baked trout, decorated with parsley and lemons, even Don was impressed. Looking at Maria, he said, "Well, little sister, you certainly can put on a big shindig. How do I get a piece of this fish?"

"Here, let me help you." Ed started to reach for the platter.

"I was hoping this cute serving girl would help me," Ed said, ignoring Ed's offer. "Maria, where did you find her?"

Don is actually flirting with Laura. He's had too much to drink.

"Eat your dinner and stop being so nosy," May snapped, dampening his mood.

"She's a friend of Chris's and goes to the same high school as he does," Ed said, flashing Don a look that told him to calm down.

But Don, who had drunk several scotch and sodas, was working on his glass of wine. He seemed to be in the mood to party. "Whoee, this is going to be a fun weekend, Ed. Are you going to take me to work with you tomorrow?"

"You bet, so go easy on the booze. I've several calls lined up with guys you'll like. Now eat. Briggie will be disappointed if you don't."

"She's Irish, isn't she? After dinner, I'm going into the kitchen and compliment her on her cooking," Don said, talking slowly and beginning to slur his words. "This here establishment is very nice, don't you think, Mother?"

"You're drunk, and I hope you get sick, old man," May barked at him.

"Maybe if you'd be nicer to me, I wouldn't drink." Don said, weaving as he stood up. "Where's the bathroom in this place. God, Ed, you have a big house."

Ed hopped up, took hold of his old friend's arm, and led him to the bathroom.

Don never returned to the table. After dinner, Ed found him sound asleep on a sofa.

Soothing May and getting Don up into bed took a lot of patience and restraint on both Ed and Maria's part. By the time Maria said good night to Amanda, she knew Ed had softened up because he'd come up to her after dinner and given her a kiss for the nice evening.

Lying on their bed, watching Maria take off her clothes, Ed said, "Don and May remind me of my dad and mom at times. Maybe that's why Don and I got along so well all those years when I worked for him. I felt sorry for him."

"I think my sister and your mother are alike. I wish I'd never invited them to come. It's so tiring listening to my sister's insipid remarks. I don't know how I stood working for her when I was a teenager." Maria slipped into bed.

"That's all over, and we're both free. Now, where were we when you said I'd have to take a cold shower? Do you still mean that?" He nuzzled her neck with his lips and whispered that he was sorry for being such an ass.

"I guess I was a little cranky, myself. My sister really gets to me, unfortunately."

"Let's forget all of them." He began rubbing her back and kissing her lips. "How about it, my beautiful woman?"

"I thought you'd never ask." Maria laughed.

The following morning Maria vaguely remembered hearing Ed's truck roaring out of the property. She had to get up, but she dreaded dealing with May all day. Her intuition told her there was going to be trouble. What kind, she didn't know, she just had a feeling.

"Mom, Mom, can I come in?" she heard her daughter calling softly.

"Come in. Daddy's gone, and I'm awake."

The door flew open, and Amanda plopped onto the foot of Maria's bed. "I forgot to tell you last night that I went to my first 4-H meeting and it was fun. There are kids of all ages there and some cute boys. We're all supposed to have a project, and Lois's and mine are ponies." Amanda got a look in her eye, and Maria knew she was going to ask for something. "When can Daddy take us to look for ponies? Now that we're full-fledged '4H-ers.'"

"Daddy's very busy this weekend with company and a big party we're having here tonight. I haven't had time to talk to you enough, but I promise we'll have another family meeting and talk about everything. That will be a good time to bring up your wish. I know Daddy's very interested in horses too, because he's building a barn for them."

"When will it be ready?"

"I don't know. Daddy will have to tell us. I haven't had time to talk to him about it."

Amanda made a pouty face. "Mom, you never have any time anymore. I don't like it."

"I know, honey, and I'm sorry." Maria hugged her daughter. "With the move, the company, the house, and now working at the clinic, I feel the same way. I promise things will settle down after this weekend." She gave Amanda a quick kiss on the top of her head. "Now, I must get up and get the party preparations under way. Will you help me? I want you to make your bed, straighten up your room, and make Chris's bed, too."

"Why can't he make his own?"

"He doesn't like to make his bed, but he's working for Dr. Glen today, so I can't be too hard on him."

Maria put out her arms. "Give me another hug and help me with my bed, too. Then I can get downstairs faster." She tickled Amanda. "Come on, don't look so sad. We'll get everything figured out soon."

Much to Maria's surprise, May sounded in a relatively good mood. As Maria walked downstairs, she could hear her sister in the kitchen laughing while she listened to Briggie tell stories about her childhood in Ireland. Maria eased herself by the kitchen door and slipped out onto the patio to see her mother for last-minute details about the party.

"Mom, can you give me a cup of coffee? I don't want to go into my kitchen and disturb May. She's having fun with Briggie."

Her mother poured from the pot she had sitting on the patio table and handed her a cup. "I know what you mean. May never seems to have much fun. But now for the plan," her mother said excitedly. She put on her glasses and read, "Cocktails and hors d'oeuvres from five to six thirty, dinner at six thirty, and dancing all evening. I asked Winston to hook up our stereo so it will be loud enough on the patio for dancing. I'm going to set up the dining room as soon as I get dressed and my coffee kicks in."

"Thanks so much, Mom." Maria sighed. "I seem to say that a lot."

"Nonsense, we have a purpose because of you and your family. I thank you!"

By early afternoon, with everyone pitching in, including May, the place looked gorgeous. May actually enjoyed herself. Perhaps with Don away working with Ed, May had time to help with preparations for the party, had nice company while performing the tasks, and didn't have any big responsibilities.

Winston had picked up her mother's order of fresh flowers and was following her around carrying the arrangements, and holding them for her as she needed so she could place them in Maria's house and patio.

Maria was pleased when she heard Ed's truck come flying in a little after three. She heard Ed encouraging Don to have a nap before the guests arrived and heard no argument. By four o'clock, everyone was dressed and ready.

60. The Entitled Ones

September 1963
(Maria)

Laura and Sarah arrived promptly at four thirty to get their instructions, dressed alike in white tops and dark blue jeans. Maria wished they'd worn skirts, but jeans were all the rage with the high school kids, and the girls looked freshly scrubbed and lovely.

It was the 60s. Maria had overheard Laura and Sarah talking about the wonderful new birth control pills. A new casualness of dress and talk about sexual freedom was in with the younger generation. Was it good or bad? What was happening to America?

By five, the music was playing, the bar was stocked, and delicious odors were emanating from Briggie's kitchen.

On her way to the kitchen, Maria almost brushed by Ed, but he caught her, and laughed as she attempted to escape.

"You and your mother certainly know how to throw a party. "I imagine this one is like those held in Washington, DC. I love you, Rosebud." Ed gave Maria a gentle kiss on her cheek. "I can't kiss your lips. I'll smear your lipstick and get it on me." He held her out in front of him. "Is this one of the dresses I bought you for your birthday? You look beautiful, even with makeup," he teased. "The guests will have plenty to talk about after tonight. This is just the beginning for us, Rosebud."

She loved his compliments, not because she needed his approval on her social skills, but rather because she saw a desperate need in him. He was proud of her, but what else was going on? That remark about the guests having a lot to talk about made her wonder what he wanted to show the "society of St. Charles." He'd spent thousands of dollars redoing their house from top to bottom and paying their monthly bills, yet never questioned her once about expenses. Even their trip to a high-end boutique for her clothes seemed out of character. But when he insisted on buying her new rings, really! The ugly thought, *trophy wife,* flittered through her head. *Is this party his attempt to help us be part of the "in crowd"? I may never know, because I don't think Ed knows.*

The insistent ring of the door chimes snapped her out of her reverie. "It's time to face our guests," she said and grabbed his hand.

"Welcome, welcome, so nice to see you," Maria said, over and over, forcing a continued smile for their arriving guests. They came dressed well, the men in elegant casualness and the women in various outfits from the reserved to the seductive. The men seemed eager to meet her, with appraising eyes—some distant, some cordial. The women were more aggressive in their greetings, especially for Ed with hugs and some cheek kisses. He took it all in stride in a very subdued manner and did a diplomatic job introducing everyone to Maria, usually adding some personal anecdote or small joke for the men. Several men made mention of the size of his place as they walked by. The women were all eyes, and everyone seemed ready for a good time.

When Babs and Bob Decker arrived, Maria gave Babs a measured smile and Babs returned it, but quickly oozed charm all over Ed, throwing her arms around him and suggesting that they dance together during the party. It bothered Maria that his ex was openly offering him implied special favors. Out of the corner of her eye, Maria watched Ed deftly maneuver around Babs, gently unwinding her arms from around his neck and speaking to Bob who had arrived already slurring his words.

Her mother and Winston stood poised as the second string of the welcoming committee, suggesting options for seating, either on the patio or in the more comfortable living room. The weather was cooperating, not too hot or cold, allowing free flow around the whole house and poolside. In fact, a small but steady breeze helped keep the air moving.

Ed waved to Chris to come inside. Chris had done a yeomen's job directing the parking in the area around the side of the house, and Ed shook his hand in genuine appreciation.

But one more car drove in at that moment, and Sharon and Glen hopped out. Ed hailed his partner like a long-lost brother. "So glad you could make it." When they came in, he added quietly to Glen, "I can use reinforcements to field all the breeders' inevitable questions."

Winston was playing bartender and congenial host while Don stood by, drink in hand, telling jokes and generally making the men feel comfortable. May was nowhere to be seen, but her mother, undaunted, moved around the living room, introducing herself to the groups of women who were absorbed in conversations with their friends of long standing, but who accepted her momentarily.

Maria slipped out to the kitchen to see if Briggie needed help and found May, Chris, Laura, Sarah, Amanda, and Lois sitting at the kitchen table drinking Coke and gobbling up assorted canapés rejected by Briggie as not suitable to serve the guests.

"Girls, after I go back to the party, I want you two to go to your room, Amanda, play games, listen to your radio, but stay upstairs." Maria said, firmly. "And Sarah and Laura, it's time to circulate and bring out the canapés. Everyone is hungry."

"May, you look lovely. Time to go out there and show off your new outfit," Maria said, trying to appease her sister and help her feel more a part of the gathering.

"Not on your life. When you invited us to your party, I thought it would be a few friends who we could sit and visit with, not a bunch of wild animals. All that loud music and craziness out there makes me sick. I'm sure Don is right in his element. He's probably drunk."

Amanda and Lois looked at each other, giggled, and whispered something to each other.

"Girls, go upstairs like your mither said," Briggie ordered, and they got up and left.

Maria smiled at Briggie as if to say, *good luck with my sister.* She opened the kitchen door, and the high noise level hit her. The blood alcohol levels were rising. Good thing food was coming out.

Laura and Sarah were trying to make their way to all the seated guests, but they were constantly being stopped by dancers and drinkers for an appetizer. Some of the men made complimentary remarks to them, but the girls seemed oblivious and ignored them. *Good for you, gals.*

Maria found her mother and Sharon sitting together out on the patio. "Are you two watching some of society's wealthiest members acting like fools? It's just like you described them to me, Sharon."

Sharon's face broke into a beautiful smile, her hazel eyes shining. "I'm glad to be here and get away from the kids and work for an evening. We had a devil of a time coming, however. Glen had a last-minute surgery stitching up a Labrador that was attacked by a pit bull, our babysitter was late, and Timmy had a fit as we were leaving."

"Well, you're here now and can enjoy your ginger ale," her mother said, sipping her club soda.

"Maria, I'm pregnant," Sharon confided, softly. "Your mother has been very kind listening to me bitch about it. Just when both kids were in preschool and school, and I thought I could really devote some time to my seed experimentation, this happens."

"Has anyone ever told you why?" Maria asked, mischievously. Maria reached over and gave Sharon a loving touch. I'll help you any way I can. Here, eat a couple of Mom's shrimp canapés. They're delicious. I stole them from the kitchen.

Sarah and Laura are now serving them to our drunken guests. Even if you can't drink, you certainly can eat."

Glen put his drink on the table, sat down, smiled at them, and devoured one of the canapés. He grinned at his wife. "Let's dance, gorgeous," and off they went.

"It's nice to see how much they love each other," her mother commented. "Glen's a good dancer, too."

"They're made for each other, and Glen has such a stabilizing influence on Ed."

As they were sitting there observing the fray, someone called out, "conga line," and Maria watched couples go wild, grabbing onto each other, laughing, jumping, and falling into a long line that was led by Raymond Farmingdale, one of the wealthiest men there and a big client of Ed's. Soon a snake of bobbing bodies was weaving around the patio, through the living room, down the hall, back out onto the patio, and around the pool. Out of the blue, Babs Decker either slipped or purposely fell into the pool.

Maria watched several big men help her out of the shallow end, running their hands over parts of her body as they did, making Babs squeal. Maria quickly sprang into action. She asked Laura to get Babs a towel. Babs wrapped it around herself, laughing, and enjoying the attention. The next thing Maria knew, Babs was back up dancing with Lydia Farmingdale's husband, his hand pressing her into his body. Human nature being what it was, Maria wondered how many couples would end up after tonight exchanging partners.

Visiting the kitchen to make sure Amanda and Lois were safely upstairs, Maria eavesdropped on Briggie, who was in rare form giving firm but kindly support to Sarah and Laura when they complained about serving the dirty old men out there.

Maria ducked out, looked down the hall, and saw a newly arrived couple standing awkwardly in the doorway. She raced over to them and introduced herself, hoping to make them feel welcome. A moment later, she felt Ed's hand on her back.

"Glad to see you could make it, Earl, my astute lawyer. This must be Mrs. Markham," Ed greeted in a friendly tone.

"This is Nadia, my partner." Changing the subject quickly, Earl said, "My, you have quite a spread, here, Ed. Now I can see why you keep my office busy. Congratulations to both of you. By the way, thanks for steering Winston to me. He's quite a guy. Is he here tonight?"

"I've kept him busy tending bar and entertaining everyone."

"Come on, Nadia, let's go meet him. Then we can drink some of Ed's free liquor, and dance," Earl said, giving Ed a congratulatory nod.

Ed grinned at Maria. "How about it, Rosebud? Are you up for dancing?" As soon as they hit the dance floor, he gave her a questioning look. "So, tell me, what's a partner? Are they just friends, or is he sleeping with her? I really put my foot in my mouth, didn't I? Times are certainly changing." He held her tightly, and they danced until Maria finally asked to sit down and have a ginger ale. She was tired.

"So, Nadia looks to be about fifteen years younger than Earl," Ed said, drinking his beer. "She must be quite a partner."

"The sixties are roaring in, my friend, for better or for worse. I think the word *partner* implies a live-in girlfriend in every sense of the word except marriage. Birth control pills are changing relationships between mostly young men and women in this country. Earl isn't letting any grass grow under his feet.

"I read about sexual freedom all the time in my magazines—no marriage, just the sexual benefits. But I think men are coming out ahead. I wonder what the final price tag will be, especially on the children who are born, but not claimed legally by their natural fathers, if the pill fails. Nothing is really free."

"You've really been thinking about this, Rosebud. My main concern is my practice. I can't control any of that other stuff," sounding disinterested.

"And then there is the new music. Chris is playing music from an English group called The Beatles, of all things. Imagine naming yourself after some bugs. On the west coast, there are the flower children, hippies, and gays. I can remember growing up feeling happy and gay. I can't say that anymore. Gay means homosexual. I'm beginning to feel old-fashioned, but I don't want to change."

"Let's not worry about the world right now. Just dance with me and help me take care of our guests. That's what we need to do." He led her back to the floor and they began moving to the music again. Beads of sweat were standing out on his forehead from the physical activity. His jacket had fallen by the wayside an hour ago. His short-sleeve shirt was open, actually showing a few chest hairs.

"You're working hard, aren't you? You need a handkerchief."

The music stopped and Ed grinned. "I don't like them. I'd rather use a towel. I'm going to the guest bathroom to wash up and dry off."

"I'm going to take a quick break and see what the girls are up to. Sleep, I hope."

Maria ran upstairs and walked by her bedroom door—it was ajar. She had purposely closed it before the party to indicate off limits. A sound inside made her stop. Two women were whispering in her bedroom. Standing quietly and listening, Maria recognized Babs's voice. She was using her soft breathiness that was so phony it made Maria gag. *I wonder if she would deflate if someone stuck a pin in her?*

The other one must be Lydia Farmingdale. Maria strained to hear their conversation. They were just on the other side of the door, getting ready to leave.

"That bed over there was quite a playground for us," Babs said softly. "We used to spend hours in here, and we weren't sleeping. Let me tell you, Ed is one hot guy. The only problem with Ed was his ungodly need to work all the time. He acted like a poor farm boy." She paused. "You have no idea how sexy that man was and still is. Have you checked out his body tonight? Uh . . . is he sexy," she said, giggling.

"I've been watching him all evening," Lydia said. "He's one hunk of a man. I wonder what it would take to get him in bed? Raymond is so boring in bed and in general. He drinks a lot."

"Hands off, girl, if anyone sleeps with him, it's going to be me. Bob's never been good in bed. But he'd rather drink than do it with me anymore." Babs cleared her throat. "I'm going to start taking a very active interest in our farm and be sure to stop by the barn when Ed and my continuously drunk husband are going over the breeding program. Now that Ed is so successful, he really appeals to me."

Maria backed into the guest room quickly and waited until they'd gone down the stairs. She was surprised by the two women's honesty with each other. They didn't leave anything to the imagination. Maria had heard enough. At least she knew what she was up against. Second marriages had many pitfalls, including unhappily married women like the two at her party, not to mention crazy ones. Maria instinctively rubbed her tender arm.

The girls were out like lights when she peeked in. That was a relief. She would have hated for them to see the drunken adults downstairs.

Thoughts of Babs ceased when Maria joined the party scene and saw Chris tending bar. Winston was circulating around the room, talking to many men with great interest. *Why?* She heard Don telling a joke to a group of men standing by the bar while Chris mixed drinks. By the grin on his face, Chris was obviously amused. *By the time he's grown, he'll have been exposed to all kinds of attitudes, ideas, and habits of men—some good, some bad—but all part of life, and there was nothing she could do.*

May was having a nonstop dialogue with Mom. Poor Mom, but at least May had finally ventured out to the party. May was sipping a drink. Had she broken her rule and decided to imbibe? Over by the pool, Ed was entertaining several couples, and she could hear one woman shrieking with laughter. Occasionally, strains of a melody were heard through the high level of noisy conversations, and Maria wished the music was louder and the voices softer.

She was circling the room and heading for the kitchen to help Briggie when Bob Decker caught her arm.

"Not so fast, my pretty hostess. I've had my eye on you all evening, dashing around in that low-cut dress of yours, tempting me." He grabbed her roughly around the waist and started to dance, holding her tightly, his alcoholic breath nearly suffocating her.

Take it easy. Play along and dance with him until he either gets tired or I can catch Ed's eye and ask him to rescue me. Bob was sweating profusely, his eyes were half closed, and he was very drunk. "I like what I feel, Mrs. McDermott," he said, slurring his words. "Do you give samples away?" His breath was enveloping her. He put his big paw on her butt and pulled her into him.

Dancing over to Winston, who had been watching, Maria said in a loud voice, "I'm sure Bob would love another drink, wouldn't you, Bob?" She rolled her eyes and mouthed, "Help me."

61. A Postmortem Review

September 1963
(Maria)

Don and Winston each took one of Bob's arms and almost carried him over to the bar. "Hey, you guys, I was dancing. I don't want a drink," Bob shouted, struggling a little.

Cajoling him, Winston said, "Maria has to check on your dinner, which will be served in a moment. You're hungry, aren't you?" Winston helped him sit down on a chaise lounge before he fell down.

Bob looked up at him. "You're a good fellow. Are you the butler?"

With that remark, Maria hurried away to help Briggie. Her mother was right behind her, laughing at what she'd just heard. "Winston won't forget Bob. I think that's a first, being called a butler." She put her arm around Maria's waist. "You'll just have to stop leading the men on, Maria," she said, laughing again.

Laura and Sarah looked worn down, but they kept smiling. Maria and her mother piled food onto the platters and gave them to the girls for the buffet table, allowing Briggie to concentrate on her special sauces for the meat and vegetables.

Maria carefully placed parsley around a platter of roast beef. "What a team we are."

Her mother had outdone herself, decorating the dining room with fresh flowers, china, and silver. Even John Whittaker, one of Ed's clients, remarked to Ed how impressed he was with the party as he stood with his wife in the buffet line.

"John, all the credit goes to my wife and her mother," Ed said, "She's the brains who put this together," he said, smiling at Maria.

"Actually, the credit needs to be spread around," Maria said. "Our wonderful cook, my son, my stepfather, and our two young serving ladies should be included. It takes a small army."

A stately lady who was going through the line looked up at Maria. "Mrs. McDermott, I want to congratulate you on a lovely party. It's so nice to meet you. Mr. Madden has spoken about your husband for the last ten years as an upstanding member of the community, and now I get to meet the reason why," she said, smiling at Maria. "My name is Agnes Madden."

"So nice to meet you. My grandmother's name was Agnes, and she was a Scot."

"We have something in common, Maria. I'm Scottish, and I never let my husband forget it. I'll call you for an afternoon meeting to discuss our genealogy. Perhaps we're related. I'd like that." She smiled again, her warm brown eyes sparkling.

Maria suspected Mrs. Madden moved in a whole different social circle than the rough and tumble breeders and their wives. Perhaps she was a member of the DAR and was on the board of the Chicago Symphony or something equally impressive. In any case, she was a pretty woman who was warm and gentle. Maria liked her immediately.

"Thank you so much, Mrs. Madden, for your kind words and invitation. I'd love to visit with you anytime. Your husband took a chance on a young, untried veterinarian twelve years ago, and it paid off. I can now thank him for his support of Ed all these years."

"He's right behind me and heard you," she said, her eyes twinkling as she spoke.

The patio tables around the pool began filling up with guests who were eating rather than drinking, dedicated to savoring the magnificent spread that the McDermott's were offering. As a contented hush spread over the party, the fall insects seemed determined to drown out the music from the stereo with their discordant cacophony. A welcome light breeze cooled and caressed the diners. The hurricane lights continued to cast their magic on the patio tables, creating a delightful mood for everyone.

"This is a big success, Mom." Maria sat down gratefully with her plate, ready to eat. "Thanks, for the two hundred and twentieth time," Maria said and laughed.

Maria glanced over at the empty chaise lounge where Bob had passed out earlier. "Where's Mr. Groper? Did he drown?"

Her mother laughed. "No such luck. Ed, Winston, and Don put him in your upstairs guest room to sleep it off. If you have a surprise for breakfast, be ready."

Putting a forkful of food in her mouth, Maria said, slyly, "Speaking of sleeping arrangements, guess who was in my bedroom tonight?"

"I can't even begin to guess, I'm so tired. Who was it?"

"Babs, our friend from school, with her partner in crime, Lydia." She gave her mother a knowing look, took another bite, and explained the whole incident in detail.

"Well, are you going to talk to Ed about it?"

"I don't know. That's why I told you. What do you think?"

"I'd ignore it. Ed divorced her because of her infidelities. He'll never go back to her again. He loves you, Maria. He gets a certain look in his eyes sometimes when he's looking at you, especially when you're completely unaware."

"Thanks, Mom, I sort of thought the same thing."

Laura and Sarah began circulating among the tables, bringing more water, offering seconds from the buffet table, and taking orders for coffee and dessert. "Aren't Briggie and the girls wonderful?" Maria asked, sipping her water, thirstily.

"Let Winston reward them and Chris too, Maria. Humor an old soldier. He's dying to do it. Chris has been on duty all evening, parking cars and tending bar. He's turning out so well, Maria. I know George is proud of him, wherever George is now. By the way, where is Chris?"

"Wherever the girls are. I bet Chris is sitting as close to Laura as possible. Briggie's resting in her bedroom and watching her 'telly.' I insisted. Laura and Sarah will do the clean-up."

"It's almost over," Ed said. "You did it, ladies, and thanks for everything. The party was a whopping success. I'll find Chris to help with the cars. I don't want any of these well-lubricated guys to dent someone else's car trying to leave. Meet me at the front door, Maria."

As they stood there, most of the couples left unceremoniously, thanking Ed and Maria. However, there was one exception. Maria watched Babs reach up and give Ed a big good-bye kiss on his lips that lasted as long as she could make it, and Bob stumbled and fell out the door. *What a pair. Babs is beginning her campaign on Ed, but it won't work, and Bob is oblivious.* Maria reminded herself of that over and over again as she was being thanked by her last departing happy guests.

As soon as they reached their bedroom, Maria dropped onto the sofa. "Well, it's over for another year. Now I hope our lives can become extremely boring." She pulled off her clothes and left them in a heap. Crawling into bed, she said, "Thank goodness Winston drove the girls home. He was wonderful tonight. I hope the Dawsons found their room. I was too tired to help them." Ed lay inert in his clothes, listening to her, his eyes fluttering.

"Don't lie there, you'll fall asleep."

"No, I won't," he muttered, but he did. His breathing deepened, and he was gone.

Poor guy, she mused, attempting to make him more comfortable by taking off his shoes, unbuttoning his shirt, pulling off his belt, and unzipping his pants. He'd worked seeing clients since the crack of dawn, taken care of Don, was a great host at the party, and he was finished. Pulling the sheet up over them both, she fell asleep.

The house was silent Sunday morning. No one was moving. Maria's eyes opened and then shut again. She moaned and then turned over, her body stiff from lying in a comatose position for so long. She must be getting old. Maria had never felt so stiff before, but a hot shower would fix her. Then she felt herself drifting off to sleep again.

The next time she opened her eyes, she could smell coffee. Where was it coming from, and where was Ed? Sitting next to her bed on the night stand was a warm cup of coffee, but Ed gone. She sat up with a start. It was Sunday—Ed didn't have to work. Or did he? Gulping her first cup of the day, she quickly gathered up her clothes, showered, and dressed.

She could hear Don as she hurried down the stairs. He and Ed were out on the patio playing a round of cribbage, and Don was complaining that Ed was cheating.

"It's not humanly possible for one man to get such good hands time after time," Don said, as he reached in his pocket for the fifty-seven cents he owed Ed.

"You agreed to a penny a point, so pay up, Doc. We've got to go. I promised Glen I'd share calls today." Seeing Maria standing in the hall, he stopped. "Did you get the breakfast I left you this morning?"

She looked at him, feeling concerned. "Are you okay, handsome? You had a big day yesterday and last night was pretty tiring as well."

"You're sweet, I'm tough. We have to work. When we get home, we'll have a game of water polo." He gave her a peck on her cheek and grinned. "Be home as soon as I can, Tiger Lily. Smile! Remember, you're married to a veterinarian. Our work is never done."

Maria heard Don teasing Ed about turning into a pansy, wanting to play water polo.

For the life of her, she couldn't believe how Ed was as perky as he seemed. She was exhausted after the party. She got another cup of coffee, went out on the patio, and sat in a chaise lounge to read the Sunday paper. One by one, the other members of her family appeared, Briggie being the first. Everyone was moving slowly, and her sister stayed in her room all morning. Maria had a delicious thought. Perhaps May had a hangover.

As the caffeine kicked in, Maria helped Briggie make brunch for everyone. She saved two plates of eggs and bacon for her two hard-working men, but when Ed called her early in the afternoon, she tossed out his food, made sizzling bacon, an omelet for each of them, and fresh coffee. When she heard his truck, she put Briggie's sweet rolls in the oven too.

A subdued May had come down for coffee by the time the men returned, saying quietly that she'd packed their bags. She asked Maria for some aspirin, but offered no explanation for her request. She looked pale as she sat on the patio, sipping her coffee and reading the Sunday paper their mother shared with her. Maria couldn't figure her sister out. Her moods seemed to change with the wind. If she was confusing to Maria, what was she to Don?

Amanda wandered into the kitchen, and Maria put her to work taking the men's meals out to the patio, paying her with another sweet roll to eat.

Maria took fresh coffee out to her mother. "How's Winston this morning?"

"He went to hit some golf balls at the club's range. I was too tired, but he wasn't."

"Why are the women so tired or hung over and the men are full of pep and energy?"

"Don't ask the men. They'll attribute it to men being stronger. Winston teases me with that statement all the time."

"Well, I know one young man who's tired and still in the sack," Maria said.

Her mother raised her eyebrows. "The what?"

"It was the word Bill used for bed when he was here with Elena. Probably a term he learned in the war," Maria said, making idle conversation.

"I'd like to say something before the men come out," May said, firmly.

From the tone in her voice, it wasn't going to be a casual remark. "Yes, sister dear, what is it?" Maria braced for the worst.

"This weekend has been an eye opener for me. After seeing what Maria has done this year since she remarried, I've decided to go to art school and stop spending my days making meals and just taking care of the house. I'm bored with my life and have been for a long time. I talked with so many interesting women last night. I want to have an interesting life, too."

Her mother glanced at Maria. "I'm delighted you're going to go back to school, May. You were always so talented growing up, and I wished you'd gone to art school then."

"I'm sorry I didn't invite you to Elena's art show last weekend," Maria said, apologetically. "I'm happy for you." Maria patted her sister's hand for encouragement.

Amanda had been listening, but was getting bored with all the talk. "Mom, do you suppose Lois could come over and go swimming with me this afternoon?"

Maria nodded. "Of course, go call her now."

"Daddy," Maria heard her daughter squeal in the hallway. "You're home so early. Will you come swimming with me this afternoon?"

Maria smiled, thinking, poor Ed, he just gets in the door and is assaulted by his eager daughter.

"Yes, Petunia," he said loud enough for them to hear before he stepped outside. "As soon as I have something to eat, we'll discuss swimming," he said over his shoulder, quickly coming to the table.

"My, it's certainly nice to have a cook like you have, Maria." May's tone relayed a little jealousy resurfacing. "Being here has been an education for me. I'd like to get together again soon," she said, surveying her mother and sister.

"Ruth, where are my swim trunks?" Winston's voice boomed through an open window. "I'm hot, and I want to take a swim."

She hopped up. "I'll be right back. Winston and I have something to say to all of you before you go home, folks."

Maria leaned over to Ed, who was enjoying every bite of his meal. "You're eating like you're starved."

"I am. I didn't want to take time to cook and eat. Briggie and you weren't up, so we just worked, didn't we, Doc?"

"Yes, but I didn't mind. I drank and ate so much last night, I was still full this morning. What a feed bag you put on. That must have cost you a pretty penny." Don chuckled. "That's why you were so delighted to take my money this morning at cribbage. You need it."

"I see everyone is assembled here this morning, having post-mortem reviews of the party, no doubt, " Winston said, striding out onto the patio in his swim trunks, looking very fit for his sixty-three years. "There's no need to beat around the bush. While I have you all together, Ruth and I have a proposal for you. We're in the process of selling our big place in Miami and buying a boat that Ruth insists is a yacht, and an apartment that has boat moorings outside its door. Our place in Washington has sold, and we want to reinvest our money in a frivolous way.

"In November, we're going to Florida to look for a boat and a place to live in Ft. Lauderdale. I have a real estate broker looking as I speak, and hopefully everything will be all set by Christmas so you can all come and stay with us and take a ride on our boat."

"You mean a cruise, Winston," Ruth said, smiling at her exuberant husband.

"Whatever, my dear. We're going to take a course in navigation while we're there, and then I'll be a fountain of knowledge, knowing all kinds of nautical terms."

Maria glanced at May and then Don to see their reactions. They were both quite stunned by the invitation. It was probably a first invitation of this kind for Don. His parents were hard-working Iowan farmers, not even remotely interested in boats and cruising.

"Grandpa, when can we come, and where will we cruise?" Amanda asked, breaking the silence with her two-part question.

"Leave it to children, they get right to the heart of the matter," Winston said. "As soon as you have Christmas vacation. I want to explore the Keys in our boat."

Amanda tugged on her mother's sleeve. "Was I ever in Florida, Mom? I remember something."

"Yes, we used to go a lot," Maria answered. "Especially when your daddy was away, which was often," Maria added, softly.

Her last comment wasn't lost on Ed. He reached over, smiled, and took her hand.

"Well, it's all settled then. The women will work out the details, which they do so well, and we men will act like we are in charge," Winston said, laughing at his last comment. He stepped into the pool and began to swim. He dove under the water, then came up for air. "Let's have one last game of water polo before the folks go home. Come on, set up the net and choose up sides."

Don was a good sport, wearing one of Ed's suits and trying to play water polo. It wasn't a medium he was comfortable in, being primarily a horseshoe enthusiast. But Chris came running when he heard the splashing and noise emanating from the pool, and the men had a wild game. Chris played with his Uncle Don and Winston, and Ed teamed up against them.

When they dragged themselves out of the pool, Don said, "Let's go home, Mother, before it gets too late. Ed's beaten me in cribbage, and now water polo, and I'm sick of it. Thanks for the invite to Florida, Winston. Mother and I will talk it over. Sounds like fun, but we have a lot to talk over."

"I wouldn't miss a trip like this for the world," May said quietly to Maria. "We're going, make no mistake about it."

Maria handed them a bag of sandwiches, fruit, and cookies for the trip as they all stood around saying their good-byes.

"See you at Christmas, if not before," Ed called to Don. They pulled out at the same exact moment Alicia drove in. Lois was bouncing in the front seat to see her friend.

While Lois got out of the car, Alicia leaned out of her window. "I'll get her at seven. Let's get together for coffee when you have a minute." She smiled and drove away.

The two-way traffic continued. Chris said he'd be home later and went out to wait for his ride. He gave the excuse that he was going to the park to see the gang, but they knew better.

"Be home by seven. I want to have a family meeting, Chris," Ed said, firmly.

The house seemed suddenly quiet as everyone had splintered off into their different worlds. Ed took Maria's hand, led her upstairs, and locked the bedroom door. "Briggie is in her room resting with the telly, Lois and Amanda are in the pool, and guess what, we're all alone on a Sunday afternoon." He took her in his arms. "I want to make sure I'm the only man in your life."

"What do you intend to do, handsome?" she teased.

62. Life Moves On

September 1963
(María)

Ed didn't say a word. He just started to undress her, kissing every part of her body as he took off every stitch of her clothes. Backing her up slowly until she fell onto their bed, he seemed a little rougher than usual. Giving her that look, he tore off his clothes and answered her question.

Ed turned over and fell asleep immediately, leaving her disappointed. He must have been overly tired. Maybe something was bothering him. Maria covered him up with the sheet and got up quietly to put away her clothes. Standing in her closet, she noticed the box holding her winter gloves had the top off. Her shoes were rearranged as if someone had tried them on and put them back in a different place. It gave her the creeps when she remembered who had been in her bedroom. Her lingerie drawer had been rearranged. The boxes from George were not in their usual places. They'd gone through everything, even her perfumes, because they were out of place, too. How could they? How childish.

As she closed the bedroom door on her exhausted husband, the need to write about her new and different world was stirring inside her. Her marriage to her loving, volatile, deeply sensitive husband was pushing her to lay her concerns out in front of her in her journal and take a look at them. Ed was building up another head of steam about something, and she found writing about it kept her from worrying.

She opened the bottom drawer of her desk in their quiet and cool study and there it was, her latest journal lying on top of her other journals. She held it lovingly as if it were alive. In a way it was, pulsing with her feelings, plans, and desires. *No one has found you, you are safe.*

Keeping all her journals in the study was a stroke of genius. She'd have been distraught if those intruders had found them. It was one thing to rummage through her clothes, but another thing to invade her mind and heart.

Spending a quiet afternoon writing in the aftermath of the party felt very satisfying. Her thoughts came pouring out. *I love writing and everything that goes with it. Someday I want to work for a paper or magazine again. I miss my job in Washington. Until Ed came along, my job was the part of my life that kept me sane.* Lost in thought, Maria jumped when Amanda touched her shoulder.

She leaned around in front of her mother, smiling. "What are you writing, Mom? Do you have homework like me?"

"Sort of. I'll be doing a lot more of this from now on because I want to write a book someday, and you'll be in it, cutie."

"That's nice, Mom, but can Lois stay for supper?"

"What time is it anyway? We need a new, big clock in here, Amanda."

"It's six, and Daddy wants a meeting at seven."

"Okay, sweetie. I made sandwiches for us when I made some for Aunt May and Uncle Don. I'll put them out along with some yummy leftover salad and dessert from the party. Lois can stay, but she has to go before the meeting."

When seven o'clock arrived, Ed started checking his watch periodically. "I'm going to the park if Chris doesn't show soon. Maybe he wasn't able to get a ride home. Of course, he could call. There are phone booths in St. Charles," Ed said, sounding a little perturbed.

"Just remember how it was with your first girlfriend," Maria said, thinking back about how silly she'd been around Bill.

Just as Ed was getting his keys out, a car pulled up in front of the house, and a minute later, Chris came flying in, and the car went roaring away.

"Hi, everybody," Chris said, his face bursting with happiness.

Chris was in love and Maria was thrilled for him. How many love affairs would he have before he found the right girl? He probably thought he'd be in love with Laura for the rest of his life, but he wouldn't.

"Everyone comfortable?" Ed sounded anxious to begin. "Let's hold hands and take a minute to be thankful that we're all here together." Maria watched Ed bow his head, something he'd never done before.

"First, I want to tell you that the barn is almost finished, except for some plumbing and carpentry work. Another month and it will be ready.

"Our plans for the rec room have sort of been on hold, but I think your mom and I will be able to get together and work on it now that our weekends will be free.

"As you know, Winston and Ruth have invited us again to spend Christmas with them in Florida. What does everyone think about that?"

"The rec room sounds cool, Ed, but I don't want to go away at Christmas," Chris said.

"I know why," Amanda piped-up. "Chris is in love."

"Shut up, squirt," Chris said, angrily.

Ed looked at his two stepchildren. "Family takes precedence over friends," he said calmly, "and who knows, maybe Laura will be away for Christmas. It's a long way off. Grandpa is going to look for a boat, since his big house in Washington has been sold. And, I want you to know, so has your mother's."

"So, Dad's house is gone," Chris said sadly.

"It is, but the money from the sale is in the bank for you and Amanda's college education," Maria added quickly. "Your dad would be pleased that what he worked hard for will go toward your future, and Ed was the one who suggested it."

Her son was smarting from Ed's decree about Christmas, and he still missed his father. For as neglectful as George had been, he and Chris had bonded when Chris was a little boy.

Chris folded his arms over his chest, and Maria saw him give Ed the same look she'd seen on George's face when he was furious. Maria hoped that Chris would be a happier man than his father had been.

"Daddy, when can we go looking for a pony and a puppy?" Amanda seemed completely oblivious to her brother's anguish.

"How about next weekend? I know of two farms that will have what we're looking for."

"Oh, Daddy, I love you."

Ed had made one kid happy and one miserable. Sometimes there was no way to please everyone.

"For the time being, Mom will have to fill in at the clinic, so remember to call her there if you need her. I haven't had time to interview anyone. Besides, your mother is the best we've ever had, and I hate to let her go."

"Oh, and I almost forgot. I'll be away for a weekend a few weeks from now with Uncle Don at a horseshoe meet. We just decided to do it on the spur of the moment before he left for home," Ed said, looking at Maria for approval.

Remembering Peter's advice for Ed to take some time off doing nothing but having fun, Maria gave him the thumbs up. *Good for you, darling. You're going to practice for our trip to Florida.*

"I'll be counting on both of you to help your mother while I'm gone."

"We did just fine before you came," Chris said, quietly.

Ignoring Chris's mean remark, Ed said, "Let's all hold hands before we leave." He waited for Chris to uncross his arms, then Ed took hold of his hand on one side and Amanda's on the other. "Thank you, God, for all of us being together," he said, surprising Maria with his prayer.

After saying good night to Amanda, Maria found Ed in the study absorbed in paperwork. He didn't look up, which was unusual for him. She took out her journal, put her head back in her chair, and shut her eyes. Maria decided mentally where she wanted to go with the story and continued writing her first novel.

After an hour or so, Ed looked over at her. "Let's go upstairs. I have some things to say to you." Maria felt a little premonition flutter through her. She knew all the signs. She'd seen it many times in the last year. He would bottle things up inside until he was so mad, he'd blow like a teakettle, and this was going to be just like that.

Ed closed the bedroom door and locked it. "Do you have any idea how you make me feel when you allow guys to paw you?"

"Who do you mean?" Maria asked, knowing the answer.

"Bob Decker, that creep. I watched you let him hold you so tight, I knew he felt your breasts, hips, and butt while you were dancing."

"Ed, I was so surprised at first, I didn't react as soon as I should have, and then I decided not to make a scene for your sake. I steered us over to Winston and Don, who were closest to me. I didn't see you anywhere."

"For my sake, what the hell do you mean? I've been waiting since last night for you to tell me about it, and you haven't. Why not? Are you planning another meeting with him?"

"His drunken attempts were ridiculous. It wasn't important to me. In fact, I'd forgotten about it until now. I knew nothing would happen with you and Winston on the patio. I didn't want to act like a school girl. He gives you lots of business. Get the picture?" she snapped. "Besides, he's a fat, out-of-shape alcoholic who has no sex appeal whatsoever."

How could Ed think for even a second that she'd be attracted to that oaf? Maria struggled to hold back tears. "I knew something was wrong when we had sex this afternoon. You weren't making love, you were laying claim to your territory. And remember this, I'm no man's territory."

"Maybe I was, Maria. I was so hurt."

She'd try to let him out of the argument gracefully. "Stand over here next to me and look in our full-length mirror, my silly, jealous husband. What do you see?"

"I see you and me looking in the mirror."

"True, but look at what I see. A handsome man built for action with muscles everywhere. Not a broken down, overweight, ugly drunk." She grabbed a pillow, stuffed it under Ed's sweater, rumpled his hair and handed him a glass. "This is how Bob Decker looks. Now make a face like this." She crossed her eyes, let her mouth fall open in a slack position, and slurred out, "I need a drink."

Ed started to laugh. "You little devil, I was pretty foolish, wasn't I? Remember when we were first dating, and I used to ask you to help me see the funny side of things? I still need help to lighten up." Ed's soft, brown eyes gazed at her like a wounded deer. "I can't make it without you."

"Yes, you can, Dr. Ed McDermott, who put himself through vet school, started a practice by himself, and has made a big success of it. If something happens to me, you'll be okay. You're made out of strong stuff."

Ed grinned, looked in the mirror, pulled out the pillow, and hugged her. "We do look pretty good together. You still have a cute butt." He gave her an apologetic smile. "Look, I'm sorry I got so upset. Can I have a do-over from this afternoon?"

"Maybe," Maria said, running her hands down his chest. "If you promise not to let Babs kiss you on your soft, desirable lips again."

63. Testing the Waters

October 1963
(Bridget/Ed)

Bridget

For the first time in her life since she had started working for Maria, Briggie was lonely. She wished for her life with Amanda and Chris when they were little. She was important to them, and they to her, as they grew up. But now they were older and had found new lives of their own.

Amanda was still her sweet self when she was around, but that wasn't very often. She spent a great deal of time on the phone with her friends, at her 4-H meetings, or doing homework. Chris ate his meals silently, kept his thoughts to himself, worked every weekend for either Ed or Glen, spent time after school in his sports program, and used any free time to be with his friends or girlfriend. Briggie rarely had a conversation with either of them longer than a minute or two.

But the biggest adjustment she'd had to make since the move was centered on Maria. Maria no longer confided in her. Ed had replaced her as Maria's confidant.

Along with these changes, her emergency trip to the hospital suffering with the terrible pain of a gall stone stuck in a duct had been a wake-up call. After she successfully passed it without surgery, the doctor had prescribed a preventive diet to keep it from happening again. She'd followed it religiously, terrified the pain would reoccur if she didn't.

But the good news was that her youthful figure had been returning slowly over the past two months. With it, her energy level had skyrocketed, and her feet didn't hurt anymore.

A new restlessness had appeared, and the idea of doing the same old cleaning chores for the rest of her life seemed boring. It also served as a catalyst to push her out into the world. She didn't know where or in what direction, but she couldn't ignore it. It wouldn't let her.

A tiny feeling of guilt gave her pause as she sat at the kitchen table sipping a cup of coffee and reading the daily newspaper, instead of busying herself cleaning the kitchen. But she had no interest. Her mother would have called it lollygagging, God rest her soul.

An urge made her check the classified section, and before she knew it, she was scanning the ads for car and truck sales. Taking another sip of coffee, she took a pencil and began circling possible buys. She needed her own safe, old reliable car so she had some freedom.

It was all so confusing, so many trucks and cars advertised. She'd never had any interest before. She asked herself, *why now*, but got no answer.

Briggie would ask Ed to help her look at ads when he got home. He was the only one who'd noticed she'd changed—no one else in the family had paid attention. Maria never asked Briggie how she spent her days or what plans she had for the rest of her life. The entire family had gotten caught up in their own worlds, and they were taking Briggie for granted. She wiped tears from her eyes with a hankie. Even Ruth had begun to volunteer at the local hospital. It was time for Briggie to change her life too!

Just the other night, she'd checked her burgeoning bank balance. Ed had insisted on giving her a big raise when they moved. *What a generous, darlin' man.* He said the money he paid her was for her good work and her retirement. He even suggested she see his accountant to help her make investments. That could come later, but for now, she wanted to see the money in her bank account where she could get at it when the need arose.

Feeling euphoric with her new decision to change, she did something she'd always wanted to do—play music while she worked. *Why do I feel I shouldn't enjoy myself? I can play music.* Turning on the radio, she heard familiar music of the forties and fifties. She began singing the songs louder and louder, and she danced as she sang, discovering her singing voice and her ability to dance again. The music Chris liked had such silly words. She couldn't imagine singing a song about a yellow submarine.

To assuage the guilt she felt, she forced herself to give the kitchen "a lick and a promise," while her mind tried to picture her new vehicle. That was difficult. She hadn't allowed herself the joy and excitement of fantasizing about anything for herself since she was young.

Briggie usually had several doughnuts or cookies with more coffee as a reward for cleaning, but not that day. She snapped the lid down firmly on the box and put it away for the family. *I'm not hungry, I'm bored. I'll do what the doctor said. I'll take a walk. Me feet don't hurt anymore!*

Always avoiding the mirror in the past, she made herself look. An old lady in a baggy house dress, hiding behind an apron, stared back at her. *Horrors, I look like me grandmother. Saints preserve me, I've got to spruce up.* She threw on her old coat and walked out of the house and up the road for the first time since she'd moved there.

Life had been changing all around her it seemed, and she'd stood still. But now, in the twinkling of an eye, her whole attitude had shifted. *Where had she been?* She scolded herself as she walked, huffing and puffing up the road to the new barn she'd never seen.

Another idea popped into her head as she walked. She'd go shopping for new clothes. The smile that brought quickly turned into a frown. Where would she go? Who could she ask? Suddenly, her panicky feeling changed to euphoria, and a large smile spread over her face. She'd ask Maisie!

Before, she would have asked Maria. They'd been so close when she was married to George, but now she didn't feel comfortable asking for such personal advice. *Am I mad at her for leaving me emotionally?*

No, that wasn't the real reason Briggie was feeling restless. She needed to establish independence from the family. She understood Chris pulling away from the family little by little. In a few years, when the kids were gone, there would be no need for a cook. It was time for Briggie to find her future. Maisie always seemed so friendly toward her. It was time to make her acquaintance. After Briggie returned to the house, she picked up the phone and made the first move.

As if planned for her benefit, that afternoon both Maria and Ed breezed in earlier than usual from work. It was a perfect opportunity to talk to them. Briggie was excited as she hurried down the hall to greet them.

"Begora, something came over me today, and I need help. I want to buy an old, reliable car to get meself about. Missy, with you gone to the clinic, I need a way to get me groceries." Groceries were only a small part of her wish, but she couldn't tell them yet that she really wanted her freedom. Her hands flew to her hips in a posture of new resolve.

"I know just the guy to fix you up, Briggie. I'll call and we'll go this evening if he's home." Ed put his arms around Briggie and danced her around the kitchen.

"Dr. Ed, are you daft? The likes of me hasn't danced with a man since I was a girl."

"You're getting skinny, aren't you?" Ed asked, ignoring her protests and whirling her faster to the radio music.

As she caught her breath after their dance, she listened as Ed called Hugh.

"Buddy, I've got a question for you. Is Fats McHenry still in business? He is? Good. Would you take a spin out there tonight with me to look for a car for a friend of mine? You will?" Ed laughed at something Hugh said. "You're not rusting, Hugh, you mean resting. You don't? Okay, I'm saving you from rusting."

They ate as soon as the kids got home. Briggie was so excited she wasn't hungry for the first time since she could remember. She began fluttering around the kitchen, wiping the countertops over and over, waiting to go.

"You can stop cleaning," Ed said, taking her arm and walking her out to the garage.

"Let's take your truck, Ed. They're big and strong, they can take the bumps, and they always start."

"I never knew you liked trucks. Do you want one?"

"Me brother had a wee one before I left for America. I liked his and would have had one in DC, but Mr. George said he'd have no trucks parked in his driveway."

"Well, we'll look for one tonight. We like trucks in the driveway. We'll pick up Hugh and see Fats McHenry. He's a great mechanic and an honest man who sells trucks."

When Hugh climbed into Ed's cab, Ed gave him a grin. "You're getting pretty spry."

"Yah, Doc Bentley did a swell job on me. My legs feel good." Hugh gave Briggie a look that lasted so long it make her feel a bit uncomfortable. "Hello, are you the gal who wants a truck? I think I met you when you first arrived. Have you lost weight?"

"Me name is Briggie, I work for the McDermotts, and me weight is me own business!"

"The lady has spoken, Hugh. Now, help me find Fats's place. I can't quite remember, and it's hard to find it in the dark. For your information, both Briggie and I want to look at trucks. I'll need another one soon. I freeze in the winter and swelter in the summer in this one."

They bounced along on the back roads with Hugh giving Ed a continual stream of directions. Briggie was glad she didn't have to find her way back on her own. "Is it always so dark, Ed? I haven't been out at night around here. Are there are no street lights?"

"No, and it's a challenge at night."

The same little misspelled sign saying, REPARES, was still the only marker into Fats's property. The same rutted road led them to Fats's house.

"Honk, Fats is used to that," Hugh said.

They didn't need to honk with the dogs barking, however. Fats opened his door, towering in the doorway with the light behind him illuminating his size. "Who's out there? Is that you, Doc? Still driving the old girl?"

Hugh leaned out of his window. "Yes, he is, and we're back for another go around," he yelled. "Get off of your porch and come help us, you old goat."

Shushing his dogs, Fats stepped down slowly. "So you're lookin' for another truck? Yourn's still good."

"Fats, meet Briggie, a friend of mine. She wants a reliable little car or truck to get around in, and I need a newer one too. We both want air conditioning for summer and a good heater for winter."

"Getting soft, Doc? A young guy like you don't need no air conditioning."

"Don't be telling the doc what he needs, just help 'em," Hugh said, climbing out of the truck and holding a hand out for Briggie. She held his hand and got down easily.

Briggie felt chilly in the October evening breeze. She wasn't used to it and wished she'd brought a sweater. Since taking off so much weight, for the first time in a long time, she'd lost her insulation. But it was a nice sensation.

"Ah got one of them foreign trucks in the other day. It's smaller than what you need, Doc, but might be nice for this here lady," Fats said, smiling his almost toothless grin at Briggie. "Of course, maybe you'd like a car? Ah gets them in occasionally."

Fats McHenry was a black man. Briggie had never known a black man, but she was glad to know one now. He talked as much as Irish men when they were buying horses or machines. She listened to the three of them, wishing they'd come to some conclusions.

Fats hadn't moved. He just kept petting his dog's head.

The next thing she knew, they were talking about dogs. Ed was telling Fats how he liked Fats's dogs, and Fats was standing there, smiling and agreeing.

"Ah have a bunch of puppies from this here bitch. Lady's a good dog and mostly Border collie. Her pups are the same. Ah think, if Pepper is their daddy," Fats said, scratching his dog's ears.

Briggie was cold, out of patience, and relieved when the men finally began climbing up the hill to the garage. Why didn't they drive up there? As she walked up the hill, she was struck by the fact that it was easy for her to keep up with them. It put her in such a good mood, she was able to ignore the men and their buying ritual.

In the garage-like barn, every tool imaginable in perfect condition was laid out on the counter in a neat pattern. But looking up into the rafters, Briggie shuddered. They were dusty, dirty, and cobwebby. The barn needed a good cleaning, but thank goodness it wasn't her problem.

Standing off to the side, Briggie couldn't take her eyes off of Fats. He was a big man and dwarfed Ed. *I wonder if he ever played football?* His black skin glistened in the light. Was it as smooth as it looked? If only she had the nerve to touch it. Did Fats have a wife and family? She hoped so—he seemed like a nice guy.

"This here is that Japanese truck Ah was telling you about. It's a year or two old, and only has five thousand miles on it. Ah had to go and buy a whole set of tools to work on it. Ah niver thought them foreign fellas could make anything like trucks. Ah just thought they made knickknacks. It's a good little piece of machinery, only they use a lighter grade of steel in it so it's not as strong as a good ol' 'Merican truck."

No one said a word. Briggie watched Ed and Hugh walk around the vehicle, peer under the hood, feel the finish, and examine the inside of the cab.

Ed approached Fats. "What do you want for it?"

"Things have gone up some since we did business years ago, Doc. But with the fender that's a mess, the tires that aren't too good, Ah could let you have it for a thousand."

Ed went over and felt the dented fender. Doc was a real Irishman and a regular horse trader. Briggie had never seen this side of him before.

"I tell you what, if you throw in a repaired fender and new tires for

437

the price, I'll talk to Briggie and get back to you. In the meantime, keep looking for another truck for me. If we buy two, maybe you can give us a better price." Ed took Briggie's arm, and as they picked their way down over the ruts and holes, he asked Fats, "When will the pups be weaned?"

"In a couple of weeks. Why? Are you interested?"

"I might be. I'll take a look at them when I see you again." Ed reached into his pocket and pulled out a business card. "Here's my card. Just call me when you're ready," he said, shaking Fats's massive hand.

"Fats will give you a good price," Hugh said as they were driving back, "if'n you buy two trucks from him. He still talks about the good work you did on his dog years ago, and I guess we didn't charge him. He never forgot it."

"Thanks, old buddy," Ed said as they dropped Hugh off. "See you tomorrow at work."

Hugh nodded, waved, and gave them his slightly crooked smile.

"So, what did you think of the truck? I want to be fair with him. He's a good guy. We'll see what he can do for us if I buy a truck from him too."

"I'm beholding to you for helping me," Briggie said. "If you like the truck, I'll get it."

"It will be good for you to have wheels," Ed said.

Ed

A week later, Fats called Ed and said the little truck was ready to go if his lady friend was interested. When they went out to check on Briggie's truck, Ed took Amanda and Maria along to see the puppies. He left them playing with the pups while he took Briggie out on the road so he could give it a test drive.

Amanda was still playing with one little male pup when they returned.

"What do you think, ladies?" Ed bent down and scratched the puppy's stomach. "Shall we take him home in a couple of weeks?"

"Oh, Daddy, can't we take him home today? I love him, and he picked me out and likes playing with me." Amanda's eyes pleaded with her dad.

"He can't leave his momma for a couple more weeks. We'll get him soon. Stay here with the pups while I do a little horse trading with Fats. Then I need to help Briggie drive her truck home. You and Mom can drive home together."

They took the truck for another spin, only this time, Ed gave the driver's seat to Briggie, and he climbed onto the passenger seat. "It's like riding a bicycle. Once you learn, you never forget."

They rode along with Ed directing her up one back road and down another. "You're ready," he finally said. "The truck sounds and feels good. Let's go back to Fats and sign the deal."

Before they got out, he turned to her. "You've changed since you've come to St. Charles, Briggie. What's happened?"

"I'm finally growing up. You and Maria have shown me a new way to live. Your generosity will allow me to find me way in my truck."

Ed's horse trading paid off. Buying two trucks did it. Both Fats and Ed were satisfied. They shook hands and the deal was sealed.

Bridget

The following morning, after the family had left, Briggie sailed through her household chores, looking forward to her day. She showered, put on her best-looking dress, and forced herself to look at herself in the full-length mirror again. She grimaced at what she saw.

Where had that young woman with roses in her cheeks, who had come to America looking for work in the land of milk and honey, gone? She brushed her long graying hair roughly, then combed and wound it back into the same tight bun she'd been wearing for the past twenty years. When her face had been young and her hair a coppery red, it had been acceptable. But now, it just made her look old.

Why had she been hiding in a fat body, stuffing herself with food? *Why, why, why?* Tears welled up in her eyes. So much lost time, being content to be a good cook and friend to her adopted family. But now, it wasn't enough.

After carefully locking the kitchen side door, she felt giddy getting into her new truck. She ran her hands over the smooth interior of the cab, grasped the leatherette steering wheel, and turned the key to start the engine. She smiled as she heard the engine purr. For the first time in her life, she was free, and she had Maria and Ed to thank for her financial position. God had been good to her when he'd led her to Maria long ago.

Her heart was pounding with excitement as she pulled into one of Maisie's parking places in front of the restaurant. Saying a quick prayer and crossing herself, she grabbed her old purse and stepped into her future.

64. Daring to Grow Up

October 1963
(Maisie/Bridget)

Maisie

Maisie had been enjoying a quiet moment between customers waiting for Briggie to come. A red truck parked in front of the café, and her new friend, Briggie, got out. Maisie hardly recognized her anymore since she'd lost so much weight. She hurried over to the door and leaned out. "I've been waiting for you since you called. Come in and tell me about that truck you're driving. Are you hungry?"

"No. Just coffee, Maisie. I want to lose a wee bit more weight; doctor's orders."

Maisie grasped Briggie's hands and looked at her. "What's wrong?"

Briggie gulped, then paused. "I need your help," she said, lowering her voice. "I need some clothes in the worst way, and I don't know where to go. Imagine a grown woman not knowing," she said, looking embarrassed.

"Let's sit down in a booth and talk," Maisie said, excited.

"I really need one of those makeovers that they talk about on the TV," said Briggie.

"After my lunch crowd leaves, we'll go shopping for clothes. I've been putting it off myself for weeks because I couldn't face those dressing room mirrors. Helping you will be much more fun."

"Saints preserve us, you're an angel, Maisie Davenport. I niver thought you'd want to take the time to do this with me."

"What are friends for? See you after lunch! I'll be delighted to have a change of scenery. We'll go and take a ride in your little red truck."

"I'll be back around two," said Briggie.

Bridget

Briggie felt jubilant as she walked under the magnificent trees lining Main Street and mentally made her plan. She'd visit the bank, walk in the park, and then maybe take time to just sit on a bench and relax. She was free to do anything she wanted.

It was one of those lovely, crisp fall days that required only a sweater. Briggie felt lighter than air. On her last visit, the doctor was pleased that she'd lost seventy-five pounds. No more hiding behind all that fat.

She moved easily in the fall sunlight, casting her eyes in all directions. Her feet felt wonderful. On impulse, she began skipping down the quiet sidewalk. A well-made sign stopped her: St. Charles Public Library. She looked across a lawn and saw a red brick building. She'd explore the library on her way back from the bank. Briggie couldn't believe how much she'd been missing.

The bank had big double doors set close to the sidewalk with only a couple of steps separating the outside from the inside. As she stepped in, she quickly removed her sunglasses, took a moment to adjust, and realized she hadn't been in the bank since Ed helped her set up an account. *Where had she been?* Briggie proudly shoved her bankbook in under the metal guard at the teller's window. He immediately disappeared. *Where had he gone? What was wrong?*

Her little bank book showed clearly that she had a grand sum of money in there. A well-dressed man appeared at the teller's window. "Forgive me, but do you have some identification, Miss Coyle?" he asked, giving her a reserved look.

"Why, of course I have." Briggie produced her new driver's license.

"So nice to meet you again, Miss Coyle. It's been a long time," he said, apologetically. "Jeffrey Fulton, Dr. McDermott's accountant, always deposits money into your account."

She watched as the teller counted out a stack of bills and gave them to her. Unable to contain herself, she said with a broad smile, "You'll see much more of me after this," and slipped the bills into her battered wallet.

She literally danced out of the bank, so full of life she wanted to scream. Briggie had begun a new adventure, and it was thrilling. She walked joyfully back to the library.

The quiet atmosphere brought back poignant memories of her money-starved little library in Ireland. She shook her head in dismay.

This library was a grand place with hundreds of books. She'd never find her way around before she had to meet Maisie. Briggie needed help.

Why she had niver gone to a library when she lived in DC with Maria and George? Once an avid reader, she was embarrassed to admit she hadn't read a book in ages. She had read the travel magazines George had brought home, featuring his articles and photographs of exotic locales. Pity he niver took Maria with him; he only took his mistress.

"Excuse me, may I help you?" an older woman asked, startling Briggie from her reverie.

"Yes, I need it," Bridget said, smiling at the friendly white-haired lady.

"Is this your first time at our library? If so, would you like a card?"

"Here's me identification," Bridget said again, proudly.

Moments later, the librarian gave Briggie her card. As the librarian showed Briggie around the library, her head felt like it was spinning as she tried to remember all of the woman's suggestions.

Pressing a small book into her hand, the librarian smiled. "This would be my first choice for a new adult reader. It's a collection of bits of wisdom by one of my favorite authors, Kahlil Gibran. What do you think? If you want it, I'll stamp the return date on the inside cover, and it's yours to enjoy for a couple of weeks, Miss Coyle. When you come again, I'll suggest few more books you might like."

Glancing at the clock, Briggie nodded. The librarian checked out her book, Briggie tucked her card into the book pocket, and thanked the woman for her kindness. Filled with a new sense of herself, and happy that she was going in a new direction, Briggie hurried out onto that beautiful lawn to a bench surrounded with fall flowers she'd seen from the sidewalk. An urge to open that little book was too much to ignore.

The bench was under ancient trees losing their leaves all around her. Stretching her legs out in front of her, she admired her thin legs and ankles. "Hello there, new legs, nice to meet you." Briggie quickly looked around to see if anyone had overheard her.

She quickly crossed her legs, another new action most people took for granted, but not her. Cradling her precious book, she read the title, *The Prophet*, by Kahlil Gibran. Immediately, she felt a kinship to him because his name sounded Irish. Maybe he was an immigrant like her.

Briggie closed her eyes and opened the book. The pages displayed were from a chapter on self-knowledge. She read his prophecy several times before she closed the book and thought about his admonition to discover herself. The town's large clock intruded on her peace, pealing the time from its bell tower.

Maisie was just finishing her luncheon receipts when Briggie hurried in. "You're right on time, Bridget," Maisie said, smiling in anticipation of the fun they were going to have.

"You called me Bridget. How did you know I've wanted to use my real name?"

"I didn't, but something is different about you—maybe the way you walk. You act like a new person." Maisie grabbed her purse. "Come on, Bridget, let's go find you some new clothes for the sixties."

On the way to Marshall Fields, Bridget recounted her noon adventures to Maisie.

"Who lit the fire under you?"

"I just woke up somehow. Isn't it grand?"

In Marshall Field's, Bridget was amazed at the myriad new styles of clothing available to women. "Saints preserve me, I don't know where to start."

"Leave it to me, my girl, I'm a champion shopper. I'll find 'em and you try 'em."

Giving into Maisie's judgment as to style, Bridget aggressively began trying on everything Maisie brought her. But she was unsure of one thing. "I don't think me sainted mother would approve of me wearing pants like a man."

"They're called slacks. They're part of a new style called leisure suits; they're comfortable, and everyone is wearing them. With your new figure, you'll love them."

After much trial and error, Maisie was satisfied and Bridget was tired. She also felt guilty spending so much money on herself. Just when Bridget thought they were finished, Maisie insisted she have accessories—lingerie, shoes, and sleepwear to complete her first shopping trip.

"Next time," Maisie announced, "we'll look for more sporty things and a coat or two."

"The next time? Saints preserve us, I've niver had so many things in all me born days."

"Winter is coming, and believe me, it gets cold in Illinois. We'll come again, you can count on it. And today, on our way home, I'm going to introduce you to my adorable hairdresser, Norma Jean, a friend of mine. She works out of her home. You need a new hairdo to go with all your pretty new clothes and your new figure. I hate to admit it, but I'm jealous of your shape. It's more salads for me from now on."

"I'm not sure I should spend any more money on meself."

"You deserve it. You earned it, now enjoy it," Maisie argued.

Bridget met Norma Jean and loved her professional manner, her friendliness, and her clean home. She made an impetuous appointment for the following day. When she said good-bye to Maisie and went home in her new truck, she felt odd, almost scared. Her whole life seemed to be changing drastically.

What Bridget needed was some good, hard work. But once home, her guilt gave way to the excitement of trying on her clothes once again. As she did, she turned on her radio and danced around her room. Picking out a pair of cotton slacks and a blouse to wear to prepare dinner, she stopped at the utility room, went in, and tossed all her old house dresses in a pile to wash and give away.

65. Embracing Change

Late November 1963

(Bridget)

When Ed came through the door, he stopped and looked Bridget up and down. "Who is this young gal in my house peeling potatoes?"

Bridget's cheeks warmed. "Get on with you, I have me peeling to do if this family wants dinner." *Dr. McDermott, I wish you had an older brother, you handsome devil.*

She hadn't allowed herself to have many romantic thoughts since the spring of her seventeenth year in Ireland. A handsome young man had lightly brushed her lips with a kiss one glorious spring evening, and she'd spent a sleepless night afterward. Three more times, she'd stolen away from her cottage to feel his arms around her and his kisses on her lips. But before they were tempted to break the church's rules on intimacy, her young life as she'd known it came to an abrupt end with the death of her mother, who had died in childbirth with her eighth child.

Bridget had to assume the household duties of her seven younger sisters and brothers. There was no way out. In a moment, her life had been turned upside down. Somewhere along the way, Bridget had lost herself in the insatiable demands of her siblings.

Angry for years about her mother's early death and Bridget's subsequent servitude, she blamed the church for banning birth control for married couples. If she heard one more priest give a sermon from the pulpits admonishing married couples not to have sexual relations except to produce an offspring, she'd scream. She knew for a fact that one of the priests who said Mass on Sunday usually spent Saturday night with a friend of hers, and they weren't praying. Bridget resented the fact that the male hierarchy of the church controlled women's bodies, while there was no worry of pregnancy for them, or worse, death from childbirth.

The sound of Maria's car going by brought Bridget sharply back to the present. Grabbing the last potato, she guiltily finished peeling.

"Briggie," Amanda said, as she opened the refrigerator, "you're all dressed up."

"I had to buy some new clothes now that I'm thinner." Did she sound like she was apologizing to Amanda? "Have a crisp, fall apple," she said, changing the subject.

Maria stopped in the doorway and screamed. "Briggie, what have you done to yourself? You look lovely. You're changing before my very eyes! We'll have to have a long talk, like we used to, so I can find out your secret."

"That's a date," Bridget replied, but Maria had disappeared from the kitchen without hearing her. All during dinner, Bridget struggled to share her burning request with the family. With time running out before they all scattered, she blurted out, "Maisie said I should be called Bridget from now on, and I agree. Maisie said Bridget is a beautiful name."

Everyone stopped and stared at her.

"When I first met you, I never liked the name Briggie," Ed said. "It didn't fit, but being a visitor to the family, I didn't want to step on any toes. I, for one, am glad you've changed it back to your real name. It has class."

"Briggie was a childish name made up by childish people," Maria said. "Forgive us."

Amanda smiled. "Brig, I mean Bridget, I'm going to miss Briggie, but I like Bridget."

"Well, that settles it then." That was easier than expected. Bridget had underestimated her family's wish for her to be happy. They loved her. With that out of the way, Bridget could change the subject. "I'll save some food for Chris. He must be at a track meet."

The following morning, it felt like Christmas, only better. Bridget was so excited about her hair appointment, she woke up before anyone and made Ed breakfast before he left.

"What a nice surprise, Bridget." Ed, sounding pleased, gave her a warm smile. "What's going on?"

Real attention from a handsome man was something she'd never had, and it made her tongue-tied. She just stood there awkwardly, smiling at him, wishing she could find the right words to tell him how much his support meant to her.

"Okay, if you don't want to tell me, I love you anyway," he said. Ed gave her another smile and carried his half-full coffee mug out to his truck.

After the family had gone for the day, instead of washing the breakfast dishes, Bridget sinfully left them in the sink, then got dressed and watched the clock. She wasn't hungry. She was more interested in getting out in the community.

Driving her new truck solo to Norma's, Bridget remembered the landmarks Maisie had shown her and arrived easily on time. While she waited anxiously for her first hair appointment in her whole life, Bridget thumbed through several magazines full of hairstyles. What should she tell Norma? What style did she want? A feeling of giddiness overwhelmed her. She felt like a young girl again and wanted to giggle.

"I'm ready for you now, Bridget. Want a doughnut? I just bought them from the bakery."

"No, thank you," she said, her mouth watering for one.

"You don't have to diet, a slim gal like you. I bet you can eat everything and never gain a pound. Have a seat and let's decide what you want to look like," Norma said, confidently.

Bridget smiled. "As for my new style, I'd like something easy to take care of, and I'd like the color it was when I was a child. Could you put a bit of curl in it, too? Make it shorter, but don't make me look like a lad."

As Norma worked her magic on her, Bridget shut her eyes, enjoying the luxury of having a beautician fix her hair. After her mother's death, Bridget was lucky to get a bath once a week. There was no time to keep her hair clean, soft, and fluffy.

No one in her family ever noticed that Bridget had gradually lost her youth mothering all them. The high and mighty priest told her it was her responsibility, and her father easily concurred. Why had it been her responsibility? Who had given them the right to decide her life? Hot tears filled her eyes from the pain of it all as Norma's gentle fingers carefully placed the curlers.

"Is the perm solution making your eyes water? I'm sorry. We'll be done in a minute."

"I'll be fine. You just do what you're doing. Saints preserve us, you're doing a fine job."

"You'll love your new do. It will be so easy to care for. Just run a comb through it, and it will look lovely. You have wonderfully thick hair."

Bridget watched Norma comb out her russet curls in the mirror. Who was that young woman staring back at her?

"Bridget, with that peaches and cream complexion you have, those big blue eyes, and your new 'do,' you look absolutely gorgeous. I bet your boyfriend won't recognize you. Call me when you want it trimmed and colored again, perhaps a month or two from now."

"Thanks, I will." Bridget was dazed by Norma's compliments. "Here," she said, groping in her purse for her new wallet. "I'm thrilled with me looks, and I want you to have this extra." Bridget barely heard Norma's thank you. Imagine the stylist thinking Bridget's boyfriend wouldn't recognize her. Did she have a peaches and cream complexion? Were her eyes that big and blue? She really didn't know who she was anymore.

Bridget stumbled out of the beauty parlor into the bright sunshine. She needed some new sunglasses—ones that would be big enough to cover her eyes. Glowing with happiness, she almost drove past the drug store. While searching for glasses inside the store, she walked by an aisle with boxes of condoms stacked on shelves. Impulsively, she thought of buying at least one package to see what the forbidden fruit looked like. Bridget glanced around to see if anyone was watching, then she picked up a package, but quickly replaced it. Her cheeks burned. *Oh, my goodness, can I do this? Me, who has trouble buying monthly pads.*

She peeked around the corner of the aisle to see who was working at the counter. *Drat, it's a young man, probably a friend of Chris's who will mention what I've bought. Perhaps, if I buy some sunglasses, put them on, buy a newspaper, and slip the box of condoms casually on the counter, he won't notice.* Quickly executing her plan, she waited in line, sweaty palms and all. She gritted her teeth as she placed her purchases on the counter. The kid took her money, tossed the first two items in the bag, and asked her if she wanted to wear her glasses.

The saints be with me, and let that be a lesson, Bridget Coyle, not to think everyone is looking at you. She made her way to the front of the store, but stopped to adjust her new glasses before she stepped outside.

"Pardon me, aren't you Sally Owens, the actress?" a man with a deep voice asked.

"Who?" she asked as she turned to him, almost in a panic. She couldn't believe a strange man had spoken to her. "No, you're mistaken," she stammered. Why was she embarrassed? Unfortunately, it was probably obvious that his question had made her feel uncomfortable. Imagine a man speaking to her and thinking she was an actress. Bridget glanced at him. My goodness, he was a good-looking man. He was every bit as tall as Ed, his salt and pepper hair was thick and cut short, no doubt, for coolness. His face was tan, a few crow's feet cornering his grey-blue eyes, clean shaven, with a beautiful smile. But what she really liked was his confidant and calm demeanor.

"I'm sorry, I could have sworn you were her. I don't usually speak to strange ladies. Please forgive me." He flashed her a smile, and her knees went all wobbly.

She gave him a weak smile and walked to her truck, half wishing he would follow her. Sitting in her hot cab, she rolled down the windows to cool it off and was surprised to see him approach her door.

"I can't believe you drive a truck. It doesn't fit you, if you pardon me for saying."

"I just bought it yesterday, and I like trucks, especially red ones." She couldn't believe she was talking to him and actually making sense.

"Could I ask you a favor? I just came into town and was looking for a place to stay and have a meal. Would you help me?"

She wanted to say, *I'd love to help you, you handsome darlin',* but instead she answered mildly, "Maisie's Café has good food. It's about three blocks down on the left side of Main. You can't miss it." He thanked her and returned her smile.

Bridget put her truck in gear, backed out, then turned to look at him. He waved and smiled—he'd been watching her. All the way home, she couldn't stop thinking about him. She scolded herself. *The first man to smile and talk to you and you go all to pieces. Get hold of yourself.* But she couldn't.

At dinner, Maria complimented Bridget over and over. Amanda sat next to her, touched her hair, and said how pretty she was. She'd never had that much attention from them.

But Chris was silent. When he walked past her in the kitchen, he mumbled, "I miss the old Briggie."

The following morning, Bridget was bursting to leave for Maisie's. She had no interest in housekeeping anymore.

Slipping into a booth, she waited until Maisie came by, then asked for a cup of coffee.

"Certainly," Maisie said, as if she were talking to a stranger. Then she stopped in her tracks. "Bridget, it's you, for heaven's sake! You look like a million dollars."

"Thanks, Maisie, for all you've done for me. I hope I can do something to repay you."

"Nonsense, you've given me a reason to get out of this place once in a while. I love it."

Thinking about her encounter yesterday, Bridget was dying to ask Maisie about the handsome stranger. She decided to make it seem like a silly incident. "Maisie, yesterday in the drug store, you'll niver guess who someone thought I was—Sally Owens."

"Was he a tall, good-looking guy in his late forties with streaks of gray in his hair?"

"Yes! Did he say who he was or why he was in town?"

"I asked him. His name is C. W. Peck. He's looking for a job with a breeding farm. He's had a lot of experience with racehorses, and he's worked on racetracks all over." Maisie got a wicked look in her eye. "I'll tell him you were asking for him when he comes in again. I did send him to Ed. If anyone would know who's looking for that kind of help, it would be Ed."

"You are me darlin' friend, and I'm going daft with everything that's happening to me so fast. Now, I must do my errands for the family. I feel a little guilty, but not so much that I want to stop enjoying myself. The laundry is piling up, and I don't care," Bridget said, giving Maisie a brilliant smile as she hurried to her truck.

When Ed came home that night, he stopped in the kitchen and poured himself some lemonade. Giving her a sly smile, he said, "Bridget, a fellow stopped in at the clinic today, looking for work. I liked him, so I took him on several of my calls to some breeding farms. I didn't know much about him until he opened up with the breeders and impressed both them and me. He has quite a background in horse racing and is a fount of information." Ed grinned at her. "I invited him for dinner tomorrow night, if it's okay with you. I told him I'd have to check with the cook before I made it official. I also mentioned she was quite a dish. He's renting the same apartment from Maisie that I did when I first blew into town."

Bridget's heart started to pound as she listened to Ed asking permission to bring home the man she'd felt drawn to in a way she couldn't explain rationally to anyone.

"You old charmer, you're full of blarney, but of course you can bring your new acquaintance home for dinner. He sounds interesting. I'll invite Ruth and Winston too. I haven't seen them yet this week."

"They're in for a surprise when they see you. Whatever you're doing, keep it up."

"Go on with you, I'll see you for dinner," she said, trying to hide her blushing.

That night, before she went to sleep, she tried reading her book. But ideas for dinner interlaced with worries about meeting Mr. C. W. Peck, and what she would say to him, invaded her concentration. Why had Ed invited him home for dinner? He hardly knew the man. The logical reason was that Ed wanted advice about horses for the family, what with the new barn and all. *But I know we're supposed to meet. I wonder what C. W. stands for?*

She turned off the light, but laid there in the dark, tossing from one side of the bed to the other. In the past, she was always able to sleep, but not now. It felt as if she were in a tornado.

66. Finding Herself

Late November 1963

(Bridget)

The following morning, tired as she was, she hurried to the grocery store where she usually bought the same favorite foods for the family every week, but today was different.

It was special. She'd serve Winston's favorite, stuffed roasted chicken with cranberry sauce, a nice conservative meal. All men, including C. W. she hoped, loved roasted chicken.

By four o'clock, Bridget was as ready as she would ever be. Her energy level had risen all day in anticipation of the evening. Showering again, she decided to wear her new slightly dressy, blue wool dress. Its color matched her eyes. Fluffing her hair, she felt light as a feather. Her cheeks were slightly pink from excitement, and just a dab of lipstick was all she needed. She grinned at herself in the mirror, then turned and ran to the kitchen, almost colliding with Winston.

He gave her an incredulous look. "Briggie, is that you? I don't believe your transformation." He took her by the arm and led her out onto the patio. "Ruth, look at our girl, can you believe this?"

"Wait a minute folks, you've been watching me lose weight for the last few months. All I've done is buy some up-to-date clothes that fit and have me hair colored and cut this past week. I'm the same person I've always been, just thinner and feeling good."

Ruth rushed from her chair and hugged Bridget. "Let me help you serve dinner so you can sit and enjoy the evening with us and our guest."

"Two more wee things," Bridget said, her heart warmed by the compliments. "I've gone back to my God-given name Bridget from me mither, God rest her soul, and I would appreciate it if no one mentions anything about me past looks when Mr. Peck comes tonight."

"We understand completely," Ruth said, patting Bridget's hand.

Winston sat back in his chair. "Who is this Mr. Peck? Do you know much about him?"

"Ed told me C. W. knows all aboot racehorses and is looking for a job. I don't know much more than that." Bridget put her hands together and gave them a big stare. "Now, let me finish putting the finishing touches on our dinner. I'll join you all on the patio when I'm finished. Maria wants me to socialize more since I can now walk easily."

"I agree." Ruth grinned. "We'll see you in a little while."

As the clock hands made their way to the appointed hour, Bridget paced up and down the hall. Where were the men? She fussed. *I'll make myself relax and sit on the patio with the folks.* "Bridget, I'm so glad you're back," Ruth said, pointing to the chair next to her. "I must say again, I'm delighted with your metamorphosis."

Bridget thanked Ruth. "I'm having a terrible time now. When the doctor scared me into losing weight, I did it because I didn't want that pain again. At first, that was all it was, but gradually as the weight dropped off, I began to realize that there was another person hiding inside waiting to come out who is completely different from the old Briggie. I don't like to clean or cook much anymore. I want to see people. I'm not content to stay home."

"Get a job somewhere," Winston said. "In the meantime, have one of these." He handed her a strawberry daiquiri. Bridget didn't want to offend him, but she'd niver drunk any liquor. Her mother had always said it was the divil's brew and people who drank went to hell.

"Here's to our new Bridget." Winston raised his scotch and soda to her and took a sip.

"If you're not drinking because you're worried about dinner, I'll help you get food on the table." Ruth took a deep breath. "I can smell the chicken. It's going to be wonderful."

Bridget sipped her first strawberry daiquiri, and it tasted like ambrosia. *Take it easy, girl, you don't want to embarrass yourself.* She felt a gentle breeze blowing, fanning her and fluffing her hair a little. Taking another sip, heard three male voices. Evidently, Ed had picked up Chris from high school and C. W. had followed them home.

"Hello, everybody, we'll be out in a minute," Ed called from the doorway. Cupboards were being opened, and then it was quiet. Out came the three men, with C. W. carrying a vase full of fall flowers. He almost dropped them when he saw Bridget sitting there.

"Maria and Amanda will be home shortly," Ed announced. "Maria is picking Amanda up on her way home from the office." He paused and smiled at Bridget. "I want to introduce my friend, C. W. Peck. This is Bridget Coyle, a member of our family; my mother-in-law, Ruth; and her husband, Winston Brooks."

Winston stood up, gave C. W. a mighty handshake, and put a scotch and soda into each of their hands. I know you both would like a man's drink. How about a Coke for you, Chris? I made daiquiris for the ladies. Too bad Maria isn't here, but she'll be along shortly."

C. W. smiled at the group. "I met Maria in the clinic this morning. She was very helpful."

Bridget caught him glancing at her occasionally as she sipped her drink. As a strange new feeling stole over her, she began to laugh more than she wanted at the banter of the group.

Oh, dear, she'd forgotten about dinner. "Excuse me, I must see how me dinner is doing," she mumbled, her brogue getting thicker by the minute.

Ruth got up immediately. "Let me help, Bridget."

Barely making it into the kitchen, Bridget moaned. "Saints preserve us, things are twirling around in my head." She leaned over the sink, threw up, and sat down.

"Bridget, go lie down until you feel better," Ruth commanded. "I'll take care of dinner."

Bridget nodded, stumbled down the hall, threw herself on her bed, and the twirling got worse. She closed her eyes, praying she wouldn't vomit again, and the next thing she knew, Maria was bending over her.

"What's happened? What time is it? Is the dinner party over?"

"It's nine o'clock. You've been asleep, and we're all in the living room." Maria sat on the edge of the bed. "How are you? Are you up to joining us? The dinner was delicious, in case you were wondering," Maria said, laughing.

How embarrassing to pass out with that handsome C. W. here. What a terrible impression I must have made on him. I certainly can't hold my liquor!

Bridget got up slowly, washed her face, dabbed her lips with lipstick, fluffed her hair with a comb, and made her way to the living room. Easing herself into a chair near the door, she felt her head pounding. Glancing quickly around, she locked eyes with C. W. and felt an indescribable surge of energy between them.

454

He smiled at her, then continued his description of one of the most exciting races he'd seen in Chicago, but kept an eye on her as he talked.

Ed slid to the edge of his chair, looking eager to say something. "C. W., what do you know about ponies and small horses? My girl here has been on my case about getting a pony."

Amanda came back to life when she heard Ed's question. "I've been going to my 4-H meetings, and they've been teaching us all about taking care of horses and ponies. They're a lot of work, but I love ponies. Will you help us pick out a smart pony?"

C. W. laughed at Amanda's directness. "Sure."

"How about making calls with me tomorrow? With your background, you'll have a position sooner than you think. Everyone is looking for expertise in recognizing good horse flesh."

C. W. nodded. "I surely appreciate your interest in me, Ed. I hope I can to return the favor sometime."

"Picking your brains will be payment enough. Knowing a little more about the racing world helped me out yesterday with a couple of hard questions from John Whittaker."

"Excuse us, C. W.," Maria said, "it's bedtime for Amanda. See you later."

With two of the four females disappearing, Bridget immediately got nervous. *What if Ruth decides to retire? Should I leave too?* She tried to hold her hands still and not rub the arms of her chair. It was so difficult sitting around talking socially. She'd always been able to hide in the kitchen. Bridget didn't want that anymore, but this was hard.

The conversation began to soften as the men enjoyed Winston's famous sippin' whiskey. C. W. was quiet for the most part, listening to Ed and Winston bantering about life. And occasionally, Ed would joke about an unusual situation that occurred on one of his calls, producing a chuckle or two. With her head pounding, Bridget excused herself and took several aspirins, hoping for relief before returning. She looked at the social smile Ruth had pasted on her face and wondered if Ruth was as bored as she was.

As the aspirins kicked in, Bridget began to feel better and more friendly.

But C. W. said, "I better get going, we all have to be up early tomorrow morning. I'll meet you at the clinic, Ed. Nice to have met you, Ruth, and thanks, Winston, for your hospitality." He got up and crossed the room to Bridget. "I enjoyed dinner. Thanks so much for all you did. I haven't had a home cooked meal in a long time."

As Bridget stood to say good-bye, he touched her elbow, ever so slightly. "Hope to see you again," he said, and then left before she had a chance to answer him.

To say she was disappointed with the way the evening turned out was a monumental understatement. She couldn't hold her liquor, converse, or relax. She felt like the ugly duckling she used to read about to the kids when they were little. C. W. probably thought she was a social outcast and boring.

Bridget looked at herself in the mirror. Her outward appearance had changed, but her insides were the same. She'd never be charming enough to appeal to C. W. Judging from the stories he told, he was a man of the world. She was a little misfit. Lying down on her bed with tears streaming down her cheeks, she reached for her book, *The Prophet*, and hoped she could read something that would make her feel better.

Turning to the tiny chapter on love, she read all about it. The last sentence had the most meaning and gave Bridget some peace. To her, it said she couldn't change what was going to happen between C. W. and herself. Satisfied, she reread the chapter, told herself to trust in God, and turned off her light.

67. Daring to Love

Late November 1963
(Bridget)

During the next several weeks, as the weather became crisper and threats of frost were forecast, Bridget made several more trips to Marshall Field's with Maisie. She couldn't believe all the clothes Maisie talked her into buying, including all kinds of outdoor gear.

"I'm not moving to Alaska in the near future, Maisie." Bridget put her hands on her hips and shook her head in amazement.

"Wait until snow is piled up against your window. Then you'll love your boots and all."

"I'm also not a skier, so why did you have me buy a ski jacket and pants?"

"Because they're really warm, nicely styled, and they give you a glamorous look like Sally Owens. Listen, I see a lot of guys watching you when you come into the café, and yesterday, two different men asked about you."

"What did you say?"

"I told them your name and gave them your phone number. Just make sure they aren't married. Sometimes guys want to play around."

"Saints preserve us, I niver thought of that," Bridget said. Was C. W. married? Maybe that's why he hadn't called.

As she was getting into her truck, C. W. and Ed drove in and parked next to her.

"Hi, Bridget, we're coming in for a late lunch." Ed gave her a subtle smile. "We've been out dickering with John Whitaker."

She felt C. W.'s eyes on her as he walked by. They reminded her of George's eyes, only much warmer.

He gave her a soft smile. "Will you be home later today?"

Bridget, tongue-tied, just nodded and got into her truck, remembering what Gibran had written about love and to follow when a loved one beckons.

She sat in her truck for the longest time, unable to move and thrilled by his question. He was actually coming to see her, finally. How long had it been? It felt like forever.

C. W. was a fine broth of a man, strong and hard as Ed. Not an extra pound on him and a lot of it in the right places. Driving home, her mind began racing. What did he want? Was he going to confess his wife was joining him, and he'd like Bridget to meet the little missus? Or worse yet, what if he wanted to play around?

Bridget heard Amanda's new puppy whining as she opened the door. She checked on him in the laundry room and cuddled him in her arms for a while. "Are you lonesome too? Amanda will be home soon and love you." Putting him back down in his bed, she laughed at herself, talking to him like he was human.

I'll wear my new slacks and sweater that Maisie likes. I think it's too tight, but she doesn't. My sainted mither would turn over in her grave if she knew I was wearing men's britches. It seems sinful, somehow, but they are warm and comfortable.

She thought about Maisie shaking her finger at her and saying, "No more baggy clothes for you."

As Bridget prepared dinner, she glanced at her new watch. It was another thing that was hard getting used to, but she loved knowing what time it was at a glance. Just a few more minutes and he would be there. She'd invite him to dinner. Hopefully, he liked chicken and rice casserole, which was Ed's favorite, but the kids didn't care for it. All they wanted were hamburgers every day of the week.

Bridget heard his truck pull up and park across the road. His door slammed, and then there was a sharp knock on the door. She smiled weakly as she opened it. He took off his brimmed hat, stepped inside, and smiled back at her.

If only he'd say something. She finally blurted out, "Will you stay for dinner?"

"Maybe." He smiled. "I'd like to see the barn. Would you take a walk with me?"

"I'd like that," she said, following Kahlil's love admonition and hastily scribbling a note to her family about dinner and where she was going.

They didn't touch as they strolled up the road. He asked her if she was cold, and she replied that her jacket was nice and warm. She loved the sound of his voice—deep with a mature resonance to it. Instead of feeling like a forty-two-year-old woman, she felt seventeen again.

He stopped for a moment and turned to her. "Do you like it here? Ed told me you moved with the family from DC this past summer." As he talked, he gently pushed a bit of hair out of her eyes.

"Yes, I'm their cook, and I used to babysit, but now the kids are big." She tried to speak without such a thick accent. It didn't used to matter, but now it did.

C. W. didn't comment on her remarks. "Could I hold your hand?"

He waited for her to say something, his beautiful eyes, searching her face. She slipped her hand into his big, strong, calloused hand and loved the feeling. Her mind had gone blank, and she began walking to cover her embarrassment.

"It's a wonderful barn," she said when they arrived.

He smiled at her. "Do you really think it's wonderful?"

"Yes, I love barns, especially clean, new ones. Let's go inside." Bridget said, complimenting herself that she'd actually made a reasonable remark or two.

"Most of the gals I've known didn't have any interest in barns," he said, simply.

They walked around inside, the hay bales in the haymow scenting the place with a sweet, strong odor. She breathed deeply.

C. W. glanced around the building. "Do you like horses?"

"I was born in Ireland, as you can tell from me brogue, and I'll have you know some of the best horse flesh is raised there. It's the national pastime to trade, buy, sell, or steal horses."

He actually chuckled at her remark. "Would you go out to dinner with me?" C. W. was asking her out on an date—the first one in her life.

"I'd love it."

"Good," he said, "how about tomorrow night? Something happened to me today, and I'd like to celebrate with you." He paused as if deciding whether to say more or not. "Mr. Whitaker asked me to work for him as a racing consultant. I'll oversee the transportation of his horses to the various racetracks and make sure they're ready to run and win races. There's more to it than that, but the rest isn't important. I have Ed to thank for my job. He was very generous in taking me around to the various farms." C. W. stood there, quietly smiling at her as her knees went all wobbly again.

"I'm happy for you," Bridget choked out.

"I'm glad you are. Where should we go?"

"Maisie's, of course. She's a friend of mine," she said, giving him a genuine smile.

He took her hand as they left the barn. The whole landscape came alive with excitement to Bridget as she walked down the hill. The sun was slowly sinking in the sky, and there was a chilly breeze beginning to blow. She shivered, and he immediately pulled her in close to him.

"You'll be inside in a minute," he said, and she could feel his breath in her hair. Before he opened the kitchen door, he stopped, and smiled down at her as if to memorize her face. "I'll pick you up around six, Bridget Coyle," he said and left.

That evening after dinner, when everyone had scattered, Bridget sat in her room and hugged herself. She was actually going out on a date with a man she hardly knew, but he had the silent seal of approval from Ed. Otherwise, Ed would never have taken the time to help C. W. land the job with one of the biggest racing farms in the county.

She was eager to know everything about him, where he was from, if he'd ever been married, or worse, was he still married? But how would she be able to explain who she was to him when she didn't know herself? If he asked her what she dreamed about doing, she'd have no answer for him. She wasn't allowed to have fantasies when she was growing up. They produced too much guilt. *Oh, dear God, help me to break free of all those shalt nots I had pounded into my head as a child.*

A new little voice whispered inside her head, telling her to read her book. Who was speaking to her? Was it her guardian angel? She picked up her beloved book, *The Prophet*, and read more from the chapter on love.

Bridget read and reread the chapter, the meaning filling her heart. She lay there with her eyes closed. Out of habit, she made the sign of the cross and thanked God for giving her Kahlil Gibran's inspiring messages. *What kind of man could write this book?* It was filled with the most intimate details between a man and a woman and their God. *Could this happen to C. W. and me? Oh, dear God, help me.* She closed her eyes and prayed.

Bridget woke early and went through the motions of her daily routine, automatically. Her mind was centered on her date with C. W., and she worried she wouldn't measure up to his expectations. He seemed like such a man of the world. How could he possibly be interested in her? What would it be like to talk to a man as a woman? Could she do it? She was hungry to try.

As she was putting the finishing touches on dinner for her family, she heard a truck. Was it Ed or C. W.? Her heart turned over as she looked out of her kitchen window and saw him. Such a handsome man he was, coming to pick her up and whisk her away. He was a half hour early. Was he as anxious as she for their date to begin? She grabbed her coat and bag from the kitchen table, propped her note to the family on the counter, and opened the door, thrilled to see him walking toward her.

"Ready to go? I'm a little early, but I wanted to come," he said, giving her a beautiful smile.

She shut the door and ran to meet him. "Hi," she squeezed out, as she hurried around the truck and climbed in as fast as she could.

Slightly breathless, she watched him as he got in and looked at her. He took off his hat, leaned over, and gave her a light brush of a kiss on her cheek. "You smell nice, like soap and water. Here we go. Hope you're hungry, I am."

He drove silently, occasionally looking over at her and smiling. She could smell his aftershave, and her cheeks felt warm. Thank goodness it was dark.

He reached over and touched her hand. "Find some good music, why don't you?"

"I'll try," she said, fumbling with the radio. "How's this? I love Henry Mancini's music."

"Good choice, Bridget. I like Henry and his orchestra. Do you dance?"

Here come his questions. How do I tell him I niver learned to dance? Bridget cleared her throat. "I came from Ireland, and the priests frowned on people dancing together," she said quietly. "Also, I had to take care of me brothers and sisters, so I niver learned."

"So, you're a country girl. They're the best kind. Do you have freckles?"

"Yes," she said, feeling her cheeks getting hot again. "I know how to milk a cow, kill and skin a chicken, and grow vegetables. I went to school until my mither died, and then I had to stay home and take care of me brothers and sisters. When they were old enough, I left and came to America." She set her jaw and stammered, "Now you know what kind of a woman I am." She quickly wiped away her tears of embarrassment.

C. W. pulled over to the side of the road, took a handkerchief from his pocket, and wiped her eyes. "Did I make you cry?"

"No, and I don't know why I got all dewy eyed when I told you aboot meself. And I don't know why I blathered on and on. I couldn't stop."

He smiled. "Bridget, there are lots of things about me that make me feel uncomfortable, so we're even. Maybe we can help each other."

At that moment, she fell in love with C. W. Peck.

She leaned over and gave him a tiny kiss on his cheek and lightly smoothed his salt and pepper hair. Ignoring that angry voice in her head that said she was acting like a hussy, she moved over a little and luxuriated in the closeness of him.

Maisie's face lit up when they came in, and she came flying over to talk and seat them. Bridget felt like people were watching them until they sat down.

C. W. slipped in next to her in their booth. "I'd like to sit next to you," he whispered.

He was so close that when she turned to answer, they were only six inches apart. He looked at her lips, and then he gave her a light but meaningful kiss. It was her first kiss since she'd been seventeen, and as she melted under his touch, she hoped she'd be able to speak coherently afterward. The words from her beloved book had come true. She felt like a running brook.

Suddenly, she heard a loud brassy voice say, "I'm Billie, your waitress for tonight. Can I interest you in our specials?"

Bridget wanted to scream for her to go away. But she listened as C. W. asked what the specials were and what she'd like.

"I'll have the baked lake trout."

"I'll get the steak, and I'll give you a bite of mine," he said, smoothly. When the waitress left, he turned back to Bridget. "You look warm. Your cheeks are pink. Let me see if you have a fever." He put his hand on her forehead. "I pronounce you perfect in every way."

His hand lingered a moment, touching her cheek as if he wanted to keep it there. "I'm sorry. I didn't ask if you wanted anything to drink. I was caught off guard. But I imagine you aren't much of a drinker. I remember the dinner party. I couldn't figure out where you'd gone. I thought maybe to bed, I didn't know. And then when you came back and sat down quietly over across the room from me, I thought, well, old boy, she's not interested in you.

"Ed encouraged me to call you or come over again, and you know the rest. I'm not so good at reading signals from women. I guess

462

that's why I've been married and divorced twice," he confessed quietly, searching her face for some kind of reaction.

All Bridget cared about was that he wasn't married, and she wanted desperately to believe him. "I have two dear friends, one who has been married and divorced twice, and one whose husband died. But they're all happily married now."

"So, there's hope for me. You don't hold it against me." He cleared his throat. "What about you, Bridget?"

Just as she was fumbling for words to explain how sheltered she'd been as far as boyfriends were concerned, the waitress appeared with their dinners. Bridget said a silent prayer of thanks for the interruption. How could she tell him she was a forty-two-year-old virgin and an old maid who had weighed so much her feet hurt. And up until the last few months, she'd given up, content to cook, and eat a lot.

Sitting so close to him, she could feel his body heat. What would it be like to feel his warmth in bed?

She shivered slightly from her sinful thoughts.

"Are you cold?"

"No," she lied. "Sometimes, I just shiver from happiness."

"I'm glad you're happy. Now, open wide, I'm going to pop a piece of steak into that beautiful mouth of yours."

For some reason, she closed her eyes, and he kissed her instead. It was a warmer, more passionate kiss than before.

"No fair," she blurted out.

They traded bites throughout dinner, and she could hardly remember what she'd eaten. She only remembered his lips, his beautiful white teeth, and his smile.

"Let's take a walk over to the city park, sit on a bench, and act like a couple of love-struck kids," he said as he helped her into her new warm coat. "I like your coat. It has a hood. That was a smart move in this cold country."

"Maria suggested it before I went shopping. I'm glad you like it."

"I like everything about you," C. W. said. "I think I'll kiss you just before we leave the café and give the townsfolk something to talk about."

"Saints preserve us, don't you do that," she said, but hoping he wouldn't mind her. He didn't.

As they crossed the road to the park, Bridget loved the way her first pair of boots felt—warm, comfortable, and nice looking. "Let's keep moving, it's too cold to sit aboot."

"Okay, we won't sit aboot, Miss Ireland. I love your accent."

"I wish I could talk more like an American. Sometimes, I feel so conspicuous."

"Don't ever lose your accent. It's refreshing. In fact, everything about you is so innocent, somehow. You seem so young."

"How old do you think I am?"

"You're as old as you feel." He grinned. "I'm forty-seven, and tonight I feel like a kid."

"I know what you mean," she said softly, stopping and looking at him.

C. W. immediately picked up on her cue, put his arms around her, and kissed her with passion.

She never wanted it to end. He released her slightly, then held her tightly again, and kissed her until she began to feel shaky. The blood rushed through her body and brain until she felt like she wanted him to take her to his bed and let the devil take the hindmost.

He stopped and put his face in her hair, inhaling the slight perfume lingering about her. "Things have really escalated, Bridget. I'm not going to apologize, I like what has happened between us. One thing I know, we're on the same wavelength so far," he said, smoothing her hair with his hands and looking into her eyes. "You have the most beautiful, big blue eyes. I love them."

"We'd better walk some more, and no more of those kisses." Bridget tried to slow her breathing. "It's getting late, and you have to be out to work early tomorrow for Mr. Whittaker."

He took her hand and began walking. "When am I going to see you again?" He stopped and turned her to face him. His eyes were full of excitement. "I just remembered something. Why don't we take some dancing lessons? There's a dance studio in Naperville. I called and they said they have a new class starting next Friday night. How about it? It will be fun, and that way I'll get to hold you without that big coat of yours getting in the way." He laughed just like a kid, and for an instant, looked like one, too.

So, this is how it is to be with a man. To tease and laugh, love and kiss, and know I'm special. She smiled. "I'd like that, but I know you aren't a beginner."

"I can dance a little, but I've spent most of my life around horses and racetracks. This would be something new for me too. Besides, I know you'll be good once you get started, and then when we go to fancy parties. All the men will be watching my girl as we dance."

Bridget was thrilled when she heard him refer to her as his girl and imagining them together at parties. *Thank you, God, for C. W.* Riding home in his truck, she sat as close to him as possible, and when he put his hand on her leg, she didn't object.

As they were pulling up to the house, she said, "Thank you for a wonderful evening. Call me, I'll be waiting." She gave him a light kiss, hopped out of the cab, and hurried to the door. She paused for a moment to wave before she went into Maria's home.

The next day, Friday, November 22, her beloved Irish president, John Fitzgerald Kennedy, was shot and killed in Texas at 12:30 p.m. The children were excused from school, Ed closed the clinic except for emergencies, and Ruth and Winston called from Florida. Everyone gathered around the television, listened, and watched the replay of his death scene in the motorcade with his wife by his side. He was shot by Lee Harvey Oswald from a building overlooking the parade route. Vice President Lyndon Johnson was sworn in as president as John Kennedy's wife, Jacqueline Kennedy, splattered with her husband's blood, waited to fly home with her husband's body to Washington, DC, for the burial in Arlington Cemetery.

Amanda sat cuddled next to Maria on the rec room couch with tears streaming down their cheeks. Amanda alternately watched, then hid her head in her mother's shoulder. Ed sat leaning forward with his face in his hands, glued to the scene. C. W. had come when he heard the news on his radio, and he sat tightly next to Bridget on the other couch, holding one of her hands. Bridget had her eyes closed and was holding her mother's rosary beads in her other hand, her lips moving in a silent prayer. Chris sat next to Ed. He was holding his father's medals, coughing, and occasionally wiping his eyes.

"Daddy, what will we do without him?" Amanda sounded frightened. "Will we be all right?"

"We'll be fine. Our country is strong, and President Johnson will be a good and honest president. Our country is founded on a wonderful constitution. President Johnson will uphold it, and we'll remain a country that is respected around the world." Ed's voice was full of confidence.

"Our family is also strong." Maria hugged her daughter. "We love each other."

"At this moment, I want to add that I'll protect and take care of us as the new husband of my dear wife and stepfather to my adopted kids," Ed said. "Together, we'll have a good life, even as we all miss

President Kennedy. This country will remember him for all he did and tried to do for the country, even though his time as president was cut short."

As their sad little group sat together and mourned their loss of John F. Kennedy, they listened to his stirring wish for all American citizens broadcasted by the news media, asking that people be more concerned about what they could do for their country than what it could do for them.

Chris's face was tight with emotion when he stood up holding his father's medals in his trembling hands and announced to the whole group that he was going to fly for the army when he graduated. "My dad gave his best for this country," he said, holding up George's medals, "and so will I."

No one spoke immediately, but Ed finally said, "I admire your spirit, Chris. I hope you reconsider, but I'll support you in whatever you decide to do."

"And I know your father will be watching over you, no matter where you go." At that moment, Maria felt George's presence. An incredible feeling of love enveloped her, and she felt it swirling around the room. He was making another visitation. It was so powerful and breathtaking, she had to close her eyes. And then he was gone. There was silence in the room for a moment or two. Everyone had felt it.

"Mommy, will we still have Thanksgiving?"

Maria hugged Amanda. "Of course, and a big turkey, like always. Then we'll go see Grandma and Grandpa in Florida for Christmas and have a wonderful time."

"Something beautiful has happened here," Bridget said softly. "Everyone, let's stand, hold hands, and ask God to bless our country and our family." Holding her rosary beads, she stood and waited. "It is a grand family we have here. Including our new friend, C. W."

They stood up, held hands, and Maria quietly began singing "America the Beautiful" in a strong, steady voice, and soon everyone was singing, "America, America, God shed his grace on thee. And crown thy good with brotherhood from sea to shining sea," in a loud chorus. They sang it several times, then the room got quiet.

Ed laid his hand over his heart. "Let's make the rest of this day, and every day, count for something in this great country of ours."

About the Author

Ella Murphy was born and raised in Chicago, Illinois. Her Midwestern roots are reflected in the settings of her books.

After Ella and her husband had raised a son and daughter, Ella returned to school, earning a BS degree from Northeastern and two MS degrees in education, school psychology, and special education from Fitchburg State in Massachusetts. She then taught special education in Massachusetts.

Now retired, she resides near her daughter and grandchildren in Virginia, where she enjoys gardening, writing, church, social activities, and sports such as tennis and golf. Her lifetime of experiences—marriage, children, traveling, and teaching—serves as inspiration for her work.

Maria's Awakening, A Matter of Choice, All About Hope, Promises, Lost and Found, and *Rebound* (the six books in the Maria series) are available at bookstores and from online retailers. Direct links to these sites are available on the author's website:

www.ellareamurphy.com

Or you may use the form below to order books directly from the author.

Maria Series Order Form

Please send _____ copies of *Rebound* at $17.00 each, plus $5.00 per book for shipping, to:

Please send _____ copies of *Lost and Found* at $17.00 each, plus $5.00 per book for shipping, to:

Please send _____ copies of *Promises* at $17.00 each, plus $5.00 per book for shipping, to:

Please send _____ copies of *All About Hope* at $17.00 each, plus $5.00 per book for shipping, to:

Please send _____ copies of *A Matter of Choice* at $17.00 each, plus $5.00 per book for shipping, to:

Please send _____ copies of *Maria's Awakening* at $17.00 each, plus $5.00 per book for shipping, to:

Name _____

Address_____

City, State, and Zip_____

Make checks payable to Ella Murphy and mail your order to:

Ella Murphy
PO Box 581
Earlysvllle, VA 22936-9998

MAY - - 2019

Made in the USA
Columbia, SC
18 August 2017